C

CW00458665

This is a work of fiction. Names, characters, places, and incidents either are the product of the author's imagination or are used fictitiously. Any resemblance to actual persons, living or dead, events or locales is entirely coincidental.

For more information contact: clivelamb@yahoo.com

First paperback edition March 2023

ISBN (paperback)
ISBN ebook)

Chapter 1

Jennifer's early years might be described as unstable. It wasn't her fault; it was just the cards that she had been dealt. Her parents had barely known each other just spending enough time together at a drunken party to ensure her conception.

Her father, Ben, was too young to have had to sign up for military service and so he had suffered the war at home. He had the good fortune to have been born too late to have to risk his life abroad trying to kill other young men who knew no better. In many ways he was disappointed. He thought he would have made a good soldier. He was well built for his age and thought he could handle himself quite well. He had come out bloodied but on top in most of the routine school skirmishes in which he was involved.

He had been apprenticed to an electrician whom he followed from job to job and county to county depending where the money was. The money was currently in London, repairing buildings which had suffered damage during the war. There were also contracts on offer fitting out newly built properties, commissioned by local authorities, to replace the housing stock lost to the war.

Ben shared digs with some of the other lads who had travelled south to follow the opportunities rebuilding offered. Jim Wilson, with whom Ben shared a room, was helping to rebuild a property, damaged by a bus which had accidentally run into its side as its driver fell asleep at the wheel. Ironically, this particular property and those surrounding it had come through the bombing unscathed. It was particularly unfortunate to be damaged by a simple, if stupid, peacetime accident.

Jim, who was a good-looking young man with a cocky outgoing nature, had become acquainted with a local young woman who had taken a shine to him whilst visiting her friend, who lived in the damaged house. She let it be known that there was to be a party in a friend's place, close by, that evening. She encouraged him to come. The house owners were out of town and their son planned to take advantage and throw a wild party. Jim didn't need any encouragement and brought the good news back to his digs. The boys were all single and always up for fun, particularly if there were members of the opposite sex involved. There was soon a posse of interest and Jim was one of the five lads who ventured along to the address that evening and blagged their way in.

Sheila Johnson was not particularly looking to meet anybody that evening, in fact she just thought she would get tipsy with her mates, have a laugh and head off home. She knew the lad whose parents had made the mistake of leaving their son in charge. His name was Neville. Sheila had actually spent time with him at the end of the war a couple of years back. They had wasted little time to discover life's carnal pleasures. For weeks they met in secret and enjoyed exploring each other, both physically and mentally. After time the thrill and excitement of clandestine intercourse began to wear off and they backed uncomfortably away from developing the relationship any further There was no ill feeling from either of them, each had taken a good deal of pleasure in the other and both were happy to move on. She had been through a war and who knew what was around the corner? Enjoy life for the moment was her motto. Sheila's moral compass was uncontrolled.

The girls had already been enjoying more alcohol than they could properly handle and found plenty of opportunity to scream with laughter. The party was becoming a blur for Sheila's group of friends as it was for most of the young people there.

Sheila found Ben as he passed a quart bottle of beer out of the window to one of his friends from the digs. They had each brought a bottle with them to ease passage through the front door. Once into the party they fully expected to take at least one back to their digs for later. Ben wasn't particularly good looking, well-groomed or even hygienic but he had a certain charm. His hair was red and his face spattered with freckles. He gave the appearance that he had Celtic blood in his veins. His engaging smile, edgy good humour and strength of character registered with most of the ladies whose company he had kept and Sheila was drawn to him.

'Naughty' she said "You'll have to look after me if you don't want me to spill the beans" Ben laughed and admitted his guilt. "I have always been a bit naughty" he said "ever since I was a little boy. In fact, you haven't seen the half of how naughty I can be."

"Well, you had better behave whilst I am around or deal with the consequences!"

Sheila and Ben laughed through the early evening and inevitably found themselves entwined in each other on a pile of coats left in the hosts parents' bedroom. The coats were pushed aside as the couple frantically tore at each other's clothes. Both parties were consumed with the moment, Sheila perhaps more inebriated than Ben but both not to be stopped. There was no romantic notion, just a sense of fun and pleasure to be had and sex. Sheila had by now developed quite a taste for sex and Ben was more than capable of both taking and giving pleasure. At the age of 17 Sheila was relatively experienced, if naïve. She left the bedroom to tidy herself up, reapply lipstick and suchlike. She looked forward to spending the rest of the evening with Ben – maybe dancing and drinking downstairs – maybe returning to the bedroom later. Her friends found her coming out of the bathroom and wanted to know all about her encounter. Sheila was happy to talk the girls through the experience and exaggerate where required. Some of the girls were quite naive and shocked at her antics but all listened intently. Others prompted Sheila for more intimate details and laughed openly at some of Sheila's outrageous answers.

From downstairs the sound of raised voices was heard - not unusual at one of these do's; some of the high-spirited lads drinking too much. Something was kicking off.

Sheila arrived down in the hallway in time to see the back of two lads heading down the front path, each nursing head wounds. The music was still playing but there was a buzz of conversation, everybody giving their accounts of events, which were confused to say the least. Sheila listened with interest, not realising for one minute that her new friend was involved. As far as she could see it was just another drunken brawl which men seemed to get drawn into so easily.

She sought out Ben interested to hear his version what had happened. He was nowhere to be found. As she asked around it became clear that he was one of the bloodied men she had seen lurching off down the path. This was a huge disappointment; it didn't seem to be in his nature during their brief encounter. He had been such fun. She had been very attracted to him and the night was far from over but he was gone. Sheila was not inclined

to chase after him, so she got herself another drink and returned
to her friends

The party was three weeks before Sheila's eighteenth
birthday. She celebrated at a dance with friends and once again
consumed far too much alcohol. This time there were no liaisons
beyond those on the dance floor. For the next few days, she was
sick every morning. She blamed the alcohol. A month later she
realised that the relentless sickness was a sign of pregnancy,
although there were few other symptoms. The uncomfortable
feeling in her stomach, was fear of the future more than the pain
of pregnancy. She didn't know where to look for Ben and wasn't
sure that the impending new life was his responsibility. Even if he
was the father, she wasn't sure that she wanted him involved. It
would just cause more complications and she had enough of
those in her life already.

Both of Sheila's parents had died when she was in her early
teens. First her father, who was sent to fight in France but never
made it back, then her mother who was killed by a bomb in a raid
in London, wrong time, wrong place. There was no other family
that she knew and she was still a child. She couldn't look after
herself properly, never mind afford to keep up the meagre flat
which her parents had rented. Winnie, whom she met when she
found a job in a local factory making overalls and protective
clothing, became a firm friend. When Sheila's mother died,
Winnie invited Sheila to come and live with her family in their
small terraced house in Mountfield Road. Winnie's mother was
glad of the extra income, much of which was spent on alcohol.
She left the girls to themselves, fully consumed by her own grief
having lost two brothers, a husband and a son to the war. She had

little time for her teenage daughter who was not a particularly easy child. She had no energy left. It was better to let Winnie get on with her own life and make her own mistakes. So, Winnie and Sheila were left to their own devices. They set their own boundaries and made their own rules.

Sheila's mother had encouraged her to leave school at the earliest opportunity to bring in extra cash for the home. Education, she felt, was wasted on girls who would soon enough marry and have domestic chores to manage.

Sheila's job was very repetitive and not particularly skilled. She soon picked up the basics and fell into the drab routine demanded. Whilst working Sheila met up with many other girls of a similar age, with a similar lack of ambition and the same focus on enjoying their free time to the full. Dancing, clothes and men were the main topics of conversation at break time.

Sharing a room with Winnie was fun but not ideal in view of her pregnancy. Where could she live with a baby? Not in Winnie's room for sure. The enormity of responsibility for the well-being of a new child was yet to fully dawn on Sheila. Her first concern was how her own life would be thrown out of kilter. What would happen to her job, what would her friends think? The partying would not be easy with a baby to look after.

Winnie was great. When Sheila finally had the courage to tell her that she thought she might be pregnant, Winnie stood by her. "Oh God that's going to be difficult" was her first reaction followed by "don't worry we'll be okay".

Sheila had become a special friend to her and Winnie felt some responsibility for the loose moral perspective that Sheila had developed. It was clearly this which led them to their current plight and it might equally well have been Winnie. She took some ownership of the situation and accepted that she had a significant role to play.

It was amongst this confusion of emotion, morality, maturity and responsibility that Jennifer Johnson developed in her mother's womb. Warm and nourished, comfortable and protected but perhaps unconsciously uneasy about her creation.

There was never a time when Sheila seriously thought to get rid of her child. Society would look down upon her as a single mother and probably treat her quite cruelly, but most of the people she knew would take even more unkindly to the manslaughter of an unborn child.   Back street abortion, the only abortion available to her at a cost she could afford, was highly dangerous.

Sheila was emotionally immature. Perhaps a sense of foreboding combined with ignorance of the weight of responsibility, hard work and emotional strength that was needed to properly give a child a good start to life, prevented her from taking the idea any further. Perhaps it was the tales which she heard about back street abortions, the pain which was inflicted and the long-term mental damage which helped her make a decision to keep the baby.

In the early stages little changed in Sheila's life, she didn't stop working or even announce her situation to the bosses at the factory. She continued to party with Winnie and others and even had sex on two or three occasions, with two or three men who she met. She drank and smoked as if nothing had happened and apart from the really uncomfortable morning sickness, life continued as normal.

One day, after a particularly bad bout of sickness, Sheila looked in the mirror and faced the reality of what was happening.

Her body shape was a clear sign of her condition now. Panic set in and emotion flooded out. Sheila didn't go to work; she stayed home and cried. When Winnie came in that evening, she said the foreman had been asking after Sheila and whilst Winnie had tried to keep a lid on reality, she knew that the cat was out of the bag. The foreman was not particularly sympathetic and was more concerned about production figures than Sheila's plight. He had asked to see her in the morning. If she could not guarantee coming into work, he would be offering her job to somebody else. As people were queuing up for work, he would have little difficulty in replacing her.

Sheila turned up for work the following morning. The foreman was actually affronted by the young pregnant girl in front of him. He was a religious man. Sheila might have hoped that would bring a degree of sympathy. It didn't, it brought disgust. Disgust at Sheila's attitude, disgust at her morals and disgust at the life style which had led Sheila to the state in which she found herself. His charity extended to offering her a cleaning job instead of her production line work. Cleaning would not affect the efficiency of production which he needed but at least would not totally deprive Sheila of any income. Cleaning, however, did not pay the same wages as the production line. Sheila had little choice but to accept the change until she could find something less taxing and better rewarded. There was never really any prospect of that happening.

As time went on, Sheila was often left at home with Winnie's mother June with whom she started to develop a bond - and a drinking habit.

By the time the life inside her had been growing for twenty-five weeks Sheila's health had deteriorated significantly. She visited the doctor as she felt weak and constantly nauseous. She was given a tonic and told bed rest was best for her and the baby. Of course, bed rest did not earn her any money. As close as she had become to Winnie's mother, she was still required to find rent, so she continued to work.

It was a Wednesday evening in January 1949. The house shivered with cold. There was one coal fire to provide heat for the whole building. Alcohol provided some inner warmth but the women in Mountfield Road were cold on the outside. Fingers white, toes numb and bones aching, they wore coats in the house to fight against the elements.

Sheila was close to collapse and had become delirious, a mixture of undernourishment, alcohol and the growing new life inside of her. Winnie and June knew that they must get her to hospital. It was just six months after the formation of the National Health Service which was proving to, literally and metaphorically, be a life saver for many. If they could get her there, heat and food would be on hand and care for both mother and baby. The hospital was 20 minutes away and the journey, which they made on foot, was arduous but between them they deposited a very sick mother-to-be in a waiting area and left her to the care of the staff.

That night Sheila gave birth to a very weak undernourished daughter: Five pounds two ounces but with all her fingers and toes. Jennifer Johnson had entered the world.

Chapter 2

Sheila recovered some strength and became well enough for the hospital to release her and her baby into the world of rationing and rebuilding that she had left. She had nowhere to go but back to Winnie and her mother and see if they would accept her and the new bundle, wrapped in blankets kindly supplied by a hospital charity.   She was also loaned some basic starter clothes which had been worn by numerous babies on the understanding that they were returned, clean, once the baby had outgrown them. Sheila had not had the foresight to prepare for the baby and suddenly she was in desperate need of help from Winnie and June.

Quite unexpectedly June was very welcoming and understanding whilst Winne who had been so supportive in the early months was now less keen to accept a new little stranger into her already limited life space. June busied herself clearing out what had been her son's room. This had been left untouched since the telegram announcing his death.

New life presented an opportunity for June to start a new chapter to her life and she took to the baby like a mother. Sheila was surprised not to be feeling the all-encompassing love for the baby, who had fought to get out of her and practically killed her in the process. She had understood that there would be an immediate bond – unbreakable for life. She didn't feel it. She thought the baby was very cute and she liked to hold her but she just wasn't ready for this in her life.

"What's her name" June asked.

"I hadn't really decided" said Sheila dispassionately.

"Well, she must have a name" June insisted "What girls' names do you like"

Sheila had been to see one film in her lifetime – *"The Song of Bernadette"*. The film had been a revelation to her and in her mind had transported her to France and taken her on the journey with Bernadette. Bernadette was played by Jennifer Jones and Sheila thought she was probably the most fabulous girl she had ever seen.

"Jennifer" she blurted out "We'll call her Jennifer"

"Jennifer it is then"

Jennifer was cared for largely by June. June sobered up with this responsibility and put alcohol behind her completely. She felt blessed to have been gifted a child, albeit somebody else's child, and wanted to do the best for her. Jennifer filled the void left by her husband and son, and whilst she would have preferred a little boy, Jennifer was, to a large degree, her saviour. She was out of touch with Winnie, her own daughter. Neither of them was sure quite how it had happened but the tragedy which hit their family in the war, had divided rather than unite them. Sheila was able to get back to work and some form of a normal social life whilst June doted on the child.

This state of affairs continued for five years. Sheila brought in money to keep them and after time Winnie married and moved out herself and when she had her first child stopped working at the factory. Sheila met men but was very wary of them and their intentions and found it difficult to form a bond with them. She didn't pine for Ben but she often wondered what might have been if they had seen each other again.

On a bitter day in February, June developed a cough and went to see the doctor who told her to stay inside and avoid the cold. He prescribed some cough medicine. The cough persisted and got worse; June soldiered on.   Winnie came to visit some days later and found her mother shaking on the sofa.   Jennifer was playing happily on the floor. Winnie rushed to the telephone box on the corner of her mother's road and called for an ambulance. The ambulance arrived some twenty minutes later and carried her mother off to hospital.

When Sheila arrived home, Winnie told her what had happened then rushed off to the hospital. The news was bad. June developed pneumonia and passed away within days of being admitted.

How do you tell a five-year-old that the most important person in her life would not be coming back again, ever? Sheila had not been the best mother so far and was definitely second in Jennifer's affections. She didn't know how to handle the situation.

Jennifer had started at school but that was only for some of the day. She needed dropping off and collecting. She needed packed lunches and snacks. Tea and love in the afternoon, someone to play with and talk to, someone for bath time and bedtime stories. All this had been happily undertaken by June. It had filled her day and made her happy, she made no demands of Sheila and Sheila could get on with her own life. Now, all that had changed and Sheila didn't know how to tell Jennifer, so at first, she didn't. Apart from anything else, of course, she no longer had a built-in child minder.

Sheila took some time off work and spent her days with Jennifer. During those few days when she behaved like a real mum Sheila started to warm to her daughter.   She avoided talking about June, passing her absence off by saying she had gone away for a while. She hoped that the loss would be easier to take after

Jennifer had been with her for a few days. The little girl was persistent. She missed June who had been a better mother than Sheila was proving to be, despite trying very hard. There was no real connection between mother and daughter and Sheila felt it, which made her feel inadequate. The longer it went on with Jennifer asking for June, the more frustrated and angrier she became until finally she blurted it out "She's never coming back, she's dead"

Jennifer looked at her mother in shock and disbelief "What do you mean" she said. "She's dead and that's the end of it, she got ill and the hospital tried but couldn't help her. I'm sorry but she won't be coming back so you have to get used to me, whether you like it or not".

Jennifer burst into tears and ran upstairs to her bedroom which she had been given when Winnie moved out. She lay on her bed and sobbed uncontrollably until she fell asleep. Sheila left her with her grief and turned to June's redundant drinks cabinet.

Chapter 3

Andy McDonald married Maggie Tulloch, who was, and remained, his partner for life. How much love was involved is open to debate. They certainly both admired each other and shared a set of values but the concept of romantic love was probably lost on them both. Both grew up in Glasgow, both were keen to better themselves. They moved south to Coventry when Andy was offered an opportunity to join a small firm of book-keepers. Andy was a Presbyterian and very strict about the way he ran his life, as was Maggie. They met at the church, realised that they had the same interests and ambitions in life and married young, without having given anybody else a chance to win their affections. Theirs was a marriage both instigated and blinded by religion.

Maggie was a stern lady who had little sense of fun. What was right, was right and what needed to be done, needed to be done and the Lord would provide. Cleanliness was next to godliness and she lived her entire life by this mantra. She was generous with her time but also with her opinions. The church benefited from the time that she was prepared to give, cleaning, flower arranging and helping out at whatever fellowship activities the clergy deemed appropriate for the community. Maggie had few friends but knew and was known by many people. She was the opinionated one at the church coffee mornings. She was also the one with the clipboard and the instructions at the church fundraiser.

The couple lived a modest life with which they were both content. Happiness was not a concept which either particularly understood and having had so little of it in their lives, did not notice its absence.

God blessed them with three children Alice who was her mother's favourite, Ronnie who was his father's favourite and Ben, whom God had given them unexpectedly. Ben was born twelve years after Ronnie and fourteen years after Alice. Alice took great joy in mothering Ben which was just as well because Maggie was very put out by God's decision to give another soul into her keeping. Maggie regarded Ben as an unwanted gift for which she would have to outwardly show some gratitude but which, in fact, had upset the perfect balance of their simple, planned and mundane existence.

Andy worked long hours, balancing the books of random local businesses. He could work with figures but found the aspects of his work which involved human interaction challenging. He was unsure of himself and awkward in the presence of most people, except those in church on a Sunday. His social life was a stagnant mix of coffee after church, chess or bridge at one of the homes of his fellow church goers, or, as a real treat, a beetle or whist drive in the church hall. For exercise Andy took his children for a brisk walk around the local park and allowed them some time on the swings whilst he read the paper.

Alice and Ronnie were created in the mould of their parents and fell into the patterns which their parents had so clearly carved out for them. They both had friends, albeit the circle was rather limited. Maggie did not entirely approve of some of Alice's friends who were "less than godly" in her opinion, however, they proved invaluable when it came to Ben's wellbeing and up keep. Maggie allowed herself to believe that God had introduced them into Alice's life and therefore her own life, for a purpose. The purpose she chose to interpret was childminding. Ben's early years were thus somewhat different to those of his siblings. He enjoyed much laughter and fun with his elder sister's friends and when school days were upon him, he sought out those with a smile on their face, a sense of mischief and somewhat more of the rebellious types.

As Ben grew and developed, he leaned towards a different life style from that of his parents. His parents always made him feel as an unexpected guest might feel when arriving at an inconvenient time. The words that they spoke to him were the right words but felt hollow and without depth. The feelings that he and his parents shared amounted to no more than friendly acceptance of the situation. A situation that had just happened to them all which was beyond everybody's control. Perhaps there was an underlying love, the bond that blood demands but it felt shallow.

In nineteen forty-one the McDonald family was devastated. Andy had been drafted to the Royal Scottish Greys at the start of the war and had been stationed in Palestine. The Royal Scottish Greys were a cavalry unit and retained their horses until 1941 when the real horsepower was replaced by manmade horse power in the form of armoured vehicles. The regiment were moved to fight in Syria and it was there that Andy took his last breath. Ironically, he did not lose his life in the heat of battle – there was an accident with one of the newly acquired vehicles. Andy was in the wrong place at the wrong time and was crushed to death.

Maggie put on a brave face for the family and for the world at large. She had feared the worst for her husband on the day he was called up and she had suffered a sort of bereavement as she waved him off to join his regiment. His forced absence from the family home and her heavy involvement in the church made the news of his demise less catastrophic than it might have been. For the children it was a different matter, they were devastated. Ronnie had also been called up and was serving in the Navy on HMS Barham, he got the news some weeks after his father died and for days was inconsolable. Alice was a land girl and had stayed at home with her mother, she too, took her father's death very badly. Ben was eleven and bewildered by the absence of his father and brother, the resoluteness of his mother and the distress of his sister. He sought solace and support in the company of his friends.

Later that year came the news that HMS Barham had been sunk in combat and Ronnie was lost to the family as well

Ben knew he was not at all like his father or his brother but he still missed them and was stunned by the news, particularly of his brother who, despite their differences, had been a figure to look up to.

His friends at school became increasingly important to him. He found himself in the company of boys who were outgoing and athletic. The school his parents had chosen for his brother and sister was, naturally, a church school. Both siblings had done well academically and were regarded by the school as ideal students. They were focussed on their work, well behaved and always willing to help out. Ben was not a model student. He excelled on the sports ground in most things – he discovered physical talents which appeared to have bypassed both his mother and father. It was possible that his parents had latent untapped physical potential but had been steered away from its development.

For some time, Ben had been bullied at school. He had some of his parents' accent and his red hair attracted abuse from one group of boys in particular. The boys were not especially bad but once formed into their pack they liked to show off to each other and they took turns to pick on Ben at any opportunity. They call him the "spots man" on the basis of a problem with acne and the accent shared by his parents. He had done nothing to warrant any ill feeling except by being different and he found himself in several scraps. He became disinclined to remain at school any longer than was necessary.

Ben did not take to academic learning. It was not that he was unintelligent but more that he wasn't particularly inspired, either by his teachers or by the subjects they taught. He was just unable to focus on academic subjects. He worked hard at the physical – games, woodwork etc. The life of a book-keeper would not be for him.

His father and brother had been well built and both six foot tall, as was he, six foot two inches in fact. He was an outstanding football player and was rarely second to anyone in sporting endeavour at school. His physique would have lent him an advantage in most sporting careers. Sadly, there were few career paths to follow in the world of sport, which is where his choice would have taken him. He could not countenance a life spent within the confines of a building, either an office or a factory, so he opted to become an apprentice electrician.

A footballing friend from school, Jim Wilson, was starting as an apprentice electrician with his father, Bobby. As luck would have it, Bobby sought another pair of hands to learn the trade in return for hard work and a modest wage. Ben was known to Jim's father and was a good fit. He felt that Ben's family background, whilst a little strange, was likely to deliver the characteristics which were important to him - honesty, dedication, hard work, trustworthiness and reliability. Ben delivered on all of these and, apart from that, he was a nice engaging boy with a bit of character.

Ben enjoyed his work, being in different locations, meeting different people and was happy to be under the stewardship of his friend's dad who was a well-known local character. His skills as an electrician developed during the next couple of years as did his friendship with Jim and now Bobby Wilson.

Bobby Wilson was a good electrician, a good businessman and had an eye for an opportunity. The end of the war offered plenty of opportunity. Whilst the Midlands was not short of work there were much richer pickings to be found further south in London and the suburbs.

Ben learned about a different way of life. Laughter and fun now filled life. He found facial muscles which had hardly been used whilst in his dour presbyterian home. He developed his own sense of fun, his own sense of humour and a winning character, He was by no means a lothario, but the ladies generally found him engaging and it seemed there was a relaxation of morals which followed the relief of the war ending.

Ben shared digs with his friend Jim and they socialised together most nights. Usually, a couple of pints and a game of darts or dominoes during the week, perhaps a dance hall at the weekend and the occasional party.

It was at one of the parties that Ben met Sheila.

Jim had told him about a party to which he had been invited and, ever game, Ben had agreed to tag along. Jim brought a number of the electricians who were lodging in the area including some of Ben's old adversaries from school. They were all in high spirits and excited at the prospect of female company and a few drinks. There was no animosity but general bonhomie. There were six of them and each carried a couple of quarts of pale ale. The group had been to parties together before and usually managed to bring back 3 or 4 of the bottles that were their passport to entry. Four would arrive ahead of the others and enter the party displaying their alcoholic contributions to the host. The others would hang back and seek a side gate which usually allowed access to the kitchen. The early entrants would then pass 4 quarts back out through the kitchen window. These were stashed away to be collected later on their way home. It didn't always work but they had saved a few bob over the weeks. This was one such occasion and Ben was in the act of passing bottles out the window when Sheila came into the kitchen.

Sheila was rather unkempt. She cut and styled her own hair which was borne out of necessity and in particular a lack of money. Her hair was fair, not blonde. It was cut to shoulder length, was naturally very curly and often tangled as a result. Her skin was pallid and needed the rouge which she applied generously (her only real extravagance). She stood quite tall at five foot six and had quite a generous figure considering how little she ate. She was not overweight but she couldn't be described as skinny either. Generally, men found her immediately easy on the eye.

Ben and Sheila experienced an instant mutual attraction. To Ben, Sheila was young, pretty and joyful and looked to be up for fun. She was very attractive to Ben and during the course of the evening the pair found themselves separated from the crowd and in their own bubble. One thing led to another and the couple took off to a bedroom where guests clothes were stacked.

Ben was not a novice in the bedroom. His initial moral discomfort with the idea of casual sex had been overcome with the sheer pleasure which he drew from it. He had been taught by the Wilsons that young women were as keen as he was to engage in one night activity. They were there of their own free will and that was the way of things. Sheila was no shrinking violet. The vodka had loosened what were already relaxed morals. The couple had a frantic, breathless sexual liaison and in no time, it was all over. Sheila excused herself and went away to sort out her dishevelled appearance whilst Ben returned to the party and Jim. As they stood talking two of Ben's old adversaries from school, both of whom worked for Bobby and had tagged along on Jimmy's invite who Jim had invited along came in. They had been doing more than their share of drinking.

It was clear to them and probably most people at the party what had happened between Ben and Sheila. A mixture of jealousy, alcohol and remembered animosity started some bad humoured goading. Ben gallantly tried to defend both himself and Sheila. The school bullies were relentless and became blatantly insulting about both. Ben swung a fist at one, then the other. The first fist connected and its recipient went down like a sack of potatoes. The other missed and left Ben wide open to the quart bottle held in his opponent's hand. The bottle crunched against the side of his face and spilt it open from his eye to his jaw. There was blood everywhere and Ben and Jimmy knew it was time to go. Nobody had wanted this to happen and the fight stopped as quickly as it started at the sight of so much blood.

Someone grabbed a tea towel; Ben pressed it against the gaping wound. This was going to need stitches. Jimmy and Ben left the party immediately in search of medical attention.

Ben had hoped to spend more time with Sheila that evening and she had felt the same. Sheila had been upstairs "freshening up" and telling Winnie all about her encounter before returning to the party to meet up with Ben again. They had heard the fracas and came to see what it was all about but Ben and Jimmy had gone by the time they got down to the kitchen where a sober mood had taken over whilst the host tried his best to clean up the mess.

"Who was that?" the host asked. Nobody admitted to knowing the troublemakers and everyone spoke about northern ruffians spoiling the evening. Sheila was keen to find out more but nobody would own up to having any knowledge of these strangers. The bullies had upped and fled the party closely behind Ben and Jimmy so there was no one who could help. Sheila and Winnie sat down and tried to make sense of it all. The party ended fairly soon after the trouble, everybody's mood had changed. The girls made their way home, wondering if they would ever see Ben again. Jim had left with him so there was no one who could help.

Ben and Jim got to the nearest hospital, thankfully within reasonable walking distance. Ben was attended to and sent home to rest. He wasn't able to work for the next week so decided to return to Coventry and recuperate at home. He knew his mother would be horrified by the events at the party, so he changed his story to favour him and win what sympathy he could. His mother was led to understand that he had been set about by a group of drunks turning out from a pub. She found the story credible and typical of many in the godless south.

Chapter 4

Sheila attended June's funeral and shared Winnie's grief. For the moment Jennifer stayed with a kindly neighbour who had more sympathy for the child than the mother. There was a wake in the church hall, sparsely attended by neighbours and distant, unfamiliar relatives, plus one or two older friends who had lost touch with June during her alcoholic post-war collapse.

Sheila and Winnie stood sipping tea and remembering the good times they had enjoyed with June. "What will you do now" asked Winnie

"I don't know, I have to work so I'll need someone to look after Jennifer. The house is rented in your mother's name so I don't know what will happen. Even if I am allowed to stay, I don't think I can afford to keep it. I won't easily get a council flat and any money I can get from the government won't keep me fed, never mind me and a child. I don't know what I can do. I need to go back to work Monday or I will lose my job and then where will I be?"

Winnie felt deeply for her friend and to some degree felt complicit in the act which had brought this state of affairs all about. She had been there with Sheila, at the party. She had encouraged her to drink and even egged her on when Ben had made a play for her. She wanted to help but she had a life and family of her own. Her husband didn't particularly care for Sheila.

"Perhaps I can look after Jennifer whilst you work, until you can sort out something permanent. Annie goes to nursery in the morning so I could call by and take Jennifer to school on the way and pick her up afterwards till you get back from work"

Sheila grasped at the offer like a drowning woman reaching for a lifebuoy.

"Really Winnie, that would be incredible if you could manage that. Just till I can sort things out properly"

Winnie made her offer in the midst of an emotional farewell to her mother; she was in emotional shock and at a low ebb. It was an offer she almost regretted as she spoke the words. She came to rue her kindness as the weeks and months passed.

June's landlord, Mr Sweeney, called to visit his property. He was a fat unpleasant man, with rubber lips constantly wet with spittle. He wore an old Crombie coat which he wore across his shoulders without putting his arms in the sleeves as if he were some sort of film magnate. He sprayed spittle as he spoke and to be in his company was generally very disagreeable.

"I'm very sorry to hear about Mrs. Smith's untimely demise" he said unconvincingly "She was a good tenant, always paid on time and caused me little trouble. It was because of her attitude that I agreed to let her have you stay here, for an extra consideration of course. I will have to review the situation with regard to your staying. Can you afford the rent?"

Sheila didn't know exactly what rent June had been paying, she only knew what her own share had been and that was all she could manage. She knew she could not afford to keep on the whole house but might be able to get somebody to share with her which might make it possible.

"I think so" she said nervously "I will need to make some adjustments but I should be able to keep up payments" Now she was lying.

"Well sleep on it and let me know by the end of the week. Mrs Smith has paid up until the end of the month. I'll need a month's rent in advance if you are going to stay. I'll be back on Friday to collect your rent or to make arrangements for you to leave."

"Could you give me a little longer? This whole thing has been a bit of a blow and I have got lots of things to sort out"

"Yes, I am sure, unfortunately my rent is one of them and I can only delay for so long. You have until Friday week then, to produce the rent. After that I will make arrangements to move in a new tenant. I am not short of people looking for accommodation"

Sheila didn't know why but she thanked him as he turned and left the house.

During the next 10 days Sheila did all she could to find someone to share the house with her and Jennifer. She asked around at work and even put a notice up in the staff room. She asked her friends but nobody was interested. Finally, the day of Mr. Sweeney's visit arrived. He called in the evening after Sheila had collected Jennifer from Winnie's house.

"Good evening, Miss" he said to Sheila, looking pointedly at her through his fat watery eyes. Have you thought your options through?" Sheila was used to the disdained expression on Sweeney's face. She had seen in so many other faces since she became a single unmarried mother six years before. People were not sympathetic in the main. British society was intolerant and the treatment of single mothers was far from charitable. Most single mothers were treated in a similar way to the criminal classes, Sheila allowed Sweeney's nasty attitude to penetrate her defences She collapsed in a sea of tears.

"Tears won't pay the rent I'm afraid" said Mr Sweeney "You should have thought of this when you were having your fun" he said waving a fat finger at Jennifer.

"Please can you give me a little more time? I am sure I will find a way to get your rent."

"How much are you able to pay?"

Sheila told him and he laughed.

"I don't think you are going to be staying here young lady. I am not a charity I have to make a living! This is no more than I expected to happen." He paused and let her wallow in fear for a moment,

"You are a very lucky young lady though. I do have a bedsit which might suit you It is in need of cleaning and freshening up. I did have a rental fee in mind but I don't think you could even afford that; however, I do have a proposition for you. If you are prepared to move in, take it as you find it then set about cleaning it up and making it homely again, we might have found a solution which is to our mutual benefit. You can make up the shortfall in what I was expecting and what you can afford by working part time for me. I need a cleaner. The bedsit is furnished but it is as the previous old gentleman left it, I am sure you will be able to freshen it up."

Sheila looked at Jennifer. What choice did she have? They both needed a roof over their heads. Right now, the responsibility for her daughter felt like an anchor round her neck. Life would be a lot easier without a child to worry about. Reluctantly she accepted Sweeney's solution and found herself thanking him again.

"I am sure it will be for the best." said Sweeney "The flat is quite close by but perhaps the neighbourhood is less salubrious than here. Mrs. Smith's contract here finishes next Thursday. Please be ready to move out then. As I said your new home is already vacant so if you care to start moving your things there and cleaning it up from tomorrow you are welcome to do so. Please don't be surprised by the odour in the room. Unfortunately, the previous tenant died in his bed and was not found for several days."

Sheila agreed to pay a week's rent in advance which was as much as she could muster.

The next few days, Sheila spent the hours after work and the days of the weekend between her new and old "homes". She had an unexpected sense of excitement with the thought of actually taking on a place of her own, no matter how basic. Jennifer shared her mother's anticipation of a new start and trotted happily alongside as they made their way to their new flat for the first time. It was Friday afternoon. The road was quite grand in Sheila's eyes, semi-detached houses with large high-ceilinged rooms, net curtains at the windows and Romanesque columns on either side of the front doors. Steep and imposing steps led up to the front door; six steps to reach the door. A further set of steps led down to the basement. In the main, the houses were very well-maintained Sheila's hopes and expectations rose as she tried to peer inside each sash corded window. She counted the house numbers and looked eagerly for number 49.

Number 49 turned out to be the black sheep of the road, a sad neglected version of its sibling dwellings. Clearly it had once boasted a similar pedigree to the rest of the street. Now it was a sorrowful wreck of a house. Some years ago, the owners had died without children or relatives to whom they could leave the property. Mr Sweeney heard about the property and made an approach to the accountants dealing with the affairs of the deceased. He managed to persuade the disinterested partner of the firm, to part with the property for a song. He could not believe his good fortune at acquiring such a property. He was not a man to worry about the condition of the building as long as it turned a profit. He chose not to pay any attention to the repairs and maintenance badly needed. His first and urgent need was to fill as many rooms as he could with paying tenants. This he achieved relatively quickly and provided an income to cover the borrowings required for the acquisition in the first place. He had always said he planned to attend to the building's many shortfalls but there was always a good reason for leaving it till the following month.

The condition of the building grew worse and worse, the tenants were effectively hostages, unable to make a difference to their surroundings. They existed and paid their rent. Sheila was just the next in line.

Sheila's heart sank. It had all been a bit too good to be true. An old stone wall covered in moss and ivy stood between her and the steps leading down into the basement. Refuse was strewn across the small paved area between the house and the wall. Sheila's key number was 49 A. She looked up at the once imposing building and then down to the darkened door which was the entrance to 49A. Carefully, holding Jennifer's hand, she stepped down the broken concrete steps leading to the peeling green wooden front door. A brass lion's head door knocker which had seen better days dared visitors to knock. Sheila imagined there had not been many who took up the challenge.

The key Sweeney had provided was stiff in the lock and reluctant to let Sheila continue her journey to her future life. She twisted and turned as best she could, back and forth until finally it succumbed to her persistence and the door to moaned open.

Sheila walked into a wall of putrid odour unlike any smell she had previously encountered. It was tangible. Instinctively she pulled the door closed again and turned away. This was not how she wanted to introduce Jennifer to their new start, so they went back home and Sheila determined that she would leave Jennifer with Winnie and come back the following morning.

As Sheila approached the house for the second time, she felt nothing but dread. It seemed to be her only option. What choice did she have? Armed with cleaning materials supplied by Sweeney, Sheila wrestled with the reluctant lock again and with all her ten and a half stone forced open the door. Cleaning materials were dropped to the floor and with a kitchen towel wrapped around her face to protect her from the stench Sheila made for the sash windows, tripping on the edge of a curled rug. She caught herself on an old dining table with folded down leaves. Cleanliness had not been a strength during her life to date but even she had never seen such black, sticky net curtains. The previous occupant had clearly been a heavy smoker with a reluctance to open the windows for fresh air. Sheila tore down the nets and cast them aside revealing a view of three sash window shaping the bay front of the room. After struggling for some time, the sashes relented and opened to allow in some much-needed cold, fresh, clean air.

Sheila went out as quickly as she could to recover from the toxic atmosphere. She bathed in the luxury of relatively unpolluted street air. Her second foray took her to the back of the bedsit. There was a reasonably sized kitchenette at the back with windows which looked onto the wall below the garden. She flung open the windows and pushed open the door to the crumbling brick steps leading up to the garden.

The garden was an untamed jungle. It was difficult to get through the overgrowth, nobody had paid any attention to the space for years. However, it was a garden and Sheila was able to breath in comfortably again.

It took Sheila most of her weekend to get any semblance of order in the place she was to call home. Furniture was to stay despite cigarette burns and frayed edges. She had no choice. Everything was going to be difficult to clean but she would try. Reluctantly bed clothes were scrubbed by hand in a large ceramic basin in the kitchenette. She rolled up the rug in the living area and heaved into the garden, for now. The electric meter was discovered in a cupboard by the front door. Sheila couldn't believe her luck to find a tin half full of coins intended for the meter. It was early March and the weather was spring-like but this weekend was abnormally cold. Sheila burnt the two-bar electric fire to keep herself and the building warm. The coins had presumably belonged to her deceased predecessor and Sweeney had clearly failed to spot them. He would have spirited them away without a doubt.

The odour had invaded the fabric of the building. As the cold fresh air invaded the room the smell was becoming more bearable but the traces of odour would take weeks to deal with completely.

Sheila stood back to inspect her work. It was cleaner but didn't feel clean, fresher but still stale, poorly lit and decorated but this was to be home. She pulled the stubborn door closed behind her and set off to collect Jennifer.

Chapter 5

The day that Sheila and Jennifer moved into their new bedsit Sweeney came round.

"Everything to your satisfaction" he spluttered, as if he cared for their well-being at all. He was grateful to have had the bedsit cleaned up and for what it was the rent that Sheila was paying was more than enough. There was no rent book and Sheila had to settle in cash each week which Sweeney insisted on calling for every Friday evening between five and seven. This of itself was an irritation.

"Now in order for you to make up the balance of rent payments I will need you to clean for me each Saturday morning from 8 till midday. For a start you can come to my house and get me sorted out for the first few weeks. After that we can look to the other properties and see where you can be of help. It will be fine to take the little girl with you as long as she behaves herself. I don't want her running amok"

"She will be fine," said Sheila.

There was something uncomfortable about Sweeney today which she hadn't noticed before. He had been quite cold and calculating up to date, not pleasant but at least she had felt that she was dealing with a hard-nosed landlord whose only interest lay in his property and the cash it could generate. She had thought she represented no more than a cog in the money-making machine of his business, but today was different. She had left the house that June had rented from him. Somehow it was her domain not his and she had felt quite safe there. Now she was on his ground, not yet settled and here he was making his demands already. She felt there was a different attitude in his approach.

Sweeney gave Sheila the address of his house: 31, Railway Mews and said he expected her to be there promptly at 8.00 am as there was much to do. Sheila agreed and saw him out of the front door not daring to mention the lock or the difficulty which it presented merely opening and closing. That would have to wait. For now, she needed to establish this as their home. She looked at her daughter and felt herself welling up. Her poor child had not had much of a start in life. Her mother seemed to not care, and had left her in the hands of an old lady. The old lady, whom she had grown to love, had now died and was never to be seen again. Now this, a new home, smaller and less inviting, dark and visited by a slobbering unpleasant old man.

Sheila resolved to change her attitude towards her daughter. She would try and improve things for them both. She would do all that she could to make things right for them. Early next morning Sheila set off for the Sweeney house. She wrapped up Jennifer as warmly as she could. The child carried her rag doll and was happy to be going somewhere.

Railway Mews was a disappointment to Sheila. She expected that her landlord, as a wealthy man, would be living somewhere grand. Not so. Railway Mews was a street with terraced houses on one side and a raised railway track on the other. As Sheila and Jennifer made their way down the road in search of number 31, a steam train clattered by. The smell of smoke intensified with the outpouring from the funnel of the passing locomotive. It was noisy enough to scare Jennifer as it rattled by. The houses were narrow and dark. It was early Saturday morning so many curtains remained drawn. Dark, dirty curtains. This was a road of railway workers, coalmen and labourers. It was not the expected location of a landlord. There were no front gardens; the doors of each property opened directly onto the street. There were signs of fires being lit as smoke bellowed from some of the chimneys to add to the already lung-choking air. A milk cart pulled by a plodding old black mare, who had followed the same routine for years and knew when to stop without a word from the milkman. She heaved her load forward to the next property. At her rear end balanced below her tail a canvas contraption caught most of her excretion which added character to the atmosphere of the Mews. As Sheila and Jennifer passed by, Jennifer was both fascinated and scared by the horse. She kept her mother between her and this enormous beast but kept her eyes on it until they were well past what she perceived as danger.

Sweeney's house was at the end of the long terrace and at the end of the road.

Sheila and Jennifer arrived at 7.45 sharp and knocked at the door. It took Sweeney some time to open the door and to her surprise he was still in pyjamas and a dressing gown "You might as well get used to seeing me in my PJs" he grunted "You'll be seeing a lot more in the future!"

Sheila wasn't sure what he meant so she just pretended to have misheard. She smiled and eased pass the fat landlord, tugging a reluctant Jennifer with her.

"You will have to behave little girl; your mother has got things to do around here and we don't want you interfering, do we?" He sought confirmation from Sheila. It seemed Sweeney had hoped the child would not have to accompany her mother.

"She will be fine" said Sheila "Where do want me to start"

"Well, the bedroom of course!" He said with a sneer.

Again, Sheila was unsure. She was keen to quickly establish a routine so that this sort of uncomfortable conversation wouldn't be necessary again.

"Can you show me which rooms need cleaning please" Sheila asked trying to pull the conversation away from the unsavoury direction which Sweeney seemed to be taking.

"Well yes of course, follow me!"

Sheila and Jennifer were given a full tour of the house. There was not a lot to see.

The dark narrow hall was lit by two pairs of yellowing bulbs sitting in brass wall mounted candle style holders. A huge mahogany mirror which did its best to make the space seem wider. Sheila caught her reflection and saw the cleaning lady which she now was.

To the left of the passageway two doors opened onto small living rooms each with an open fireplace neither lit but both with signs of fires in recent days. The first room might be described as a sitting room. Two deep wing backed chairs convivially faced the fireplace each with a small occasional table beside it. On one table an ashtray spilled its contents alongside a whiskey glass and a dirty cup and saucer. Sheila imagined Sweeney sitting smoking and poring over his accounts here. She found it difficult to imagine him having any leisure pursuits. The other room was set up for eating and reading. A circular leafed table was half opened against the wall. There were four chairs in the room, three around the table and one tucked uncomfortably in the corner against the floor to ceiling book shelf.

The end of the passageway opened onto the kitchen. Two identical green, open flapped, kitchen cabinets stood side by side like sentries. Both hinged flaps were open each crowded with kitchen flotsam and jetsam. An open can of corned beef with its key and lid still attached. Half a loaf of bread surrounded by its crumbs. Butter on a saucer designed to hold a cup. A sticky jar of half-eaten strawberry jam. Sardines in a dish. Sheila tried to imagine the order in which Sweeney might consume these delicacies. At the end of the kitchen a door opened to a scarcely populated larder. Outside was a toilet in a small shed like room attached to the building.

The stairs up to the first floor were steep and led to two bedrooms. The first was at the front of the house, obviously where Sweeney slept. The second a smaller room which was crammed with junk. There was a sort of passageway through the various piles of books, gramophone records, furniture and ornaments. Sheila guessed these had come from some of his properties. Everything was stacked in piles in order to allow as much use of the space as possible rather than for the sake of tidiness. Beyond this room was a tiny bathroom with a bath and basin but no toilet facilities. These as she had learned were outside – not a welcome prospect.

Overall, the house was far from filthy but nor was it clean. This man probably had never cleaned for himself but relied on somebody to tidy once a week. Sheila had become the latest somebody. In Sweeney's bedroom, clothes from the week lay strewn across the floor. The wardrobe door hung open exposing its contents which were packed in tightly. In the kitchen the week's washing up covered the surfaces and half empty tins sat alongside them. This was very clearly the home of a single man with no sense of hygiene or cleanliness. Sheila found herself feeling a little sorry for Sweeney. Her sympathy was short lived.

"Well get on with it then" Sweeney barked.

"I think I will start downstairs," suggested Sheila. "I can move upstairs once you have dressed and come out"

"Very well" said Sweeney clearly not expecting this turn of events.

"Did you have a cleaner before?" Sheila enquired timidly

"Of course, Tilly," said Sweeney testily. "Things started getting a bit uncomfortable between us and so she took herself off."

"Can I just be clear what I am required to do exactly?"

"Well clean the house as we discussed, what else do you think I mean? Don't go in my private things. Don't go through my drawers. If I need clothes cleaning, I will give them to you"

"Okay, I can see washing up, floors and surfaces and general tidying which will probably take all of the morning."

"I like the bed changed and the sheets washed every Saturday as well," said Sweeney

"Okay "said Sheila hesitatingly "What did Tilly use to clean the sheets"

Sweeney looked at Sheila with incredulity "Well the bath of course. She would heat up a bucket of water and clean them in the bath on the washboard, with a bar of soap. There's a mangle and a hanging clothes horse in there too so she would hang them up to dry indoors in the winter and in the backyard in the summer"

"Fine" said Sheila realising that Sweeney was not a man to invest in modern facilities like a twin tub. Sweeney's cleaner was provided a Bex Bissel floor sweeper, various cloths and dusters which had all seen better days. Sheila was beginning to confirm her opinions of Sweeney – he was a man who liked collecting money more than he liked spending it. She just needed to get on with it and see how much could be done but clearly, he wanted his sheets changed so she must allow time for that.

"Do you have clean sheets spare?"

"Of course, "said Sweeney "they are stored in the top of my wardrobe, if you can't reach them, I can give you a bit of a lift"

"I'll be fine, why don't you get dressed and I will make a start in the kitchen" said Sheila and hurried to the kitchen. Jennifer had followed her mother around sullenly.

"I'm hungry "she said

Sheila realised that this was not going to work. "Fine" she said and got out a bread-and-butter sandwich with a smear of jam. Jennifer sat in a deep chair and tucked into it ravenously as though she hadn't eaten for a week. Sheila resolved to seek Winnie's help looking after Jennifer again on a Saturday morning. Sheila started into the dirty dishes

Sweeney dressed and went out. "I'll be back in time to see you off" he said. Sheila was polishing a table with some help from her young daughter.

"Okay Mr Sweeney" she said and continued with her polishing.

As soon as he was out of the door Sheila rushed upstairs followed by Jennifer. She realised that she must get the sheets done and bed made quickly. The sheets would take some time to wash and get hung up and she felt this and the dishes were the most important things to keep Sweeney happy. It was more relaxed without Sweeney in the house. Jennifer could be left to explore and play with some of the things she found. Sheila just kept an eye on her.

The sheets were soon off the bed and Sheila found that her worst fears had not been necessary. The sheets were reasonably clean if rather rumpled. The clean sheets were folded away where Sweeney had pointed out and while they were not ironed, they were reasonably presentable. She remade the bed with the clean sheets and the less clean blankets. She picked up the clothes from the floor and put them into a wicker basket in the corner. The room already looked much better.

She'd had the foresight to heat a bucket of water and set about washing the sheets in the bath. There was a washboard and soap to hand.

Sheila had brought the child's rag doll along. Jennifer had named her Junie and wouldn't go anywhere without her. The child made up stories in the new rooms in which she had to play. As any child of her age Jennifer was curious. She had particularly liked looking through the piles of junk in the second bedroom. Sweeney's room held no less interest. There were cupboards and a chest of drawers, boxes under the bed, curtains to hide behind. For now, she was happily sitting with her doll on the floor discussing the doll's next bath time. As she stood to take Junie to the bathroom her foot slipped on the threadbare rug covering the dark varnished floorboards. The rug went with her and she fell and banged her head. There was little harm done, although the ear-piercing scream that came out of that little body would suggest otherwise. Sheila dropped the soap-soaked sheets and ran to her daughter.

"What happened" she asked, although it was quite clear from the scuffed rug that Jennifer had come a cropper as a result of the rug slipping. Jennifer sobbed and heaved her lungs not really knowing why. She had no pain but was very angry and a touch embarrassed at her fall. As Sheila sat and comforted her daughter, she noticed a small string between the floorboards and easing

Jennifer away from her tugged at the string. She thought she was tidying but the string was firmly attached.

As she pulled it a loose floorboard started to rise. Sheila grasped the floorboard and pulled it towards her. The board came free to reveal a space between the joists containing a cardboard shoe box. Sheila felt a tinge of guilt but her curiosity was overwhelming. She reached down and retrieved the shoe box carefully; Jennifer's sobs were becoming less intense as she shared her mother's interest in the box in front of them.

Sweeney had taken himself off for a haircut, which was long overdue, a newspaper and a bottle of whiskey. The off licence was shut so he would have to venture out again later. He visited the corner shop for some groceries and was on his way home to see how this new girl was getting on with his flat. She would come in handy for a number of his properties, he thought and if she is nice to me, I might even pay her a basic amount for the extra work. Sweeney's mind was racing to a place where Sheila and he were friends, more than friends, fantasy land really but he had little else to think about that morning. He turned the key in the door and entered. There was no sign of them downstairs so he made his way to the kitchen and put his shopping away in the larder. He was pleased with the way the kitchen looked. The washing up was done and things had been put into cupboards. The floor had been swept of all the crumbs and dropped food particles. The floor had actually been mopped and was looking good. He heard the child upstairs and loudly announced himself.

Sheila had been unable to resist a peek inside the box. She had lifted the lid carefully to reveal bundles of ten-shilling, one pound and five-pound notes. They were rolled neatly up and equally neatly packed into the box. This was probably the best kept and neatest item that she had found in the house so far. Sheila touched the rolls. They were mostly ten shilling and one-pound bundles but it was more money than she had ever seen or could imagine. She thought each roll must contain about fifty notes except the five pounds which were much bigger and folded rather than rolled – there were much fewer of those. It looked like there were about ten rolls. Sheila was trying to calculate how much there might be when she heard the front door open. Putting Jennifer aside Sheila hurried to return the room to its former state and move quickly back to the bathroom and the wet sheets. Jennifer's sobbing had ceased and she clung to Junie for comfort.

"I'm back" hollered Sweeney "Kitchen looks nice. Very good. Let me see how you're getting on up here."

Sheila heard his weight on the stairs. The stairs creaked one by one. He reached the top of the stairs and peered into the bedroom.

"Looks alright" he said "have you swept the floor"

"Not yet" said Sheila, she felt certain that Sweeney would notice something that she had missed and she was not sure what to expect from him if he suspected her of going through his things.

"I thought I'd finish washing the sheets and get them hung out first and then sweep up, I won't have time for much more" she said. Sweeney harrumphed and went to his wardrobe. She thought he looked down at the floor but he said nothing and went to the inside pocket of a jacket in the wardrobe.

He turned and looked at her looking at him.

"Well get on with it then "he said.

Sheila finished the sheets and hung them up to dry. She swept the bedroom and tidied the cleaning tools. It was five past midday and she was relieved to have finished.

"I'll be off then" Sheila said.

"Very well, young lady I'll see you next Friday for the rent, and see if you can find somewhere for that child next Saturday. She can only interfere with you doing a proper job for me. She would be happier somewhere else where she can play."

Sheila didn't want to argue.

"I'll see what I can do "she said and made her way downstairs to the front door with Jennifer in tow.

"Just a minute! "Sweeneys voice stopped her in her tracks. What has he noticed? Her heart was racing and she was trying to formulate an excuse for having been looking under the floorboards.

"You'll be needing this for next week"

Sweeney proffered a key.

"I suppose I can trust you with this. Please don't let me down. I won't want to be getting out of my bed at eight o clock in the morning next Saturday. Let yourself in and bring me a cup of tea at about eight thirty would you"

Sheila wanted to throw the key at him but knew that she couldn't

"Of course, Mr. Sweeney. Thank you for your trust in me"

Sheila and Jennifer shuffled up the road and made their way to the hovel they now called home.

Chapter 6

The following week Sheila arranged for Jennifer to go to Winnie's on a Saturday morning early. Winnie and her husband were not overjoyed with the arrangement but Winnie continued to feel compassion for Sheila and had come to love Jennifer as one of her own. Their own daughter Annie was actually easier to manage when she had Jennifer to play with, so another day was not the end of the world.

Sheila arrived at Sweeney's house at eight o'clock and no earlier this time. She made tea for Sweeney to drink in bed and took it up to him. Sweeney sat up in bed with the bedclothes covering his rotund stomach but exposing the gaping pyjama top and underneath a mass of greying hair on his chest. He was unwashed, ungroomed and unshaven. The room hung with stale air which had no doubt circulated Sweeneys lungs several times during the night. His body contributed the smell of dried sweat to the room's ambiance.

"What a pleasure" he said and sipped at his tea with his little finger pointed at the ceiling, as if a titled lady in her drawing room. He smiled a filthy smile at Sheila "Would you like to join me?" he said and patted the bed by his side. Sheila ignored him and went to work on the cleaning. This pattern was repeated over the coming weeks. Sheila was never comfortable with taking Sweeneys tea to him first thing. There was always an undercurrent of suggestive behaviour which might one day lead to him overstepping the mark.

Habitually Sweeney went out for two or three hours on a Saturday morning whilst Sheila cleaned up behind him. Sweeney would try to make conversation whilst he was there but mainly in the form of complaining about the behaviour of his other tenants.

Sheila was uncomfortably aware of the stash of money sitting in a box under the floorboards in Sweeney's bedroom. Part of her wanted to check again to see if what she had seen was real and whether it was still there or not. Part of her was scared that Sweeney might somehow find out that she knew. So, she left well alone and pretended she had not seen the hidden cache.

One Saturday morning whilst Sweeney was out, there was a knock at the door. Sheila was not sure whether to pretend not to be there and ignore it, or open up and find out who it was calling on her landlord. Curiosity got the better of her and she opened the door.

"Oh, Hello is Mr. Sweeney here?" the voice belonged to a young man probably in his early twenties. He was quite dark and Mediterranean looking, unshaven and scruffily dressed. Sheila was most struck by his dark blue eyes which sparkled with life. The man was clearly surprised to see Sheila.

"No, I'm afraid he has gone out for a while"

"Pity, when will he be back?" said the man.

"I really don't know exactly but he is usually back by the time I finish which is midday"

"I don't suppose I could wait," said the man. He had an accent which was unfamiliar to Sheila. She didn't come across many foreigners in her life.

"I am sorry, no. I can't let complete strangers into somebody else's house. Can you come back?"

"Looks like I will have to" he said with a smile "If he comes back, please tell him that Mickey Godoy- Orellana from Glengall Road called round with his rent. He was getting a little concerned because I didn't have the cash to give him last night so I brought it round"

"I live in Glengall Road," said Sheila

"49?" he asked

"Yes" she said "how did you know?" she wished she hadn't said it as soon as the words left her lips.

"Well, Mr Sweeney owns that house" Mickey said

"Of course," said Sheila "How silly. I haven't seen you there?" Again, she felt foolish, she hadn't seen any other tenants at 49 Glengall Road since she had been there.

"Yes, we're not a very outgoing bunch, are we?" he said "I only know one other tenant in Flat B, an older lady Miss Philpot who I help with the shopping sometimes. I am in the attic, Flat G. What about you?"

"Basement, Flat A"

"Ok how is it in there? Mickey asked

"Horrible actually, but you know how it is, beggars can't be choosers" Sheila smiled uncomfortably

"Yes" he said "I suppose you know about the old man who lived there before you?" he asked gingerly.

"Not really?" Sheila said "except that all of his furniture is what I am living with now and moving in was not a nice experience. The flat smelt terrible and was very dirty, I had to clean it up as best I could and I don't think I will ever be able to completely lose the smell. We have to live with it. What else is there to know?"

Mickey was wishing he hadn't asked and wasn't sure what to say now.

"Well, there's not much to tell really. He died as you know and wasn't found for several days, nobody is completely sure what killed him. The police were called when somebody complained about the smell. Sweeney took his money monthly in advance from the old man and paid little attention to him, so he didn't notice. Sadly, nobody did, till it was far too late. The police were unsure about the cause of death at first and to be honest I don't know what has happened since. I didn't even realise that the flat had been relet. Sweeney doesn't hang about with money matters. He must have got the all clear from the police. I feel very sorry that you had to clean it up"

"Yes, well I must get on" Sheila realised that she mustn't talk too much as she'd not have enough time to get finished. It was a pity, conversation with Mickey seemed very easy. "I will tell him you called"

"Okay, thank you I will look out for you at 49, perhaps we can have a coffee one day?"

"Yes perhaps" Sheila said and closed the door.

As she cleaned and tidied Sheila thought about Mickey who seemed like a very gentle and caring man. She thought him very handsome and remembered the sparkle in his eye. Strangely he held no particular sexual attraction for her at all, which surprised her, nothing within her was excited by their meeting. The morning passed slowly and Sweeney finally returned from his expedition. Sheila told him of the visit of Mickey Godoy- Orellana during the morning. He was irritated to have missed him and muttered something about unreliable foreigners. As had become the norm he was content with her work and invited her to stay for lunch and as normal she politely refused, bade him goodbye and left to collect Jennifer. She had no desire or intent to befriend her landlord. She remained courteous but distant.

Jennifer was pleased to see her mother and looked forward to getting back to what was now established as home. The relationship between mother and daughter was growing slightly better since they had move to Glengall Road. It was a shared adversity through which they were helping each other. Sheila being at work all day Monday to Friday and Saturday morning made their time together more valuable. The bedsit was cleaner and becoming more liveable.

As they arrived home, they saw Mickey coming down the road. He waved and hurried towards them.

"Hello" he said with a smile "and who is this?" indicating Jennifer.

"Hello, she said "this is Jennifer, my daughter" Sheila expected the same disapproving look which most people gave her on realising her status as a single apparently unmarried mother. Mickey was far from disapproving and got down to Jennifer's level to say "Hello Jennifer, what a lovely name, my name is Mickey and we live in the same house. I have the top and you have the bottom!"

Jennifer was unsure and shuffled behind her mother's legs.

"Don't be shy, I won't bite. I promise. Here do you like fruit drops?" he looked to Sheila for approval before producing a small paper bag from his pocket with a variety of brightly coloured sweets. Jennifer sheepishly reached into the bag and pulled out a bright red sweet, studied it for a moment, quickly checked with her mother then popped it into her mouth. Sweets were not a regular occurrence in her life so this was a real treat. Jennifer remained behind her mother's legs but smiled warmly at Mickey.

"I didn't ask your name" he said to Sheila

"Sheila" she replied "Sheila Johnson"

"I didn't realise you had a lovely daughter" he said "but why would I – I suppose"

"Can I invite you up for a tea or a coffee?"

"That's very kind but we have to get Jennifer her lunch, thank you"

"I could manage a sandwich and a biscuit if that would do?"

Sheila didn't feel the sense of distrust that she felt with Sweeney and most other men. She quite liked the idea of sitting down and talking to someone about something different. She heard herself saying "Well, yes thank you, that would be nice". She was also curious to see another part of the building. So, Sheila, Jennifer and Mickey climbed the broad concrete stairs to the front door. The door had a small coloured glass semi- circular window at the top to shed some light in the hall. Mickey went to get his keys but found that the door was slightly ajar. They entered the hallway which had a patterned tile mosaic floor. The stairs were heavy dark wood with a carpet which just covered the centre of each stair. The carpet was held in place by two brass arms on each riser. Mickey switched on the light which was a bare yellowish lightbulb and hopped up the stairs two by two. Sheila and Jennifer followed more slowly, taking in the new surroundings.

On the first floor Mickey indicated two doors side by side, Flats C&D. "I think there is an Irishman in C and an old German Jewish couple in D." He whispered "I have never met them". They carried on up the stairs to the next floor again two doors faced the stairs Flats E & F. Sheila looked enquiringly.

"A young couple in one and an older man in the other" said Mickey "I have seen them but never really spoken to them. I hear the young couple arguing sometimes and the old man plays classical music late at night but I can't tell you much more. I bump into them from time to time but that's all I know."

The staircase continued up with a single doorway at its head. "This is me!" Mickey said proudly and flung open the door.

The room beyond came as quite a surprise to Sheila. The floor area was vast but the room was limited by the sloping roof. Still, it felt spacious. Cupboards were built into the eves making sensible use of the space. A Kitchenette filled one corner; a dining table sat alongside the kitchenette with four open fold-away chairs. Between the kitchenette and the dining area was a door which led off to a WC and shower area.

In the opposite corners a small sofa and single chair sat facing a sideboard with a record player on top. The record player resembled the His Masters Voice record player seen on the covers of 78RPM records. Mickey had a collection of, mainly classical, 78's. The other corner was the sleeping area with a neatly made single bed, chest of drawers and bedside table. Sheila noticed an artist's easel and brushes tucked away against the wall alongside the bed.

Sheila was struck by how tidy and ordered everything appeared. Mickey went to the four-bar electric fire and switched it on. Sheila hadn't really noticed the chill. They all kept their coats on for the moment.

"It'll warm up soon, what can I get you to drink? Ovaltine for Jennifer, tea or coffee for Sheila? "Mickey asked

"Jennifer and I love Ovaltine – that will be great for us both thanks" Sheila said

Mickey poured milk into a pan and set it onto the gas stove. "We'll all have Ovaltine then "He opened a drawer and took out a box of matches and lit the gas. "What would you like in your sandwich Jennifer. I'm afraid I only have jam, marmite, spam, cheese spread, fish paste, sardines"

"Jam" said Jennifer

"Jam it is and what about mummy?"

"Sardines please," said Sheila

"Tomato?"

"Yes please"

"There's not much to see but have a look around, while I make lunch." He found some paper and coloured pencils in one of his cupboards. "Can you draw me a picture Jennifer"

Jennifer nodded and pushed her tongue into the side of her cheek. Mickey helped her sit at the table and set her off drawing. Whilst Mickey made their modest lunch Sheila looked around Mickey's home. There was a replica of Michelangelo's David which she liked although she didn't know that was what it was. Various pictures adorned the walls, one or two which were apparently the amateur work of Mickey.

"You paint?" she asked

"Yes, badly as you can see but I like to try"

"Oh no they're not bad, they're pretty good actually" Sheila said "You have promise!" she hesitated teasing him and then said with a smile "As if I know what I am talking about"

He smiled back but said no more.

After a while they sat at the table and ate their sandwiches and drank their Ovaltine.

"Well," said Mickey "So what brought you to 49 Glengall Road"

Sheila didn't really know where to start. She told Mickey about June and what had happened leading up to meeting Sweeney. She was careful not to say anything out of place. She didn't really know what Mickey felt about Sweeney and now was not the right time to be completely honest about how she felt. Mickey listened sympathetically and made the right noises as Sheila told her story. She avoided talking about Jennifer's father or the circumstances that lead to her conception. She had experienced nothing but bad reactions to her being a single parent and didn't want to invite more from Mickey.

Jennifer sat quietly drawing and listening to her mother talk about their recent lives. She looked at Mickey frequently, sizing him up, the way only a child can. She was forming the opinion that he was trustworthy and could be fun, but for now she was not going to open up to him.

Sheila asked Mickey about his background. He told her that he wasn't currently with anyone and that he had only recently stopped living with his Spanish parents. He went on to explain his background and how he came to be living in 49 Glengall Road.

Mickey's actual name was Miguel. He had anglicised it early on at school, wanting to fit in with the others so he told them to call him Mickey. His mother and father were Spanish. They had been reasonably comfortable, living a normal life in Madrid. They had an apartment and lived well. They had met at a socialist group meeting and their joint political views had brought them together to eventually marry.

Their political beliefs led them to sign up for the communist party. General Franco was in the ascendancy and his politics diametrically opposed to those of the Godoy- Orellana's. At the outset of the civil war Miguel's parents had decided to stay and fight for their cause. Months into the turmoil, with the violence going on around them, they changed their minds. They had a four-year-old child and their first concern was his wellbeing so they took up what they could reasonably carry and fled to France. Most of their possessions they left behind. They became nomadic for a while.

They had heard that England was welcoming and heard stories of other Spanish refugees settling there. They used what money they had to pay for their passage from southern France. They had been told of a small Spanish community in North West London so that was where they headed, finally settling in a small flat in Maida Vale recommended by Spanish friends. To make ends meet they had started cleaning for a family in the area. They were diligent and hardworking and their employers recommended them to others. Life was not easy for immigrants. War was brewing and there was a general distrust of all foreigners.

The Godoy- Orellana's were lovely warm-hearted people and those that employed them offered other work – general maintenance and the like. The war came and Mickey was evacuated to the coast – quite an unstable start for an 8-year-old whose first language had not been English. After the war Mickey briefly went to school in the Kilburn area of North London until he was fourteen years old. At fourteen he left and joined his mother and father's growing cleaning business, which was where he remained. The parents built a business" Clean and Tidy" which did well. By chance one of their employers had heard of a position as house keeper and general maintenance man for a married couple in a grand mansion in Hertfordshire. There was accommodation offered with the position. The Godoy- Orellana's expressed their interest and, following a successful interviewing process, relocated.

Mickey was 21 years old and decided to stay in the area and keep the cleaning business running. He renamed it "Spic and

Span" which amused him, his school friends had called him both names when he had first come to England. He found a place to stay and settled into his work, cleaning and developing the business.

Jennifer interrupted Mickey's story.

"Can we go home now?"

"In a while" Sheila was enjoying hearing about somebody else's life.

"Why don't I make you a paper aeroplane," said Mickey, who then fetched one of his sketch pads, ripped out a sheet of paper and folded a plane shape. He demonstrated how it would fly and gave it to Jennifer to try. Her first attempt was successful and she was hooked, throwing Mickey's basic origami work all about the room. For a while she forgot about going home.

"So how long have you lived here" Sheila asked

"Oh about 18 months – it was going to be temporary but I have made it habitable and just got used to it really" he replied. "I am thinking about moving on now. I 've managed to put some money by from the business and I've heard that I can get a loan from the council to help me buy somewhere"

Sheila felt disappointed she was just making a little progress with someone who might become a friend and he was talking about leaving.

"Oh, that's good" she said "Good for you I mean, not for me!" She felt herself flushing red, not comfortable with what she had just said "It must be lovely to be able to visualise things getting better! My future looks much the same as far as I can imagine. Not a prospect that fills me with hope!"

"Then you must trust yourself, imagine more and imagine better things," said Mickey earnestly. "With hard work and desire, you can achieve many things"

Sheila smiled "I am sure you are right" She didn't really mean it

"May I ask about Jennifer's father?" Mickey felt a little uncomfortable asking but was interested to know more about Sheila's situation. Sheila flushed red again and braced herself for the inevitable tut tutting, but found she felt quite comfortable talking to Mickey as the story unfolded and felt no judgement from him. Mickey smiled and said "Thank you for trusting me with your story. I think you are very brave. Now I will tell you, my secret."

Sheila said nothing but looked intently at Mickey.

"Some time ago" said Mickey "I realised that I was not the same as my friends in school. They all fantasised about the femme fatales in films or dancing girls or beautiful singers. For me I felt more that I related to them, the girls that is. I tried to join the boys in their fantasies about some of the girls in our school but it just didn't work for me. I thought I must be too young or immature and that I would start to understand their feelings as I grew older, but as I grew, I began to realise that it was the boys that excited me. Sheila I'm a homosexual. I hope you understand, Society looks at me in much the same way as it looks at an unmarried mother, with contempt. I'm sure you can understand. I didn't choose to be this way and life would be a whole lot simpler if I wasn't but I can't change the way I am made"

Sheila was shocked. She had no idea that Mickey might reveal such personal information. She had only met him twice and very briefly. She didn't know how to react. She was programmed to feel disgusted at the thought of two men together and yet she felt empathy with Mickey. She understood some of the problems he would face being different.

"So do you have a boyfriend?"

"No, I never have – I just know I'm different – I know that I shouldn't be, I know it is illegal but I can't change myself, so I have never tried. I focus on work and building the business."

"Have you ever had a girlfriend?" Sheila asked

"Not in that way no, but I have girlfriends"

Jennifer buzzed her paper plane passed Mickey's ear.

"Crickey, I don't know what to say"

"Well actually I would rather you didn't say anything to anyone. Can you keep it our secret, otherwise I could end up in prison? Oh, and should you ever meet my parents – even they don't know – it would kill them. I just feel that I can trust you"

"Of course."

Sheila and Mickey talked and talked for about an hour and would have gone on but for Jennifer demanding attention.

"We really should go "said Sheila "Thank you for lunch, it was lovely" She meant it was lovely to be able to talk to somebody for so long and to be so comfortable. Mickey felt the same, he was quite lonely and the time he had spent with Sheila had been welcome.

"Perhaps we could do this again" he said

"That would be great" Sheila said almost too enthusiastically "Why don't you come down for a drink this evening once Jennifer is in bed, say 7.30"

"I would love that "Mickey beamed "I'll bring a bottle of sherry"

"Great, see you later then"

Sheila and Jennifer made their way downstairs, both happy with their new friend.

Sheila put Jennifer to bed that evening with a warm feeling that things were going to get better. Jennifer was her daughter and their fragile bond was growing slightly stronger. Mickey was a lovely man although he was homosexual which everybody said was wrong. Sheila could not understand what made him like he was, but he seemed like such a nice person. She was looking forward to seeing him again that evening and made an effort to make herself look nice.

Mickey arrived at seven thirty as arranged and he too had made an effort. He had put on his favourite beige flannel trousers with turn-ups and a striped tee shirt underneath a double-breasted blue jacket. He presented Sheila with a bunch of tulips, which was a first for her, she had never been given flowers before in her life. Sheila realised that there was no romantic intention in the gesture, purely one of friendship which somehow made the flowers all the more special. She beamed as she greeted him.

"Thank you so much they are lovely"

Mickey also produced a bottle of Sherry as promised.

"If I didn't know better, I'd be questioning your intentions" Sheila laughed "I am sorry about the state of the bedsit"

"Its fine" said Mickey who was slightly taken back by the décor, which was more befitting of the old man who had died, than of its new incumbent. "M intention is to have find out more about you, your daughter and hopefully have a bit of fun. That's not too much to ask for a bottle of sherry, is it? "

"Not at all "Sheila readily agreed

Jennifer was asleep on a small mattress in the corner.

"We'll have to keep the noise down; I don't know how Jennifer will be. This is the first time I've had company with her asleep close by"

"No Flamenco then?" Mickey laughed

Sheila smiled "I don't have much to offer you to eat. I was unprepared for anything this evening. I can do some cheese on toast if you like"

"Welsh rarebit would be divine!" Mickey laughed

"What's that?" Sheila laughed bemused

"It's what they call cheese on toast in Wales" Mickey said with a smile

Sheila made cheese on toast and they consumed it with gusto and a glass of sherry.

Conversation was easy. They spoke of the war and how it had affected them. Mickey explained the situation in Spain, of which Sheila knew nothing. Sheila told him about her work and the consequences of pregnancy. She confessed to having been a party girl following the release from the war and how nothing seemed to matter except having a good time, since there was no longer a death threat hanging over their heads. She was frank about her sexual appetite. She told Mickey how she regretted some of the things that she had done and how for the first few years of Jennifer's life she had felt disconnected from her. She spoke of June and what a lifesaver she had been, although she had also probably been in the way a proper relationship with Jennifer.

"What's he like, Sweeney? "Sheila asked as if talking about a complete stranger

"Well, you must know him better than me" Said Mickey "I just pay him rent and that's it"

"Oh, I assumed that you knew him better when you came to his door. In fact, I thought you were a friend"

"No! I'm nothing like a friend. I'm a tenant. I nearly did some work for him which is how I came to be a tenant."

"Really, what happened?"

"Well, I told you I took over Spic and Span, Mum & Dad's business??"

"Yes, you told me at lunchtime"

"Well, Sweeney was one of mum and dad's main customers. He didn't pay very well but he had been a Godsend in their early days in England. They needed work and he wanted cheap labour to clean his places. It worked well for them both really but they had to work very hard for their money. When they got the opportunity to get out and leave me the business, I decided to drop him because there was better paid work to be had. I did need accommodation though and he came up with the loft here. It wasn't ideal but it sort of suited me, so I took it.

Sweeney resented the fact that I stopped doing his cleaning but he was happy for me to fill one of his places and take my rent. He's not a nice man. I don't know his background so I don't want to be judgemental but I don't hear much good about him. You need to be careful Sheila! I don't know what happened to the girl who cleaned before you arrived but she left very hurriedly and not on good terms. I suspect that he tried it on with her. So be careful!"

"I don't feel at all comfortable with him" said Sheila "He often seems to say things with two meanings and he leers at me whenever I see him. I have to take him tea in bed every Saturday which I don't really want to be doing. He sits in bed and looks at me. I can't explain what it is like. I know I'm always glad when Saturday mornings are over"

"That's awful Sheila, be careful. I don't know what he has in his life. All he seems to do is collect money. God knows what he spends it on. He probably sleeps on a mattress stuffed with notes"

Sheila suddenly felt very uncomfortable. She felt that she had been discovered. She didn't know what to say and stayed silent.

"Sorry" said Mickey sensing her discomfort "I didn't mean to frighten you. I 'm sure he's harmless but you never know. Just keep your wits about you."

"I will "

Mickey felt a change in the atmosphere.

I really am sorry I didn't mean to upset you. I said too much. It must be the Sherry."

"No Please!" Said Sheila "It's me. You are just being kind and concerned. I went a bit quiet because, well I do feel uncomfortable in his company and I have probably not behaved properly in his home

"What do you mean?"

"OH, no, nothing like that "Sheila realised that Mickey might be getting the wrong idea.

"No, well, I don't know if I should say really" Sheila was feeling the effects of the Sherry and felt inclined to trust Mickey with her secret.

"Look" she said earnestly" I know I shouldn't have done this but – well I did it and I can't change it now."

Sheila proceeded to tell Mickey about her first time in Sweeney's house. How Jennifer had unwittingly uncovered a secret hiding place and how she, Sheila, had found further exploration irresistible. She told him about the box full of bundles of notes. As she spoke, she felt relief on the one hand but incredibly foolish on the other. She barely knew this man, Mickey, and she had just told him about a pile of money under the floorboards in her employer's house, the location of which Mickey knew all too well.

"I have never taken any money and I never would but I know that even having looked and found it I behaved inappropriately"

"Sheila don't lose any sleep over that. I'm not surprised to hear what you have told me. He has a lot of money coming in and I can't imagine how he might be spending it. A secret stash is only a surprise, in that I would have thought he would use a bank. Perhaps it's not all legitimate! Anyway, it makes no difference to me. I am more concerned that Sweeney may try something physical on with you. I mean more than just innuendo"

"In you what?" Sheila asked

Mickey laughed "Double entendre? Double meaning? You know when he says one thing but seems to suggest another"

"Oh that" Sheila laughed "What did you call it?"

"Innuendo" he said and they laughed together.

"I don't think I have heard that word before. I am learning English from a Spaniard"

They spent the evening laughing and finding out about each other, very at ease, both enjoying the opportunity to talk. Later Mickey made to leave and go back upstairs to his flat, Sheila felt disappointed and encouraged him to stay. A lot of sherry had been consumed their conversation reflected their lack of sobriety.

"Pleeese stay a bit longer "Sheila implored

"You'll only take advantage of me" Mickey teased "and unfortunately, I have an early start tomorrow so I must go and leave you and your lovely daughter to your beauty sleep. Perhaps we can do it again sometime"

"Do you know Mickey, I'd love that" Sheila slurred and wrapped her arms around Mickey's neck. She kissed him on the cheek and said "I wish you weren't a Homo; you could stay the night"

"Well, sadly I am not Heterosexual and even if I was, I still have work to do in the morning"

He bent and kissed Jennifer's forehead, kissed Sheila on the cheek, said goodnight and left.

Sheila reflected on the day's events. This morning she hadn't even met him, now he felt like an old friend. It seemed to her that they would be friends for a long time to come. She was a little unsure how to deal with the fact that he was homosexual but she knew she mustn't let the cat out of the bag to anybody. Sheila went to sleep that night and strangely dreamt of Ben, Jennifer's father. Perhaps it was the close contact with a man that set her dreaming. She didn't remember having thought about him for a long time.

Chapter 7

A week passed for Ben rather slowly. His mother and sister looked after his dressing and made whatever sympathetic noises they could muster. They were interested in his life in the suburbs of London, where he was going to church, who he was seeing and what his life was like in general. His absence seemed to have promoted a warmth and family love which he hadn't felt when he lived at home. Ben did his best to settle back into his home surroundings but he had clearly moved on emotionally and grown into his independence. He felt suffocated by the spartan, straight jacketed, correct life that he had left behind. His mother and sister now seemed sad, limited people, trapped by their own belief system. Ben was grateful to be looked after for a few days. He was pleased to see his family but soon realised that a return to the south, to work and to his lifestyle couldn't come soon enough.

He spent much of his idle time at first thinking about the girl at the party who had been such fun and so full of life. He was sad really that things had turned out how they had. He thought he had matured beyond street fighting and was a little disappointed in himself for getting so angry, losing control and turning violent. If events had happened differently and those idiots had not been such, well idiots, he may well be spending more time with the girl right now. He seemed to remember her name as Sheila but he had had a few drinks and he hadn't used her name very much that evening, so he was not sure his memory was real. He knew she had come with a friend and wondered if Jimmy knew anything about her. Ben did not really feel an urgent need to find her but he was curious and felt a little guilty about what had happened.

As the week passed Ben's thoughts of Sheila faded. He listened to the wireless, and read a little, something he hadn't had much time for in the past. His mother was determined that he not been seen in the neighbourhood in his current condition and encouraged him to stay in. She did not want local people to know that he had been fighting. She had always told neighbours and friends that Ben was a solid, respectable and hard-working young man. He was making a good Christian life for himself in the south, which was largely true. Perhaps he visited church less frequently and didn't spend the time she might have suggested doing charitable works, but he was working hard and making a respectable living. The appearance of a scar from eye socket to jawline might be difficult to explain to gossiping neighbours. The week dragged by. Finally feeling better and with the medical clearance to go back to work, Ben headed for the station and a return to normality.

Meanwhile in the south, Bobby Wilson had heard all about the events at the party and, whilst he was not pleased by what had happened, he valued Ben as an employee and knew that he was decent enough. Jimmy had given his father a good account of events that evening. Bobby made arrangements for Ben's work to be covered for the week, readjusting his schedules at some considerable inconvenience, loss of good will from some customers and consequential financial cost. On Ben's return he was given a conditional welcome back. Bobby secretly had admiration for Ben's actions and thought he would have done the same thing in the circumstances. The other participants in the fracas had already been given a stern warning. They had been served chapter and verse on the consequences of any future repetition and allowed to return to work immediately.

The conditions laid down for Ben to be able to return included an agreement that he would not seek reprisals, he would avoid mixing with the other two, either at work or socially and he would give Bobby assurances that there would be no further action taken against them. Ben happily agreed, he was not keen to start things up again and already had a scar on his face likely to remain with him for the rest of his life. He certainly had no desire to socialise with them either. Life returned to normal.

A few days later Jimmy and Ben found themselves teamed up on a job in Willesden.

"Well, well here comes Freddie Mills" said Jimmy with a smile. Freddie Mills was a hero of theirs who had brought boxing glory to England several years before. "You look like you've done a few rounds with him actually" Jimmy laughed. "How are you feeling?"

"Oh, a bit sore and a bit stupid but I don't actually regret it" Ben spoke the words but didn't convince himself. "Who was that girl, by the way?"

"Really" said Jimmy "Are you really asking me? You're the one who disappeared upstairs with her not me"

"I know, but I thought you might know one of her friends, or a bit more about her"

"No" said Jimmy "we hadn't been there five minutes before you and she were laughing in a corner I thought you would have at least got her name and address."

"Shame" said Ben "She was great fun and a bit of a looker. Oh well there's plenty more fish, as they say"

"Yeah, we had better crack on with some work. Next time, remember to make a note in your little black book if you want to see the lady again." They both laughed and got on with their work.

Ben put the party behind him. From time to time his thoughts wander to Sheila, but he decided to leave the past in the past, he couldn't do anything about it now. Move on.

There were other parties and there were other girls, Ben didn't of course possess a black book and didn't really feel the need to use one. Girls came and went. Work was plentiful and Ben was happy with things as they were.

A couple of years passed quite quickly, as they do when life is good. Ben had moved down to London permanently and had taken rented accommodation in Kilburn. The area was central to most of his work and he had become fed up with temporary board and lodgings. His life in London until now had mostly been spent in somebody else's house which was very limiting. Ben sought more freedom and found it in a small flat in a large converted house which was actually in Kilburn but very close to West Hampstead. He liked to tell everyone he lived in West Hampstead.

Jimmy was taking more responsibility for his father's business and had become attached to an Irish girl he met on a bus. They had hit it off instantly and were courting quite seriously, such that Ben found himself alone much more when he wasn't working. This actually did not bother him too much; he had his own space in the flat and was getting to know himself better. He was still only nineteen and had his life ahead of him. He had started to read a little whilst he was home and found that he was becoming more and more interested. He read a few novels, one or two Charles Dickens books and the occasional business-related book which he enjoyed very much, to his surprise.

One day he went to his pigeonhole for mail in the tiled hall of the house in which he lived. There were six pigeonholes mounted in the front door each allocated to one flat. Ben's pigeonhole seemed to be troubled the least by the postman. A weekly letter from his mother or sister, who took turns to write to him, a regular demand for money from the housing association, some bills but little else was stuffed into his box. On this occasion an official looking government letter in a brown envelope with a cellophane window marked for the attention of "Mr Benjamin Macdonald". Governmental communications did not spell good news. What could it be, unpaid tax? some sort of census? Ben opened the envelope reluctantly.

The letter was from the Ministry of Labour and National Service advising him that he would be required to support his country's armed forces for a minimum period of eighteen months on a full-time basis.

Conscription!

The thought of being tied down for eighteen months filled him with horror. He had heard terrible stories about the treatment of squaddies in the army and wasn't about to volunteer for that. He had a pathologic fear of the Navy since his brother had been so horribly killed and he wasn't sure how he would fare at sea anyway. It looked like the RAF was the way to go for him. There was a romance about flying and whilst he had no desire to be a pilot, there might be an opportunity to at least experience it in some way

Ben was duly accepted for the RAF and started his national service that September. He gave up his rented accommodation in

Kilburn and was stationed at RAF Manston in Kent. At the outset he asked if he could be assigned to the kitchen. He thought he might learn to cook and he was sure that if he was involved in the preparation of food, he would never be hungry. He liked his food and supplies were not plentiful generally. He had heard that some of the armed forces were not at all well fed and he did not relish living on limited rations. His request was denied. He was assigned to the aircraft support team, given his electrical background. He threw himself into his maintenance and support role. Plenty of other young men from all over the country found themselves in the same situation. Ben was soon part of a friendly group who were determined to make the best of their time in service of their country. In many of ways, life in uniform suited him.

There were plenty of opportunities to engage in sport. His physique and background saw him entered into boxing, football and even rugby tournaments within the force and he did pretty well, collecting several trophies for his endeavours. A local boxing match was organised within the camp and Ben put his name forward.

The competition was a knockout affair. Literally in some cases. There were lots of conscripts who fancied their chances. Victory in the local competition would deliver the opportunity to represent RAF Southern Region in a national RAF competition. Victory at a national level offered the potential to represent the RAF in an inter-services competition where there was fierce competition between the Army, Navy, Territorial Army and RAF. Over the years the Army had won the overall inter services competition most often and bragged loudly about it. The RAF had won three times prior to the war but had been unsuccessful since. The Southern RAF Boxing Club based at Manston was now headed by a new Squadron Leader whose family had a proud boxing history. Squadron Leader Cummings was a mountain of a man who had the battered face which reflected hours spent in the boxing ring. He had a personal drive and ambition that the RAF team would win the inter services competition if not in his first year in charge, then definitely in the next. Squadron Leader Cummings appealed for a sense of honour within the service. He wanted to make history by winning back the Noble Statuette. Fighters came from the numerous RAF bases around Kent to train at Manston.

As a further incentive, the Squadron Leader convinced senior brass to set up a flight experience in a two-seater Spitfire for the victorious fighters. Most Spitfires were single seaters but there were training craft built with two seats. The Spitfire had become an iconic plane during the war and Ben was delighted to have had the opportunity to work on the maintenance of those stationed at Manston. The sound of the Merlin engine roaring off the runaway had become very familiar to him and the chance to actually fly in one really appealed. He set about training hard. He wanted to win.

The training facilities were fairly spartan although a boxing ring was set up in a large prefabricated building used as a gymnasium. Ben found himself there most evenings getting fitter for the battles ahead and also keeping him from both the mess and the local public houses, where many of his fellow conscripts spent their time. Training alongside him was a lad from Stepney in London, Bertie Buckle, who had adapted very well to military life. He came from a large family of Cockneys and had to hold his own with his older brothers. Fighting came naturally to him. He fought as a heavy weight whilst Ben was a middle weight. The two men liked each other from the start and became sparring partners despite the weight differences.

Squadron Leader Cummings made arrangements for extra food rations to be available for members of the boxing club and as word spread, the numbers in the gym at night started to swell. The atmosphere in the temporary structure thickened night by night. Body sweat and paraffin heater fumes mixed to create a memorable fug. After weeks of training and sweat the time came to identify the camp's team that would travel to the RAF's national competition to be staged at RAF Farnborough. Competitors would compete for the right to take on the other services.

The competition comprised three, three-minute rounds per bout. The winner of each bout went through to the next round, the winner being decided on points awarded by three judges. Most of the boys from the barracks were present cheering on their mates and cat calling the opponents. Others arrived from other sites in Kent and Hampshire and there was much rivalry between camp teams. The "Scuffers" or Military Police were in attendance make sure no unofficial fights broke out in the audience. Each of the other teams arrived on RAF lorries. This gave them the opportunity to smuggle in alcohol, despite camp and competition rules. The atmosphere was charged and noise levels grew as the evening passed.

Ben fought his way past 4 rounds of opponents before winning the camp title. His face was red and puffed up with the pounding of boxing gloves but he won each bout reasonably comfortably. Bertie Buckle sailed through his bouts and came through as Southern Heavyweight champion with barely a mark on him. Six other fighters were successful in their weight categories and the team was complete.

Cummings called the team together the next day, it was a cold dark night in December. Three of the victors were from Manston, Ben, Bertie and a skinny, mean looking North Londoner who had the nickname "Biffer". The rest of the victors were from other southern based camps and had been housed overnight at Manston. Cummings was there to give them their instructions for the nationals and to meet some of them for the first time.

"Well done everybody" said Cummings "We obviously have some tough fighters amongst you but not many of you are boxers yet. Obviously, there are one or two of you who have been fighting in the ring for some years and have learnt a lot about ring craft. Others are just tough and good street fighters"

Ben, Bertie and Biffer looked at each other with a knowing smile.

"You have four weeks, including Christmas, to train for the championships in January, where there will be proper boxers who will be doing their level best to lay you on the floor. We have the makings of a good team here and I would like to see some of you competing for the RAF, at the Combined Services Boxing Association annual meeting in March. There is a lot of work to do to get you into shape to give us a chance of being well represented. Are you up for it?"

Every man shouted their agreement enthusiastically. Each of the camps represented had experienced boxers and novices. The experienced boxers were to instruct the others in ring craft. Three of the winners were gifted boxers already and agreed to share their knowledge. They were to come together once a week at Manston for team briefings but otherwise would train at their home camp. Cummings would oversee training and travel between the four camps to ensure that progress was being made.

Ben, Bertie and Biffer became known as the three B's. They trained hard together and Ben and Bertie improved their boxing skills. Biffer was a slugger and always would be. If he didn't land his punches, he would be outclassed, if he landed them, he would probably knock his opponent out. Christmas came and went. The boxers were allowed home to spend some time with their families but Cummings made it very clear that he wanted no excesses during their leave.

The weekend of the national finals came. It was a Friday and a cold, winterly January night, the ground white with cold. Three B's, Cummings and the trainers set off for Farnborough in a RAF lorry, diverting to pick up two other boxers. The other three boxers and their trainers made their own way. It was late afternoon as they pulled up to the sentry post at Farnborough.

" More meat for the market" the sentry quipped cheerfully. "We've got some ugly ones here tonight. In you go lads, good luck"

The truck pulled up outside a large hangar which was being used for the competitors and their entourage. Each team had their own roped off area to change and prepare for the bouts ahead. As Ben's group were led to their area, they passed the RAF East of England team. He saw a familiar face. It was the face of the man who had given him the scar that earned him his boxing nickname.

Peter Cauldwell was one of the school bullies who seemed to plague Ben's life. Cauldwell had been called to do his military service just as Ben had. It turned out Jimmy, Ben's school friend, had been called soon after. Jimmy had been posted to the Army to a base in the north of England. Cauldwell had also been posted to the RAF, his posting was in North Weald in Essex, from where famously Douglas Bader took off to lead the VE victory celebration flight. The north weald team proudly called themselves Bader's boys.

Cauldwell had followed a similar path to Ben and joined the local boxing team. His category was the same as Ben's and there was a chance if the draw went that way that they could find themselves up against each other in the ring. Neither boxer realised this as they saw each other and gave a reluctant wave of acknowledgement.

Eleven areas of the country were represented including Scotland, Ireland and Wales. For many this was not only a boxing tournament but also a few days away from normal duties and a chance to "hit the smoke" and see some of London's sights. Each of the eight weight categories had sixteen contestants, one from each region. two in some cases. To reach the final a boxer would need to fight 4 knockout bouts, each comprising three rounds of three minutes, with a minute's break between rounds. Two hangars had been assigned and four boxing rings from around the RAF bases had been assembled, one at either end of the two hangars. The preliminary rounds would be fought that evening with the semi-finals and finals taking place the following day. All the finals would take place one after the other in one ring. There were bleacher seating facilities around the finals ring, for all the unsuccessful candidates and any travelling supporters to watch.

Of the nine participants from the south-eastern region five made it through to the next round. Then four to the semi-finals the next day. The three Bs all came through their rounds, each supporting each other, when the scheduling allowed. Ben checked the results sheet which were posted in the hangar to which he had been assigned. He noted that Cauldwell had also been successful. They were on track for a final showdown if both made it through their semis.

Ben was not sure how he felt about facing Cauldwell in the ring. He remembered his promise to Bobby Wilson not to get involved with either of his assailants in the future but surely this was different? For now, he needn't worry. They both had to come through their semi-finals, if that happened then he might feel a little guilt but he would go ahead with the fight. In fact, the more he thought about it, the more he found himself relishing the prospect.

Semi-Finals started early afternoon on the Saturday. The grand hangar provided an interesting acoustic experience as the shouts bounced around the great roof space. It towered high above the rings and even higher above the benches and bleachers brought in for spectators. Those who had made the next round were able to invite supporters along. This opportunity definitely played to the advantage of the southern based competitors. Groups of excited onlookers cheered on their favourites loudly. They also booed any decisions which didn't suit them. By six o'clock the final contestants knew who they were. The standard of boxing was higher than in the earlier heats, as was to be expected. Some semi-finalists bore the signs of their earlier fights but all were given at least 2 hours respite between their semi -final and final. The three B's all came through to the final round.

Ben watched nervously in anticipation of his final as the other bouts were played out. Biffer's ferocity and focus saw the referee stop his bout in the second round. His opponent was not prepared for the brutal attack he encountered. He went to ground twice before the referee put an end to it, raising the arm of a jubilant Biffer. Three other outcomes were delivered before it was Ben's turn to enter the ring. Cheers from the Southern based groups welcomed Ben as he climbed between the slightly sagging ropes. He was a little embarrassed at first but soon entered the spirit and danced around the ring, shuffling his feet and jabbing at an unseen opponent.

Peter Caudwell's entrance received a roar from Bader's boys. He also hunched up his shoulders and threw some meaningless punches into the air. The seconds called their boxers to the corner before the referee called them together in the centre of the ring. He reminded them of the rules and his expectation of a fair fight. He also reminded them that this was the RAF and this was a marvellous opportunity to represent the best of the services. He wished them both good luck. Ben and Cauldwell looked each other in the eye as meanly as they could until one of them broke into a broad grin, rapidly followed by the other. Neither was sure who caved in first but they both knew that this fight would settle things once and for all. They might even become friends.

The first round was edgy, neither boxer wanting to over commit. At the break Ben's second reminded him that this was a final with only three rounds to make an impression on the judges. He recommended that Ben start boxing and stop dancing, if he wanted to collect a winner's medal. It appeared that the same message had been delivered in both corners. The second round was a battle, both boxers summoning up all their history and hurling it back at each other through their 10-ounce gloves. The gloves were intended to protect their fists and softened the blows to their bodies. No blow felt soft to either boxer. Ben drew blood from Cauldwell's nose possibly, he thought, breaking it. Cauldwell pounded Ben's sides till both men were gasping for breath. The bell rang for the end of the round.

"Better" said the second.

"What are you playing at?" came a voice from behind the trainer, the voice belonged to Bertie. "Biffer has won his medal, I'm going to win mine but you look like you don't want to hurt him. Where is the aggression you show when you spar with me? Seriously Ben if you don't do something different, you're in danger of losing this!"

Ben looked at his friend, heaved another deep breath and winked.

"Just saving it up for the last round" he managed to gasp.

The bell rang and both fighters came to the centre and touched gloves. There was a sneer on Cauldwell's face, his bloodied nose had been cleaned up and he looked deranged. His attitude projected more than the hostility of the boxing ring. Ben remembered seeing the same look that evening at the party. He remembered the specific words which Cauldwell had used that night, he had mocked the girl and ridiculed him. He remembered the bullying and name calling at school. He remembered the frustration he had felt laid up in a hospital bed and the disappointment of losing touch with that girl that night. For a split second he wondered how things might have turned out if it hadn't been for Cauldwell.

If you asked Ben what happened at that precise moment, he would not be able to explain. Something inside took over and for the next three minutes he boxed like a professional, with control and style but also with power. A power which he had not known he could muster. A power fuelled by anger. Cauldwell fought hard but without the passion which Ben had found. Ben had stepped up a gear and was untouchable for those three minutes. One moment laying a vicious punch, the next pulling his body away.

The Judges unanimously gave the win to Ben. His arm was raised by the referee and Cauldwell had the good grace to nod an acceptance and offer Ben his outstretched gloves in congratulations. Ben had not expected a sporting gesture like that from Cauldwell. From that moment their past was behind them and would not rear its head again. They had found a mutual respect and a form of bond which neither comprehended completely.

Biffer and Bertie were leaping up and down with joy outside the ring, along with an exuberant crowd who were enjoying a great evening of boxing. Ben caught sight of Squadron Leader Cummings who was looking directly at him. Cummings nodded his congratulations, punched the air and smiled victoriously. He was building an RAF team which would be hard to beat.

Unsurprisingly Bertie wiped the floor with his opponent in the heavyweight fight which was top of the bill for the evening. The team was complete. The interservice event would take place in March and this was an RAF team with the heart, enthusiasm and talent to win.

The Manston lorry set off later that evening to return to base. It was loaded with five boxers, four of whom had won their titles. Supporters who had come up for the final night had clambered into the back and brought the remaining crate of beer for celebration with them. Spirits were high.

The lorry made good time on the dark roads back to Manston. Most of the passengers were unaware of their surroundings, they were too busy singing and drinking to notice the journey passing. The driver had enjoyed some of the hospitality through the day and was enjoying a bottle of beer whilst he steered his vehicle down the icy lanes. He joined in the singing and celebration from his place behind the wheel. Although it was a little tight, three of his passengers shared the cab with him.

Half a dozen revellers were dropped off outside their base before the lorry set off again for Manston.

When asked later the driver couldn't remember exactly what had happened. He had lost control and in what seemed like an instant, the lorry was rolling down a bank onto a railway track. They were lucky that it was the early hours of the morning and the train service was limited.

Fifteen men were taken to hospital. Some with minor injuries others less fortunate. Amongst the less fortunate were the three B's. Bertie was thrown from the vehicle. As it tumbled down the bank, he was concussed and suffered injuries to his ribs, arms and face. Biffer and Ben both sustained fractures to bones, both of Biffer's legs were broken, Ben broke his arm and was burnt in his attempts to get clear of the burning lorry. He passed out trying to scramble up the bank.

Ben woke up in hospital under the watchful eyes of a young nurse. She was busy taking readings of his vital signs and was clearly pleased to see him come out of his state of unconsciousness. He had been unresponsive since being hauled up the bank by his fellow passengers. The nurse explained where he was and what had happened. He had some memory of events but it was some days before it all sank in.

Cummings, who had escaped with severe bruising and a couple of broken fingers, came to visit his team the following weekend. He did the rounds of those hospitalised and counted the cost to the RAF Boxing team. His hopes of victory in March were zero. The team was devastated and whilst he could patch a team together it would be missing the talent and character of the four broken bodies. He gave each of his boys a well-meant chin up speech, which rang hollow. They all knew that their chances of competing were zero. They would have to wait till next year when for two of them conscription would be over.

That night Ben went to sleep and dreamed of the girl at the party.

He was hospitalised for four days, his right arm encased in plaster of Paris. During his time there, he grew attached to his nurse, Caroline and when the time of his discharge arrived, he suggested meeting for a drink at some point. Caroline was a young girl with a slight figure. She stood five foot three inches tall and was very smart in her light blue and white nurse's outfit. Her brown hair was swept back into a bun to accommodate the white nurses cap which she was obliged but proud to wear. Her face was fresh and beautiful with a just washed glow. Makeup was neither worn nor needed. She was often propositioned by her patients, particularly those from the forces. She didn't often accept but felt differently about Ben there was a warmth, honesty and vulnerability about him which she found attractive. She looked forward to finding out more and readily accepted his invitation.

Chapter 8

Life for Sheila went on, a drab routine. Winnie was amazing and supported her with childminding all week and Saturday mornings. Sheila's work at the factory was no different, she didn't enjoy it but she got on with it. It provided a structure, some income and some social contact for her. There was no escape that she could imagine so she just plodded on and put the best face on it that she could. She thought and hoped that herself and Jennifer were growing a little closer. She started to learn more about her daughter and Jennifer started to brighten up a little. June's death slowly fading from her memory.

Evenings with Mickey became commonplace. They would often arrange to share meals. He would bring Sheila small gifts for her home and help her decorate. Together they changed the room around to make it a more acceptable place to live. Gradually the thought of an old man dying there passed from Sheila's mind and she began to build their own memories.

They both looked forward to their evenings together. They caught up on the day's events and got to know something about each other's acquaintances from work. They shared gossip. Mickey loved to gossip. He listened avidly to the stories Sheila told about the supervisors' antics with some of the girls on the shop floor.

They told each other about their dreams and desires. Mickey had few friends to really, he had been ostracised at school, a slightly effeminate boy with a foreign accent didn't fit well at St, Marks Catholic High School. He still saw one or two of the boys but not as friends, only in passing. He had made more friends from working with his parents and developing the business himself. He was still only 22 but seemed more mature to Sheila.

Mickey told Sheila that he would like to engage with his sexuality more. It was one thing to recognise himself as homosexual but another thing completely engaging with others. He knew there must be thousands of others like him. The only evidence he could point to was an occasional scandal in the local or national newspapers, somebody exposed for their "unnatural" and criminal behaviour. It seemed this was mostly more about men than women, but that was perhaps just his perspective. Regardless it was frustrating beyond belief.

By engaging with his sexuality, he meant he would like to meet a man in the same situation, with whom he could at least talk about his feelings. He didn't suppose he would "fall in love" with the first homosexual that he met but he thought it might open a door to meeting others.

One evening after what seemed like a very long day the knocker on the front door sounded softly. Sheila knew Mickey's knock by now, it always had the same pattern and was always considerate of the fact that Jennifer was likely to be asleep in the room. She opened the door quietly and welcomed Mickey into the room with a peck on the cheek. Jennifer had gone to sleep easily that evening. Mickey brought a bottle of wine for them to share and Sheila fetched a couple of glasses, eager to sit and catch up on the news since they last met. Mickey was like a dog with a bone.

"You've splashed out haven't you! Wine! Its normally pale ale!"

"I know, I know but listen, I've got news!" he said excitedly and with a glint in his eye.

"You always have something to tell me "Sheila laughed

"No this is real news "he said bursting to let her share his excitement.

" Come on then, spill the beans!"

"Well," he began "You remember I have told you about Dyllis, one of my favourites and most reliable cleaners" Sheila nodded

"Well today she didn't turn up for her cleaning rota, which left me in a bit of a jam. Thankfully she sent word, so I knew from the start of the day that I would need to fill for her. I managed to move some of the girls around and fill most of her work but there is a new customer I didn't want to let down. I haven't even met them and I don't want them to have a bad experience. So, I took the job on myself."

"I went to a very nice apartment on the edge of West Hampstead, one of those lovely high ceilinged three-story Victorian buildings, you know the ones?"

Sheila nodded again; eyes wide open in anticipation but not wanting to interrupt Mickey's flow.

"Well, we have spare keys for many of our cleans as the homeowners are often out at work when we go round. I opened the front door and went into what was a beautifully decorated hallway. I loved the décor and just knew I was going to like the flat. There were some wonderful paintings hanging and one piece of sculpture which I adored. It was two gladiators fighting but the muscle definition and the strain of the battle was so well captured. Anyway, each location has a work sheet describing exactly what is expected by way of cleaning, so I got started on the living room.

I was dusting the frame of a picture when a door opened! It scared the life out of me! I didn't know what to think, it all happened so fast. A man came into the room with just a towel around his waist. I assume he had just showered and was in the bathroom when I arrived. He was as surprised as I was but I was standing with a feather duster in my hand so not very threatening to him.

I explained that Dyllis was unwell and that I was filling in, which seemed to amuse him. "Not really a man's thing, cleaning" he said and laughed. "Well, no I suppose not" I said "Most men wouldn't know where to start, but I'm not like most men."

He looked directly at me quite calm, saying nothing then left the room.

Later he came back in and offered to make me coffee. We sat and talked largely about his paintings and in particular the sculpture which turned out to be an original bronze which had been cast for him by a friend. Perhaps I was a little over enthusiastic about the work but he seemed to be pleased that I liked it. He was interested in me as well, my background and the business. He told me he was in the rag trade and it seemed he was doing very nicely for himself.   He suddenly realised that he was late for a meeting and excused himself. Before he left, he asked if I would be interested to attend a gallery in a few weeks where a friend would be showing a collection of water colours.

Of course, I said yes."

He said "wonderful, I'll get the details and perhaps we should talk again"

I can't wait to go, but I haven't got a clue how to approach it. What to wear, whether formal or informal? I am not sure whether he intends me to go with him or whether he just thought I would like the art. I'm not used to situations like this"

Sheila found herself sharing Mickey's excitement. "Well, what did he say?"

"He didn't really. Just that he would send an invitation to the office"

"Well, you'll have to wait and see."

"I think he is homosexual although he is not particularly camp or effeminate. It is just a feeling which I got from talking to him, we seemed to be on the same wavelength"

"Fingers crossed for you Mickey; I am sure that whatever it turns out to be you will have a lovely time. Did he say where the art gallery was?"

"Yes, Portobello Road" the person who runs the gallery also has a stall at the market where he sells more commercial art works to the general public."

"Sounds great. I hope you'll tell me all about it afterwards"

"Of course," said Mickey "Every little detail"

"What was his name?"

"Don, Don Mosely."

"Oh, dear not one of the black shirt Mosely's I hope"

"Well, his shirt was white and we didn't talk about politics but I very much doubt it. I can't see him as a fascist"

The rest of the evening Sheila and Mickey talked about Jennifer and her news. Sheila repeated that she would love to move on but felt she was just stuck. Somebody at work had said that she should have had Jennifer adopted because she would get a better life than Sheila could give her. Sheila wondered if they were right. She knew of other girls who had given their babies up for adoption shortly after birth and they seemed to be getting on quite well with their lives. The thought of losing Jennifer now was unbearable and Sheila knew that they would get through the tough times somehow. Mickey agreed with Sheila and said she should never even consider the idea of adoption; he would help her if she ever got in trouble.

"Perhaps I can start to help now" he said "and you can help me as well. Listen, I have settled down with mum and dad's business now, I have it under control and it pays me quite well, but I will never be wealthy or even comfortably off unless I change things a bit. I need to put more effort into promoting the business, attracting new customers and new cleaners and also pushing through some new ideas which I have. Unfortunately, I don't have the time that I need but perhaps with your help we could do it together and have some fun at the same time. It would mean us working together into the evenings and giving some time to it at the weekends for the first month or two, but if the business picks up, I may be able to employ you on a more permanent basis."

The idea of escape from her situation was too wonderful to contemplate. Sheila was hopeful but unconvinced.

"How would that work?"

"To start with we would need to identify a lot more cleaners for the future, so we can put some adverts in local shops, speak to the labour exchange and set up a time for interviews. The work is ideal for working mums. We can make it flexible and those that perform well can grow the number of hours offered. A larger cleaner list will make cover for illness and the like much easier – although I wouldn't mind filling in more often if today is anything to go by. You can help me with the interviews to start with and once you have the hang of it you can take over."

"Oh no I've never done anything like that, I wouldn't know where to start"

"That's why you start with me! To be honest a mother's perspective will be really helpful in choosing the right people. If it goes well, we can help them set up a co-operative baby-sitting club so they can help each other out when they have to work.

I'll need help organising rotas, visiting customers to check they are happy, visiting new customers to agree what is to be done. At first, we can do a lot of this together, in the evenings and at weekends but once it has built up, perhaps, we can get your factory to take a contract from us which will keep your work with us but free you to help with the business. It will also get Spic and Span into the commercial cleaning world."

Sheila was not at all sure that she was capable of doing what Mickey was suggesting, but he was insistent that they could make it work between them.

So, a new chapter in her life began.

Between them they wrote an advertisement for young women with an interest in earning additional housekeeping money and suggesting the availability of a child sitting club

Mickey produced leaflets describing the services they could offer and they targeted areas as close to them as possible, to minimise the travel requirements, selecting streets where they thought the household was likely to be able to afford cleaning services. Each evening for an hour or so they took Jennifer for a walk in her push chair and whilst they walked, they distributed their leaflets. Jennifer took great pleasure in putting a leaflet through the letterbox when Mickey lifted her up.

The leaflets invited potential customers to do one of three things; phone between 8.00 AM and 10.00 AM to request a visit;

write and request a visit; or call in to Mickey's rented office space in Kilburn High Road.

Sheila was impressed that Mickey had his own office and use of a phone. She didn't know anybody else with access to a phone except for the factory where she worked.

Mickey taught Sheila how to use the phone and gave her a script to use when she answered. She was to talk about the services offered but never to talk about the cost. When people enquired, she was to advise them that the nature of their property was likely to dictate the cost and that the company estimator would visit them at their convenience. Mickey and Sheila practiced her telephone technique at Mickey's flat. They roared with laughter at Sheila's attempts to sound posh on the phone and finally agreed that she should just be herself.

Mickey was surprised at the instant response they received. There were lots of mothers interested in the baby club, some not even wanting work, just somewhere to leave their children for a couple of hours. There was also many home owners and businesses who wanted cleaning services. Mickey and Sheila worked hard in the evening and the next weekend to respond to the interest. They came to the conclusion that they would need a date to work towards, maybe in a month's time, to launch the services

There was too much for Mickey to deal with alone by day. The backlog of interest built daily, so with Sheila's agreement he went to visit her factory. He explained that he was a friend of Sheila's and that they had been talking about her job and how it could be much better done by a professional company with the backup of a number of cleaners on the payroll. Properly contracted it could cost no more than they currently paid Sheila. They could also opt into other services which "Spic and Span" could supply as and when they wished.

Sheila's manager was very receptive to the idea and agreed to a six-month trial, if approved by the business owner at their next weekly meeting. Sheila's contract was severed and she would be free to support Mickey in the business. Mickey was overjoyed and saw Sheila in the offices to tell her the good news.

"That's wonderful" Sheila said hesitantly, starting to realise the enormity of what was happening. "Let's talk about it later when I'm finished here"

"Well, I can't tonight, Sheila, I am off to an art gallery!"

"Oh, Mickey I 'm so sorry, we've been so busy over the past few weeks I had forgotten all about it. Are you excited?"

"More nervous than excited, but I am looking forward to it, yes!"

Chapter 9

During the day Portobello Road was home to a street market, mostly fruit and veg stalls, clothes and shoes and the odd stall selling arts and crafts. Rufus was an artist trying to build a reputation for an art gallery which comprised the ground floor of two buildings, which had previously been used as a production unit for various items of clothing. The clothing business had become very successful and the owners took the decision to move to Great Portland Street, fast becoming one of London's centres for the rag trade.

One of the successful businessmen was an art lover and had befriended Rufus. Rufus ran his stall outside on the road selling his work alongside locally crafted pottery and knickknacks. There was time left on the lease for the Portobello location so it was agreed to set up a gallery at the premises for the remaining months of the lease. The premises were sparsely decorated with bland white walls and drapes against which budding artists were invited to present their work, in the hope of making some sales. A mixture of reclaimed furniture was tastefully used to create a reception area for drinks and nibbles for patrons The business was beginning to get off the ground but the young artist was spending his time seeking new artistic talent with a body of work to display, whilst developing a network of potential buyers. Tonight, it was Rufus' turn to display his own collection

Mickey had never been to Portobello Road before. The invitation was for a viewing at 6.00PM, cocktails were promised and attendees were requested to arrive promptly as there would be a presentation of the artist early in proceedings. The viewing would last until 9.30 after which any patrons still remaining were invited to adjourn to the wonderfully named "The Sun in Splendour" public house.

Mickey walked down the grey, narrow, gently curving street. The evening light was fading and there was a gloomy air about the place, a feeling that the day's activity had long passed and everybody had long gone. It was five to six as Mickey approached the address on his invitation. He knocked hesitantly on an uninviting black door with a big brass knocker in the centre. A young man with beard and wire glasses opened the door.

"Hello" said the young man "Rufus" and he offered Mickey his hand.

"Mickey" said Mickey returning the smile.

"Please come in," said Rufus. "You're very keen,"

Mickey entered the strangely presented shop space. It was not at all what he had expected. This was clearly a temporary arrangement, pictures and various other art forms were presented around the room against a backdrop of bare whitewashed walls. Every so often a drape was hung to break up the blandness and to highlight a particular painting. The room, practically devoid of people, was quiet and Mickey felt quite uneasy as those who had already arrived turned to look at him. He smiled uncomfortably.

"Keen?" he said

"Well, yes, most people won't arrive till at least 6.30"

"The invite said six" Mickey's words stumbled from his mouth "am I too early?"

"No, no relax, "said Rufus. Can I offer you a drink? Basically, its white wine, beer or lemonade. We can't afford to be too posh, not yet anyway and besides it seems to go with the bohemian feel to the place"

"Beer would be great thanks"

Rufus poured a small glass of pale ale and handed it to Mickey.

"So, Mickey, how do you come to be with us this evening?"

Mickey explained the circumstances of his meeting with Don Mosely and their shared enthusiasm for art.

"Don kindly sent me an invitation and here I am, although I've never been to anything like this before."

"I don't think there is anything else like this "Rufus laughed. "It's pretty ragged around the edges but we are trying to get it off the ground on a shoestring and those who come seem to like it here. We have sold quite a lot of work and the numbers who attend are growing so we must be doing something right."

As Rufus and Mickey chatted the door knocker started to get busy and Rufus had to pull away to greet new arrivals. Mickey felt a little more comfortable and moved into the room to start taking in some of the pieces of art on display. There were some very traditional landscapes, with nothing particular to be said for them. Disappointing really. One or two portraits which had a particular style to them but again nothing really note-worthy. Mickey moved on to some abstract works which he found much more interesting. He became absorbed by the first abstract that he came across and was staring intently at it when a voice alongside him said "Why I am I not surprised to find you looking at this, I didn't think you would go for the commercial stuff"

It was Don.

"Hello Mr Mosely, "said Mickey

"Please call me Don, and say hello to Hazel"

Mickey felt a surge of disappointment to find a beautiful girl on Don's arm.

"Hello Hazel" Mickey said as cheerfully as he could

"What do you make of this then" said Don indicating the rather obscure and unusual painting in front of them.

"I don't know really "said Mickey "I am just drawn to the strange way that the artist sees people, there is a sort of melancholy about it which pulls you in"

"Interesting "said Don "I hadn't even considered that the forms represented people. Just shows you, doesn't it? Have you met the artist yet?"

"No", said Mickey "I just arrived and met Rufus but he had to concentrate on letting people in and making them welcome"

"Well, you have met him then, Rufus is the artist."

"Oh, sorry I had no idea I thought he must be the gallery owner or something"

Don smiled "I am not sure that Rufus owns the clothes he is wearing, never mind a gallery. No, it is Rufus's collection on show tonight. The Gallery is his project but it is financed by the clothing business which I run with my partner. Rufus knows a lot of up-and-coming artists who need an outlet and we have a lease on this property for another year. So, with my interest in art and having met Rufus on the market it seemed like a good match."

"Is it going well?"

"It's actually is going better than I had expected, we've sold a lot of work. The problem we have is maintaining the numbers of interested art lovers who have any cash to spend. I am constantly seeking new faces to come and show an interest"

Mickey felt suddenly deflated. He was clearly just another "new face" for the gallery.

Don and Hazel made conversation with Mickey for the next half hour talking about the art world and how fortunate one had to be to be successful. The numbers in the gallery had grown significantly since Mickey had last noticed. Don apologised and left Hazel and Mickey together. "I have to do some marketing" he said as he left.

Don moved to the front of the gallery and tapped his glass with a spoon.

"May I have everyone's attention please?"

Another tap of the glass

"Good evening, ladies and gentlemen and welcome to the "The Gallery Bello". I am pleased to welcome back so many friends of the gallery, and also those of you for whom this is your first visit. This evening you are enjoying the work of a fine young artist who plies his trade outside on the street during the day – he runs a market stall by day and paints whenever he can. Please put your hands together for Rufus who you will all have met, either tonight, or on a previous event at the gallery. "

Rufus stepped forward and acknowledged the introduction.

"Rufus is my artistic partner in "The Gallery Bello" and tonight is his night to shine. His works are exciting and varied so please, enjoy them and don't be frightened to get your cheque book out – you could be investing in the next Picasso. Please don't forget the Gallery will close at 9.00 and we will adjourn to the "Splendour" afterwards for those who want to continue the evening."

The evening went well. Mickey found himself talking to lots of people with similar interests and, he suspected, many with the same sexual inclinations. Rufus sold enough work to make him enough money to live for a couple of months and Don covered his lease expenses. As advised the gallery closed at 9 pm and a large number of the party moved on to the pub, including Mickey.

Inside Mickey caught up with Rufus.

"Did you have a good night?" Mickey asked

"Yes, I sold a lot of pictures and I got one commission for an abstract to be hung in the reception of a local business. There were a lot of new faces tonight and some of them put their hands in their pockets which was great"

"I know, I am sorry I couldn't afford to buy anything tonight; I really liked a lot of the work"

"Oh God "said Rufus "that sounded terrible, didn't it? I didn't mean to say that you should have bought something" Then he laughed and said "but it's a shame you didn't. Perhaps you'd like to choose one to hang in your home until you can afford it – no obligation. I 'd like to see my work in someone's home on display- one condition though – I will have to help you hang it so I know it has the right lighting"

"Really" said Mickey "That would be great, can I choose the piece of work?"

"Of course," said Rufus

"That's wonderful, I really liked an abstract called "Uncertainty", I would love to be able to study it more, it really touched me"

"No problem we can arrange to get it to you as soon as you like but we will probably have to take it on the bus"

They talked about where Mickey lived and the logistical challenges of getting it there. They laughed a lot and the rest of the evening passed quickly.

Mickey remained curious about Don and his beautiful lady friend.

"I notice Don didn't stay in the pub long" he observed casually "Who was his lady friend?"

"Oh, that's Hazel she used to be a "Kipper" when Don started his business. Now she is the hostess of their Saville Row office where they meet and greet important customers"

"What's a Kipper. I thought you had kippers for breakfast!" Mickey laughed

"You are probably closer to the truth Mickey but when young girls are employed to learn to be tailors and dressmakers, they have to do their time as dogsbodies basically and for some reason in the rag trade they are known as "Kippers".

I suspect Don may enjoy a hearty breakfast tomorrow though, don't you?"

Mickey was thrown, he wasn't sure what to think and his face showed it.

"Oh, dear" said Rufus "Did you think you were on a date with Don – whoops."

Mickey's defences rose immediately "A date, I don't know what you mean"

"I think you do Mickey. On another night it might have been a date but Don is not the same as us, he likes to bat for both sides. Tonight, he was on their side, another night he is on ours"

"What do you mean our side?" Mickey protested

"Come on Mickey we both know what we are – or maybe you haven't owned up to it yet. Listen we all have to deal with our sexuality and what society thinks of it sooner or later. I know how tough it is being a homosexual – so we have to stick together and be discreet. But first we have to own up to it to ourselves"

Mickey didn't know what to say, Rufus was right of course but he had never been so frankly confronted before.

"I suppose we do." Mickey said weakly and from that moment his life was changed.

Chapter 10

Caroline became an important part in Ben's life. She was living in Guildford near the hospital to which Ben had been ferried after the accident. Guildford was about 90 miles away from the RAF camp at Manston and without any means of transport any relationship was doomed to failure, so Ben bought himself a second-hand motorbike. It was a Triumph Speed Twin, which became very special to him. It enabled him to see Caroline at the weekends when he was not on duty and even some evenings. Their relationship grew closer, and Ben found himself covering hundreds of miles on the bike, firstly, just to see Caroline but increasingly the bike itself became a form of relaxation and pleasure.

After six months of Caroline's voluntary and quite unnecessary outpatient "care", they realised that their relationship was far from fleeting. They would need to change things if they wanted to get serious, and it appeared that they both did. The journey between their homes was taxing and restricting, despite the pleasure that Ben took from his new love (the bike). Caroline started to watch out for nurses' jobs in the Kent area and finally secured one at Kent and Canterbury Hospital, locally known as the K&C. The role moved her up the pay scale by several notches, an added bonus resulting from seeking a move to be nearer Ben. In order to reach her immediate goal of ward sister there was still plenty of studying and exams to be completed, but the money was better, and the accommodation was relatively modern as the K&C had been rebuilt in 1937.

Ben renewed his boxing training as soon as he was able, but he missed the inter services competition through his injuries. The RAF team was depleted, and the Army took most of the honours, much to the disgust of Squadron Leader Cummings, who vowed to rebuild his broken team for the following year.

It occurred to Ben that he would not still be in the RAF in a years' time as his conscription term only ran until February 1952. Surprisingly Ben felt a tinge of disappointment. He had grown accustomed to the RAF and enjoyed the structure and discipline that it gave him. Ben was well thought of and the possibilities of staying on for a further term on a full-time basis started to be spoken about. Ben was not averse to the idea of moving his career to the RAF. Apart from anything else, if he chose to leave the service, his relationship with Caroline would become complicated and distant again. He had always planned to move back to London to pick up where he had left off with his electrical career. The Midlands were not home any more.

Boxing training was conducted most evenings on the basis of circuit training, each element of the training lasted three minutes with a thirty second rest between. During one of his rest periods Squadron Leader Cummings approached Ben and took him out of his circuit pattern. Ben was completely recovered from the accident as were most of the others, with the exception of Biffer whose legs were taking much longer to heal than he had hoped.

"What's the plan then Ben"

Ben was a little perplexed.

How do you mean sir?" he asked

"Well, the interservice competition next year is in March and your conscription ends in February. I need to plan the team to beat those other bastards and I need to know who is available and who isn't. At the moment you are not available to me as you will be back in civvy street!"

"Well, I'm not sure what I can do about that sir. I would like to compete, of course but as you say my time will be up in February and I guess I will have to go back to my old life."

"You guess, you guess!! This is your life we are discussing here Macdonald. You had better stop guessing and take some decisions. You seem to like our way of life in the RAF. You seem to be doing quite well. You keep your nose clean and get things done in good order. There could be an opportunity for you to sign up properly and get yourself a career, if you thought it through. But do not guess your way through life or nothing will ever happen for the good. Think about it!"

With that Squadron Leader Cummings made his way to the door, turning to look briefly at Ben before marching out.

Ben was quite taken aback by this unexpected attack. It was clear that the Squadron Leader was thinking as much about his team structure as Ben's welfare but none the less he had posed some serious questions and quite emphatically made a point. Ben was sort of drifting through life. He didn't have a plan and was allowing events to dictate what he should do rather than deciding what to do and dictating events himself. He resolved to change all that. He would map out a plan for the next few years at least. It would definitely help to bounce his ideas off Caroline who was usually quite level-headed and well-reasoned. He would talk to her next time they were together and hopefully clear up his thinking about his future.

Ben didn't sleep well that night. He finished training early and made his way back to the barracks wondering why he felt so attracted to the idea of staying on. He had heard that he could take on a two-year extension to his conscription which would convert him to full-time, fully-fledged RAF personnel. He was not frightened of the idea in fact it quite appealed. There was just something nagging at him and as he lay in bed, he couldn't work out exactly what!

The next time Ben met Caroline was on the Friday evening. Ben took her out on his motorbike. Fortunately, Caroline loved the exhilaration and excitement of high-speed cruising through the country lanes of Kent. Caroline had seen evidence of the damage which could result from motor cycle accidents, and yet the thrill of the speed was intoxicating. She loved the sense of the air blowing through her hair, whilst the bike pitched from one side to the other. She had to catch her breath whilst they leaned into bends in the road. The sheer power of the engine beneath her, far outweighed any reservations or thoughts of danger which she might have. She loved to cling on to Ben and was confident in his ability in handling the machine.

Ben drove to the Old Red Lion a favourite country pub which they had visited on many occasions. It had become familiar to them, and he knew they could find a quiet corner and talk. He bought a local ale for himself and a coca cola for Caroline. They found themselves a familiar table tucked away in the corner and settled into a conversation about their recent activities. Caroline was enjoying life in the hospital; she liked her colleagues and was finding the extra load of studying quite manageable and rewarding. She talked enthusiastically about her ward and the patients for whom she was currently caring. She always seemed to have a particular favourite and was usually sad to see them leave, almost ignoring the fact that their recovery was her main objective. Ben was interested to hear Caroline's anecdotes and knew some of the characters of whom she spoke from previous conversations. They laughed and joked, both of them comfortable with Caroline's clear contentedness. Caroline was keen to hear about Bens past few days. She had felt a certain restlessness in him recently.

Ben described his encounter with the Squadron Leader. Caroline listened intently; she was not a fan of the Squadron Leader from what she knew of him. He seemed more concerned about his Boxing team than he was about the wellbeing of the boxers themselves. However, this exchange at training seemed to have had a positive effect on Ben. She felt he was behaving and talking in a more mature way than she had heard before. She had always felt, and enjoyed the fact that, he was quite easy going about life, lived for the day, enjoyed a good laugh and didn't take himself too seriously. The Squadron Leader had clearly made him stop and take stock of his situation, whether this had come about for the right reasons or not. Caroline was surprised but inwardly happy about the fact that Ben was discussing his future with her, albeit it was about him rather than them.

"I am seriously thinking about signing up for another couple of years" said Ben "I never in a million years thought that I would end up even considering staying beyond the conscription period, but I have enjoyed my time in the force. It has given me a focus and I think I have grown up quite a bit since I've been here. I have made a lot of friends. I am much fitter than I ever was in civvie street and I have really found the boxing an exciting and positive thing to be doing"

"Except it ruined your boyish good looks "Caroline teased him

He laughed "It would be hard to ruin my rugged features. But seriously do you think I am being foolish? I do want to see the boxing thing through. I was really disappointed not to be able to compete this year and I've got an eye on the interservice competition for next year, but that's not the whole story, is it? I can get a reasonable, reliable wage here. New opportunities are bound to develop if I commit to the service. There doesn't seem to be any likelihood of me being involved in hostilities anywhere on the horizon. The commercial flight business is growing, they will need skilled people to support their fleets of planes. I am sure this will open up opportunities for me. Oh, and of course I will still be close to you."

This felt a bit like an afterthought but Caroline did not dwell on it, she took it as a positive that she had been mentioned at all.

"Follow your heart" she said genuinely not meaning anything romantic. "It seems to me that your mind is made up and you are looking for confirmation, or someone to blame if it all goes wrong. No, seriously follow your heart. Whatever you might go back to, if you leave now, will probably still be there in another two years anyway. I don't think there is any risk at all and of course we can carry on as we are now which makes me happy too"

"I think you're right. I think my mind was made up after that intervention by the Squadron Leader at training. I agree it will be lovely for you and me to carry on as we are. The worst that can happen to my civvie electrical job is that they won't take me back in another three years, but I doubt that and even so I can look to the aviation industry for work if needs be. Perhaps I can sign on for another period with the RAF is all goes well. "

He paused. "So that's that then. I'll go and see about signing up tomorrow, make the commitment and look to the future. Let's drink to that – I'll get us another drink"

Cummings was delighted to learn of Ben's decision. He had another piece of his precious boxing team cemented into place, certainly for the next two interservice tournaments. They would just need to avoid any more traffic accidents.

Some of Bens colleagues were astounded. They couldn't wait to escape the military structure which they found constricted their lives. They were desperate to get back to the normality of their pre-conscription freedom with all the opportunities on offer, but Ben started to focus away from social time with the other conscripts and spend most of his time training for boxing. This involved multiple bouts of circuit training, copious amounts of skipping and running every morning. When he wasn't training, he was spending time with Caroline, socialising or helping her with her revision work. His duties on a daily basis started to change.

The months came and went with Ben getting ever fitter and ever stronger. He fought off all challenges to his entitlement to a place on the boxing team and became a favourite of the Squadron Leader. He found it easier to get time off his duties when he needed it .and was definitely given better food rations that the other lads. The three B's Ben, Bertie and Biffer were reunited as each came back from injury. They became the beating heart of the boxing team once again. The team managed to win through again at Farnborough and many of them were now in position to represent the RAF at the interservice knockouts in March.

The tournament was to be held at HMS Nelson in Portsmouth. Such was the interest and rivalry from the different teams and their supporters, the building there was filled to the rafters with wildly cheering servicemen and their families. Ben had never been inside this Naval establishment before and here he was performing under pressure at a well-attended, highly-charged event ,representing the RAF in general but Squadron Leader Cummings in particular. The boxers had changing areas from which they could hear most of what was happening. Following last year's disappointment there were very high hopes for the RAF. The team was well represented in all eight weights being contested Flyweight, Bantam weight, Feather weight, Lightweight, Welterweight, Middleweight, Light Heavy Weight and Heavy weight.

This year Ben was boxing at Middleweight. The bouts were scheduled in weight order with the Flyweights starting and the Heavy weights closing the evenings programme. By the time Ben's contest came around five titles had been decided. Two had gone to the Army, one to the Navy and two to the RAF. The team competition was finely balanced and Ben felt a further weight of responsibility on his shoulders. Ben's opponent was a slugger from the navy who seemed to feel nothing and kept on coming no matter how many punches landed. The first two rounds were even. Ben was bruised but he was the better boxer and entered the final round confident of a victory. Two minutes into the round disaster struck. Ben's opponent took a huge risk dropped his guard and swung wildly. The blow landed square on Ben's jaw and he was knocked clean out. The Navy supporters went mad with delight as the fly-boy hit the deck. There was a shocked and worried silence from the RAF support. Ben was carried from the ring unconscious and eventually brought round in the changing area. He was loaded into an ambulance and rushed to Portsmouth hospital. The RAF did go on to win the team competition but without the help of a point from Ben.

Not much made sense to Ben until the next day. Caroline who hadn't been either willing or able to attend the boxing match was taken to visit Ben by an RAF driver, dispatched by Squadron Leader Cummings.

"I wish you wouldn't box" Caroline said when she thought Ben was listening.

Ben didn't react, He was lost in his thoughts about what had happened. He didn't remember it all clearly but he knew that he had expected himself to win. He was looking for somebody else to blame. He was very angry and disappointed. So much effort had been put into arriving in that contest, so to lose it, to what he felt must have been a wild opportunist swing, was really galling. It started to make him start to question his decision to stay on in the RAF.

" It seems like every time you box, you end up in hospital!" she said

Ben opened his eyes and smiled "Yes, but that's how I met you"

He closed his eyes and drifted back into semi-consciousness.

Next time he came round Caroline had gone and he was able to think through all that had happened to him over the past two years. He started to consider his pursuit of the noble art and how much he actually liked boxing. Was it the boxing itself, pitting himself against another individual for personal satisfaction in victory or was it the discipline of regular focussed training? He concluded the latter. The tournament gave him a goal but it was not actually the objective. The objective was personal application and fitness management both of which could be achieved from other sporting activities with less potentially damaging outcomes. Ben determined to change direction and apply himself to a new activity once he had recovered from this setback.

The doctors were not entirely happy with Ben's condition. His brain had been shaken and he had experienced some internal bleeding. Injuries such as this could have long term effects which might not surface for some time to come. Ben was kept in hospital for a week under observation, until the pressure, which had built inside his skull, had subsided and the medical team were happy that any immediate danger had passed. He was released from hospital with clear instructions to take things easy for the next month. He was advised to neither box nor ride his bike for that time and preferably to consider whether it was worth pursuing boxing as a hobby at all. They suggested it might further aggravate the damage that he had already suffered. Caroline was privy to this advice and intended to encourage Ben to more sedate pastimes. Both the medical team and Caroline were lagging behind. Ben's decision to stop boxing was already made.

Chapter 11

For the immediate future had Sheila continued with cleaning the factory. She arranged more suitable hours and she taught another of Mickey's current cleaners what was required at the factory. Gradually she phased herself out and became a liaison between Mickeys company "Spic and Span" and the factory.   She even convinced the owners to use Mickeys business for their domestic cleaning. Mickey agreed to match her wages for the time being and hoped to be able to increase them as time passed.

Sheila spent more time in the office manning the phone, interviewing potential cleaners, explaining the childminding scheme and drawing up work rotas. It seemed she had an inborn organisational ability which may never have surfaced without Mickey's kindness and support. Winnie continued to support her by looking after Jennifer when Sheila was at work.

Sheila could not have survived without Winnie and she knew it. She was the closest thing to family that Sheila had known since she lost her parents and had a very special bond with her. She told Winnie all about her life. From the start Winnie knew about Sweeney, his demands and innuendo, in fact she had experienced it herself in the past when Sweeney visited her mother for the week's rent. She knew about Mickey but not his sexuality, so was excited by the possibility of Sheila finding a potential husband. She knew about the business development which Mickey and Sheila planned and was actually secretly very interested in the child minding co- operative idea, which she thought she would find useful. In fact, the more she thought about it the more she would like to be involved in the running of it.

One day whilst Sheila was visiting to collect Jennifer, Winnie blurted out her thoughts about the childminding.

"Sheila, you know how much I like having Jennifer"

Sheila flinched, fearing Winnie was about to back away – and really, she couldn't blame her.

"Well, I have been thinking about your child minding idea and I would like to be involved, if you think I could help"

"God Winnie, don't do that, I thought you were going to stop helping out with Jennifer for a moment; but yes, yes it would be great to have you involved, did you have something specific in mind?"

"Well not exactly but I do like being with the children and most of my time is committed to minding children anyway, so I think I could help"

"Of course, you could" said Sheila "You'd be marvellous. All we have really done is talk about it because we are so busy getting new business and interviewing cleaners, we haven't actually got round to the nitty gritty details of what the childminding part of things looks like. We don't even know where the children would be minded. In fact, the more I think about it the more there is to do. I am sure that Mickey would agree. Perhaps you can come and meet him and we could all talk it through"

"Well, yes I could and I have an idea for where we might look after the children?"

"Really where?"

"Well, you know I go to Mass don't you"?

Sheila nodded.

"Well, it's at the church in Quex Road."

"I know it, "said Sheila

"The priest is very friendly and helpful and is always looking for ways to raise funds and of course help the community. There is a sizeable hall next door to the church which to say the least is underutilised. I feel sure that for a reasonable regular donation to church funds and with running costs covered, Father David would be happy to see it put to use. I actually think if I was to propose it and be involved directly, he would jump at the chance. We get along very well."

Sheila's eyes brightened "Can you come to mine tomorrow evening?" she asked

"Well, I will have to check with Liam when he gets home but yes, I don't see why not"

The next evening Sheila, Winnie and Mickey took turns to read a bedtime story to Jennifer and when she was finally asleep sat down with cups of tea to talk about the childminding business. Winnie's enthusiasm for the project was unexpected, almost breath-taking. There was a pent-up need for her to get involved in something outside of her day-to-day routine. She threw her energy into it wholeheartedly. Mickey and Sheila were impressed with her ideas and her enthusiastic approach. She realised that there was not likely to be much to be gained financially at the outset as the whole objective was to provide young mothers with the space to go and earn some badly needed funds to support themselves and their children. There would be no rich pickings here, but there was opportunity to be of value and Winnie could see the project developing in the future. It could become bigger as time passed and probably more financially substantial.

It was agreed that Winnie would take the lead on the childminding business whilst Sheila and Mickey concentrated on the cleaning and services business. Sheila would provide office support and continue to be involved with the selection and rostering of cleaners. Mickey would deal directly with the customers and seek to bring in more commercial work.

Sheila and Mickey agreed that for as long as she could stand it, she would continue to clean for Sweeney as he provided a route in to other landlords in the immediate area and possibly beyond. Mickey had also noticed that Sweeney and his fellow landlords needed other services beyond cleaning; plumbing, electricity, drains, decorating and many more. He had already met some tradesmen whilst out cleaning and was starting to build a contact base of locally based people who were constantly seeking work. The Spic and Span cleaners could look out for opportunities to introduce tradesmen to their customers through the Spic and Span Services company. This would attract a finder's fee for the cleaner and a percentage commission for the company. It looked like, and proved to be, a vehicle to growing money streams for little effort.

Sheila continued to visit Sweeney, every Saturday morning at 8.00am, take his morning tea up to him in his bedroom and put up with his increasingly objectionable lewd suggestions.

Spic and Span started to take off. Father David was happy to see his church hall being used as a social facility and agreed to allow free access for the first month, to help get things off the ground. It had the double bonus of allowing him to meet some of his less pious parishioners and even to meet many non-Catholics, whom he might persuade to see the light.

Mickey was able to convince a local bank manager to lend him money for investment and they were able to take bigger and more accessible offices in Kilburn High Road where they could establish a new base for the next steps of their business. The offices themselves were populated with about twenty other small businesses each of which offered a new opportunity for Spic and Span.

Chapter 12

"Good morning, Mr. Sweeney" Sheila said and put down the tea and papers on his bedside table. She drew the curtains and awaited the first lewd comment of the morning. Nothing. Not a word. Come to think of it not even the sound of his heavy breathing filled the air.

"Mr Sweeney, Oh my God!!" Sweeney was dead and with the curtains now drawn back Sheila could see the grotesque outline of his gross lifeless body. He wore his usual old, worn, striped pyjamas and something sticky seemed to have had dried around his mouth. It wasn't clear what it had been but looked quite disgusting, some flies buzzed about the room eagerly anticipating decay and detritus. Sheila unconsciously opened the windows to address the heavy, thick atmosphere in the room. He must have been in his bed since Thursday.

After the initial shock Sheila felt surprisingly calm. She was emotionally unmoved to see Sweeney dead. He had been unpleasant in life and in death his pallid, motionless figure spread heavily across his ruffled bedclothes was pathetic. For the first time Sheila was struck by the emptiness of his life. There was probably nobody who would care that he was gone. She knew of no friends of his, she never saw any signs of social activity in the house. Only ever one plate, one knife one fork, a lone whiskey glass but often more than one empty whiskey bottle.

"Poor Man" Sheila addressed the corpse "what a miserable life you led, what could have brought you to this misery? A pile of unspent money and a life of emptiness. Well, whatever your story was this is where it ends."

Sheila was not unfamiliar with death; the war had taken care of that but she was not sure what she should do in these circumstances.

"I suppose I'll have to call a doctor, or an ambulance and probably the police" she thought. She wasn't aware of any family who would need to be told. She expected that the police would come and want to know what had happened and deal with any relatives that there may be. The doctor would examine him and then an ambulance or maybe a hearse would take him away. There was no need to clean this Saturday – or probably ever again for her. What would become of the house if there was no family to claim it. Well, it didn't matter, she could just walk away and leave that to the authorities. She had never felt comfortable here and felt no remorse for Sweeney's demise.

All these thoughts ran through her mind as she made her way downstairs and to the front door. She must advise the authorities quickly. Thank goodness that she had not brought Jennifer with her this time. What an awful sight for a young child to see.

The thought of Jennifer suddenly brought back a memory of her daughter playing in Sweeney's room when Sheila had first started cleaning. A memory of a loose floorboard hiding a shoebox full of money, of Sweeney noisily arriving home and of the cold sweat which she had felt at the prospect of being found out. Sheila had largely managed to put that discovery out of her mind since, although she had never forgotten completely and when cleaning had occasionally glanced in the direction of the now hidden loose floorboard.

In many ways she had wished that she hadn't seen the string in the first place, but now a new thought was forming. Who else knows about that box? Who else knows anything about Sweeney come to that? The money was clearly kept secretly so presumably nobody else was aware of its existence. How much was in the box? There were rolls of notes so it was likely to be in the hundreds, perhaps more, a fortune to Sheila.

Sheila 's progress towards the front door slowed and finally stopped. She turned and looked back at the stairs she had just descended and up towards where the stiff body of her now ex-employer and tormentor lay lifeless. Could she bring herself to take advantage of this situation? Did she have the nerve? Would she be caught out? Suddenly she was looking around to make sure there was nobody watching. Ridiculous, but she couldn't help it. She had changed from a shocked dutiful citizen about to report a death, into nervous opportunist potentially about to lay hands on more money than she could have imagined.

Sheila crept up the stairs silently, as if not to disturb anybody or anything. She peered slowly round the door to where Sweeney lay sleeping his final deathly sleep. She inched forward, careful not to awaken the corpse. She was checking once again, to be sure he was dead. As she reached his corpse, she questioned herself." Why am I doing this? I know he is dead", but she felt for a pulse nevertheless. Sweeneys pulpy flesh was cold and firm and there was no chance of finding a pulse. Sheila felt there were other eyes in the room watching, as she quietly made her way to the loose floorboard, now covered by a threadbare rug. "Was that there before?" she wondered.

Sheila pulled back the rug and saw the string which could open the door to a small fortune. Carefully she took the string and started to pull gently raising the floorboard with a wooden screech. The old battered shoebox came into view. Sheila carefully lifted the floorboard to one side and reached forward to pull the box from its hiding place. She leaned right into the darkness under the floor. As she tried to grasp the box something furry brushed her hand. She screamed and fell backwards onto the floor. Was it a mouse or a rat which had quickly scurried away under the boards,or just some random material she had connected with? She didn't know but it really spooked her. She turned to check that Sweeney wasn't looking at her, perhaps laughing at her stupidity. Happily, he was still dead.

Sheila took a deep breath. She hated what she was doing but couldn't stop herself. She gingerly reached into the hole for a second time, this time holding her breath. The shoebox came awkwardly out. She carefully replaced the floorboard, covered it with the rug and made her way quickly but quietly down the stairs.

The shoebox sat on the kitchen table for five long minutes. Sheila knew that if she opened it her life would change, perhaps for the better or maybe for the worse. What should she do? The lid lifted by about an inch and rolls of banknotes became evident, the lid came off and the banknotes were frantically moved from their hiding place into the shopping bag used for her cleaning materials. Sheila took the shoebox and put it into the dustbin outside. The shopping bag accompanied Sheila out of the front door and back to her flat where she pushed it and its contents under her bed. The journey home had been a breathless rush. She had tried to keep calm and keep the air of an innocent nonchalantly passing from A to B but felt as guilty as she was. She couldn't believe how many people were out and about. Perhaps they were always there at that time. She wouldn't normally notice. The milkman walked alongside his tired old nag as they slowly made their daily deliveries, the cart lumbering slowly behind.

"Morning Miss," said the milkman. Sheila wanted to vanish but managed a smiled "Good morning" and hurried by. How many others had seen her? Did they notice what she was carrying? Would they remember if asked?

Once indoors, Sheila stayed frozen to the bed. She sat and stared ahead, thinking about what she had just done. Thinking about Sweeney still lying in that bed. She didn't know how much money there was and she didn't really care. At the moment she was battling her conscience and struggling to convince herself that she was doing the right thing.

A knock at the door snapped her out of her hypnosis.

"Who is it "She asked and checked that the shopping bag was out of sight before opening the door.

"It's me, Mickey. I thought you were working at Sweeney's this morning!"

"Yes, I am but I had couple of things to do first. I'm just going."

"You Okay Sheila? You look a bit pasty if you don't mind me saying "smiled Mickey

"Yeah, fine just a bit tired. I better get going. He will be wondering where I am, I've usually done some cleaning, and brought him his tea by now"

"He'll probably still be in bed if I know him. "Said Mickey "Mind you he'll notice you're late, miserable old sod"

"I am sure you're right. See you later" Sheila said as she grabbed her coat and sped off.

Sheila went back to Sweeney's as if to start all over again and ignore what she had just done. She didn't feel the need to go upstairs but tried to make herself believe that she hadn't just stolen his money. She waited for a couple of minutes, then set off on foot for the police station to report the demise of her employer.

The police station was intimidating. Dark wooden panels lined all the walls, occasionally decorated by posters offering a variety of advice for members of the community. A red faced, rotund and quite serious looking police sergeant who towered over Sheila stood menacingly behind the front desk. He was focussed on filling in the details of what was presumably a very important form. Sheila couldn't see what he was writing but she was overwhelmed by her surroundings. She hadn't been into any police establishment in her life but this one lived up to what she might have expected.

The sergeant hardly looked up, apparently irritated by the intrusion into his workspace.

"Can I help?" he asked, sounding more like "What do you want?"

Rather timidly Sheila said "I want to report a death" This seemed to grab his attention. He put down his pen and looked up from his paperwork and down directly into Sheila's eyes

"What happened?" he asked.

Sheila's mind was racing – he knows there is something not quite right here, he can see that I am guilty of something.

"I just found the man I clean for dead in his bed" she said and proceeded to explain some of the events of the morning. The policeman, it seemed, took her obvious discomfort to be the reaction of a woman finding a man dead in bed – of course she would be flustered. He took down details of Sweeney's address and Sheila's name and address, which she had to prove to be accurate. Luckily, she was carrying her latest gas bill.

"Do you have your key to the deceased residence with you Miss?"

"Yes of course "Sheila quickly added "I came straight here when I found him so I have my keys with me."

"Perhaps you could leave the key with us, it will save our officers having to force an entry. Will you be needing them back at all, given the circumstances?"

"Probably not" Sheila conceded

"We may need you to make a statement"

Sheila nodded obediently and asked what happens next.

"Well, officers will attend the address and evaluate the scene. If all is in order as you describe and I am sure it will be, the police doctor will be called to attend the scene and certify the gentleman's death. All being well, we will have the body removed to the morgue. We will try and find next of kin and let them sort out funeral details. Unless there are any suspicious circumstances that will probably be that."

"What sort of suspicious circumstances do you mean?"

"Don't worry about that "he said "Leave it to us. It will probably be quite straightforward. If we need you to make a statement, we know where you are!"

We know where you are! Those words sounded close to threatening and Sheila felt an urge to blurt out her guilty secret. She managed to contain the urge and thanked the policeman for his help.

She left the police station without looking back. Sheila's first thought was to get home where she would feel safe, somehow everywhere felt a little threatening and uncomfortable. She thought of collecting Jennifer early and spending the morning with her but she didn't feel very much like playing games or entertaining her. She would pick her up later as usual. Winnie wouldn't mind. For now, she needed time to think. She really was not sure what to do, who to tell if anyone! The journey from the police station was much slower than her earlier breathless rush. She couldn't decide if she was excited or frightened. Perhaps both.

Sheila opened her flat door and made straight for the kettle. A cup of tea usually makes things feel a bit better and this was no exception. Sheila sat down with her tea and looked at the bed. She thought about the shopping bag and its contents. How much money was in there? Would anybody else know about it? Should she own up to the police? She was already feeling really uncomfortable. She was also feeling an increasing sense of excitement and wanted to tell somebody. This would be lifechanging.

Sheila mulled over what to do "First things first. Count the money, let's see what I'm dealing with, then decide what a cover story might be if I was to be discovered with it. How I might hide it away and how can I spend it without attracting suspicion." Her calm and apparent logic surprised her.

Sheila pulled the curtains of the flat shut. She did not want anybody passing by to have any chance of seeing her in the act of counting. She checked that the door was properly closed and locked. When she was happy that she was secure, she took a deep breath and emptied the contents of the shopping bag onto the table. It was a breath-taking moment as bundles of notes tumbled out, a couple falling to the floor. Sheila pulled it all together, picked up those that had fallen and set about counting. She had never seen so much money. She felt as, she imagined, a wealthy high-born lady might. It was a serious business. Sweeney had been fastidious about the way the bundles were arranged as it turned out. Each bundle contained exactly 250 notes. Each denomination of note was carefully arranged in the same direction. A rubber band was placed round the middle of the bundle both as they lay flat and another in the rolled-up position that Sheila found them. There were six bundles of ten-shilling notes, four bundles of one-pound notes and one bundle of five-pound notes. Sheila counted twice. Three thousand pounds was a fortune. She sat and looked at it unsure whether to laugh or cry. She was snapped out of her trance by a sharp rap on the front door.

"Christ, who's that" she thought and hurriedly threw the piles of banknotes back into the bag, Sweeney's neat stacks gone forever. She shoved the shopping bag under the bed. Guiltily she straightened her hair as if she had been caught in a lover's clinch. She made her way to the door and opened it gingerly expecting to see a member of Her Majesty's constabulary standing there ready to arrest her.

It was Mickey.

"Thank God for that, come in" Sheila virtually pulled Mickey into the room with her and burst into tears.

"Crikey, Sheila, what's the matter" Mickey was worried something terrible had happened.

Sheila sobbed. She tried to control herself but found that her pent-up emotions were overwhelming. It was some moments before she was able to get some semblance of control.

"Sorry" she said

"For God's sake what's happened?" Mickey demanded

Sheila told him the history of her morning but left out the mention of floorboards and cash.

"Well at the risk of being unfeeling, I didn't think that Sweeney was one of your favourite people but I do understand the shock of finding a dead body must be awful, no matter who it is. On the bright side he didn't realise that you arrived late, did he?" Sheila managed a smile

"So, what did the police say?"

Sheila told Mickey about her visit to the police station and repeated what she had been told by the sergeant.

"Look Sheila it's always a terrible thing when somebody dies but I don't think they will be queuing up to say goodbye to our Mr. Sweeney. He was not a very nice man and very likely didn't have a lot of friends to miss him"

Sheila was desperate to share her secret and release some of the tension she felt. If she couldn't trust Mickey, who could she trust. So, she told him. She told him everything and went to the shopping bag under the bed as if to prove what she was telling him was truthful

Mickey's jaw dropped when he saw the money.

His instinct was that Sheila should return it before things got out of hand. She would probably be reprimanded but no more than that.

On the other hand, she was a partner in the business now and that sort of money could make life much easier for them both. He subconsciously assumed that having told him her secret she would be willing to share some of her good fortune. Then he assumed it consciously and felt bad about himself.

"Are you sure nobody else knew about it?"

"No, not really that's been going through my mind, but I don't think Sweeney was the type to have anyone else and certainly not where his money was concerned. It seems to me that most of the people he knew were his tenants and the very people who were contributing to his pile of money."

"Have you counted it"

"Yes, I'd just finished when you knocked on the door and put the fear of God in me"

"How much?"

"Three thousand pounds exactly. I counted it twice. It seems that he only put it under the floorboards once he had two hundred and fifty notes, so presumably somewhere in the house there will be other incomplete bundles, waiting to be stashed"

"You're not suggesting we go back for that are you?"

"No but it will make it seem more normal if the police find money. You might expect that there would be some."

"That's true. What are you going to do with it if you decide to keep it?"

"Well, I don't know really, I can't just suddenly become rich. I can't explain that away. Perhaps we could use some of it to help the business. It might be easier to hide if we invested it in the business. I don't know exactly how that would work and I don't want to involve you but it seems I have already and the business could benefit."

"Okay, let's think about this some more. I have things to do, I only knocked because I could see that you were in and I wondered why you weren't cleaning. Now I know. Don't do anything for now. I have to carry on with my day, there are things which can't wait but perhaps we can meet this evening and talk about it then."

"Great, I feel a lot better. Thanks Mickey, even though I am sorry to have involved you. A problem shared and all that! I'll go and get Jennifer from Winnie's and spend the day with her, that will take my mind off it and once she's asleep tonight we can talk further. Do you want to come for dinner?"

"That would be great, thank you and don't worry. This could actually prove to be the making of you and give Jennifer a much better start to life. See you later"

Mickey pecked Sheila on the forehead and left

Sheila stashed her shopping bag back under the bed with slightly more confidence and the beginnings of feelings of ownership. Perhaps things would be all right. For now, she set her mind on what to tell Winnie. Just the facts about Sweeney's death would be enough for the pair to chat about before they took the children to the park together. Sheila looked at the bed and went to the bag. She took a five pound note out and slipped it into her purse. At least she could buy something nice for dinner tonight and maybe a little gift for Jennifer, after all no one would notice a fiver!

Later that evening Sheila prepared Jennifer for bed. She had left Winnie at the park gates and headed towards the butcher's where she had brought two steaks. Meat was in short supply and not cheap so she felt very happy to be able to afford such a luxury. She had told the butcher it was her friend's birthday and that it was a big celebration, which was why she was being so extravagant. She had taken Jennifer to a toy shop and brought a little rag doll, nothing too expensive, but enough to make Jennifer's eyes light up with excitement. Now Jennifer cuddled her new doll as she closed her eyes to sleep.

Sheila waited for Mickey to arrive before cooking the steaks. She had never actually had good steak and was looking forward to the experience, although she didn't really know how to cook it. Between them Mickey and Sheila created a wonderful dinner and accompanied it with wine, which Mickey had brought with him. A very special occasion!

"If we are careful, we can eat like this every day in the future" Mickey smiled. "I think we should keep the money and maintain a low profile for now. We can start to sift it into the business and take it back out as the business grows. That way we would not look suspicious as we start to get wealthy. Do you like the sound of that?"

Sheila decided that she did like the sound of that and relaxed into a bottle of wine and the prospect of newly found wealth. They spent the rest of the evening talking about the business and how they could now develop it faster than they had ever previously imagined.

Chapter 13

Ben and Caroline married. It was a natural progression and seemed to make sense to them both. They had a white wedding. Ben's mother and sister both came to the ceremony, pleased to see Ben married in the presence of God. Caroline's family were well represented by her mother and father. Her two sisters were bridesmaids and various aunts and uncles and cousins dug out their Sunday best for the occasion. Bride and groom were popular at work and the boys from the RAF formed a guard of honour. Caroline's colleagues delighted in peppering the couple with rice at the gates of the church.

Amongst other guests were Bobby and Jimmy Wilson with their wives. Jimmy, had married Gillian, a girl of Irish descent who he met at a dance the previous year and Ben had attended the wedding with Caroline. Jimmy had finished his period of conscription and was back working with Bobby, his father.

During the evenings celebration Bobby found time to update Ben on things back in North London. He told Ben how the business was growing and becoming very successful. Ben was happy to hear how well the business was going but also harboured a little envy that it was doing so without him. Perhaps one day he would go back. It was comforting to know that he would be welcomed and his relationship with Bobby and Jimmy was still apparently as strong as it had always been.

The newly married couple honeymooned on the island of Jersey which was fast becoming the holiday location of choice for honeymooners, at least those that could afford it. They had a wonderful week staying in a guest house on St. Brelade's Bay.

Their married life together could not have had a better start. The RAF had a number of small houses made available to servicemen on the base for rent and Ben and Caroline happily took advantage with a view to saving up for a place of their own at some time in the future.

Life was good, they were happy. Eleven months passed before Caroline announced that she was pregnant. This came as something of a shock to them both, as they had planned for a longer period with just the two of them. They had hoped to get Caroline promoted to ward sister but nature intervened.

Pregnancy did not suit Caroline. She was ill from the outset; unable to keep food down and feeling generally unwell throughout her confinement. Her mother made time to support her, having suffered in a similar way during her own pregnancies. She came to stay for days at a time and did what she could to make life better for Caroline. Caroline felt unable to grow into her confinement and found it very difficult to come to terms with her discomfort. Things just seemed to get worse. Ben also found the situation difficult. Whilst understanding the need for her mother's support, having his mother-in-law in the house did not make for a good atmosphere. At any one time, one person or another was at odds with someone else. Mother with son in law and vice versa was the relationship which caused the most friction, both feeling somewhat inadequate in trying to help Caroline.

At twenty-four weeks things came to a head. The baby had been moving for some time, which had given Caroline some renewed excitement about the life inside her but she had also found it disconcerting. The baby's movement added a further level of discomfort. Early one morning Caroline was in the toilet trying to throw up. She felt an intense pain in her stomach which was almost unbearable and seemed to be never-ending. She screamed out. Caroline's mother was not staying at the time so Ben had to deal with her agony alone. Since the pregnancy he had acquired a second-hand motorbike with a sidecar, to help transport Caroline around. He felt that the only way to deal with their predicament was to get her to hospital and quickly. He wrapped her up and helped her to the sidecar, covered her with a blanket and closed the top of the sidecar over Caroline's head. Caroline was in extreme pain, so Ben was torn between racing to the hospital as fast as he could and trying not to bounce his wife around too much.

When they arrived at the emergency department of the K&C. Caroline was seen very quickly and rushed straight to the maternity unit where it became clear that things were not going well. The staff on duty went about their business efficiently but with obvious concern. Caroline and Ben's baby was still-born. Life had turned upside down. What had been a perfect start to their married life had come crashing down with this pregnancy. Caroline was distraught. She blamed herself for the loss of their child, although she couldn't rationalise her thoughts. Ben was distraught and felt guilty. He had been unable to help his wife or his child when they needed him. His faith did not help him, nor did his mother's prayers or his mother in law's advice after the event. The couple were required to name their stillborn baby and chose George. They registered his birth and his death at the same time and then went through the trauma of a funeral for a child they had never had the opportunity to get to know.

Life was unrecognisable for the couple as they tried to get back to what might be described as a normal existence. They tried to renew their relationship where they had left off but each knew that things would never be the same. What had happened could not be undone and it left a scar on each of them individually but also on their partnership. As time passed Ben found his in-laws increasingly involved in his life, it was as if they felt he was unable to look after their daughter. Ben and Caroline talked about their stillborn child and over time came to terms with what had happened. They would never get over it but as time passed, they became more accepting of their fate. As they started to talk about it more and more openly, they found that they were not alone in losing a child. It was surprising how many people knew someone who had miscarried. Caroline returned to work and found her colleagues full of sympathy, experience and advice. Apparently, infant mortality was not an uncommon occurrence but it put Caroline off the idea of ever having another pregnancy. She had always wanted and expected to have children but this experience was not something she wanted to risk repeating.

The general view suggested that, armed with the experience of her first confinement, the second time she would be better informed to manage her condition with more care. It took a long time and a lot of heartbreak before Caroline and Ben started to come round to the idea of trying again.

Part of their incentive was that perhaps returning to where they had been in their life, the excitement of starting a family, would bring them closer together again. Both were of the same view that marriage was a once in a lifetime event and that they would work through whatever difficulties life threw at them together. The news came that Caroline had conceived again. The news was both chilling and exciting at the same time. Caroline left her job and resolved to take things much more carefully this time.

She still had morning sickness and generally was unwell but she felt in her heart that things were actually going better this time around. She and Ben became closer to each other again and it felt that their life was getting back on track. They both treated the pregnancy with much more respect than first time around. The slightest concern took them to the doctor for reassurance. Caroline put on much more weight this time round and everybody was eager to reassure her how healthy she looked and how the pregnancy was suiting her so much better this time. For a long time, all seemed well. They had put away all of the baby paraphernalia which they had bought for George. With mixed feelings they started to prepare the babies room again at home and allowed themselves to imagine their baby laying in the cot and smiling up at them.

Ben received a message at work. He was working on the engine of a small training plane when a rather worried looking WRAF approached him. "Airman Macdonald?" she confirmed

"Yes, that's me!"

"I am afraid you wife has been taken to hospital and you are advised to get there as quickly as you can"

"Whats happened?" Ben felt a mounting panic.

"I don't know, I just have instructions to tell you to get off as quickly as you can and get to the maternity unit at the K&C hospital. You have been cleared to leave the airfield and go straightaway."

Ben left his tools where they were, grabbed his jacket and ran to his motorcycle. The journey to the K&C was one he had done many times in the past couple of years. He had never before felt as he did today. Intuitively he knew that things were not right despite the fact that Caroline was towards the end of her pregnancy, beyond thirty weeks. This was a sudden and unexpected call; his wife was in hospital and apparently in some trouble. It took about thirty minutes to get to the hospital and he ran to reception.

"My wife has been admitted, she's seven months pregnant" for a moment he doubted himself "it may be eight months" he said, as if it would make a difference.

"What is her name please"

"Of course, I am sorry its Caroline Macdonald"

The receptionist looked directly at him with a kind smile. He imagined he saw pity in her eyes.

"Please go along to the fathers waiting area up on the second floor, someone will be along to see you shortly. Ben took the stairs up to the second floor and followed the signs to the fathers waiting room. There were two other anxious fathers pacing the floor, one drinking tea, the other chewing gum, but both clearly very nervous about the wellbeing of their wives and impending new arrivals.

Ben calmed himself a little. Seeing two other men, clearly agitated, made him feel a little less anxious. He sat and waited and watched the door. After ten long minutes the door opened and a serious looking doctor in a white coat with stethoscope slung around his neck came in.

"Mr Macdonald?"

Ben stood up and took a step forward.

"Please follow me," said the doctor politely.

The doctor led Ben to an office nearby.

"Please take a seat Mr Macdonald. I am afraid I have bad news. Your wife was brought into the maternity ward earlier today by ambulance. She was haemorrhaging quite badly and had lost a lot of blood; I believe a neighbour found her collapsed at home. I am afraid that the blood loss was too much. We were unable to save her. We did all that we could. I am sorry!"

"What……. Caroline?" Ben was unable to take in what he had just heard

"Mrs. Macdonald had gone into early labour at home and was shedding blood when she arrived. She had clearly lost a considerable amount of blood even before she reached the hospital. I am afraid that we did what we could for both mother and baby but neither survived, I am sorry. There was clearly damage to the placenta and the baby had little chance of surviving the birthing process. I am afraid your wife died about thirty minutes ago"

Ben couldn't believe what he was hearing.

"Oh my God, it can't be true. Why would this happen?" Ben's voice was almost a whisper

"We wonder if she had taken a fall at home which may have brought on the bleeding and caused some damage but at this stage it is too early to be sure. She was very dazed and incoherent when your neighbour found her"

"Can I see her?"

"Of course," said the doctor "First take a moment before we go to her. This is obviously a considerable shock for you and you need to take it in."

Ben sat and stared ahead of him, sifting through a myriad of thoughts. He didn't know where to start. His mind took him back to George the child they never knew, how unfair it all was. This couldn't be happening again. He thought about what a gruelling couple of years they had endured, part of him was thinking we'll get through this together. Abruptly he caught himself in the realisation that Caroline would not be there. He just couldn't bring himself to comprehend that.

"I need to see Caroline" he said

A few moments later a senior nurse led Ben the length of the ward to a cubicle at the end. There was a palpable atmosphere in the ward. In the distance a mother screamed in the throes of childbirth. Ben didn't hear. Ben didn't really see where he was going either. The thoughts going through his head didn't leave space for other senses.

The nurse opened a door leading into a small room. There on a theatre bed lay Caroline, pale and lifeless. Ben looked at her and finally believed what he had been told. He felt his chest heave and he struggled for breath as the emotion rose up through him. He slumped over Caroline's body and sobbed like he had never sobbed before. He was completely lost. Why? Why Caroline she was one of life's good people, she didn't deserve this. She spent her life helping people, why her, why in child birth, how could life be so cruel?

At that moment Ben realised that any relationship that he had with religion could never continue in the future. How could a God, who is supposed to love all his children, allow this to happen?

Ben spent twenty broken minutes with Caroline before being helped from the delivery suite. He had no interest in seeing the baby who was also a victim of this catastrophe. He had a wife to grieve for and was not sure of his feelings towards his second still born child. George their first still born son, had been referred to as a member of the family over the months since his arrival and death, even though they had never known him. Ben had no thought of humanising this second lost infant, it was too much to bear.

The hospital arranged for transport to get Ben home. He was too shaken and upset to even consider getting onto his motorcycle. It was also agreed that the hospital would contact Caroline's parents. There were professionals who obviously had considerable experience dealing with loss and Ben didn't know what he could say to her parents to minimise the pain. He could barely speak.

The next two weeks of Ben's life were hell. He stayed home alone. He couldn't bring himself to contact his mother and sister because he knew they would come down and probably move in and he couldn't handle that just now. Caroline's parents were very supportive, they came the day after Caroline had died and spent many hours with Ben talking about what had happened.   The baby had been a girl this time and Ben was still required to go through the gruelling task of naming and registering birth and death then arranging a funeral. Ben and Caroline's parents agreed to call the baby girl Jennifer, Caroline's grandmother's name. The joint funeral was harrowing and painful.

Ben knew he had to move away. He couldn't stay where he was. There was too much of Caroline and the life they had built together. The RAF were understanding. Ben was given compassionate leave and was supplied with both pastoral and emotional counselling. He had five months left on his contract and he started to consider his options for the future. It would not be in the RAF.

Chapter 14

It was Tuesday evening when the policeman knocked at Sheila's door. Jennifer was having her tea.

"Good evening, Miss" The policeman said "Is it a convenient time to ask you some questions?"

Sheila was completely flummoxed.

"Well, it's a bit difficult. I'm about to put my daughter to bed. Will it take long?"

Sheila was scared

"Shouldn't take too long. Just some routine questions to clear up one or two anomalies Miss"

The police officer was scanning the property and making his assessment and personal judgment about Sheila's situation. Having been brought up as a good Christian and part of the Church of England his predilection for a "normal" family life, meant his prejudices were already stacking up against this single mother, living on a shoestring, with a helpless young child. However, he wasn't here to judge. He was here just to get the facts.

"It's regarding the untimely death of Mr. Sweeney".

"How do you mean untimely?" Sheila asked

"Just a figure of speech. Although I suppose there are few deaths that one might describe as timely. Do you have a moment or would you rather pop in to the station tomorrow?"

"No.no, if it is just a couple of questions, I suppose we should do it now but do you mind if I get somebody to sit with my daughter in the meantime?"

"Of course, "said the policemen

Sheila ran upstairs and told Mickey what was happening. He was naturally somewhat taken aback but rationalised that, of course, there would be follow up questions. He agreed to come and get Jennifer for a while and take her to his flat whilst the police asked their questions.

Now the officer was seated with his notebook flipped open and a pencil in his hand

"How can I help?" asked Sheila

"Thank you, Miss Johnson, we just wanted to confirm the details of your statement at the station and clarify one or two other points. You were Mr Sweeney's cleaner, is that correct?"

"Yes"

"Did you perform any other role for Mr. Sweeney?"

"What do you mean?"

"Well, you had a key to his flat and someone had taken tea to his bedside, we wanted to be sure that there were no other duties involved, other than cleaning". The police officer squirmed as he asked the loaded question. He was not at all comfortable making the unspoken, but clear, suggestion that Sheila might be providing other "services"

"What!! No, I was his cleaner, and his tenant, full stop. He asked me to bring him tea on my arrival and I have always done that"

"His tenant?"

"Yes, I rent a room here, this is another of his properties." Sheila went on to explain the circumstances.

"I see" said the police officer. Sheila felt that this policeman was drawing conclusions and condemning her on the spot.

"What time did you arrive at Mr. Sweeneys property on Saturday?"

Sheila knew she had to find something to fill the time between first arriving and then going back again later.

"I was late, I normally arrive about 8.00 but it was more like 8.30 on Saturday"

"I see"

Every time the policemen said "I see" Sheila felt that he had stumbled across something of importance.

"Why were you late?"

"Well, I dropped my daughter off as usual at my friend's and got it into my mind that I had left the gas stove on after cooking breakfast. So, I rushed back home to turn it off, which made me late."

"And did you leave the gas stove on?"

"Yes, I did, so it was just as well I came back"

"What was for breakfast?"

"It was porridge but I don't understand what this has to do with Mr. Sweeney's death"

"You're right I'm sorry. May I ask you if you saw anything different at Mr Sweeney's place on your arrival at his place, anything which was out of the ordinary?"

"No, no I didn't "

"Please be sure, this is important"

"No, sorry I don't know what you are looking for"

"Just the facts Miss only the facts. Just one final question for now, did you remove anything from Mr. Sweeneys residence when you left?"

God, they know something she thought

"No nothing "she said

"Nothing at all?" the officer pressed.

"No nothing" she repeated

"Well, thank you for your help this evening, you have cleared up one or two points for us, we will leave you to your evening"

"Is that it?" Sheila wanted to find out more now.

"Yes, for now. Please let us know if anything comes to mind that you feel may be useful to our enquiries. Sorry for the disturbance" The policeman folded his notebook and slipped it back into his tunic, got up and left.

Sheila ran upstairs

"God, I think they know" Mickey was sitting with Jennifer on his lap reading a story.

"Let's get Jennifer to bed, shall we?" he suggested "then we can talk about this sensibly – don't panic"

Mickey patiently finished off Jennifer's story and carried her down to bed. Jennifer was taking in all that was going on around her and sensed that things weren't right.

"What did that policeman want Mummy?"

"Nothing, Jennifer, he just wanted to ask me some questions about a man that I used to work for?"

"Has he been naughty?" Jennifer's eyes widened, eager for more information.

"No, he is just helping them with one of their cases" she said "Now time for sleep"

"What is a case, Mummy?"

"I'll tell you more in the morning, it's bedtime now."

It would be difficult to talk for a while as Jennifer was an enquiring child and her bed was close by.

Sheila made tea and she and Mickey sat together and whispered.

"What did he want? Mickey asked

"I'm not sure really but he asked if I had taken anything from Sweeney's place"

"What did you tell him"

"I told him I hadn't taken."

"Good, I'm sure it must be routine for them"

"Perhaps somebody saw me, I know I spoke to the milkman and there were others about."

"Just leave it, I'm sure it will all blow over once Sweeney's body has been buried. The man just died. It happens every day, the police will do their paperwork and that will be that. There's nothing to worry about"

Sheila was less confident though happy to get Mickey's reassurances. She always felt better when he was around. Why did he have to be queer!

Much to Sheila's relief she didn't hear any more from the police, except to be told when the funeral would be held. Sheila felt she should attend and Mickey agreed to go with her. The funeral was held in the chapel associated with the cemetery and was conducted by a local vicar. There were 9 people in attendance including Sheila and Mickey. Sheila recognised one or two other tenants of Sweeney's from errands he had asked her to run in the past but there was little sign of mourning. The vicar spoke generally about the sad passing of one of his parishioners but his words could not conceal the fact that he knew little about the man laid out in the coffin. After the service everyone dispersed without a word. Sweeney was gone and for most of the congregation the main thing on their mind was who would be collecting the rent in the weeks and months to come.

Unsurprisingly Sweeney had died intestate. He had a lawyer and an accountant both of whom had been present at the funeral, more in a professional capacity than from any particular affection for the man. The accountant was a short tidy individual, name of Higgins and it was he who came calling at rent time the following month. He explained that as a sign of respect for Sweeney and good will towards his tenants, tenants would be granted a six-week, rent free amnesty period, whilst Sweeney's affairs were put in order by the authorities. There were decisions to be made about property ownership and Sweeney's estate. Much of the property would revert back to the lenders who held the deeds and it was likely that the properties would be resold to the highest bidder. Any contracts or agreements with Sweeney were no longer relevant and new arrangements would be made in the near future.

Sheila and Mickey had decided that part of their new found wealth could be used to improve their living arrangements. They agreed to look for living accommodation which offered them their independence but kept them together. They were happy to share a flat or house or whatever they could find as an interim measure until circumstances changed. The plan was to rent and let the dust settle after Sweeney's demise but to get out of his world as quickly as possible. They wanted to put distance between them and those managing Sweeny's affairs.

Mickeys friendship with Rufus had been developing during the weeks since their introduction at the art gallery. They had shared a number of evenings together and were moving their relationship towards something beyond the platonic basis on which they had started. Mickey had been invited to join Rufus for drinks at his home which was a significant invitation as far as Mickey was concerned. He was flattered and excited but somewhat confused by the address which Rufus had given him.

The address read

"Freedom"
Regents Canal
Bloomfield Road
Maida Vale

It transpired that Rufus lived on a converted narrow boat owned by one of his Portobello market group of friends. Rufus's arrangement allowed him free rent of the boat in return for decorating services of both the boat and of the boat owner's property. He was also commissioned to complete works of art for the owner from time to time. The arrangement worked well for both men, except for the odd occasion when the boat owner wanted to entertain a guest aboard the narrow boat alone, Rufus had to make himself scarce.

Mickey was excited by the romantic notion of his friend's life on a converted narrowboat and was not disappointed with what he found. The boat was brightly painted in traditional green and red; the paintwork was immaculate and the brass lamps that adorned the front and rear of the boat sparkled. Along the side of the boat in elaborate Italics was written the word "Freedom" announcing the owner's dream to those who wanted to know. More importantly, at that moment, informing Mickey that he had in fact arrived at the right vessel. In the absence of a bell or a knocker Mickey tapped on the hatch with his bare knuckles, not sure of the correct protocol.

"Come in! It's open. The top just slides back and the door opens inwards" Rufus was in the galley preparing food. "Welcome to the canal" he said as Mickey climbed awkwardly down the three steps that led to the galley.

"You get used to the height of the ceiling, and the width, it's all very cosy really"

The boat, whilst by definition narrow, provided more space than Mickey had first expected. This was a custom conversion which was well furnished and suited to the life of a budding artist. One area had been left as a creative artistic space where Rufus was able to paint, although the light limited creativity to some degree. It was littered with various sized canvasses and a multitude of charcoal and pencil sketches, brushes paints, easels. One area was assigned for sleeping with a bed which might have claimed to be a double but was more like an oversized single. There was a small wardrobe and some limited drawer space.

The galley comprised a small gas cooker with hob, grill and oven tucked into one corner and a small refrigerator tucked away in another. Mickey was invited to sit at the table on a bench seat which would manage three people at a squeeze. His seat offered him a view through a side window of a similar craft on the opposite site of the canal, which had clearly seen better days.

"I didn't realise people actually lived on these" Mickey said

"You'd be surprised" said Rufus "there's a proper community around here and should it take your fancy, you can move your home anywhere you want between here and Birmingham and probably beyond. Living on a narrowboat offers all sorts of advantages. Nobody knows how to find me unless I tell them. I'm completely off the radar. Scotty, the guy who owns this boat, brought it as a shell and allowed me to convert it to suit my needs. I built in everything I need until I make a big sale of a artwork, when I will buy a studio with an apartment above. In the meantime, it's a great life on the open seas!!"

Mickey laughed and digested the being off the radar comment.

"Seems a bit small to me"

"No, you get used to it, honestly! I've been living on this for 18 months now and I love it. It took three months to convert – with a lot of help from my friends, including Scotty. Now he just leaves me to it, more or less"

"You converted it yourself?"

"Well, yes, Scotty had the boaty stuff done, you know watertightness rotten wood etc, that was all done in dry dock somewhere, then delivered as a shell to me. I have friends who are handy with electrics and plumbing and stuff and I am pretty handy with a saw. Creative stuff you know!"

"Wow very impressive"

Mickey's relationship with Rufus transformed that evening. They became an "item" and Mickey's affair with narrowboats began. A narrowboat would always hold a special significance for him. During the course of the evening Mickey told Rufus about the demise of his landlord and Sheila's difficult morning when she had found him. He kept the details of the shoebox and its contents to himself but told Rufus everything about getting a fresh start and seeking a new place to live. Rufus shared Mickey's good riddance view regarding Sweeney and understood why both he and Sheila would want to move on from their current set up.

"Perhaps you should try canal life "Rufus suggested

"Do you know that could be fun," said Mickey.

The seed was sown.

Mickey wondered how Sheila might feel about bringing Jennifer onto the water. They could give it a try and see how they got on, nothing to lose really. They would need a bigger, differently configured boat if they were to share but it all seemed possible. Mickey asked Rufus to ask around his water bound neighbours regarding availability of other boats in the locality.

Rufus was expecting a visit from the warden who collected mooring fees fairly soon and if anybody would know what was available, he would.

The next day in the office Mickey told Sheila all about his evening with Rufus and how they had got a little more intimate. Sheila was a bit uncomfortable with being confided in quite so much but she was happy for Mickey that things were moving along. He spoke enthusiastically about Rufus's unusual home and Sheila's eyes lit up. The idea of living on the water sounded like fun and to get out of her bedsit anywhere else would have to be an improvement. For Jennifer as long as the boat was moored within reasonable proximity to the school and thus close to Winnie, she had few reservations and would be willing to give it a try.

The business was growing steadily; Winnie had started her child-minding club and had taken on another likeminded mother to help her out as the numbers of children to be looked after started to grow. One or two of the older church ladies made a point of calling in more often when they found out that young children were playing in the church hall. They willingly volunteered to help out free of charge, just happy to have the contact with Winnie and the children.

The roster of cleaning ladies was longer and the geographical spread of customers expanding too. Sheila was still available and willing to clean but she found that her time was filled with administration and organisation. The final clean at Sweeney's had been her last hands-on cleaning work for some time. Both Mickey and Sheila's wages were increasing as the business grew and there was opportunity to drip Sweeney's money into the mix without raising suspicion.

A week later and Mickey was back aboard "Freedom" and Rufus had news.

"I spoke to John Mitchell, the warden from the canal company about availability of berths and narrow boats on the canal. He told me that berths would not be too difficult to find, in fact there were two or three just off Little Venice, slightly up the Grand Union. The moorings there are a little cheaper as well, since they are not in the prime locations. Narrow boats can be sourced from a number of boatyards up and down the canal and the further out you go to purchase the better the value you will find."

"That's great. How does it all work then? I hadn't thought of buying a boat really just renting"

"Problem with that is you would be waiting for somebody to move out, whereas moorings are available today. If you can borrow some money, you could buy a boat as an asset of your company and let it back to yourself at a reasonable rate. As places to live boats are relatively cheap. If it all doesn't suit you in at any time in the future you can let it out yourself – become a landlord. I suggest that we look for boats first and see what you can get and how much. Come on, for a big business man like you this should be a piece of cake!"

"For a struggling artist you seem to have an eye for business"

"I can dream but I can't do. My skill is in creating. I am not really a business minded person but this looks like an easy decision, if you can raise the money!"

Mickey knew exactly how he could raise the money. It was sitting in his office safe in bundles. He would just need to agree it with Sheila.

This was, of course, no problem.   The plan would relieve two worries at once, where to live and how to hide some of Sweeney's money whilst using it productively. So, a trip to a boating yard was arranged. They agreed to look locally first to get some idea of what might be available and what sort of costs might be incurred. Afterwards, perhaps, they would take a train ride to the Midlands and see if their money would deliver better value. If they found a suitable bargain it could be driven back to the mooring points in London. That would be something of an adventure in itself!

Mickey started to research the availability of narrowboats and found himself getting sucked into the history of canals. It seems the canals had been nationalised in 1948 after the war and that the commercial use of them was getting less and less important, as roads and railways were taking over. The canals were run by the British Transport Commission (BTC) which included the Grand Union Canal carrying company (GUCCC). BTC had a fleet of three hundred or so boats many of which they were looking to offload as they just represented a cost. They had started to abandon the boats in a number of sites up and down the country, the nearest of which was Harefield. They were told that there was another at Braunston, which Mickey thought may prove to be the best place from a cost point of view.

Mickey also discovered that there were wider boats which might be more suitable for their needs. It seemed that these wider boats could not travel everywhere on the Canal network but since they did not plan to travel, one of these might turn out to be an even better option.

One Friday Mickey, Sheila and Jennifer went to meet Mr Hobbs from the British Transport Commission. They met him on the canal in Hayes where there were several boats berthed. The location was not the pretty country canal side that Sheila had envisaged. The area had a more industrial feel to it than residential.

"Don't worry about the location Sheila" Mickey assured her, "there are berths near the Paddington junction which are available and much nicer"

Mr Hobbs explained that the BTC would be happy to take a token payment for the boats, as they were effectively obsolete and would end up being scrapped if they were not "moved on". The BTC was eager to keep canals open and alive. They expected, and were keen to encourage, a move towards residential usage as well as leisure and recreational activity in the future.

Sheila and Mickey were shown round 4 or 5 craft in various states of repair. One in particular stood out: a wider boat called "Melody", a wide beamed boat attached to a second with no engine, which the gentleman called a "butty". The second boat was more or less a barge towed by the first making the carriage of goods more efficient. Both boats were badly in need of a coat of paint from the waterline upwards. There was no knowing what needed attention under water. "Melody "had an enclosed area from where the skipper steered the boat, within this area, down three steps was provision for a galley and two rooms with 2 berths for crew. The boats were relatively clean as they had not been used for the carriage of coal at any time and probably had mainly handled textiles between Birmingham and London.

"This would be ideal for us. We could have one each," said Mickey.

Sheila was not so sure. The romantic notion which she had first felt was fading as the reality of seeing these older boats, which were in need of a complete rebuild, hit home.

"I don't think I want to live on there!" Sheila had yet to see a boat which suggested warmth, comfort or home. She just could not see how she could make Jennifer safe and comfortable on what was effectively a barge.

"Please keep an open mind, come and see what Rufus has done with his boat before you decide. I think that "Melody" will transform into a dream boat and we can pick it and its "butty" up for next to nothing. We can invest in converting them as we want them and if it all doesn't work out for any reason, we can sell them or rent them for a profit."

Sheila reluctantly agreed but was definitely cooling about the prospect. Jennifer was very excited by her outing. She had never been near a canal before and thought the boats and the wildlife were magical. Along with her mother she was finding it difficult to imagine actually living on one of the boats that they had visited. Just to be in this new environment had captured her imagination and she was becoming a real fan of Mickey, who could do no wrong in her eyes.

Mickey and Mr Hobbs exchanged information. Mickey provided the office address, wanting to de-personalise any transaction or suggestion of a transaction. Mr Hobbs promised to send Mickey a firm proposal for the sale of "Melody" and her "butty" within the week. He would co-ordinate the berthing permits which actually belonged to another department. He could minimise the work needed from Mickey. He also suggested that he send details of dry docks and boat builders in the relatively near proximity so that Mickey could start to calculate the costs they might be facing.

"That's great, Mr. Hobbs this has been very interesting and your enthusiasm for the canal and keeping it alive have been inspiring for me. I hope we will be able to make something happen in the near future." With that they parted and Sheila, Mickey and Jennifer started to make their way home.

"I'll have a word with Rufus to arrange for you to see his place. You'll love it and it'll give you a whole new perspective of what living on a boat will be like. I know this has been a bit of an eye opener and might have put you off a bit but those boats can be turned into something wonderful. You'll see."

Sheila smiled unconvincingly, clutching onto Jennifer's hand.

Chapter 15

The next few days were busy. More women came seeking work as cleaners, plus more houses and businesses seeking the services of Spic and Span. There were inevitably problems to be dealt with as mistakes were made, or clients thought they deserved more than they received. Some of the cleaners got their timings wrong, despite the meticulous schedules Sheila had constructed.

Generally, though, all was good. The business was growing and Sheila was growing into it. She was taking on more of the management of the business by default, and as a result a lot less of the cleaning, although she made a point of doing at least one hands-on job each week. Mickey was growing the referral side of the business and spent a good deal of his time out meeting tradesmen, plumbers, electricians, builders and general handy men. These were people who had been referred or recommended to him by contacts from a number of different sources, including some of the people Sweeney had used. Mickey had pushed Sweeney to fix some plumbing in his flat several months ago and Mickey had stayed in touch with the plumber who had his own circle of tradesmen to use. Rufus had also turned out to be a good source of experts in various field: carpenters and joiners, decorators and tilers. Mickey's network was growing.

Amongst this network of tradesmen was Bobby Wilson. Bobby rented an office in the same serviced block of offices as Mickey. He was an older man in his fifties, always well-presented and seemingly doing well. He covered a wide area of North London. One of his team was his son Jimmy. Jimmy effectively ran one side of the North London business and Bobby the other.

Mickey liked the way they worked and sought to use them as much as he could when it came to referrals. They had agreed a formula which worked for them both, everybody benefited.

Over a coffee one day, having exchanged leads and finder's fee business, Mickey was telling Bobby about his plans to move onto the canal and the opportunity that he had to acquire a wider than normal narrow boat and its "butty".

Bobby thought it was a great idea and offered to help out with the electrics. He thought it would be an interesting project and he might even get himself a small boat as a hobby when he returned to the midlands, at the other end of the Grand Union. Mickey was proving to be a great source of work and the two seemed to get along very well. Both had done work for Sweeney in the past and both had a similar perspective of the man. Much of Sweeney's estate was being used up by the legal expenses required to sort out the property estate. Mickey and Bobby both kept in touch with the administrators to establish who would be the new owners of Sweeneys property, as they had a vested interest to make contact with the new owners. Mickey had the added benefit of keeping his ear to the ground regarding any suggestion of money gone missing. Of course, Mickey was still in a Sweeney property so had an interest as a tenant as well.

Since he had shown so much interest, Mickey invited Bobby to come and visit Rufus' boat to get an idea of what could be achieved in a boat conversion. Bobby was happy to go along. So it was that Sheila, Jennifer, Mickey and Bobby found themselves on a brief guided tour of "Freedom". Rufus was vivacious and excited when showing off his home, speaking only of the good things about boat life. He would not be drawn into any negatives.

"There is something to find fault in wherever you choose to live, I like to focus on the positives"

Both Bobby and Shelia were captivated by Rufus's enthusiasm for his lifestyle. Jennifer was very excited to think that she might be living on a boat at some time in the future. It was a lovely sunny day and the group sat on the grass alongside the tow path beside the boat with cold drinks after their tour.

"Can we get a boat to live on please mummy" Jennifer implored

"Well, I can't promise anything but we are looking into it" Sheila said

"I am very impressed" said Bobby who had never really had any awareness of this alternative lifestyle. "I'd be happy to help refurbish *Melody, it* would help me find out about the possibilities, especially as the British Transport Commission are off loading boats for very reasonable prices at the moment. We both have tradespeople that we know and I am sure that between us we could do everything you need to transform "Melody" into a wonderful home for Jennifer, oh and Sheila of course"

"Don't forget me" said Mickey with a smile

"I think you are sold on the project Mickey. In fact, I think Jennifer is on your side as well. Its only Sheila that needs convincing it seems"

Sheila remembered her previous misgivings after their initial visit but felt much warmer towards the idea now, having seen Rufus's stylish conversion.

"Let's do it "she said "It can't be any worse than living in a Sweeney rental! In fact, today it looks like heaven in comparison."

"Fantastic, I'll get in touch with Mr Dodds and tell him we want to go ahead. Sheila, you and I will need to agree how we finance this. We'll need to arrange loans through the bank. We can talk about that later."

Rufus suggested that he join Mickey for a visit to *Melody* to measure up and start some drawings of how they would like the boats to look after construction. This was agreed and two days later Rufus and Mickey concluded a visit to *Melody* with Mr. Dodds who agreed to get the necessary paperwork drawn up for the sale.

Mickey and Sheila had some decisions to make now. It would not be sensible just to pay cash for the boats. In the event that somebody looked into their finances it would take some explaining. They discussed buying the boats as part of the Spic and Span business but concluded that it would potentially put the transaction under more scrutiny. So, they agreed to go to the bank with their finances from Spic and Span as evidence to convince a bank manager that his money would be soundly invested in their project and the lending risk would be minimal. To Sheila's great surprise the bank manager readily agreed and they were offered the full amount they requested. This represented, they thought, about seventy per cent of the cost of buying and renovating the two floating homes. Since they were not a married couple, they would have to agree to having legal documents drawn up between them clarifying what would happen if one or the other wanted or needed to opt out. This also included ownership arrangements which was agreed to be a fifty-fifty arrangement.

Sheila could not believe what was happening. She had moved from being a single mother, virtually down and out with no way of seeing an escape route, to a home owner with an interest in a business and a very bright future. How could that have happened? She remembered Sweeney with a pang of conscience but she also realised that this was not entirely a consequence of taking that money. There were other factors, not least her friendship with Mickey. If only he was heterosexual, she might find herself in a relationship as well. She knew that was never to be and actually was very comfortable with the way they were, it was uncomplicated and really suited them both. Mickey was becoming not only a very good friend but a business partner and he had faith in her to support the business. Her private life was limited but she was able to be a much better mother than the person who had given birth to her child and more or less handed her over to somebody else to deal with.

Sheila had matured. She was a much more confident woman, capable of things which previously she had no idea she would be able to handle. She dealt with money, employees, customers and even commercial partners to some degree, although that part fell largely to Mickey.

She had not had any sort of a relationship, for some years now and for the time being it wasn't even a consideration. From Monday to Saturday the daylight hours were fully tied up with Spic and Span. Evenings gave her time to focus on Jennifer for a couple of hours then take some time to relax. Sometimes she spent the remainder of the evening with Mickey, but that was becoming less and less frequent, now that Mickey had Rufus. Mickey was becoming more involved in a clandestine homosexual scene, which society had driven "underground". Many of his evenings were spent with groups of men at one location or another, which seemed to make him happy and comfortable with himself.

With all the formalities taken care of, ownership of *Melody* and butty passed to Sheila and Mickey. Mickey arranged for them to be taken into dry dock to ensure that the undersides of both vessels were sound and waterproofed. The outsides were completely repainted in what Mickey considered to be traditional narrow boat colours, green, red and gold. The names on the boats were left blank as both had agreed that they may want to change the name but also to name both boats separately. That done, the boats were transferred to their permanent moorings, side by side, just outside Paddington on the Grand Union Canal. The next six months were taken up with the renovation of the boats.

Rufus spent a few evenings with Sheila and Mickey sketching out the way they would like the boats to be configured. They changed things around several times until they had what they wanted. Sheila was to have the Butty as there was no mechanical element for her to deal with. Mickey was actually no more competent with things mechanical than was Sheila, but Sheila did not want the additional responsibility.

The layout of the two interiors were significantly different. Sheila needed two bedrooms, a luxury she only dreamed of until now. Mickey settled for one large bedroom at the front of the boat with an ensuite bath/shower and toilet facility in the bow. His galley was to be located in the middle with dining space for four comfortably seated. A large reception room was provisioned at the back. Then there was a space left for Mickey as a creative area, as yet to be defined, with stairs leading to the cockpit. Wardrobes and storage were supplied where needed. There seemed to be plenty of space.

Sheila opted for bedrooms at the rear of the boat with a shared bathroom and a walk-in wardrobe between the two. One bedroom was larger than the other with a view to a double bed for Sheila, the other with a single. Sheila's galley was to be at the front of the boat and configured slightly differently from Mickeys. The living space was at the centre of the boat and was partitioned into three areas eating, relaxing and playing. The partitioning was such that it could be rearranged as and when needed with a minimum of disruption. One of Rufus's friends was an architect and enjoyed helping with the plans of what was a really unusual project for him. Rufus and Mickey had a wonderful time agreeing the interior design of Mickey's boat and helping Sheila with her ideas.

Bobby had become engaged in the process and was really enthusiastic about the conversion of these once commercial work horses into attractive, viable living accommodation. Between them Mickey and Bobby had the contacts to address all of the build requirements including the utilities. Many of the tradespeople gave their time at special rates. Materials were largely sourced from over supply at jobs on which they were working. Perks of the job they called it and nobody quibbled. Rufus happily stepped back from further involvement as he had two commissioned pieces of work and needed to focus on these.

Mickey found himself diverted from the business towards the boat project. All the different tradespeople involved needed coordinating and scheduling which was not always straightforward. Whilst people were happy to help, they still had their day jobs and other commitments. Mickey was often travelling to meet people on site to cajole them into just getting the next bit done. What they had hoped would take three months turned into six and Mickey was often tearing his hair out with the frustration of logistics and communication.

Finally, to their great relief, they were able to move into their new homes. They had given the administrators of their current flats three months' notice and were glad to be able to extend by a month for three consecutive months. The flats they were leaving would need considerable modernisation before they could be let again so there were no new tenants waiting to put pressure on their exodus.

Sheila did not have a vast amount to move. Her rented flat had been furnished and she had not been in a position to acquire much in the way of home comforts. Most of her move was about clothes for her and Jennifer and kitchen utensils. Mickey's move involved a bit more in terms of personal belongings. Whilst his flat had also been furnished, he had been able to bring some personal touches to it. There was artwork, one or two chairs and various other pieces that Mickey had acquired over recent years. Mickey hired a van and drove it himself, some of his clandestine social group came and helped with the move for them both.

The day they left Sweeney's house was a day of great joy and celebration. There was some sentimental feeling. They had forged their friendship in those nasty rooms. They would not be here today without Sweeney and his money. Inadvertently Sweeney had become a good thing in their lives but it was hard to look back on him with any gratitude.

A new life beckoned.

Chapter 16

Whilst Ben was away in the RAF Bobby Wilson had kept the business growing. It was doing very well.

He was also developing a second life of his own in London, which was not a healthy situation for his marriage. His wife, Susie, knew that he was a bit of "a player" and turned a blind eye to some of his indiscretions. What she didn't see she didn't allow herself to worry about. In many ways she was happy not to have to bother too much with Bobby's sexual appetite. Susie had far less desire for bedroom activity than did her husband.

This attitude had worked well for them both until Bobby had met someone with whom he had started to develop a more prolonged affair. Susie instinctively knew that something more serious was going on and apparently developing into a relationship. Their marriage had reached a watershed and something needed to be done. Bobby and Susie had many long and serious discussions about their lives and what they both wanted. It was clear that they did not want to lose each other. Bobby realised that the affair would need to end and they both agreed that their life needed to get back onto a more normal footing. Bobby being away in London all week was no longer desirable or sustainable There was still plenty of work to be had in Coventry and he could soon pick up some customers and re-establish himself back in the Midlands. Bobby ended his affair.

In order to deal with his London based business Bobby, had split it in two. He made a geographical boundary north of the river which ran up Finchley Road as far as Barnet. That split allowed Jimmy to take over half of the business whilst still working together with his father on some overlapping projects. Bobby maintained responsibility for the west side of the business but appointed a foreman to manage his team whilst Jimmy looked after his own team directly. Bobby could start to transition his life back to the Midlands. There was a lot more administrative activity to Bobby's work than he had been used to, which hadn't really suited him but came with success. The more business they attracted the more electricians they required, the more management and paperwork was generated.

Bobby was actually looking forward to getting back home and becoming simply an electrician again. The transition would take some months. Bobby was not completely relaxed with his foreman and did not trust him to run his side of the business completely, so a pattern emerged. Bobby started his week in London and set up his foreman, Andy, with a schedule of work. All the electricians would meet in a café on the North Circular Road for breakfast and job allocation, Bobby would set everybody off, then hand over to the foreman to manage through the week. Of course, things never went exactly to plan and adjustments had to be made throughout the week. Andy struggled to manage things as smoothly as they should have been managed and Bobby found himself drawn back to London more often than he, and his wife would have liked.

When Ben Macdonald turned up at his office in Kilburn it was as if he had been sent from heaven. Bobby had kept in touch with Ben and had attended Caroline's funeral. During the wake Bobby had again reminded Ben that he would always be welcome back to the firm should things not work out with the RAF. At the time Ben was too confused and distraught to pay much attention. It was difficult to see beyond the day.

Once Ben had decided to get away from the RAF for good, he felt that his best option would be to return to the thing that he knew best, electrics. He did not want to go back to the midlands and be close to his mother and sister. They had, if it was possible, become even more fundamental in their religion. His sister was looking like a career spinster, there was no man in her life and with her attitude it was unlikely that there ever would be. Ben did not want to become part of that scene. Life, he felt, had already shown him enough misery. He wanted another chance.

Ben had found the new offices in London. Above the door in bold red letters were the words" Bright Sparks Electricians". The office was small but tidy. There was room for three desks, a couple of filing cabinets and a coat stand. A door to one side led to a storeroom which housed just about all that an electrician might need. Stacks of coils of wire of various thickness, plugs, sockets, light fittings, Insulating tape and more. All neatly stacked and clearly marked.

At one of the desks sat Bobby. At another was a young fresh-faced woman busily typing. As Ben entered a bell announced his presence. Bobby beamed, delighted to see Ben walk through the door.

"Good morning. How can I help you?" The young woman had looked up from her typewriter and gave Ben a warming smile.

"Sylvia, this is Ben, I'm hoping he has come to tell us he wants his old job back" Bobby shook Ben firmly by the hand and indicated the chair behind the third desk. Ben looked around and accepted Bobby's offer and sat down.

Ben immediately felt comfortable. It was as if he had come home even though he had never been in the office before.

"Tea or coffee, Mr.?"

"Please call me Ben"

"Ben this is Sylvia, she's the boss here. She keeps us in good order and makes sure we keep on top of everything. This business wouldn't function without Sylvia she is invaluable, a diamond and she makes a great cup of tea as well. You two might have met before at Jimmy's wedding?"

Neither showed any sign of recognition.

"Nice to meet you, Sylvia. Tea please, oh and congratulations if you can control Bobby, there aren't many who could manage that, as I remember"

Sylvia smiled "By and large he does what he's told, but it has taken some time to get him to understand the rules. He seems to be getting the hang of it. Anyway, he's not here so much these days. He and Jimmy leave me here alone most of the time. Bobby's foreman Andy calls in quite a lot, more for some tea and sympathy than to do any office work. Not really his thing."

"Well with any luck you'll be teaching Ben the rules soon. If we can persuade him that we are an outfit worthy of his attention"

Ben said "I am flattered, Bobby, and I have come to talk to you about the possibility of a job. By the way where is Jimmy today?"

"Where he always is, Ben, out on the tools. He doesn't really like the administrative stuff so he just calls in for supplies and coffee. Oh, and to give Sylvia a hard time"

They all laughed.

"So, when can you start Ben? We have no shortage of work and we don't need to go through any interview process really. I suppose it would be sensible to bring you up to date on the business because it has moved on considerably"

Bobby outlined the shape of the business and his vision for the future, which included him backing out of the business and selling his share to his partners. If it all worked out then Ben would have the opportunity to buy a share in the business alongside Jimmy, Andy and Sylvia.

Ben hadn't expected this. He had just come in the hope of getting his job as an electrician back. He was flattered by Bobby's apparent trust and confidence in his ability, but couldn't be sure that what was being offered was what he wanted to do.

"What about just a job as an electrician?" Ben asked

"Of course, Ben, but there is a much bigger opportunity for you here and I know that with some basic training and support you could be the best person to take over from me"

"I am very flattered by your faith in me, Bobby, but I'm not sure it isn't misplaced. I know I can do the practical hands-on stuff but the other business management area is something completely new."

"You're hard working and reliable, you have plenty of common sense, except when you are fighting of course"

Sylvia, who had provided tea and biscuits and was now listening in, was momentarily startled by the suggestion that Ben might be up for a fight.

"I'm only kidding Sylvia, Ben had a small contretemps back in the day, but he was only standing up for himself, not being aggressive."

Sylvia smiled and returned to her typing.

"I'll tell you what Ben, you take some time to think about what I've said and then make up your mind. I'd be keeping a close eye on you to start and we will agree a probationary period to be sure it works for both of us. After that first say three months we can review where we are and make some plans from that point onwards. Let me know what you think within the week and we'll move forward accordingly, is that okay? By the way when could you start - either as an electrician or a partner?

"Well, I have to see out the last three weeks of my RAF contract. I will have to find local accommodation so I thought maybe in a month"

"Really, I don't know if we can wait that long" Bobby said with a smile. "Just let me know before the week is out what you want to do. I can help with temporary accommodation. We've got several landlords on our books and I know we will be able to find something to tide you over, if it's helpful."

Ben left the office with his mind spinning. This was far more than he had hoped for and seemed almost too good to be true.

As he left the office, he brushed past a young woman coming out of the office next door. The office belonged to a business called "Spic and Span". Ben noticed neither the name of the business nor anything about the woman. She was the mother of his child. The child he did not even know existed.

Ben returned to his rented RAF home and looked at the picture of Caroline. What would she tell him to do? She would push him to take on the challenge, even if he hesitated. He would look back on the decision that was about to significantly change his life and realise that it was a decision taken in a large part by his deceased wife.

Chapter 17

Life on a boat, unsurprisingly, proved to be a great improvement on the crowded flat. Sheila felt as if she had escaped from a prison, a prisoner with no prospects of happiness or hope. Within the space of a year, she had moved from abject misery to latent happiness. She had a new and self-designed home which felt like it was the place she belonged. A proper home for both her and Jennifer. A home about which she could feel a sense of pride, an emotion which until now had been unknown to her, but she was proud. Proud to have given Jennifer a proper home, proud to be a business partner to Mickey, proud of the skills which she had learnt and displayed. Her pride was slightly tinged with guilt which surfaced each time she went to her "Sweeney Pile" as they had come to call it, but the sense of guilt faded as time passed.

Happiness was just around the corner. She had Jennifer and she had Mickey and occasionally Winnie for company but she did not feel complete. It had been years since she had had a date. She could never say that she had enjoyed a proper relationship with anybody in her life. It was not something that she desperately wanted but she was twenty-four now and her peer group were largely married with children. Many of the cleaners that she employed were of a similar age and established in relationships, not all of them happy, but none the less in relationships. It seemed that most of the men that she did meet were friends of Mickey and unlikely to be interested in her sexually.

As she and Jennifer settled into their life on the boat and as the business started to get slightly more routine and so less time consuming, Sheila allowed her thoughts to start drifting towards the idea of meeting somebody and hopefully settling down. There were not too many men who would want the added responsibility of a six-year-old child. If there was somebody out there who could accept the extra burden, she would not find him without going out to meet him. As a single mother, with no single friends, going to dances or clubs was not easy, so for the time being it didn't happen.

Jennifer moved school and had brightened up as a child. She had plenty of opportunity to play outside and along the towpath after school. Winnie was still a key part of her life; she collected her from school and kept her at home each day until Sheila was able to collect her. Sheila took the two girls to school in the morning then went straight to work. Winnie would work at the childcare business from eight in the morning to three in the afternoon, then leave and collect Jennifer and her own daughter, take them home and give them tea. Sheila would arrive sometime between five and six and take Jennifer home with her.

Jennifer had developed a sort of independence built from a life of being passed from one adult to another. Apart from Mr. Sweeney with whom she had felt very uncomfortable, Jennifer's exposure to adults had generally been to caring loving women. In her early years she felt little love from her mother but that was more than substituted for by June who doted on her as if she were her own. When June died and was taken away from her and there was a period when her mother was distant, almost resentful of her, Winnie formed a solid anchor for Jennifer for a few years whilst her mother was struggling to make ends meet virtually providing an alternative home for her. Now mother and daughter were more or less on the same page although Jennifer still spent a lot of her days away from her mother at Winnie's.

Underlying Jennifer's attitude to people was a distrust born of the instability and change which had occurred during her six years on the planet. As of now, there were no outward signs of unusual behaviour with Jennifer but inside, subconsciously a rebel was burgeoning. Her best friend both in and out of school was Annie (Winnie's daughter). The girls were like sisters and had probably spent as much time in each other's company as real sisters might have done. Over the years whilst Winnie supported her friend Sheila, Jennifer had spent many nights at Annie's home. Most week days Jennifer and Annie played together at Annie's. They mostly played with Annie's toys since, until recent weeks, there was not enough money for Jennifer to have very many toys of her own.

Jennifer was not very academic and struggled with both reading and writing at school whilst Annie sailed through the day and was amongst the brightest of the children in the class. Jennifer was more athletic than Annie, she was wiry, but strong and could outrun most of the girls in her age group. In fact, there were only one or two of the boys who could compete with her.

Jennifer was beginning to find her skill set a bit difficult to deal with. In class she often could not keep up with the academic learning. She didn't fully comprehend instructions and found herself either copying somebody else, doing the wrong thing completely or staring out of the window daydreaming. When she was called upon to answer she often didn't even understand, or hadn't heard the question. She became the source of much laughter for the other children. Jennifer was embarrassed and withdrew into herself. Self-esteem was very low whilst she was in the classroom. Jennifer was quite an insular child and did not make friends easily.

Sheila was largely unaware of the challenges her daughter was facing at school. For the first couple of years, she was too preoccupied with fighting for a home, heat and food for them both. On the occasions when she did visit the school to talk to the teachers about Jennifer most of what was said really passed her by.

Sheila didn't like to go to school for the playground gossip. Single mothers were taboo. It was clear from the way that groups of mums looked at her that she was the subject of their conversations. Apart from Winnie she had made no friends with other parents. She wondered if this pattern was repeated by the children in the classroom. Jennifer never complained, she hardly talked about school at all. Sheila felt there was little she could do to change things and Jennifer seemed to be okay to her.

Jennifer did find a friend on the canal.

Several boats along the tow path a tired, untidy boat in need of much restoration floated dejectedly on the water. It looked as if the owners collected as much old junk as they could and kept it on top of the long cabin for future use. Much of it looked like it would never be useable again. Old broken chairs sat alongside a wicker coffee table which had seen much better days and was not enjoying the weathering process out in the elements. Pots and pans, old vases and rolls of linoleum sat alongside a loose attempt at a garden area. It seemed as if at some time the inhabitants of the boat had decided to start their own "cottage" garden on top of the boat's cabin. Several long homemade plant containers stretched along the edges of the roof. Nothing resembling anything edible lay within. Some herbs mingled with the weeds and sorry remainders of plants from better times. The weeds had the upper hand. For all of its unpleasant appearance the boat drew attention and much curiosity. Jennifer always tried to peer into the dark, filthy windows as she walked past with her mother on the way home from school. Ironically the boat had been named "Neat and Tidy". It may have been once but it certainly wasn't now.

One day as she passed, a boy who was some years older than her, perhaps nine or ten sitting on the bow of the boat. He had longer than normal wavy brown hair which he habitually flicked from his eyes. His eyes had a mischievous glint and he seemed very focussed on what he was doing. He was carving a piece of wood with a penknife. There seemed to be no particular form he was trying to achieve. He just hacked away at the old lump of wood. The resultant shavings piled up on the floor below him and would probably remain there for some time. The boy looked up briefly and caught Jennifer's eye. He looked directly at her and watched as she walked by with her mother. He stopped whittling and watched her intently until she disappeared along the towpath. Jennifer turned and looked back at him as she and her mother walked towards their boat. He had stood up to his full height. His clothes were dirty and crumpled. She noticed that his feet were bare. Jennifer didn't know quite what to think of the boy or his home. The thought of him looking at her stuck in her mind for some time. She didn't see him again for weeks. Each time she passed by the boat she looked for him but each time it seemed deserted.

It was not until the early Spring that Jennifer saw the boy again. Alongside the canal path close to the berths, which Sheila and Mickey had been allocated, were rows of trees of different varieties, behind them, some rough grassy areas. As time passed and Sheila became more familiar and comfortable with the area, she allowed Jennifer to explore these areas. Jennifer took great delight in capturing and torturing a variety of insects which she found in old rotting bark. Following an experiment in school she had learned how to focus the sun's light into one small point through a magnifying glass. Sheila was quite pleased at Jennifer's seeming interest in wild life and had bought a cheap plastic magnifying glass to build on her interest, little knowing its horrific purpose.

Jennifer spent countless hours capturing and making little prisons for her captives before dispatching them in a variety of ingenious but unpleasant ways. There was so much to keep her attention in the undergrowth under the trees. During her exploration of the area Jennifer had found an enclosed bushy area. It sat beneath a tall, thick, majestic, old oak tree which was partially hollowed out at the base, it was here that she experimented with multiple defenceless insects.

One day whilst cremating a butterfly pinned to a piece of bark, Jennifer's solitude was broken. No particular noise took Jennifer's attention away from the gruesome task at hand, just a sudden awareness of somebody watching.

"What are you doing?" It was the boy from the tawdry boat.

"Nothing" Jennifer lied

"I can see you're doing something" said the boy "Can I have a go?"

The boy got onto his knees alongside Jennifer and examined her work.

"That's really good" he said "I pull some of the legs off of spiders and watch them try to get away, then I squidge them"

"I do that too," said Jennifer. "Do you burn things like this?"

"I haven't got a magnifying glass so I can't. Can I have a go with yours?"

Jennifer reluctantly allowed the boy to take her magnifying glass and torture a beetle that he found in the bark nearby.

"Whats your name?" Jennifer asked

"Johnny, what's yours?"

"Jennifer, do you live on that boat? It's a bit dirty." Jennifer said

"Sometimes, it depends"

"Depends on what"

"My mum and dad" he said

"Oh" said Jennifer as if that was a full and satisfactory answer.

Jennifer had a new friend.

"How old are you?" Jennifer asked

"Nine" said the boy "How old are you?"

"Seven and a bit," said Jennifer

Age didn't seem to matter too much. They were both pretty poor at anything academic at school, they both liked being in the woods with no adults about, they had much in common, but mostly their love of insecticide. They spent the next hour or so passing the time and finding lots of things to laugh about. Eventually it was time to go. They both went back to their respective boats, with no mention of meeting again.

Neither child told anyone about their meeting.

Chapter 18

Sheila was in the office setting out the work schedule for the next week. It was Friday. She had to juggle with the new customers that Mickey had attracted, there were three new commercial jobs and a couple of domestics. Some of the cleaners wanted more hours, some less. Sheila had identified domestic and commercial cleaners and those who she felt could do both. There were also the reliable ones, the A team, and the ones who you never really knew would be on time or even turn up, the B team. The business tolerated a degree of unreliability because the work was growing faster than the workforce. It was difficult to give all the work to her "A" team since they could not cope with it, so the "B" team were given the less important jobs or those where the customers were a little more tolerant.

A significant percentage of Sheila's work life was resolving difficulties created by some of the "B" team and managing the challenges of working with a group who were largely women, many with children and or husbands to manage. Often, when it all got a bit too much, she took herself out of the office, across the road to a café where she would find some respite. She would smoke a cigarette or two with a hot brew.

This was such a day.

She was well known in the café and had frequently noticed the woman from the office next door. She was about the same age and seemed to follow a similar pattern, a couple of cigarettes and a pot of tea, perhaps a quick look at the newspaper. In time the two women got chatting and found that sharing their frustrations of the day became cathartic. The other woman was Sylvia. She worked in the "Bright Sparks "offices.

Sylvia was there when Sheila opened the door and came in

"Usual?" asked the Italian café owner

"Yes please" said Sheila and plopped herself down in the chair opposite Sylvia.

"How are you today?" Sylvia smiled

"Bit of a day already, and it's only eleven o'clock"

Sylvia laughed "Me too! We've got a new partner starting and he seems nice enough but he hasn't got a clue about the business yet. I feel like I'm carrying him around all the time. He's been here for a week and let's just say it's a slow learning process!"

It was Sheila's turn to laugh. These twenty-minute breaks were proving invaluable in breaking down the frustration which built up during the mornings. Sheila and Sylvia were slowly building a friendship.

"You should come in and meet him. He's a nice bloke, ex RAF, in his twenties and quite good looking. He's single, apparently, he lost his wife quite recently, although I don't know the details"

"Sounds alright for you then"

"Yes, he might be if I wasn't going steady, I might have given him a try. I think you should pop in and say hello"

"Maybe one day, but today's not that day!"

Sheila felt a sense of excitement rising in her for a man she had not even met and about whom she knew nothing. It was the total absence of any male company, with the exception of Mickey, for the past seven years which fed her appetite. She was receptive to any slight opportunity to meet a man, particularly one who came with some, if modest, recommendation. The fact that Sylvia had said he had been married, rang some alarm bells but then she knew she was largely regarded as "soiled goods" as a single mother. It was unlikely that he would want anything to do with an unmarried mum. Sheila talked herself out of the hope that this might finally be the chance to meet somebody.

Back in the office with the early morning frantic rush behind her, Sheila sat and thought about what Sylvia had said. She found herself building a picture of what this man might look like. She invented scenarios which might have led to him parting from his wife, some encouraging, others frightening. She imagined him as a wife beater whose wife escaped his evil clutches, then as a cuckold who knew nothing of his wife's torrid affair with another man until it was all over. Every fantasy she made up was nonsense and she knew it, but she couldn't help herself. An angry customer snatched her from her daydreaming and back into the here and now.

It was approaching the end of the day when Sheila returned to her earlier thoughts and determined to at least go and have a look at the man who had become a bit of a mystery to her. When the time came to lock up the office, she took a deep breath, checked her appearance in her powder compact mirror and made her way towards the offices of "Bright Sparks".

Sheila had walked past this door many times over the past months but never really gave it a thought until Bobby had become involved with renovating the boats, she knew this was where he worked and that Mickey often popped in to see Bobby for one reason or another. So far she had found no reason to venture beyond the door, until now. She wasn't sure whether just to open it and stick her head round the door casually and say something relevant to Sylvia. Perhaps she should barge confidently in as if she had been there a dozen times before. Maybe knocking timidly and waiting for an invitation to enter would be better.

She decided to barge in confidently and ask Sylvia if she would be going for coffee on Monday morning. She grabbed the door handle and pushed. It was locked. Everyone had gone home. Sheila felt a wave of disappointment. She would have to wait till next week. Perhaps it wasn't such a good idea anyway. Sheila went home to Jennifer to find out about her day, but also to talk to Winnie.

Winnie arrived as usual at about 5.30 and sat down for a cup of tea with Sheila. Jennifer said hello and went to her room to change out of her school clothes and into some clothes more suited to the tow path. She returned quickly and asked permission to play on the towpath.

"Yes, but not for long I'll be getting your tea and then its bath time and bed time"

Jennifer couldn't wait to get out to the towpath and see if that boy, her new friend, Johnny was around.

Sheila on the other hand was pleased for Jennifer to be outside so she could talk to Winnie about her day. At the end of every day Winnie and Sheila spent half an hour talking about the day's events. Usually, the main thing on Sheila's mind was how the child minding was going. Winnie knew the children of many of the mothers who were employed as cleaners and it was interesting to compare the characteristics of mother and child. Surprisingly it did not always follow that because mother was troublesome their offspring would be of a similar nature. In some cases, it was quite the reverse. Knowing something about the children also helped Sheila deal with the mothers during her time managing their days. She was able to have a conversation which was not work related, besides addressing whatever issues or plans arose.

Winnie told Sheila about the day's ups and downs and the funny incidents which inevitably happened where children were involved. Wet trousers, cut knees, arguments and all the day's action. Sheila listened patiently, desperate to casually throw in her meeting with Sylvia and Sylvia's suggestion that she should come and meet the new man. Eventually her moment came and she blurted it out like a schoolgirl.

"Crikey, you seem keen and you haven't even seen him yet" Winnie laughed "Steady on, Sheila. I know you haven't had a boyfriend for a long time but I think you need to take a more cautious approach. You'll have his trousers off in the office if you're not careful. Anyway, he might not be your type, calm down"

Winnie and Sheila chatted over the subject like the pair of schoolgirls that they once were, giggling at some of the potential outcomes which might ensue. They were having such fun that they didn't realise how much time had passed.

"Oh my God" Said Winnie "I need to get back to Liam and Annie. Liam was doing tea for Annie but I haven't thought about dinner for me and him yet. Looks like bangers and mash again." And she hurried off home to her daughter and hungry husband.

Sheila started to prepare their meal and realised that Jennifer had gone out nearly an hour ago and hadn't been seen since. She climbed up the stairs at the back of the boat and looked up and down the towpath.

"Jennifer" She called slightly Worried "Jennifer" again.

Jennifer's head appeared through the bushes in a small canal side copse.

"Yes mum"

"I think you should come in now it's nearly dinner time"

"Just a little bit longer, pleeese"

Sheila allowed her another ten minutes and went in to prepare the meal and think about her conversation with Winnie and the mystery man.

Jennifer had gone off in search of Johnny when she first left the boat. He wasn't in the trees where they had met first time and was nowhere to be seen much to her disappointment. Somehow Jennifer just expected him to be there. He would have been home from school for a long time by now.

Jennifer decided to go to the boat where she had first seen Johnny whittling. She crept along inside the bushes from which she could see his scruffy boat and there he was on top of the boat with a stick and line looking for all the world like a seasoned fisherman. He sat on the roof with his feet dangling over the sides and his home-made fishing tackle resting in his hands. He was looking vacantly at the end of the string where it entered the water. He didn't seem to expect a strike and it seemed he hadn't had one yet.

Jennifer pulled herself through a gap in the bushes.

"Have you caught anything" she asked quietly.

Johnny visibly jumped out of his stupor.

"Shhh!" he said and pointed to the bushes to indicate for her to go back out of sight of the boat. He swung himself across the boat and pulled his line in with the same action. Jennifer could see the end of the string now with an open safety pin attached to the end, no doubt to surprise a disarmed passing fish. There was apparently no bait but Jennifer knew less about fishing than did

Johnny and was quite impressed that he had seemingly made his own rod, line and hook.

Jennifer did as Johnny had indicated and went back into the bushes. Johnny followed her.

"You shouldn't come here" he said

"Why not" she asked

"You just shouldn't. Mum can be difficult sometimes" he said

"What do you mean" she asked

"She just can be difficult, that's all. She's got a bit of a temper and doesn't get along with most people, especially kids. She screams at them and lashes out if they're too close!"

Jennifer was unmoved.

"My mum was like that once" she said "She used to drink too much; I think. She's okay now. Does your mum drink?"

"She does" Johnny admitted "I don't think she means to be horrible, she just can't help it"

"My mum stopped drinking, perhaps yours will too. Let's go and catch some insects" and off they went to torture the unfortunate creatures that they found in the undergrowth. The children played and laughed together with no sense of time. They liked each other's company and talked freely about anything that came to mind.

They spoke about school and their teachers and what a lot of rubbish they were made to do. Apart from play time and milk break neither could find many positives for the institution and thought they would be better off playing in the woods all day.

Time passed quickly. Jennifer heard her mother's call and signalled Johnny to be quiet whilst she went to answer.

"I've got another ten minutes" she said on her return.

"Okay let's make this our camp. We can meet after school every day, "said Johnny. The age gap surprisingly didn't seem to matter to him. She was a kindred spirit and good fun.

"Right but let's not tell our mums." said Jennifer as if hiding a guilty secret.

"What about your dad?" he asked "are you going to tell him then?"

"I haven't got a dad" Jennifer said as a matter of fact and with no emotion

"Really" said Johnny "How come?"

"Have you got one? Jennifer asked ignoring the question

"Of course," said Johnny "I live with him sometimes and sometimes with mum. They don't like each other and they both drink too much. Sometimes I have to go and stay with the other one because one is too sick for me to stay. Dad lives in the flat where we used to live, mum got this boat when grandad died and lives on it when she and my dad fight. That's why I'm not always here. I like it here best. I can get outside and play."

Jennifer listened intently then turned and ran. "Got to go, see you tomorrow after school. Bye"

"Bye" said Johnny and went back to face his mother

Sheila and Jennifer talked about their days to each other over their dinner. Neither mentioned the new arrival of a new male in their lives and neither planned to do so.

Chapter 19

Mickeys relationship with Rufus was, through necessity, clandestine. Homosexuals were considered disgusting and associated with all sorts of behaviours which had nothing to do with the way they conducted themselves. Perverts, they were called, amongst any number of other unpleasant names. "Queer bashing" was not uncommon and the police turned a blind eye to much of it considering that "the homos had got what was coming to them!".

Despite the difficulties, their relationship was developing. Mickey was becoming a regular at the gallery and other locations frequented by a certain type, Mickey's type. Rufus was struggling as an artist. He sold the occasional piece of work and was commissioned to do some portraits and landscapes but it wasn't really where he wanted his work to be going. He still had to eat and Mickey found himself supporting Rufus to a degree.

One evening on Mickey's boat Rufus let his emotions get the better of him.

"I don't want to keep taking your money, Mickey but I can't survive on the money I am getting for my art. I really don't know what else I can do. I couldn't get a job in an office it would absolutely kill me. I can't do manual labour; I just haven't got it in me and working in a factory just isn't an option"

"Well, you could supplement your income by doing some cleaning for Spic and Span, just to see you through for now" Mickey knew this wasn't really what Rufus needed but it was something he could actually offer.

Rufus looked at Mickey as though he had just strangled a kitten. "You are joking, I hope. Keeping my home clean is enough cleaning for me thank you very much"

"I just mean temporarily" said Mickey defensively "I might be able to find you some interior design work in time but right now that isn't an option, you would need a portfolio of work and some recommendations behind you."

"Well, that's more my thing, "said Rufus. "Perhaps I could get some pictures of the inside of our boats and show them to potential customers. Most of those designs were mine, weren't they?" Rufus smiled at Mickey hopefully "Well my boat's interior was completely mine and I did contribute to yours. Didn't I?"

"You did! I'll tell you what, next time I see Bobby Wilson, I'll have a word and ask him to watch out for suitable opportunities. It's not really quite his thing but you never know. He spends a lot of time in different homes and he might just hear of the odd opportunity. In the meantime, you can do some cleaning jobs for me. I'll make sure you get the best places to clean. No dodgy bedsits for you Rufus, only upmarket apartments with upmarket clients – I promise"

"Me, cleaning for a living. I can't believe it has come to this!" said Rufus, but it had and he knew it.

The next time he saw him Mickey spoke to Bobby Wilson who was still trying to extricate himself from his London commitments and move back to Coventry.

"Rufus needs to use his creative flair in some form and I know he would be good at interior design if he got the chance, look what he achieved with his narrow boat!" said Mickey

"No doubt, Mickey, but it's not my line of work. If I hear of any opportunities, I'll be sure and make introductions for Rufus"

"Thanks "said Mickey "I would appreciate any help you might be able to give. Anyway, how are your boat plans going?"

Since the completion of Mickey and Sheila's boat renovations, Bobby had been talking about buying a narrowboat as a project for when he returned to Coventry full time. He had been very impressed with the living accommodation they had created and thought there was a commercial opportunity which might also serve him as a hobby when he returned home.

"Well, I've looked at boats and I do think it has potential. I can't, however, see me being back in Coventry and re-established with enough work to justify investing in a boat up there for a long time. Down here is a different matter, I've got all my workforce and contacts to draw upon if I were to invest in one. I even spoke to Ben and he was quite excited by the idea, even though he is still trying to get to grips with Bright Sparks. It may be that I give it a go down here in London with a partner or two who could share the commitment and the investment. Susie would be livid if she thought I was starting something keeping me down in the smoke even longer, so I would need to be in partnership with some understanding partners."

"Well, I could invest and maybe Rufus could be involved in the design and decoration but I don't really have the time to get terribly involved."

"Your investment would be invaluable" said Bobby "and I would value Rufus being involved as well. Perhaps he could project manage it like he did for his current home. I am pretty sure that Ben would like to be part of the project but he hasn't got any spare cash to invest as far as I know"

"It all sounds good to me" said Bobby "let's arrange to meet up for dinner and talk about how it might all work out"

"Good idea" said Mickey "I'll need Sheila involved as well. We're very much running the Spic and Span business together these days. Any investment should really be a joint decision between us. I am sure she would give it all her serious consideration"

"Let's have a night out, what about Lyons corner house? I'll invite Ben and my wife; she'll need to agree to anything I sign up for. You invite Sheila and Rufus. We can have a nice night out for once and if it all comes to nothing, we'll all have had a nice time anyway.

Mickey was delighted at the whole idea. It would get him and Rufus a legitimate public date at the least and would potentially give Spic and Span another money-making opportunity without too much investment. He would talk to Sheila about it as soon as possible but he felt sure she would be supportive. Apart from anything else it would be another opportunity to "launder" some of Sweeney's money.

"Okay, perhaps we should set it up for a couple of weeks' time to make sure it fits everybody's calendar"

They agreed on a Thursday evening two weeks ahead.

Mickey regularly went to visit Sheila in the evening to catch up on the day's business news, gossip about their clients and their employees and also just to socialise and wind down a little. He told Sheila about his uncomfortable chat with Rufus and his reluctant acceptance of a role cleaning the homes of their more prestigious clients. Sheila unquestioningly added Rufus to their select list of cleaners who were chosen for the better jobs. She knew what was needed and agreed to place Rufus in some of their best clients' homes. He subsequentially became a very useful and reliable employee and actually started to enjoy his work.

Mickey also told Sheila about the discussion he shared with Bobby Wilson about commercialising boat transformations. There were definitely commercial possibilities.

Sheila took no time to agree to meet with Bobby and the others. Since her involvement with Mickey her life had changed and it seemed he could do no wrong. The business was doing well and there was still plenty of Sweeney's money stashed away on the boat. Why not use it to make some more? She liked Rufus and knew he was very artistic. He should be a good member of the team. She had also enjoyed her time spent with Bobby Wilson when he was helping out with the outfitting of the boats. She didn't know the others but assumed that they would be okay.

Sheila looked forward to the night out and would make arrangements for Jennifer to sleep over at Winnies. Life was getting interesting.

On Monday Sheila was back in the office. Mondays were particularly traumatic launching the week's schedule. Invariably there were phone calls about cleaners not turning up, or being late. Monday was the day for chaos. Sheila battled through and didn't really give a thought to the mystery man all morning. At eleven she left Mickey, who was working in the office that morning, to man the phones so she could have her brief respite with Sylvia across in the café.

There were a group of builders in the window seats as she entered and they welcomed Sheila with wolf whistles and some less than gentle suggestions, which she shrugged off with a laugh.

There was no-one in this group who appealed to her in the least. She took her seat and the proprietor brought her the pot of tea and buttered toast which had become her habit. She lit a cigarette and leaned back in her seat, blowing a long, controlled raft of smoke towards the ceiling. Why was a cigarette such a relaxant? She didn't know but she loved that mid-morning cigarette more than any other. She had given up for some years after Jennifer was born, unable to afford to continue. One of the luxuries which Sweeney now afforded her was the opportunity to fill her lungs with smoke four or five times a day.

Sylvia came in and received a similar reception to Sheila, which she chose to ignore, raising her nose in mock contempt but secretly smiling at their familiarity. She joined Sylvia at her table after placing her order at the counter. She was less predictable and today was taking coffee with an iced bun. As she sat down Sheila looked expectantly as if a piece of news was about to be delivered.

"Hi Sheila"

"Hi Sylvia"

A brief silence

"Well?" said Sheila

"Well, what" Sylvia answered mystified

"Well, is the new man in the office today?"

Sylvia laughed "I thought you weren't interested"

"Just intrigued really. You got me thinking last week and it is time I met somebody. I came by the office Friday evening to see you and take a look at him, but you had all gone home"

"What and you've been fretting over it all weekend?" Sylvia teased

"No, but I must admit you got me interested. It's not easy for someone in my situation to meet people. I should start to consider my options when opportunities arise. I would quite like to see him before I come to any conclusions so I tried to think of a reason to call by. Perhaps I can pop in later today."

"Well of course you can pop in but you won't see him. He is not in this week and will only be in and out next week. He has decided to get out with the electricians and get to know them. Also, he's taken on a couple of jobs himself to get his hand back in and to get a feeling for the work environment. Good idea I think, but not so good for your introduction opportunities."

"Oh, God! Steady on I don't know if I want an introduction yet. I just want to set eyes on him, then I will know if I need introducing"

"Well, you'll have to wait a couple of weeks before he is planning to come into the office."

The next twenty minutes the girls spent talking about Bobby and his inappropriate behaviour with some women. They thought he was a bit of a rogue but was too nice to feel angry with and since his wife had sort of turned a blind eye, who were they to criticise. Sheila thought of her own situation and wondered if she had the right to be making moral judgements about others.

It seemed her interest in the new man on the block would have to be put on hold. Sheila convinced herself that she had built it all up too much and was likely to be disappointed anyway. The mystery man would have to wait. Someone might just walk into the office tomorrow and whisk her off her feet anyway.

Chapter 20

The den was evolving daily. Each day after school Jennifer sought permission to go and play in the woods alongside the canal path. Sheila had, in the beginning, gone with Jennifer to find out exactly where it was that she was disappearing.

The area was behind the canal path, beyond the thick trees and bushes that lined the path. There was a clearing, then another set of trees and shrubs. At either end were large trees, a huge old oak tree at one end and a weeping willow at the other. The branches of the willow hung down producing a curtaining effect and when the dangling branches were held apart it was possible to get inside.

Sheila was quite happy that the area was fairly inaccessible and not very obvious to passers-by. She was not really sure what Jennifer found to do in this place but she seemed to be able to amuse herself for hours there. As long as she was happy and safe Sheila was happy to let her disappear there after school for an hour or so. She could call out and get a response every so often.

Inside the branches of the weeping willow was the area which Johnny and Jennifer had named their den. They preferred it to the oak because of the curtaining effect of the hanging branches. They had gathered a number of jam jars where they incarcerated insects of various types. They had even captured frogs, which they kept in a shoe box. Insect executions had to be conducted elsewhere in the clearing where strong shafts of sunlight forced their way through the tree's leafy defences.

Any spiders, woodlice, ants or other insect life which was foolish enough to try and make a life on either Johnny or

Jennifer's home boats were captured and taken to the den. Johnny and Jennifer would make decisions upon the life and death of the errant insects and carry out the executions as deemed appropriate. The children would giggle with glee as they killed a variety of insect life.

Close by there was a collection point for the boat dwellers' refuse. Black sacks full of rubbish were left out on collection day. The council agreed to take away unwanted items from that spot to save the canal sides becoming a dumping ground. Odd pieces of household flotsam and jetsam were randomly left at the collection point, which became a source of materials and furnishings for the den.

The children first started collecting when one evening Johnny came in with an old stool which he had picked up at the collection point. It was a metal legged stool with a stuffed seat which had seen better days. The stuffing had come out of the seat and the seat cover was torn beyond repair. The stool was about eighteen inches high. John had torn off all the covering to reveal a wooden circular base which was to act as a table for the pair when they attended to their insects, whilst sitting cross legged on the floor.

The den and what went on there were a matter of great excitement for the children. More and more items were added to their collection including numerous containers to keep their condemned insects captive. Both children were careful not to talk about each other to their mothers. They also took care not to be seen together. They didn't quite know why but felt that their relationship was special and their secrecy both created and maintained the excitement that they felt every evening.

Being a lot older than Jennifer, Johnny enjoyed the dominant role of leader. Jennifer was constantly in awe of her much older companion. She had no other relationship to compare. Her friendship with Annie was completely different. For now, she told Annie nothing although she was bursting to tell her, or somebody, all her secrets. She was both protective and scared of the situation in which she found herself.

One day Johnny arrived at the den with a packet of cigarettes which he had taken from his mother's bedroom whilst she lay in a drunken coma. He had seen other boys smoking and was keen to give it a try. He stole matches from the kitchen and lit a cigarette in front of Jennifer to demonstrate how grown up he was. Despite nearly choking and, as with most first-time smokers, not finding the experience at all pleasant, he insisted that it was fantastic and invited Jennifer to have a try. Jennifer was under Johnny's spell, looked up to him and thought he could do no wrong. She tried to take in the acrid smoke and nearly choked in her attempt. Johnny laughed at her and insisted that she keep trying until she got the hang of it. Which of course in time they both did.

They were both smokers now but Johnny realised that despite his mother's drinking habit and frequent comatose states, he would not be able to keep taking her cigarettes without being discovered. Between them they had no money and because of their age couldn't buy cigarettes anyway. There was a corner shop where the shopkeeper was familiar with Johnny because he often ran errands for his mother. It was quite common for him to be collecting her cigarettes. The shopkeeper knew that the cigarettes were for his mother and so he turned a blind eye. Johnny at first was reluctant to push his luck and buy his own.

To supply their desire to act like grown-ups in their den and smoke cigarettes, they both took just the odd cigarette from their mothers' boxes. They felt that these one-offs would not be noticed. As time passed, they turned their attention further afield and looked for other boat dwelling smokers. Their pattern of play started to change. They started to spy on boats from the confines of their den. They took pleasure from inventing their own stories about the people on the boats. They became familiar with the boat dwellers comings and goings. At the least opportunity they would try to get aboard other narrow boats in search of cigarettes, usually when the owners were otherwise preoccupied in one way or another.

At first it was cigarettes that they lifted, but as they became more successful and confident, they started to collect other small items. A knife here, an apple there. Small things which would be an irritation when missed but were unlikely to cause major concern to anybody. The den became a store for their pilfered bits and pieces as well as their collection of items from the waste collection point. Jennifer and Johnny enjoyed the excitement of their exploits and found it a great source of amusement. Johnny led; Jennifer followed.

One day, Johnny started to talk to the owner of an old cluttered narrowboat "The Fine Old Lady" who they had spoken with on a few previous occasions. Whilst Johnny talked, Jennifer slipped onboard, unseen at the far end of the boat. The owner was called Bert, a scruffy old man with an unkempt beard which had grown over many years. His uncut hair poked out from beneath an old flat cap. His skin was leathery and weathered by years of exposure to the elements. He clearly was not over familiar with the benefits of soap and water but he was a harmless man just living his lonely life at his own pace. It seemed to suit him. When he smiled, he revealed the few brown teeth that he had left. His weathered skin wrinkled around his watery eyes. He had the appearance of an old sea captain, which appealed to the children. Bert was quite chatty and enjoyed the company of these youngsters more than adults. They were innocent and non-judgemental.

He sat on the canal path alongside his boat fiddling with a faulty generator. Jennifer had been in this boat before and pilfered odds and ends of no particular value. The thrill was more important. On this occasion there was nothing that particularly grabbed her attention, until she spied a ten-shilling note on the galley table. They had never taken money before. Jennifer didn't give it a second thought. She didn't really know what they would spend it on but decided that it was worth taking anyway. So, she did.

As she lifted her dress to hide the note in her knickers she heard Johnny shout at the owner, "where are you going?"

Bert replied "There's no need to shout! You made me jump! I am just going inside to get my other tool box. I need a wrench; this bloody generator is proving more difficult than I expected. I won't be a minute" and with that he clambered onboard.

Jennifer could not possibly get out fast enough so she ran to the bow of the boat and looked for somewhere to hide. Narrow boats are not well provided with hiding opportunities and it seemed her only choice was to get into a very narrow and crowded closet in the far bedroom. The air in the closet was heavy with the smell of sweat, which reflected Bert's lack of awareness of his personal hygiene.

Jennifer held her breath, her little heart pounding, her ear to the door. She had never been so frightened. She could hear the boat owner as he clattered about in the galley area and she could feel his folded ten-shilling note pressing against her leg. All her senses seemed heightened at that moment. Time passed slowly for Jennifer as Bert carefully retrieved his tool box and left the boat again. He was onboard barely two minutes but it was two minutes she could have done without.

When she could hear Johnny and the owner start chatting again, she felt safe to leave. She closed the door of the closet behind her and made stealthily for the steps, to her freedom at the rear of the boat. She slipped out as she had slipped in, unnoticed, other than by Johnny who bade the, now generator focused, owner a quick farewell and ran back to the den to see what treasure they had managed to extract form their visit.

"Crikey that was close" Johnny said "I really thought he was going to catch you., did you get anything interesting?"

"I got this" Jennifer said proudly and she pulled the folded ten-shilling note from its hiding place.

"That's fantastic, that's a ten-bob note" said Johnny "that's a lot of money. Where was it?"

"Just sitting on the table partly under a mug" Jennifer was pleased with the smile on Johnny's face, which seemed to confirm his approval. She had no idea what a ten-bob note meant apart from that it was money. Regardless she was pleased that she had managed to get one. Johnny was clearly very happy.

"Do you think he will miss it "Jennifer said "I was really scared"

"Where did you hide" Johnny asked with some admiration

"In a clothes closet, it was really smelly "

"Right, well we will have to hide the money. Neither of us can take it home, it's too dangerous, it's not just some old rubbish. Let's leave it in one of the insect jars with some leaves till tomorrow, then we can decide what to buy with it"

The children smiled at each other triumphantly and set about hiding their treasure.

"Not a word to anyone, see you tomorrow" Johnny instructed and Jennifer dutifully nodded. What an adventure today had been. They both headed home full of secret excitement.

Sheila was in the galley. Mother, daughter and Mickey had taken to calling things by their nautical names as far as they knew them and if they didn't, they sometimes made them up. So, it was the Galley where meals were prepared rather than the kitchen. Jennifer went straight to the galley to announce her arrival and her sudden hunger.

"I don't know how you amuse yourself for so long in those bushes "Sheila said "Look at you, you're filthy. Go and get cleaned up. I hope you haven't brought any spiders in jars back with you this evening"

Jennifer left and went to wash her hands.

The next evening Jennifer couldn't wait to get to the Den. She told Sheila she was going and left without waiting for a reply or permission. Sheila was getting used to the routine and didn't make a fuss.

When Jennifer got to the den there was no Johnny, but that was not unusual, she often got there first. She sat on the floor and picked up one of the insect jars. It was spiders. She became quite accustomed to them and they held no fear for her. They had carefully made holes in the lid with an old metal skewer which they had found on the tow path and added to their collection. She stared at the spiders who had been disturbed when their life had been shaken up as Jennifer picked up the jar. She sat and stared for some time before remembering the ten-shilling note. She had been thinking about it all day at school but had temporarily forgotten when she got to the den. She turned to its hiding place and reached in to withdraw the jar.

"I 'm sure we left it here" she thought and looked around the area thoroughly. It was gone. Perhaps Johnny had been back for it already and put it somewhere safer. For the moment that explanation satisfied her. Twenty minutes later, she had been waiting to see Johnny for too long. She decided to go and find him and tell him it was missing.

They had agreed that they would stay away from each other's homes for fear of their friendship being discovered and possibly stopped. Jennifer thought the missing jar was important enough for her to at least go and see if she could see him on his boat. She walked along the towpath to where she knew his boat was berthed and was devastated to find it gone. No boat, no Johnny and no way of knowing where it had gone, why it had gone or how long it had gone for. Jennifer was distraught.

Chapter 21

Joe Lyons Corner House was located on the corner of Coventry Street and Rupert Street in Piccadilly. It had been years since Sheila had ventured "up west" and she had never been to a Joe Lyons Corner house. She had heard about their famous Nippies who were considered up market waitresses. A position as a Nippy was considered the cream of waitressing opportunities in London. She was really looking forward to being served by one of these girls. They wore smart black outfits with white collars and aprons and their signature black and white headwear.

Mickey, Rupert and Sheila had all put on their Sunday best clothes and hopped on the underground together. Jennifer had been dispatched to Winnie's to stay overnight with Annie. Sheila's presence with Mickey and Rupert gave a certain air of respectability to the two men going out together and they all linked arms. Sheila walked between the two homosexual men as they approached the restaurant. Mickey and Sheila had agreed to fund the evening from the Sweeney money and make it look like Mickey was paying for the evening with "Spic and Span "profits.

A table for six had been booked at seven thirty in the name of Mr Bobby Wilson. They had arranged to meet at the restaurant. When the trio from the Grand Union canal arrived, Bobby and his wife Susie were already seated.

Bobby stood up to greet everybody and make introductions. His wife had clearly made an effort for the evening and was both smart and pleasant on the eye. She was not especially confident and seemed slightly uncomfortable in this environment. Sheila warmed to her immediately and felt that they would get along very well.

"I'm afraid Ben is running late this evening. He had a spot of bother on one of the jobs and it has put him back a while. He said to continue without him and he will catch us up when he arrives. Thank God he is taking responsibility now otherwise that would have been me arriving late!" said Bobby

"Let me get some drinks and we can get started looking at the menus"

Bobby and Mickey agreed that Spic and Span and Bright Sparks would jointly fund the evening. Bobby would not allow Spic and span to suffer the whole cost. Everyone was able to relax and order exactly what they wanted without having to worry about cost. Each of them ordered a drink and the evening got off to a good start. They all agreed that the topic of boats and their refurbishment would have to wait until Ben arrived. After all, he would need to agree to what was decided if he was to be a partner in the venture. Thirty minutes passed very quickly. Sheila was getting along very well with Susie. Eventually they decided to look at the menu and make their choices without Ben.

"I'm sure he'll be here soon" Bobby said "Let's get started and he can catch up"

Ben had been held up at a site in Hendon. The electrician involved ironically was one of Bobby's long-standing electricians who, whilst being good at his job, was not the best at following instructions. The customer had been very specific about what was wanted in terms of outlet sockets in their kitchen and had left clear instructions. The electrician had seen a potential fault in the locations and had decided to use his initiative and install them where he thought would be better. The customer was away on holiday and was unavailable to ask about the alternative positioning of the sockets.

Ben remembered his own experiences of adjusting the customers' specification in their absence. He clearly remembered Bobby's advice. "Don't change the specification without the customer's approval". Since the customer was not due back until the following week it wasn't possible to get their approval. Bright Sparks protocol was to deliver the exact specification. In this case, new channels had to be made in the plasterwork and then made good.

Ben and the electrician had disagreed about re-siting the sockets. At this early stage of his management career this was a battle he had to win. He did win, but his schedule was delayed by ninety minutes and he could not avoid being late for dinner.

Showered, shaved and smelling of a decent aftershave Ben arrived at his first dinner outing since Caroline's death. He was not particularly looking forward to it but he was interested in the boat project, which might provide some distraction for him during his long lonely evenings.

Ben announced himself at the restaurant door to a young Nippy who was passing. She smiled and ushered him to the table where his party had begun tucking into their starters. The group were obviously getting along well and enjoying each other's company. They had restrained from actually ordering main courses in anticipation of Bens arrival, although they had each made their choices and discussed the merits of the menu. The mood was light and slightly frivolous.

"Your final guest has arrived" the young lady announced and deposited Ben at the table.

Sheila had her back to the door and sat facing Bobby who rose to gesture Ben to a seat. Ben nodded to those guests whom he knew then looked to Sheila. The face that met his was very familiar but he was not entirely sure why. He racked his memory for help. Sheila instantly recognised the father of her daughter and was visibly shocked. She had no words to say and gasped for breath.

"Sheila, may I introduce you to our prodigal partner Ben. I think you know he has come back from the RAF to save my skin and release me to build house boats and return to Coventry and my beloved Susie"

Sheila did not know how to react. She looked Ben directly in the eye, stood and left the table heading for where she had seen the ladies WC. Not a word was spoken. She had to escape to grab a breath and untangle her emotions. She headed straight for a cubicle, closed the door behind her and burst into tears. Sitting on the lowered seat Sheila sifted through a rush of thoughts.

"How could this happen? Where had he been? What did she feel about what had happened after all this time.? She had never blamed him at the time and didn't assign guilt to him now. Why had he turned up in her life again? Could she spend an evening with him and the others now?

Her first reaction was to flee. Whatever I feel about this all, here and now with four onlookers is no time to talk. He would probably not appreciate the news that he is a father delivered publicly in Joe Lyons Corner House. She did know she could not remain there any longer. She gathered herself up to make her excuses and leave.

As she left the cubicle Susie arrived. It was clear that Sheila had been crying.

"Whatever happened "Susie asked

"I can't explain now Susie. I'm sorry but I will have to leave. I can't return to that table now but I don't want to spoil everybody's evening. I wonder if you would ask for my coat.

"But surely, you're not leaving, we were just beginning to get to know each other"

"I have to go, I am sorry"

"But what's wrong is there nothing we can do?"

"It's all too difficult to explain right now. When I have settled down, I'll explain to everybody and make my apologies, but now I need to go home"

"Okay wait here and I will organise a taxi, but promise me you will let me come and see you at home and help sort this out, whatever it is"

194

"Okay, Susie thanks for your concern" said Sheila "For now please just help me get out of here"

Susie left the ladies and went straight back to the table and explained what was happening.

"I'll fix it "said Mickey and arranged for the restaurant to order a taxi. He then went straight to the ladies and Sheila and told her "Whatever is going on its okay. I don't need to know but I am coming home with you"

"No, I'll be fine" said Sheila "Please stay and agree whatever we need to do for Bobby and the boat scheme. I think it will be good but I just can't stay here tonight. Let's talk about it tomorrow"

Mickey made arrangements for a taxi and saw Sheila into the cab when it arrived. "Can I check on you later tonight?"

"No Mickey, I will be fine, just wait until tomorrow evening after work and come round. I will explain what is going on. Ben might remember something but he doesn't know the whole story." She kissed him on the cheek and climbed into the taxi, Mickey gave her a pound note to cover the fare and waved her goodbye.

Back in the restaurant all eyes were on Ben.

"What was that all about Ben" Bobby asked

"I can't be sure; I know that we have met before but I can't be specific. I think I met her at a party years ago but it was never more than a one-night stand for both of us as far as I can recall. I'm really sorry to have caused such consternation"

The group were silent no one knowing quite what to say.

"Perhaps I should go" said Ben feeling the weight of the atmosphere on his shoulders.

"No, it will all work itself out in good time." said Bobby. "You're a good man Ben and whatever the problem is I'm sure there will be a good outcome. Let's enjoy the rest of the evening as best we can. We'll take good care of Sheila tomorrow."

The mood of the party changed. Everybody talked politely and carefully about boats. The subject of Sheila was left hanging.

It was decided to invest in the development of one boat to see if there was any prospect of a profitable business. Roles and responsibilities were broadly agreed and a future meeting in the offices was planned. Bobby already had some idea of the investment needed and Mickey signed up to take his share of the costs. Rufus was to oversee the design and project management. He would liaise with Ben over the physical refurbishment. Susie felt relieved that this was perhaps a start to getting her husband back home. The enthusiasm for the project and the fun of the evening were tainted by what had happened between Sheila and Ben but the evenings' purpose was fulfilled. Nobody knew exactly what had happened that night and everybody went home with questions to be answered.

Sheila wept quietly until the taxi dropped her off at the tow path. She had so been looking forward to this evening, it had felt like the start of something. Now she was in turmoil. There were a million questions to answer and Jennifer, the little soul around whom the evening's events revolved, was not even at home. Sheila felt as lonely as she ever had. No-one to share her feelings. No-one to understand what had just happened and most importantly no-one to hug.

Inside the home which represented her new life Sheila took out a bottle of sherry, poured herself a tumbler full then sat, drank and cried herself to sleep.

Chapter 22

It had been more than two weeks since Johnny's boat had disappeared from its mooring along with Jennifer's ten bob note. Jennifer went to the den every evening in anticipation of Johnny returning. There was no sign of him. The overnight stay at Annie's had been a welcome interlude to her daily disappointment on the towpath.

The next day she had walked to the old man's boat from which she had acquired her best trophy yet and found everything the same. The old man sat aboard his boat in an old leather chair thumbing through a publication about coarse fishing, he looked up and waved. Normality had returned, perhaps it had never left. Maybe he hadn't even noticed a ten-shilling note missing. Jennifer didn't know and didn't care really, she just wanted to know what had happened to Johnny, his boat and curiously she wondered about his mother. She carried on to their mooring point.

There was still no sign of Johnny's home. The mooring was sadly empty. Jennifer feared that another narrowboat would arrive and fill the space and that would be that. So far, no new boat, just the space that used to be filled by the home of her new best friend. As long as the mooring stayed empty there was still hope for him to return.

With no Johnny around Jennifer returned to her own home. There was little to keep her in their den. Her mother, she sensed, was in a different mood from normal. She was unable to identify exactly what was different but she knew that something in her life had changed.

"Are you okay mum?"

"Yes, I'm fine, just a little under the weather. Nothing to worry about. I'll be back to normal tomorrow. Anyway, you don't seem yourself lately. We both seem a bit sad, don't we? Is anything upsetting you at the moment? Anything at school I should know about"

"Not really, I don't like school very much but it's okay I know I have to go. Annie is really nice and I always play with her."

"Don't you have any other friends? Other than Annie I mean"

"Not at school no"

"How was your sleep over?"

"It was fine, we played in Annie's bedroom until Auntie Winnie told us to go to sleep. We had a bit of a midnight feast and talked for a little while, then we went to sleep. It was a bit boring really"

"Did you like your dinner party"

Sheila felt her eyes fill up again but overcame the temptation to cry again. She was actually not entirely sure what her tears meant. This little girl's father had turned up out of the blue last night and her life had somehow turned upside down. She didn't know what she felt about him, anger at first, that he could have left her with a child to bring up alone, then irritation with herself. How could he have helped? He didn't even know about his daughter. It wasn't as if he had intentionally abandoned his child.

"It was very nice but I came home early because I wasn't feeling too well, which was a pity, but couldn't be helped. I wished you were here with me on the boat but I was glad you were having a nice evening with Annie. I'm pleased you've come back from your little wood this evening. You're normally out much longer than this"

"I wanted to be with you mum" Jennifer realised that this was true but largely because Johnny was nowhere to be seen

"That's nice Jennifer. I want to be with you this evening as well. I saw Mickey this morning at work and he is coming over for dinner and a chat soon so the three of us can be together and have a nice time"

"Do you think he will bring me any sweets"

"I don't remember any time when he didn't bring you sweets. Do you?"

Mickey turned up later with sweets hidden inside his Jacket pocket and flowers in his hand for Sheila. He smiled at Sheila and gave her the flowers with a little wink of the eye, then turned to Jennifer

"And how is my favourite girl"

"Hello Mickey" Jennifer smiled at Mickey who had become an important person in her life. He was the closest that she had known to a father figure.

"Have you been good?" Mickey asked

"Yes" said Jennifer

"Well, you deserve something special then!" Mickey reached into his inside pocket and produced a packet of spangles which were Jennifer's favourite sweets.

"If your mother says you have been good then these are for you. What do you say mum?"

Sheila smiled and said "Of course she has been good but she will have to wait until we have eaten before she has one. You can only have one after dinner and before you go to bed. The rest can go to school with you in the morning and you can share them with your class mates"

Jennifer knew not to argue, she also knew that she would eat some later in bed and that her class mates, with the exception of Annie, would not get a sniff of her sweets.

Dinner was eaten with small talk about the day, Attention was focused mainly upon Jennifer. The group managed to laugh about nonsense introduced largely by Mickey. They were comfortable in each other's company. Conversation was at the level a seven-year-old could understand and had nothing to do with what was really on their minds.

When the time came for Jennifer to go to her cabin, she was insistent that she was not tired and that it was not fair. Mickey intervened and took Jennifer to bed. He read her a story about pirates and hidden treasure, then kissed her goodnight and left her to dream about Johnny, her favourite pirate.

Mickey had been very patient. Sheila had come into work as normal but looked awful. He had insisted that she go home and rest. He would come round later and she could tell him as much as she wanted. Mickey was bursting with curiosity. It was clear that there was history between Ben and Sheila. Mickey and Rufus had sat up into the early hours postulating what that history might be. They had imagined a dozen scenarios, mainly romanticised, but had no real insight.

Sheila opened up to Mickey as she always did. He had become her best friend and confidant and she knew that anything she told him would go no further. Well, no further than Rufus anyway.

Sheila felt that Mickey, and perhaps Winnie, were the only people with whom she could share her secret. She had not seen

Winnie that day and here was Mickey, sitting on the edge of her sofa desperate to know what was going on.

"Mickey, I don't know where to begin."

Mickey said nothing but sat and listened intently while Sheila emptied her soul. It was difficult to explain her feelings about seeing Ben again because she had hardly known him. Were it not for Jennifer, she would probably have dealt with the whole situation much better.

Ben was a part of her life which had been long forgotten, so to have him thrust back into it in such an unexpected fashion was proving difficult. When she had first discovered that she was pregnant all those years ago she had secretly hoped that Ben might find a way back to her, she had asked around but things had moved on and nobody seemed to be able to provide a link back to him. Her life as a single mother had been particularly hard and she had found herself resenting Ben and the memory of their all too brief encounter. As time passed, Sheila had managed to blank him out. Jennifer had stopped asking difficult questions and it had become almost as if he didn't exist at all which had suited Sheila.

Mickey gasped in surprise when Sheila told him that Ben was Jennifer's father. His feelings were a mixture of shock and jealousy. Mickey found himself puzzled that he felt so jealous about the appearance of this man. He instinctively knew that his arrival would change his relationship with Sheila and Jennifer forever. Mickey enjoyed being a surrogate father and had grown into the role. To have his position threatened by a complete stranger was difficult to take.

"What will you do?" Mickey said after a prolonged silence.

"I just don't know. It seemed that Ben didn't even remember who I was.

"That's not quite true, Bobby told me that Ben had said that he did remember a party at which you two met but he said it was a one-night thing which you both seemed to enjoy but that circumstances took him away unexpectedly. He clearly had no idea that he had fathered a child. I think you should tell him about his daughter, don't you?"

"I don't know. I suppose so but where will that lead to? I'm worried that it will completely upset the status quo. Supposing he gets funny about Jennifer and insists on seeing her. What do I tell Jennifer now? Supposing he has a family, what will that mean to Jennifer? It's all just a mess. If he is to be a partner in the new business it is going to be very difficult for me to deal with. I will probably have to pull out. Oh Mickey, my life had just started to get brighter and now this! I don't know what to do"

"Well, whatever you are going to do you can't do it tonight. Let's just calm down and think this through. Have you got any sherry? "

"I think so!" said Sheila and went to the galley to check.

"Sometimes a glass of sherry can make things clearer. If it doesn't it can make you care less anyway, so, either way, my immediate advice is sherry all round."

Sheila smiled as she returned with a half full bottle "I don't know where I would be without you Mickey. Before I met you, I couldn't afford sherry. Why did you have to be queer? "

"Do you know I often ask myself that question, life would be a lot easier if I wasn't but I am and it wasn't even a choice, it's just what I am."

Mickey took the bottle of sherry and poured them both a large measure in tumblers not really intended for sherry. They were the first ones Sheila had grabbed from the galley.

"Cheers Sheila, let's not forget that we have each other"

"Cheers Mickey, thank heavens for you"

"Now, let's weigh up where we stand Sheila. Correct me if I make any false statements because we must get the facts right to come to a logical conclusion. Firstly, when you met Ben, you were very attracted to him, right?

"Well, yes, I suppose I was!"

"Okay good start. Was it just a sexual attraction or do you think there was more to it. Remember I am not judging you!"

"No, it wasn't just sexual, he made me laugh to start with and we seemed to be on the same level. We didn't take long to reach the physical attraction but it wasn't the only attraction that I felt."

"How did you feel after he left without saying anything"

"Well naturally I was very hurt but when it was explained what had happened, I was just worried for him"

"But you didn't pursue it that evening?"

"Well, I didn't know how to really. He was off to hospital and I wasn't going to chase after him there, even though I was concerned for his well-being. I carried on at the party but I was only half there if you know what I mean. I hoped he would find me once he was out of hospital, but he never did"

"How did you feel about that"

"Quite upset really. I waited for days and days, hoping that something would happen but it never did. I didn't really know where to start to look for him but it didn't seem right for me to be chasing him, it should be him finding me. I didn't know I was pregnant then!"

"So, when you found you were pregnant, did that change your attitude?"

Sheila took a large swig of sherry as she remembered how awful she felt when she found out.

"I was mortified. I was more concerned with what it meant to me and my life. I don't really think I gave him a thought at that stage. Suddenly my life was upside down and everything pointed to me getting rid of the problem myself. He didn't even feature in my thoughts at that time. I think I had given up on any hope of ever seeing him again. I had to worry about my survival and how to make sense of the situation in which I found myself. I worried for days and considered getting rid of the baby, but in the end I just couldn't. Ben was a long way from my thoughts then."

"So, you don't really blame him?"

"Well, no I don't really, it just happened"

"And do you think you would have continued the relationship had he not been taken to hospital?"

"Well, I don't know really, but yes, I suppose at the time I would have wanted to see him again. pregnant or not"

"So maybe that is your answer. See him again and see how it goes. You don't need to bring Jennifer into the conversation until you are comfortable that it is the right thing to do. See him as a future business partner. Remember the evening you had, see what he remembers and see if there are any complications. It has happened and you can't ignore it"

Mickey and Sheila talked through the evening. The conversation didn't move far from the point at hand and when Sheila went to bed, she was clear what she must do and do it quickly.

The next day Sheila arranged to meet Sylvia for coffee, as had become a frequent occurrence. She was keen to establish if the new partner about whom she had been fantasising and the man who arrived at the dinner table to join the boat development syndicate were, as she suspected, one and the same. Sylvia had heard about the goings on at the business dinner and was quick to the subject.

"What on earth happened at dinner" she asked almost before Sheila had taken a sip of her tea.

"Oh, I just came over a little strange and had to excuse myself. I didn't want to spoil the evening for everybody so I left"

"Yes, I heard. Just after Ben our new partner arrived."

"Is that the partner who we have been talking about?" Sheila asked guardedly

"Of course, how many new partners do you think we have?" Sylvia noticed a change in attitude from Sheila, she was somehow less frivolous about the subject of Ben. Equally inquisitive but more purposeful in her approach.

"He is the bee's knees, isn't he?" Sylvia teased

"He seemed okay but as you have obviously heard I did not stay around for long after he had arrived"

"It was suggested that you two may have met before!" Sylvia left the implied question hanging.

Sheila was unsure where to go with an answer and felt the pressure of silence whilst Sylvia peered over the froth of her coffee.

"I'm not sure Sylvia. What do you know about him? I think you said he was single."

"I did, I heard that he was recently bereaved, his wife died from a terminal illness but I don't know much more. I think we talked about that last time. So do you think you might know him?"

"No" Sheila was quite firm "but I might have seen him somewhere before!"

"That was quite a reaction for someone who you don't really know, I mean you missed a slap-up meal and everything"

Sheila smiled at Sylvia's ability to turn what was a fairly traumatic evening into a missed eating opportunity.

"Look it just caught me unawares, I thought I might have known him before and his sudden appearance just threw me that's all."

"Not sure I believe you but where do we go from here?" Sylvia was eager to involve herself in developments.

"I don't know Sylvia. I know we will have to get to know each other if the businesses are to have common areas of interest"

"Ooo is there something new in the offing" Sylvia was practically salivating.

"No" Sheila was backtracking now, she realised that the business meeting's purpose was confidential and that she had walked into an ambush by a seasoned gossip.

"I just mean that our businesses share leads and things, so it is likely that we will cross paths and at some point, I will need to get past this!"

"What are you going to do" Sylvia was beside herself and was cleverly leading Sheila into taking some form of action.

"Well, I suppose I will have to meet him and get this situation under control, so that we can move forward on a stable business footing"

"Whoa, that's a different conversation from the last time we met, when you were getting excited about the dishy new partner" Sylvia was now in her element and having fun. "Would you like me to set up a business lunch for the two of you to "thrash out your differences?"

Sheila couldn't help but smile she had been trapped in a corner, in the nicest way and felt that this actually might be a solution to her dilemma.

"Do you know what Sylvia; I think that might just be a good idea!" Sheila was petrified at the thought but knew it had to be confronted. She had never had a business lunch before in her life, she was really just a jumped-up cleaner but worse than that she was going to meet the father of her daughter.

Sylvia grinned like a Cheshire cat. There was romance in the air and she was playing the role of matchmaker, she would dine out on this for weeks to come.

Chapter 23

"Well, this is a bit awkward" Ben felt the need to try and relax them both. Understatement was his weapon of choice but once he had said the words, he regretted opening his mouth.

Sylvia had arranged for Sheila and Ben to have a "business lunch" in a local restaurant. It was just around the corner from the office so they had agreed to meet there rather than have a clumsy "how-do-you-do" in one or another of the offices. It was arranged for one o'clock and Ben had been held up so was ten minutes late. Not a good start in Sheila's mind, she had been worrying about this meeting for several days now and a further ten minutes seemed like an eternity. She hadn't known what to wear, normal business attire (which in her case was often dungarees in case she had to cover a "clean") or should she make an effort? Make up or not? What shoes? What would he wear? She had decided to make herself as presentable as possible and to treat the meeting quite formally. She had chosen a navy pleated skirt and a white blouse from the limited selection of clothes in her wardrobe. Smart, business like, devoid of emotion.

Ben was a in his electrician's attire which was workman like. No special attention to dress etiquette for Ben. The restaurant did not demand fancy clothing either; it was a lunchtime family run affair where meat and two veg was the main offering, wholesome food without any fuss.

The whole episode leading up to this lunch had been something of a surprise to him. On walking into Joe Lyons, several nights previously, Ben had been shocked to see Sheila. It took a few moments to place her but he soon remembered their first meeting. His recollection was of a relatively short but fun and pleasurable experience. He recalled that he would have liked to have seen her again but circumstances had prevented that and so they gone off on their own paths never to meet again. Until now.

Ben understood Sheila's immediate discomfort and embarrassment at that dinner given their first meeting. The people round the table were to some degree an unfamiliar group and explanations might have been somewhat problematic but also not insurmountable. He was not prepared for the dramatic exit to the ladies which ensued, nor was he or anybody expecting Sheila to leave the restaurant without another word to those at the table.

Bobby being Bobby felt he understood and, with a nod and a wink to Ben, helped the delicate moment pass with minimal commotion. Later Bobby and Ben had engineered a brief meeting in the gents' toilets where Bobby confirmed his suspicions that Ben and Sheila had experienced a personal intimate coming together, which was likely to be the cause of Sheila's curious departure. Bobby was quite amused by the whole thing but insisted that Ben and Sheila would need to deal with any discomfort that they felt with each other if the boating business was to go ahead.

Ben was in total agreement and felt that it could be managed with relative ease, so, when Sylvia suggested a business meeting to clear the air, Ben was keen to agree.

"I meant to say I am sorry I am late Sheila. I was caught up with one of the electricians on site in Cricklewood"

"Don't worry, it seems to happen a lot in your job" said Sheila "and yes, it is a bit awkward"

"Well, I am pleased to see you "said Ben "I must admit I never saw this coming"

"Neither did I!" said Sheila

"Have you eaten here before "Ben asked

"No, I am usually a sandwich at the desk for lunch type of girl. I don't each that much during the day anyway. What about you"

"No never, Sylvia suggested that it might suit us both as a quiet place to meet."

The couple considered the menu together and agreed on a ham and egg salad with tea and bread. A young waitress took their order and left them to themselves. For what seemed like an age neither one spoke, both looking at the tablecloth as if for inspiration.

"So how have you been?" Ben finally found a question to ask

"I've been okay" Sheila managed

"It's been a long time" Ben ventured

"About seven years" Sheila replied too quickly

"Yes, a lot has happened since that party," said Ben

"So, what do you remember about our first meeting then" Ben wished he hadn't opened his mouth, he wasn't alluding to the bedroom romp but it sounded very much like he was.

He tried to recover the situation "I am sorry, I didn't mean anything by that it's just that I have very happy memories of our brief time together, until we separated. Were you aware of what happened to me after we parted that evening? I had every intention of staying on but fate intervened"

"I remember what I was told. I remember very well. I was told that you started a fight and came off the worse, ending up in hospital. I am not sure if that is fate or just pig-headed ignorance" It was Sheila's turn to regret her words, the years of frustration, regret and anger spilled out.

She tried to regain her composure

"I am sorry, I suppose I am a little on edge. I was disappointed when I found that you had gone. I asked around and was told that you had been in a fight and had taken off to hospital. Actually, I was more than disappointed, I was also worried for your wellbeing. I asked around after the party but nobody seemed to even know who you were. Eventually I gave up and got on with my life. So, what happened to you that night, what is the story behind the fight"

"I ended up in hospital. A couple of the blokes were having a laugh at our expense, talking about us disappearing into the bedroom and making nasty insinuations about us both. It went too far and I lost my temper and took a swing at one of them. Somebody decided that a beer bottle was a fair way to fight, smashed it against the furniture and tore my face open with the jagged edges. I was bleeding badly and by everybody's reaction it was important to get to hospital as soon as possible. I had 18 stitches from my eye down to my jaw. As you can imagine I felt really poorly when I came out, so I went home to Coventry and let my mother take care of me. Bit pathetic really looking back on it but that's what I did"

"Coventry!! That's a long way to come for a party. No wonder nobody knew who you were. How did you come to be at that particular party on that particular night?"

"Fate, I suppose. If you believe in fate"

Ben went on to tell Sheila the background leading up to the party and as his tale unfolded so the tension between them began to loosen. They both talked about their lives before the party but neither wanted to take it beyond. They avoided the "what might have been" and started to try and find a basis to move forward from this point, after all they were going to become business partners – neither of them could ever have imagined that happening!

Before they knew it time had overtaken them. They were both expected back at work and didn't want to draw any more attention to their liaison than had already started. Sylvia would be straining at the leash to find out what had happened.

"Perhaps we could continue this one evening over dinner when we have got a bit more time?" Ben suggested. "I think we are both a bit wiser than when we first met and we do need to work together in the future, so another get together would be sensible, don't you think?"

Sheila had warmed to Ben but knew that there was still a long way to go before she would even approach the subject of Jennifer. She couldn't give him her trust after one meeting and still wasn't sure how the news would be received. She didn't know very much about him yet and felt it would be a long time before she felt comfortable to introduce him to his daughter.

"I think that would be a good idea" Sheila agreed trying to sound business-like.

"How about Thursday?"

Sheila was pretty sure that Winnie would come up trumps if she heard that a "date" was on the cards. It was too soon to tell Winnie about the complexities of the situation so she would describe it as a date. She was confident that Jennifer would be happy to stay with Winnie.

"That sounds fine "Sheila replied.

"Perhaps we should go back to Lyons Corner house and start again." Ben laughed

"Wherever you think," said Sheila.

"Let's stay local this time and maybe keep the Corner House on the back burner for another occasion. I will find a nice place to go close by and let you know the details."

Ben paid for lunch and they left the restaurant with an awkward handshake. He headed off for his next job and she returned to the office to face a grilling from Sylvia, who called in the minute Sheila sat down.

Chapter 24

"It's not fair. I don't want to go to Annie's. You are always shoving me off to Annie's. I hate you and I hate Winnie. I don't always want to be with Annie. She's boring"

Jennifer had just returned for the canal bank after her usual forlorn look for "Neat and Tidy". The canal bank had lost its magic without her secret friend. There was something special about Johnny. He was not like all the other children that she knew. He was wild and exciting and even more importantly he took Jennifer at face value. They had met on their own terms, hadn't been forced into a friendship, which she often thought about Annie. Until Johnny's recent disappearance he was reliable and always fun.

Jennifer knew that it was not his fault. He would have to go wherever his mother, or father said he should go. If she moved the boat then she moved him and there was nothing he could do about it. He may be with his father, but either way he wasn't here. Jennifer's magical evening escapes had been taken from her. It wasn't fair.

School was rubbish, she didn't like the lessons and couldn't do most of what was expected of her so she tended to switch off. Her teachers knew she was the child of a single mother and that brought an attitude from them, which other children didn't suffer. She didn't even like the school milk which was forced upon her each break time.

The other kids didn't like her and laughed at her in her face. They knew she was from a single parent and teased her about not having a father. Annie was okay but she was clearly in a difficult situation with the other children. She didn't want to be too overtly friendly with Jennifer but she did her best to stand up for her, as much as she could, without losing friendship with the others.

Jennifer's fathers' genes were kicking in and the red hair and pale complexion were being increasingly punctuated with sizeable freckles. Jennifer hated the way she looked. As if she didn't stand out enough from all the others, her looks picked her out for further abuse. There was an expectation that a red headed girl would be fiery and Jennifer was beginning to live up to that expectation.

Now her mother wanted to dump her off at Annie's so she could go out on a business dinner.

"I don't want to go to Winnies. It's not fair"

Sheila snapped she had been through much mental turmoil over the past few days and was not in the mood for molly codling her moody daughter.

"Now listen young lady I am working very hard for us to have a nice life and sometimes that means that I can't be here for you all the time. We are very lucky to have Winnie to help us out otherwise I don't know how we would cope. Tonight, I have to meet someone about our future and I am afraid that you will have to do as you are told."

Jennifer turned and ran to her bunk, threw herself onto the mattress and sobbed her heart out.

Sheila decided to leave her alone and wait till the rage burnt itself out.

As Jennifer's sobs retreated and morphed into deep snatched breathes, she sat up and decided to take action. "I'm not going to Winnies "she thought "I'll go and hide".

Hiding on the boat was not an option. There was nowhere to hide where her mother wouldn't easily find her. Silently she crept to the front of the boat, whilst her mother washed in the bathroom area. She slipped off and started down the canal path not quite sure where she was heading. The weather was cold and damp and autumnal. Leaves covered the towpath which made it quite slippery underfoot. There was no actual rain, but the evening was drawing in and the light starting to fade. Jennifer walked carefully onwards still not quite knowing where she would go.

Sheila finished getting ready for her evening with Ben. She didn't really have any particularly dressy clothes, but she did her best to look as good as she could. She had a brightly coloured floral dress which felt a bit too summery for the evening outside but it was her best option, she always felt comfortable and attractive when she wore it. She drew a line up the back of each leg to imitate a pair of nylons. It was a long time since she had found herself doing that. She had no stockings and had learnt that trick from the girls after the war when she used to get out.

Sheila was ready and needed to get Jennifer round to Winnies. She called out to Jennifer

"Come on Jennifer it's time to go"

There was no reply.

"Jennifer" Sheila started to get angry again.

"Jennifer please stop that silly behaviour and let's get going"

Still no sound.

Sheila went to Jennifer's bed and found the ruffled bedclothes but no Jennifer. Anger quickly changed to panic as she frantically searched the few potential hiding places on the boat.

No Jennifer.

The tow path was now the only option and the area where Jennifer tended to play the most.

No sign anywhere. Complete panic and horror now then a sudden realisation. She must be with Mickey. Sheila calmed down and thought how foolish she had been not to have even considered looking on Mickeys boat. She marched down the towpath to Mickeys boat, climbed aboard and politely knocked on Mickeys door. It took Mickey some time to open his door and he appeared in a slight state of undress.

"Hello Sheila. Sorry I was taking a shower. Do you want to come in?"

"Is Jennifer here?" she asked panic rising again.

"No, I haven't seen her. Whats happened"

"Could she have got on board without you seeing?"

"Well, I was in the shower so I suppose she could I don't think the cabin door was locked. Whats happened?"

"She's gone missing can we check she's not hiding on your boat?"

Between the two of them they searched any possible hiding places on the boat. Still no Jennifer.

"What can we do" whimpered Sheila.

"Well, she can only have gone in one of two directions along the towpath. I'll get properly dressed and head off in one direction and you take the other"

"Okay" said Sheila pleased to have a plan "I'll go back past my boat and down the path that way. You head up towards the bridge.

Ben was in his lodgings thinking about the evening ahead and what it all meant to him. It was astonishing that he found himself in this situation. He was still grieving for Caroline; the thought of her death was difficult to deal with and he had to deal with it daily. Now he was going out effectively on a date of some sort. He mentally defended himself. I have not orchestrated this situation. It has happened to me. I am not driven by any romantic motive. Sheila and I need to establish a working relationship, make some sense and come to terms with the past and move on. He couldn't help but feel some attraction towards Sheila. She was a girl he had briefly met all those years ago at a party albeit she had matured into a woman. She had showed signs of tension and he guessed that her life had not been easy since their original meeting. She had a weariness about her which belied her age. He had learnt something about her life leading up to the party. She was effectively an orphan whose parents had both been victims of the Germans in one form or another. She must have had a difficult life.

Tonight, he hoped to find out a little more about her and establish a working relationship in which they would both be comfortable. He had been recommended a restaurant where the food would be good, the atmosphere informal and the price not too steep. Sylvia had helpfully been acting as a messenger between Sheila and himself which had made arrangements easier. He was acutely aware that Sylvia thought she was acting as a matchmaker rather than a messenger. He could do nothing about that. Denial to Sylvia would merely confirm her suspicions that they were already romantically entwined. He knew to leave Sylvia to her wild imagination and make sure that he and Sheila both understood that this was about business and not romance.

The arrangements had been for Ben to meet Sheila at the restaurant in the Edgware Road. It was close enough for Sheila to walk and despite his chivalrous insistence she had declined his offer to come and collect her from her boat. Ben's lodgings were in Childs Hill which was a ride on a 28 Bus and a twenty-minute walk at the other end. He set off with plenty of time to arrive at the restaurant early, he didn't want Sheila to be sitting there alone. At seven twenty he took his seat and ordered a light ale for himself whilst he waited for Sheila to arrive.

Sheila had not thought to put on a coat when she left the boat and as she peered into each boat along the canal path, she was beginning to feel the cold. Tears streamed down her face driven as much by the cold wind in her face as by her fear of what might have happened. She found herself peering into the canal at any object which remotely resembled a little body. On a couple of occasions, she thought she had found her daughter floating in the murky, still water but her eyes and her mind were conspiring to feed her imagination. After twenty minutes heading away from her boat, she decided she was getting nowhere and should get back to the boat. Perhaps there was something she had missed or maybe Mickey would have found her by now.

Mickey had dressed and set off in the opposite direction. Looking through the bushes and woods that lined the canal banks. Peering into craft moored along the way and where there was life aboard the boats, enquiring about a little red headed seven-year-old girl. He hadn't thought to look at the floating debris in the water, his mind hadn't started to consider that even as a possibility. At approximately the same time as Sheila he decided to head back to the boat fully expecting Jennifer to be sitting with her relieved mother. She was not.

Mickey was now as worried as Sheila. Both knew Jennifer had a temper and her mood swung from one extreme to another very quickly, but they did not have any experience of her running off like this. Sheila had forgotten her meeting with Ben and even if she had remembered, what could she do about it? She sat forlornly and wept. She really didn't know what to do next. It had been a good forty minutes since she had last seen Jennifer disappear into her cabin in tears of anger. Somehow her absence was the worse because they had been at each other's throats. It was Sheila's fault.

"I'm sure it will be fine" said Mickey without the slightest conviction. "I think I should get some help in the search. We can't cover the area alone and one of us should be here for when she comes back. I am going to call the police and report her missing, they will know what to do, they are used to this type of situation. It happens every day."

"Oh my God" Sheila screamed "What do you think has happened to her"

Sheila suddenly felt a total sense of dread with the mention of the police.

"I don't think anything has happened to her. I expect she is wandering the streets lost and the police will quickly find her. I'll run to the telephone box up the road and call them now. Stay here I am sure she'll be back. Try not to worry I'll be back as soon as I can."

Sheila sobbed and nodded. Mickey left and ran the relatively short distance to the red telephone box just hoping that it would be working. It was and he dialled 999. It wasn't long before he was advised that a car would be despatched as soon as possible and to return to the boat.

Ben sat at a table in the restaurant and wondered what was taking Sheila so long. He didn't think for one minute she would stand him up. They had seemed to get along quite well if a little cautiously. He felt sure there would be a sensible explanation, but it was twenty minutes past the time he thought they had agreed to meet and there was no sign of her. He began to doubt himself and thought perhaps they had said eight o'clock rather than seven thirty. He decided to have another light ale and wait till ten past eight. If she didn't show he would order something for himself and eat alone. He hadn't any other plan and would need to eat something, so he might as well eat here alone.

Ten past eight and Ben reluctantly ordered a meal for himself and his third light ale.

"I hope nothing has happened" he thought but he had no way of finding out until the morning, so he sat alone ate his dinner and thought about his wife."

Mickey returned from the call box hoping to find Jennifer in her mother's arms. She wasn't.

"What did they say? What's happening?"

"They are sending a car "Mickey said.

"What will they do?" Sheila asked desperately

"I don't know, Sheila, have you thought of anywhere else where she might have gone?"

"We'll I suppose she might have gone to Winnie's but that was what the whole issue was about, she said she didn't want to go there!"

"That's probably where we will find her!" Mickey wasn't at all sure that was true. For a small girl the distance to Winnie's house was quite significant and despite having been there so many times he wondered if she could find her way there.

"We should wait for the police and see what they say!"

More than an hour had passed since Jennifer had gone missing. Two policemen arrived in a black police car. A missing little girl was treated as a high priority and it hadn't taken them long to be diverted from their original destination and, as luck would have it, they were close by in Paddington.

The policemen were both over six feet tall and broadly built. They clambered awkwardly into the body of the boat and stooped uncomfortably. Sheila recognised one of the policemen as the officer who had come to question her after Sweeneys demise. She was not sure if he had recognised her but suspected he would have remembered coming to a narrow boat before.

"Good evening, I realise that this is very worrying for you both "the first officer said with as much sympathy as he could. I think I have been here before, haven't I?"

Sheila reluctantly reminded him of his previous visit but quickly asked him what they were going to do about her daughters' disappearance.

"We can start by you telling us what has happened this evening leading up your daughter's disappearance. I assume it is your daughter that is missing?"

"Yes, she's my daughter" Sheila replied

"I'm a friend and neighbour" Mickey added

"And where is your husband this evening" the policeman asked.

"I don't have a husband"

The policeman raised one eyebrow and looked at his colleague.

"No husband! "He repeated, as if this was clearly part of the problem.

"I see! What is your daughter's name"

"Jennifer"

"Just Jennifer?"

"It's Jennifer Johnson"

"And how old is Jennifer"

"She's seven"

"Do you have a picture of her."

Sheila realised that she didn't have a single photograph of her daughter. She didn't have a camera.

"No, I don't, I haven't got a camera" Sheila confessed

"Well perhaps you can give us a description"

Sheila started to describe Jennifer whilst the policeman scribbled onto his notebook. Their progress was interrupted.

"Coooeee"

The sound came from the tow path. Sheila went to investigate.

Chapter 25

Jennifer had decided to head back to the den even though she knew that Johnny wouldn't be there. She was particularly missing him now. He would understand what mothers could be like sometimes, how selfish, and unreasonable. He would agree that it wasn't fair the way she was being treated. If he had been around, they could have gone off on another adventure together, but she knew that he wasn't. When she reached the den, she suddenly felt very alone, she sat on the damp leaves and cried.

"What would Johnny do "she thought. "Probably something exciting and fun"

She remembered the times they had spent away from the den, climbing aboard empty boats to see what mischief they could get up to. Then she remembered Bert. He would always talk to Johnny. Jennifer had spoken to him on a couple of occasions, he would recognise her, she felt he would be kind. She didn't really know where else to go, so she headed for "The Fine Old Lady"

Bert was sitting reading on the bankside beside "The Fine Old Lady" in an old armchair with no legs. He was wrapped up in a thick dirty old blanket and had an untidy homemade cigarette hanging from his lip. Jennifer walked along the towpath towards him. Bert looked up from his magazine, he coughed.

"Hello, young lady. You're out late this evening. I haven't seen you and your friend for a while now"

"Johnny's gone away" she said simply.

"Has he now, and just where has he gone too"

"I don't know he just went"

"I expect he'll be back"

Bert could see that Jennifer had been crying but didn't really want to get involved.

"Does your mummy know where you are?"

"She knows I have gone for a walk "she lied

"Where are you going to?"

"I haven't decided yet" she said

"Would you like to come and have a look inside my boat" Bert asked "I have got something you might like to see!"

"What is it?" Jennifer was intrigued

"Come on I'll show you"

Bert heaved himself up with some difficulty, the chair was low to the ground, and he was encumbered by the blanket. He took Jennifer's hand and led her onto the boat. Inside, Jennifer remembered the last time she was here, she had found her prized ten shilling note which Johnny had taken away with him. Her eyes instinctively went to the place where she had found it. There in a neat pile were some coins, silver ones and brown ones. Jennifer felt no remorse for her previous actions and started to wonder if she could get one of the silver coins to take away with her.

Burt said" You are going to like this I promise, just wait there a minute" and left Jennifer in the galley area. Jennifer looked at the piles of coins on the table and quickly took one from the silver pile. She stuffed it hastily into her cardigan pocket and turned to wait for Bert's surprise.

Bert came back into the galley proudly holding a round wooden board with a glass dome on top. The dome was about eighteen inches tall and inside was the tiniest little dog, stuffed. The dog was no more than six inches long and stood about eight inches tall.

"Is it real?"

"I believe it is, yes," said Bert. "One of my friends does house clearing and he came across it. He didn't think it was worth anything, so he gave it to me. He gets lots of odds and ends for me. Do you like it?"

"I think so, it's a bit scary"

"Don't be scared of him. He's been stuffed. He must have been a freak of nature he's such a tiny thing. Do you think I should give him a name?"

"Yes. Spot!"

"Spot it is then. You can come and visit Spot whenever you want"

Bert and Jennifer sat and talked inside the boat for a little while until Bert said "Right young lady you better go home to your mother, she will start to worry about you"

Jennifer left the boat feeling a bit better but still angry at her mother.

Just off the tow path runs Harrow Road. Opposite Sixth Avenue was a small parade of shops including the local newsagents run by Nancy Reddy and her sister (known to all as Sis). Nancy and Sis built their life around the newsagents. Both were spinsters in their sixties who had never married. They had enjoyed life together as sisters in their parents shop through the war and beyond. They had opted to keep the shop on when their mother and father, one by one, succumbed to cancer. Between them they kept the shop open for long hours. It represented their history, their income, their interest, and their social life. Everybody locally knew Nancy and Sis. They knew that they could get their cigarettes, newspapers, chocolates, and a variety of sweets at any time of the day between 6.00 AM, when the ladies would be found marking up the morning papers and 8.00PM when one or the other would lock up and go upstairs to their flat for an evening meal. The upstairs flat made life easier, each could rest in turn.

Nancy was upstairs preparing the evening meal whilst Sis sat in her customary position by the door watching the world go by and anticipating her next customer and with it her next conversation. It was about seven fifteen when a little seven-year-old red headed freckly girl walked up to the shop and entered.

"Hello" said Sis "Are you on your own? Where is your mummy?"

"I think she is at home, but she is going out" Jennifer said

"Oh, I see, and where is home?" Sis enquired.

"On a boat "Jennifer replied nonchalantly.

"Does she know you are here? Sis asked

"She doesn't care" Jennifer was eyeing up the sweets. "Have you got any Spangles?" she asked

"Well yes did your mummy give you some money to spend?"

"I've got money, can I have some spangles"

"Spangles are threepence for a packet, have you got threepence"

Jennifer gave her the silver half-crown that she had tightly clenched in her little fist since leaving Bert's boat.

"That's a lot of money for a little girl" Sis took the coin and handed Jennifer the sweets. Jennifer turned to run out.

"Wait a minute you need some change" Sis produced a threepence piece and a two-bob bit and handed it to Jennifer.

"Would you like me to help you with those sweets they are quite difficult to open"

Nancy appeared from the doorway at the back of the shop.

"Hello who is this" she asked.

228

"A customer," said Sis. "She lives on a boat with her mummy who might not even know she is here. I thought I might walk down the canal path with her since it is getting a bit late"

"I think you should, Sis" said Nancy "What is your name"

"Jennifer"

"My name is Nancy and this is Sis"

"Do you mind if Sis walks down the canal path with you, she would love to see your boat"

Jennifer was already feeling a bit worried about where she was and what she had done. The idea of getting back to the boat was getting quite appealing although she was not looking forward to her mother's reaction.

"Alright then!" Jennifer replied

Nancy nodded to Sis who put on her coat and a scarf, held on to Jennifer's hand and walked her back to the boat.

Jennifer knew exactly where to go she had been to that newsagent before with Johnny for cigarettes for his mother. Last time she left with Spangles as well but that time she didn't pay for them, she stole them as Nancy turned her back to get the cigarettes.

Sis and Jennifer reached the boat. Sis was not keen on the idea of stepping onto the boat so instead she called out.

"Coooee"

After a moment the door flew open, and a tearful Sheila jumped onto the towpath pushed Sis aside and grabbed Jennifer. She didn't know whether to hug her or smack her. She hugged her.

"Where have you been? I have been worried to death. Don't ever run off like that again!!"

Jennifer burst into tears.

The head of a policeman appeared from the entrance to the boat.

Sis said "I'll be off then"

"Just a moment" said the policeman" Can you explain how you come to have Jennifer with you?"

Sheila recognised Sis from the shop. "Thank you for bringing Jennifer back, what happened"

Sis related all she knew and when she had answered all of Sheila and the policeman's questions she left and headed back to the shop for dinner with Nancy.

"It seems that we are not needed here anymore. Come on Cyril back to work." The policemen said their farewells, repeated Sheila's warning to Jennifer "You mustn't run off like that, your mother was very worried" and left.

Sheila Jennifer and Mickey went back on the boat, and all sat down together.

"You must never run off like that again. It's very dangerous. We didn't know what had happened to you. We had to call out the police." Sheila was babbling. Mickey took over. "It's alright now, no harm done. We can talk about this in the morning. Why don't you get ready for bed Jennifer, and I will tuck you in. "

Jennifer still whimpering went to her cabin and changed for bed. Mickey kept a close eye on the cabin door until she said she was ready, then he went to her cabin and kissed her lightly on the forehead. "Go to sleep now you little adventurer, sweet dreams"

Sheila sat on the bench in the galley stunned. The past ninety minutes or so had taken a lot out of her and she felt exhausted.

"You okay" Mickey asked

"I suppose so "

"What started it all off?

"Oh my God" Sheila realised where she was supposed to be, which had completely gone out of her head. "I am supposed to have been meeting Ben about an hour ago"

"What! Where?"

Ben and Sheila had chosen not to mention their assignation to anybody else thinking that it was likely to start tongues wagging even more than they had been. Sheila hadn't even told Mickey, which was why she had chosen to take Jennifer to Winnies rather than ask Mickey to step in and babysit. If she had asked Mickey this probably would not have happened.

Sheila found herself explaining herself again. Mickey was sympathetic and understanding as always.

"I'll go to the restaurant and see if he is still there and explain. If he's not still there we can tell him what happened tomorrow"

"Oh, Mickey do you mind? You are a life saver. Actually, I would rather that you didn't tell him exactly what has happened" Sheila said sheepishly. "I don't want him to know about Jennifer yet. It's too soon"

"There's no need to tell him he is the father, just that you have a little girl."

"I know but he will find out her age and he might put two and two together. I don't want to risk it!"

"Okay. What shall I tell him?"

"Tell him I am unwell. Tell him it's a lady's problem and that I am sorry. Men don't like to talk about ladies' problems so he probably won't ask you too many questions and when I do finally see him, I expect he will be too embarrassed to ask me"

Sheila gave Mickey the details of where and when she was due to meet Ben. Mickey ran off to try and catch Ben before he left.

Ben was surprised when Mickey came into the restaurant and at first thought it a strange co-incidence, since he had agreed with Sheila to keep quiet about their second meeting.

"Ben" I am glad I caught you I am afraid Sheila won't be getting here tonight she is a little unwell. I happened to go to her boat tonight and she asked me to come and offer you her apologies, she feels very guilty, but she wasn't up to dinner tonight"

"Oh dear, I hope it is nothing serious" Ben was genuinely concerned.

"It's a ladies thing" Mickey said with a shrug of the shoulders.

Chapter 26

Sheila was back in to work next day, Jennifer was, reluctantly, back to school. The events of the previous evening were barely mentioned. Mickey had told Sheila that he had reached Ben before he left the restaurant last night and had told him about the imaginary sickness they had agreed upon. He said that Ben, after an initial gruffness, had been concerned to hear about Sheila's state of health and understood that such matters were not for discussion between men and women. Ben had said he hoped that they could rearrange another meeting to help clear the air.

Jennifer woke and squirrelled her laundered change away into small wardrobe before being taken, mainly in silence, to her class in school, where she sulkily parted with her mother without a word. Sheila met Winnie in the playground and, with profuse apologies for not turning up the previous night as arranged, described what had happened. Winnie seemed unphased and as ever took most of the story in her stride, she seemed a little shocked that the police had been involved but, with Sheila, she had learnt not to expect things to ever be straightforward.

Sheila arrived at the office to a series of customer phone calls. A number of cleaners had not turned up for their regular cleans and the customers were not happy. As well as reassigning some of the girls, Sheila was forced to fill in and effectively was out of the office for the rest of the day. Ben also was out "jobbing" and unable to get into the office for any type of meeting. The weekend came and went. Sheila spent more time with Jennifer and life seemed to settle down again.

Monday morning saw Sheila issuing cleaning rotas and making last minute changes, she could avoid any cleaning herself and settle into catching up on some of the administration work which she had fallen behind with on. Mickey was in the office and wanted to catch up with Sheila. He had spent the weekend with Rufus and had been constantly worried about Sheila and how Jennifer would get along through the weekend. He felt a responsibility to be there for them. Rufus persuaded him it was not for him to worry and that he should focus on himself, and Rufus, for once.

Sheila caught him up on all the details of her weekend and of course Jennifer's behaviour which had been okay, if a little sulky. There was the tricky situation of getting together with Ben without having to make alternative arrangements for Jennifer, which might just set her off again. As ever Mickey was keen to be supportive. He wanted to enable Sheila to move forward and establish how she and Ben could adapt to the situation in which they found themselves. He suggested that they both take some extra time one lunchtime and meet on neutral ground somewhere that they could talk without being disturbed. Mickey agreed to act as go-between. They agreed to set up a meeting on his boat which was neutral, if slightly favouring Sheila since she had spent a lot of time there. The location would enable the pair of them to have their chat in the context of the business in which they were proposing to partner.

Mickey kept Bobby in the loop. They were both keen to move the business forward but wanted everybody to be in agreement. Bobby agreed with Mickeys proposed meeting arrangements and made sure that Ben got there on time. He took all of Ben's responsibilities for the day and effectively gave him a day off to get things straight with Sheila.

Everything was arranged for Wednesday morning. Sheila sat in the galley of Mickeys boat with butterflies in her stomach. Ben also approached the meeting with an unexpected nervousness.

Mickey let Ben in and left the pair to their own devices.

"Hello again" Ben said

"Hello Ben. I am so sorry about the other night I just couldn't get there I wasn't up to it. I hope Mickey explained"

"Yes, he did. I must admit that until he arrived, I was getting very worried. I thought I had been stood up and I had no way of getting in touch with you."

They both laughed, Ben's comment was more suggestive of a romantic liaison than a business meeting and loosened the tension they both felt.

"Well, we learnt a little bit more about each other last time but didn't really get up to date, did we?"

"No, not really" Sheila shifted uncomfortably

"Right well let's cut to the quick. Do you mind if I am very direct? I think it will probably save us a lot of shilly shallying about" Ben was keen to move things forward with the least discomfort for them both.

"Okay" Sheila said slowly "What exactly do you mean"

"Well, our past is only known to you and me, isn't it?"

"I suppose so" Sheila Lied

"Well here goes. Do you have anybody in your life who would be upset to know that we have met in a previous life, a husband, a boyfriend or anybody"

"No, I suppose not! "Sheila was unsure how Jennifer would react when she found out.

235

"Good, neither do I, so as long as we are both comfortable to be in each other's company there is no reason for our past to be a problem, is there"

Sheila didn't know how to react. Of course, Jennifer was a massive problem and would need to be addressed in time but for now she was not ready to let Ben into that side of her life. His knowledge of Jennifer's existence would doubtless complicate what was already a tricky situation. Sheila wanted the same clarification which she had just given up to Ben.

"So, you have no wife or girlfriend who might feel uncomfortable about our past?

"No Sheila, I was married but my wife died last year"

"Oh my God, I am so sorry!" Sheila wished she had kept quiet.

"It's okay. It is taking some time, but I am beginning to come to some sort of terms with it. Caroline and my daughter died in the process of childbirth. There was nothing that could be done"

Sheila felt physically sick.

"Your daughter?"

"Yes, she was still born. We lost an unborn son before our daughter"

"Oh, Ben I don't know what to say that is just so tragic. I am sorry I have pried; you didn't have to tell me all of that. I feel terrible for you"

"Please don't. I was the one who suggested being direct and I expected to tell you and anybody else that needs to know eventually. Of course, Bobby and his wife know. It was as a consequence of Bobby's kindness that I come to be here today"

Ben went on to tell Sheila his story. The days after their meeting at the party, his call up to the RAF, how he met Caroline which included his boxing career. Sheila listened and found herself drawn to Ben as she had been all those years ago. He told her everything about his hopes for a family with Caroline and the devastation he felt in losing both is wife and his unknown children. At one point Sheila found herself on the verge of tears, Ben spoke with emotion and was clearly still hurting. Eventually their conversation moved on to the present and the boat they were sitting in. Sheila was relieved that Ben hadn't tried too hard to delve into her circumstances and she had manoeuvred the conversation back to the business.

"Shall we have a look around the boat? Mickey gave me his approval, in fact he suggested that we should."

"Good Idea" Sheila agreed.

"You have one of these as well I understand."

"Yes, it's right alongside this one but it's a bit of a mess at the moment so I would rather not look at it just now" Sheila knew that it wouldn't take long for Ben to notice the trappings of a seven-year-old girl. "The fundamentals are pretty much the same, but the layout is different to accommodate our different needs. We chose to use the wider berth boats to maximise the space available, then we considered what we would each need included in the design. Rufus who was the original inspiration for the idea designed both layouts and then we, well Mickey mostly, used tradesmen from your company and elsewhere to complete the fit outs. We did both boats concurrently so we could maximise peoples time and we learnt from mistakes on one boat to the benefit of the other. My boat is the "butty" to this boat so it doesn't have an engine of its own"

Ben had lots of questions for Sheila, and she was surprised how much she knew and how few questions were left unanswered.

"I don't know too much about the financial implications for the business venture" Sheila said. Mickey is dealing with that side of things and our investment will come from the Spic and Span business."

"I am very impressed Sheila, that young girl that I met at that party has come a long way. I am surprised that you haven't found a husband, you would be a great catch for someone."

Sheila felt a blush rising and ignored what he had said.

"Well do you think we can work together?" she asked

"I am sure it will be no problem for me. What about you?"

"I think we will be fine" Sheila felt a pang of guilt about her secrets. "No doubt there will be more to learn about each other but if we can accept the past for what it was and move forwards from here, I hope we can overcome any hurdles that come along."

Their meeting on the boat had lasted for more than three hours. "Well, I had better get back to work" Sheila said.

"Okay "said Ben "I have got the day off but I think I will go to Harefield and take a look at some of those abandoned boats that we are planning to give a new life. We should reconvene a meeting to replace the abortive Joe Lyons meeting. We need to formally kick the business off and agree our roles and responsibilities."

"Crikey" Said Sheila "That all sounds very structured."

"Well, we will need to be clear about who is doing what. I am really excited about it all aren't you?"

"Yes, I am actually" Sheila realised that her original enthusiasm for the project had been lost to her since the events in the restaurant. Now she was re-energised and eager to get started.

"I will talk to Mickey and let's see if we can all get together in the next few days"

"Brilliant"

Ben and Sheila shook hands awkwardly again and said goodbye. Ben headed up the canal path towards Edgeware Road. Sheila locked up and went back to her own boat to gather her thoughts.

Chapter 27

Jennifer was at school. It was a Church of England school which inhabited an old Victorian building that had seen better days. The wooden sash windows were rotting, the paint was peeling through the effects of neglect and weathering. The walls were built of red London brick and were dark and dirty. This was not a building in which to stimulate fresh, eager, young minds.

Jennifer sat by the window staring out at the clouds drifting by, she was not at all eager to learn. Her mind was detached from the monotonous drone of her teacher explaining the basics of the alphabet and the "ch" combination. She was far away in the den with Johnny talking about their adventures, stashing away their stolen paraphernalia, cunningly acquired from a variety of boats and local shops. In her mind she saw them laughing about the various acquisitions which they had just thrown into the canal to see if they would float. She remembered the toy duck which had been liberated from the bow of one visiting narrow boat. They had spent hours throwing stones at it until eventually the water seeped in and the canal swallowed the duck whole.

"Jennifer Johnson, are you paying attention"

"Not really" she replied without thinking

The rest of the class laughed which only made the situation worse. Jennifer was thought unusual and disliked by the other children in her class. Their parents had told them to stay away from her, they all knew that she didn't have a father.

"Well, I suggest you do young lady you are not the brightest girl in the class and you need to concentrate more than the rest. I will be having a word with your mother."

Jennifer's teacher, Miss Williams was a middle aged, thin-lipped, matronly spinster, who wore her hair in a tight bun. She peered over half-moon glasses at the children in her care and found little sympathy for any of them but particularly this one. She considered that Jennifer had been born illegitimately, which was against the will of God and deserved less attention than the others in her class. She had a very low opinion of her mother and doubted that "having a word with her" would make the slightest difference. Being illegitimate was synonymous with being troublesome.

Jennifer reluctantly straightened up and looked in the right direction. It was not the first time she had been admonished and she found it all rather tiresome.

"Sorry "she said, without a hint of remorse. She had no respect for her teacher or any of the other children around her.

Miss Williams looked over her spectacles and tutted, there was nothing she could really do to help this child, the rest of the class were suffering at her expense. At least she was quiet, which didn't disrupt the class. She was unlikely to learn anything but that would be her problem. She decided, as she had many times previously, to leave Jennifer to her daydreams and avoid any disruptive confrontation. Some children wouldn't be helped.

Jennifer's thoughts wandered off in a new direction. Her focus moved on, to the people around her in the classroom. She looked around and considered each of them. There was Annie, the one person, other than Johnny, who she could remotely call a friend. She liked Annie who did her best to be nice to her at school, but Annie had other friends who stole her away but wanted nothing to do with Jennifer. She had no axe to grind with Annie.

The identical Wilson twins were particularly spiteful, the creators of a variety of nicknames, each of which she hated. "Gingernut, Nodad, Spottyface" The twins competed with each other to think of the worst names for Jennifer. Their measure of success was determined by the amusement of their classmates and the uptake of the name. The longer it stuck the better it was considered.

"Nodad" was the worst for Jennifer, who was not scared to hit out, scratch or even bite any child that she heard call her by that hurtful name. This aggression was misunderstood by the teaching staff. It was interpreted that Jennifer was initiating attacks on the other children rather than defending herself against cruel bullying

Jennifer stared at the back of the heads of the twins whose hair was neatly tied in identical pigtails. Each twin had different coloured ribbons to help tell them apart. She imagined setting fire to each of the pigtails, causing the twins to run screaming from the class. If only she could.

Her gaze wandered around the class. She didn't like any of them but who were the worst?

Her eyes settled on Jack Blair who was a spiteful character. She had fallen foul of his bullying on many occasions. He was physically much bigger and stronger than the other children in the year. He was a September baby and the eldest in the class, he had an older brother in the school and everybody looked up to him. Everybody except Jennifer who he had pushed over in the playground many times. He had given her Chinese burns, pulled her hair, tripped her over and punched her body many times. He was mostly showing off and was largely capable of containing Jennifer's attempts at retaliation.

"What could I do to Jack Blair" she thought "He needs to be taught a lesson. Jennifer remembered how Johnny and her had used their magnifying glasses to kill insects. She visualised Johnny knocking Jack to the ground, Johnny was much the stronger and fearless. He would hold Jack down whilst Jennifer focussed the sun's rays on different parts of his exposed body. She imagined Jack screaming for mercy and enjoyed the power that she felt.

Jennifer was abruptly brought back to the world by the scraping of chairs and the rush for coat pegs.

"Slowly now children. Take care and walk!" Miss Williams issued her instructions.

Outside children ran to meet their parents, mothers in the main. There were two gates one at either end of the playground, parents and children habitually went to the same gate every day. Jennifer started to walk ruefully to the awaiting Winnie who was animatedly talking to Annie about what she had learnt at school and whether she had eaten her lunch. Winnie was, unsurprisingly, more interested in Annie's day than she ever was with Jennifer's. She did her best to take an interest but her heart wasn't in it in the same way.

Jennifer decided that today she was not going to put up with playing second fiddle. She stopped and did an about turn heading purposefully for the other gate. She slipped through past a group of doting parents and their excited children and headed off into the unfamiliar. Nobody noticed. She felt a sort of freedom. She had a vague notion of her whereabouts but was not completely sure. She decided to keep the school in sight and circle back to the normal gate from outside the school perimeter. As she reached the point where Winnie stood, she crossed the road with a large group of others and wandered off. Winnie was beginning to get a little worried as the other parents drifted off, she had not seen Jennifer and whilst it was not unusual for her to hang back, Winnie would have expected to at least see her crossing the playground by now. She grabbed Annie's hand and silently cursing Jennifer headed into the school to find her.

Miss Williams was clearly in a hurry to leave and greeted Winnie just outside the classroom door wearing her hat and coat.

"Hello Miss Williams, I didn't see Jennifer come out, do you know where she is?"

"She left with all the others." Miss Williams said sniffily

"Well, she hasn't come out yet" Winnie said "Where else could she have gone? She knows where to meet me perhaps she's in the toilets."

Winnie, Miss Williams and several other members of staff looked high and low throughout the school and its immediate vicinity. Jennifer was nowhere to be found. Winnie was angry and very worried.

"You can't just loose a child, it's ridiculous"

The headmaster decided to call Sheila at the office.

"No, she's not here – what do you mean gone missing?" Sheila could not believe this was happening again. She was alone in the office and shouldn't really leave for another hour or two but she had no choice.

"I'll go to the boat and see if she has found her own way home"

"Do you want me to call the police" the head asked.

"I suppose so yes"

Sheila locked the door and popped her head into Bright Sparks. "Sylvia, I have to go Jennifer's gone missing from school.

Mickey is due back soon but I can't wait. Would you explain please and let him know I have gone home in case she is there"

"Of course," said Sylvia "Let us know what happens good luck"

"Anything I can do" Ben was standing at a filing cabinet behind the door. Sheila had been unaware of his presence.

"No thank you its fine. I need to get going but thanks anyway"

Sheila disappeared out the door and rushed back to the boat.

"Who is Jennifer" Ben put Sylvia on the spot.

"It's Sheila's daughter" Sylvia said reluctantly

"I didn't know she had a daughter. She's gone missing, how terrible. How old is she?"

"I'm not sure to be honest but she is very young I know that!"

"Well, she must be" Ben thought out loud "Sheila's not that old herself.

Ben felt concerned for Sheila but wasn't sure how he could help. Hopefully the child would turn up at home and it would be panic over.

Jennifer walked down the street. The further she got from school the fewer the numbers of schoolchildren with parents were evident. Nobody had bothered to challenge her. She wasn't exactly sure where she was heading but she thought it was in the general direction of the canal.

Her plan was to find the canal and head off in the other direction from her last sortie in search of Johnny's boat. She hadn't walked far that way before and perhaps he might be close by. As she walked along, she noticed a small Scottie dog had tagged along. She looked around for an owner but there was no-one to be seen. She bent down and stroked him.

"Hello" she said "Are you lost"

The dog looked sadly up her.

"You are lost aren't you. Come with me and we will see if we can find your owners."

Jennifer walked on and the dog followed closely behind. She walked on for five or ten minutes by which time it was clear that the dog was staying. Up ahead she saw Sis and Nancy's newsagents. She knew the way to the canal from here and headed back in the direction of her home. Her new concern was her adopted dog.

As she approached the boat she was only concerned with the Scottie and had talked to him all the way. The Scottie wagged his tail enthusiastically, pleased to have found a new friend.

Sheila was running urgently towards the boat from the opposite direction.

"Hi mum. This dog followed me home. I don't think he's got a home. Can we keep him?"

Again, Sheila didn't know whether to smack her or hug her.

"Where have you been"

"Walking home from school."

"Well why didn't you go with Winnie back to her house like you always do"

"I couldn't see her" Jennifer lied "All the other children's mothers come to collect them so I thought I would just come home. You never collect me"

"Jennifer you are seven you don't just decide to come home, you wait for an adult to bring you home and you know that Winnie will always be there to collect you!"

"Well, I didn't see her today. So, I came home. It's not fair I always get told off for everything"

Sheila looked up to see two uniformed policemen walking towards her.

"Everything all right here?" the first one asked sarcastically "We seem to be regular visitors to the canal lately. We had a call from the school regarding a missing seven-year child. I think we have been called out to look for this one before. I think you will have to be more careful with your daughter in future. We have criminals to catch you know!"

"I am so sorry!" said Sheila "there was obviously some kind of mix up at the school gates and Jennifer made her own way home."

The policeman got down on his haunches, put his hands on Jennifer's arms and looked directly into her face. "Are you alright young lady"

"Yes" she said boldly

"Well, you must pay more attention to the adults in your life and stop wandering off"

"I found this dog; can I keep him?"

The policeman looked at Sheila who was equally perplexed. "She just walked up the towpath with the dog following behind, I have no idea where it is from"

"Where did you find the dog?" the officer asked

"He followed me in the street"

"Which street?"

"On the way home"

It was clear this was going nowhere. The policeman looked at Sheila "I suggest you hold on to him and I will report that you have found him. His owner will probably call to report him lost and we can send them here to collect him. Alright?"

"I suppose so" Sheila didn't know whether she was coming or going.

"We will inform the school that Jennifer has been found. I believe that the lady who normally collects her is still at the school and in a state of shock and worry!"

"Oh my God poor Winnie"

The policemen left Sheila, Jennifer and Scottie on the canal bank

Mickey flew down the tow path seconds later.

"Thank God "he said breathless "Sylvia told me what had happened. I came straight away. Did the police find her?"

"No, she just turned up here with this dog"

"Where did you get the dog?" Mickey asked not sure what else to say

"He followed me home" Jennifer said lightly

"Where from?" Mickey asked

"We've done that" said Sheila "Let's get on board, we can talk about this over a cup of tea."

"I need to go back to the office and finish up. I left as soon as Sylvia and Ben told me your news. They were very worried so I will need to let them know that she has been found. What did you tell Ben?"

"Just that she was missing, I didn't know that he was there when I was telling Sylvia. He just appeared from nowhere"

"Who's Ben?" Jennifer asked

"He's a man that we work with" Sheila said quickly "You had better go Mickey. Come round later and we can talk about it then.

"I can't tonight, I am attending a gallery launch with Rufus and I can't let him down. Sorry Sheila, I will call round tomorrow if we don't have a chance to speak at work"

Chapter 28

Mr Ronald Hudson stood six foot five inches tall. He looked down on most people. He was uncomfortably thin and his skin had a tinge of yellow suggesting a liver problem. Mr Hudson kept a bottle of scotch locked in his desk for those moments when stress overwhelmed him. He found his position was particularly stressful. He wore a malignant smile, intended to disguise his general dislike of the human race. He hid behind circular wire glasses; the cheapest money could buy.

As the headmaster of Jennifer's school, he was a formidable presence for all of the children and regarded with an element of fear. His style was authoritarian which produced tension and disquiet in the staff room. He chose to wear his black gown every day and was often seen striding around the school premises, carrying the cane which he used to administer punishment to the little people who persistently refused to abide by his rules.

If you were known to the headmaster it was generally not for your strengths or good behaviour. Jennifer was known to the headmaster before he had cause to call the police to his school, something which would need to be fully reported to the board of management. He had stayed later than normal, whilst the police sought out the errant child. He laid the blame squarely at the door of Miss Williams, who should take more care with her children.

Miss Williams had defended herself and her actions. She had further reminded Mr. Hudson of Jennifer's parentage and her record of "incidents" both in the playground and the classroom. Finally, she had explained Jennifer's attitude on the afternoon that she went missing, suggesting that she had probably wilfully avoided those trusted with her safety.

It was as a consequence of this that Sheila found herself sitting opposite both Mr. Hudson, in full headmaster regalia, and Miss Williams.

"Jennifer is a very difficult child Mrs. Johnson. Oh, I am sorry I meant Miss Johnson you aren't married, are you?" Mr Hudson smiled.

"No, I am not but I don't see what that has to do with Jennifer's behaviour"

"We tend to find that the absence of a male role model to introduce discipline to the child is often the cause of ill-mannered children such as Jennifer. Is there a man in your life at all who could help with discipline? Clearly a masculine presence would be invaluable in this instance"

"Are you suggesting that I am not bringing my daughter up correctly?"

"Well clearly, she is hardly a model child, is she? We would not be all sitting here if there wasn't an issue to resolve, would we?" Miss Williams chirped

"Look I know that Jennifer finds school difficult. It isn't helped by the other children, who at best don't play with her and at worst bully her"

"I am not aware of any bullying Miss Johnson. In fact, Jennifer has been reprimanded on several occasions for attacking other children. We have managed to deal with this within the school until now and without resorting to the cane" Mr Hudson's eyes went to his cane, proudly displayed on the wall, alongside his educational certificates.

"I am reluctant to use the cane on a seven-year-old and particularly a girl but I am afraid that we are getting close to the point where we will have to introduce discipline with a little more impact. Miss Williams has tried her best with normal methods but is just not getting the results that are needed."

"Please let me talk to Jennifer. I am sure we can resolve this without the use of the cane" Sheila was practically begging.

"Well, you will need to administer firmer discipline in the home. You will have to behave as a father as well as a mother and that won't be easy," said Miss Williams

Coming from a middle-aged spinster this was hard to take but Sheila didn't want to make things worse than they already were.

"I am sure I can. I will just need to take a firmer stance at home."

"Well, we will leave it to you Miss Johnson but we will expect to see an improvement in behaviour in the coming days and weeks or we will be forced to take more decisive action within the school. We cannot afford to have this sort of disruption, it isn't fair to the other children."

"I realise that and I will take action but please can you watch out for the bullying which Jennifer says she is suffering"

Miss Williams rolled her eyes" Of course we will, we are trained to spot that type of behaviour and I can assure you, I will not tolerate it"

Sheila took her leave. It had been two days since Jennifer's latest disappearance and she had been summoned to the school for this meeting before Jennifer was allowed back. Jennifer had been left in the office with Mickey whilst Sheila went for her humiliating dressing down. She had already been to Winnie's child care group with flowers of apology for Winnie but also to try and understand how it could have happened. Winnie as always was understanding and accepted Sheila's apologies with a sense of relief. She actually felt responsible to a large degree and was happy to put the incident behind them. Losing a seven-year-old would not be a good reference for the leader of a child-minding group.

Sheila returned to the office to collect Jennifer and return home. It was Friday and a return to school that day seemed unnecessary. Sheila decided to spend the weekend with Jennifer and use whatever means necessary to make Jennifer realise that she must behave better in school. She was convinced that her daughter was not malicious but more a victim of circumstance. Next Monday would be a new start. She had already discussed the issue with Mickey regarding taking and collecting from school. It was agreed that Sheila could tailor her hours to be there for Jennifer both before and after school. The hours spent with Winnie would be significantly reduced.

Mickey had taken Jennifer to the park despite it being a cold and damp November morning. There was little to interest her in the office. Once again, she felt her mother had pushed her aside but enjoyed the freedom to run around in the park. They had taken "Mac" with them to give him some exercise. "Mac" was the name they had given to the lost Scottie; he had no collar, so no way to identify him. Mac had remained with them since Jennifer appeared with him on the towpath. The police had promised to advise the owners where he could be found if they came to claim him. The following day, Sheila had tied some string round his neck and taken him and Jennifer to try and retrace her steps. The dog showed no signs of recognition nor any desire to leave them.

Sheila brought a can of dog food and brought him back to the boat fully expecting an owner to appear very quickly. There was no sign of a loving owner yet!

Mac, it appeared, was staying!

Mickey and Jennifer appeared in the office shortly after Sheila. Jennifer went to get Mac a saucer of water and give him one of the treats which Mickey had brought along the way.

"How did it go?" Mickey asked

"Not well really. The headmaster is daunting and very difficult. Miss Williams, Jennifer's teacher, hasn't got a good word to say about her. I think I would run away if faced with those two."

"What are you going to do?"

"I'll talk to Jennifer over the weekend and try and explain that she needs to behave better. I think that taking her and collecting her will be a great help and I will try and call in to see Miss Williams at least once a week to see how it is going. I actually think that "Mac" might prove to be a God send. Look at them together, he is the unconditional friend that Jennifer needs."

"Don't rely on that, Sheila I am sure the owners will turn up any day now. He was too well fed and groomed to have been a stray. Anyway, whilst we are here, Ben and Bobby are both in the Bright Sparks office so we thought it might be a good opportunity to get together and get the boat business kicked off. Sylvia is happy to mind Jennifer in their office whilst we meet in here. What do you think?"

Sheila was torn. She would be passing Jennifer off again but the business opportunity would be good for them both in the long run and it was only likely to be for an hour.

"Okay" she said but we will have to keep it brief.

Jennifer and Mac were delivered to Sylvia. Bobby and Ben came back to the Spic and Span office. It was the first time that Ben had seen Jennifer. He tried to be nice to her, but Jennifer was unresponsive.

"How is your daughter?" Ben asked Sheila "You must have been very scared when she disappeared like that!"

"Yes, it was a horrible mix up but I think that it will be fine now" Sheila was defensive.

"She looks like a lovely little girl" said Ben "but I think she might be a little bit nervous with strangers. She wouldn't even look at me."

"She needs time to feel confident with anybody." Sheila left it at that. Mickey looked at the pair of them and wondered how the situation would play out.

The meeting was productive. Money and shares were agreed. Roles and responsibilities were discussed and next actions. On his trip to Harefield, Ben had seen some boats and since made tentative enquiries about procurement. He had identified a sixty-foot narrowboat called "Work Horse". It had a cabin at one end and was open at the other. It has been used in the main for transporting coal so would need a thorough cleaning but the boat was sound and would provide the foundation for their first attempt.

Mickey and Bobby would go to Harefield and, if in agreement, make the acquisition there and then. Mickey contacted Mr. Hobbs and made arrangements. The new business venture was launched. To formalise matters Bobby instructed his lawyer to draw up contracts defining decision making rights, ownership and modus operandi. Spic and Span's recently appointed accountant was engaged and the business was launched.

"We need a name for the business" Bobby said

"Let's keep it simple what about Union Boats?"

"Or Union Houseboats"

"Or Grand Union house boats, give it a bit of class!"

So it was, on Friday thirtieth of November 1956 Grand Union Houseboats was born.

Chapter 29

Sheila was not looking forward to Monday at the school gates. She remembered the beginning of Jennifer's first term, how the other mothers were obviously talking about her, giving furtive glances in her direction, a leper in their midst. She had avoided going to the school as much as possible since and the arrangement with Winnie had allowed her to largely stay away.

The weekend passed surprisingly slowly. Sheila had determined to spend every moment with Jennifer. She talked to her about school at every opportunity and seemed to find some common ground in their joint dislike of Miss Williams, although Jennifer was not very forthcoming. Sheila took the view that any daughter should feel that their mother was on their side but at the moment, it seemed that Jennifer didn't feel that way. Rather than spending the weekend punishing her and trying to enforce a change of behaviour in such a short period of time, she resolved to try and get closer and seek insight into what was happening.

Jennifer regarded her mother with some scepticism expecting to be scolded or off- loaded to somebody else at any point in time. She was not convinced by the leaf that her mother had apparently turned over and was not entirely sure what was expected of her, however, she was completely distracted by Mac, to whom she gave all her attention.

On Saturday Sheila took Jennifer and Mac out for a long walk along the towpath to Camden Town. Whilst they were there, they bought some dog treats and food for Mac. Jennifer's treat was a visit to a Wimpy Bar where she and Sheila enjoyed their first ever hamburger. Later they went to a toy shop and Jennifer was allowed to choose a fishing rod for the canal. Sheila used some of her Sweeney money which was now being slowly laundered through "Spic and Span". Jennifer was actually as happy buying the dog food as she was the fishing rod, it represented a permanence to Mac's status.

"Can we buy him a proper lead please" She begged her mother

"Not today, Jennifer. Let's see what happens first"

Jennifer already regarded Mac as her own and could not contemplate the idea of him having another owner.

On Sunday Mickey cooked a roast meal for them. Rufus also came for lunch and was captivated by Mac.

"I've always wanted a Scottie" he said "They are such cute little things but they can be quite feisty. A bit like me really" They all laughed except Jennifer who didn't see any likeness at all.

"Are you going to keep him? "

"Yes" said Jennifer without hesitation

"We will have to see" said Sheila "Firstly Macs owner is probably looking for him now. We should put some signs on trees saying we have found him. Secondly Jennifer and I have been talking about school and how children should and shouldn't behave. Jennifer has promised to try and be better. I have promised to take her to school every day, collect her and listen to anything she has to tell me about her day. If everything goes well, we can think about keeping Mac"

Sheila instantly regretted her words. She had linked keeping the dog with being good at school but had little control over the fate of the dog.

She quickly added "So if Jennifer is good and the owner does not come for their dog, Mac can stay"

The beam on Jennifer's face had not been seen for a long time. Sheila and Mickey had become used to the permanent, morose demeanour of a sad lost little girl. Perhaps this was turning point?

Later that day Ben and Bobby came round to talk about Grand Union Houseboats first project. They were keen to have some discussion and input to Rufus's design ideas. Mickey had warned Sheila that they would be coming, so it was no surprise. The moment Ben stepped foot on the boat Sheila gathered Jennifer and her things, including Mac, made her excuses and left.

They went straight back to their own boat, where they left all their bits and pieces before heading off for a walk. Jennifer ran past the den without a glance, or a thought for Johnny, too wrapped up in Mac to think of anything else. They passed and said hello to Bert sitting wrapped in a warm blanket beside his boat, cigarette and magazine in his hand.

As Jennifer and Mac ran off ahead Sheila's thoughts turned to Ben. Something would need to change. She could not just run away every time he came close to Jennifer. She would have to break the news to him sometime soon. He seemed like a personable man and her initial reservations about introducing him to his daughter had diluted to some extent. She thought about the effect on Jennifer who was already having a fairly traumatic time with everything at school. It wasn't time yet but the moment was approaching.

Inevitably Monday morning and a new routine arrived. Sheila could see Ronald Hudson peering at her across the playground through the window of what he laughingly called his study, the room allocated for the headmaster was seven foot wide by ten feet long, barely room to swish a cane. The look he gave was chilling. Sheila pictured him gleefully punishing her daughter, as if exacting some revenge on humanity. He momentarily caught her eye and acknowledged her with a gentle nod of his head, his smile fixed upon her face. She looked away.

The mothers around her shivered with cold, waved goodbye to their children and left to get on with their days. They were completely disinterested in Sheila's presence, not a head turned as far as she could make out. This was a surprise and a blessing but also in some ways a disappointment. She had avoided dropping her daughter off at school for months to avoid the conflict which might have arisen through their intial attitude towards her. This now seemed cowardly and unnecessary. It even seemed that last week's drama had escaped their attention. One or two women stood and chatted but there was barely a nod in her direction. The school, Winnie, and even the police had kept the incident low key. It suited nobody for a child's disappearance to be common knowledge, so it had been carefully contained.

Sheila took Jennifer to the classroom door, said a brief good morning to Miss Williams and quietly reminded Jennifer of the promises which she had cajoled from her. Jennifer walked to her hanger and took off her coat. Sheila watched sadly as the other children barely acknowledged the fact that her daughter had arrived. They were far too busy catching up with each other after the weekend. Jennifer walked quietly to her seat, sat down and stared out of the window. Another day of boredom ahead.

Sheila left reluctantly and hurried back to the boat where she had left Mac.

"Come on Mac you will have to come to work with me" she said grabbing the makeshift collar and lead. "If nobody comes for you this week, we will have to buy you a proper collar and lead"

Mac looked up at Sheila excited to be going out.

The week passed quickly. Each day after school Sheila called in to see Miss Williams to get an update on Jennifer's behaviour and demeanour. The reports she received were short and uninspiring but at least there had been no incidents to report. Miss Williams had allowed Jennifer to day dream as much as she wanted and hadn't tried to involve her in the lessons if she didn't show any interest, this seemed to work for everybody. This was not reported to Sheila who was relieved to hear nothing bad and for now didn't question the education her daughter was receiving.

Mac trailed along after work to meet Jennifer at school, an arrangement that the school were not keen to encourage but would turn a blind eye to, for the short term. The dog greeted Jennifer with great enthusiasm giving her all the affection that was missing in class. One or two of the children came across to make a fuss of Mac, who responded to them all with much tail wagging and excitement. This was as close to a sign of friendliness as they had ever shown. Perhaps it was a breakthrough!

Grand Union Houseboats was beginning to breathe life. The first project had been started. A price was negotiated for the first boat. Mr. Dodds was a soft negotiator. It seemed that his company were keen to get rid of their stock of boats and he had a large margin for discounting the price. He shared this information with Bobby at an early stage and after agreeing an unexpectedly low-price Bobby made a financial gesture to Mr. Dodds privately ,which Mr. Dodds was very happy to accept. Bobby hoped that this would cement their future relationship and enable negotiations to run as smoothly on each future occasion that he came for another boat.

The dimensions of the narrow boat were provided for Rufus who eagerly set to work on the boat's future design. The boat itself was transferred to the dry dock at Harefield, where it was treated for canal worthiness and where the shell would be rebuilt as somebody's new home. Mickey had secured a berth on the canal not far from his boat and very close to old Bert's, where Jennifer had stolen the money.

Ben and Sheila were to input into Rufus's plans, Shirley from her experience of living on the boat and Ben from the practical point of view. Where would a generator need to be, how would the wiring and plumbing work, what height should the ceilings be? There were lots of considerations for them both and many of the decisions they would take needed to be co-ordinated. All the partners needed to agree upon whom they should target. Who typically would be attracted to living on the canal. The consensus was that a young newly married couple would likely be their first customers, so provision should be made for a minimum of two bedrooms.

Much of the planning would take place at the office but everybody had their normal work to manage as well, so sometimes it might become difficult to fit it all in to an eight-hour day. Each of the partners spent a fair amount of their time out of the office. It became clear that extra hours would be needed to get the work done in the timescales which had been agreed. Ben and Shirley needed ongoing meetings, some of which could be managed in the office but some would need to be out of normal office hours. Sheila made it clear that she was loathe to leave Jennifer at home alone or ship her off to Winnies or anywhere else for that matter. She decided that Ben could come to the boat after Jennifer had gone to bed and they could get on with their work through the evening. She hoped that there would be little cause for Ben and Jennifer to meet. Ben was aware that she had a daughter now, so that hurdle had been crossed but she knew she would have to tell him sooner or later that Jennifer was his flesh and blood.

With each visit to the boat, Ben became more and more interested in Jennifer, largely because she was never evident to him. Sheila would check that she was in bed and asleep two or three times during their meetings.

"I haven't really met your daughter" Ben said one evening "I would like to get to know her a bit more."

"Yes" said Sheila a little taken aback by his directness. "It's a shame that we have to meet after she has gone to bed but she does need to sleep undisturbed. I think if I let her stay up to meet you, she wouldn't sleep properly"

"I suppose so." Said Ben "How is she doing at school now?"

"Okay" Sheila said uncomfortably. She was relieved to be interrupted by a knocking on the outside of the boat. She excused herself and got up to see who was outside.

"Hello" A middle aged man in a dark overcoat, scarf and trilby hat stood alongside the boat, replacing a glove. "Sorry to disturb you, the police sent me"

"Police, what do you mean"

"Well, I understand that you might have Jock"

"Jock, who is Jock?" Sheila was confused

"Oh sorry, Jock is my mother's dog. A little black Scottie. The police said that you had reported finding him and that you were looking after him until we arrived to reclaim him."

"Oh, yes" Sheila said "Oh no" she thought

"You had better come on board" she said. The man struggled aboard. He clambered down into the lounge area where he came face to face with Ben.

"Hello" said the man

"Hello" said Ben

"This gentleman has come to collect Mac" Sheila explained

"Er Jock – I think you mean"

"Yes, sorry we have been calling him Mac since he has been with us. Would you like a cup of tea?"

"If it's no trouble "said the man "It's very cold out there tonight and it has taken some time to find you"

" No trouble" said Sheila "Please take your coat off and have a seat Mr. er"

"Wilkins" said the visitor "Joshua Wilkins, please call me Joshua"

As the kettle whistled to the boil, a crack of light appeared unnoticed at Jennifer's cabin door. Jennifer peered through. She had been disturbed by the extra movement on the boat and the unfamiliar voice. She listened noiselessly and nosily"

"Do you still have Jock?" Joshua Wilkins asked politely looking around the cabin.

"Yes, he's asleep in my daughter's bedroom" Sheila told him

"Oh good. Thank you so much for looking after him. You must have been wondering where he came from."

"Well, we did, of course, but we had moved on really and just accepted that he was part of our life now" Sheila said whilst considering the effect that this was likely to have on Jennifer.

"I know, I am sorry. Let me tell you what has happened. As I said Jock is my mother's dog, her companion in fact. She has had him for three years and he has been vital for her well-being.

Unfortunately, mum had a fall in the garden a couple of weeks ago and knocked herself out. Jock found his way out of the garden and was probably looking for someone to help her. They are such clever little creatures, aren't they?"

"Well, yes, they are Joshua. Mac, sorry, Jock, followed my daughter Jennifer home from school, we had no idea about your mother's situation"

"Of course, not neither had I at the time. I live by the sea in Clacton with my wife. Mum has been managing alone since dad died a couple of years ago when we brought Jock to keep her company. One of her neighbours found her unconscious in the garden and called for an ambulance."

"I suppose that she wants Jock back now?" Sheila asks

"No!!!" Jennifer was standing in the doorway. "He's not Jock, he is Mac and he's mine. You can't have him"

"Jennifer, I didn't see you there," said Sheila. "This is Mr. Wilkins whose mother owns Mac and he has come to collect him for her. His mother has been unwell so she couldn't look after him for a while but now he has to go back to her"

"NO!!!!" Jennifer Screamed

"Well, that's not quite true" said Joshua "Sadly mum died in hospital the next day. We have been busy tidying up her things. I am embarrassed to say that Jock was overlooked at first and only came to mind and attention when we got to mums to sort out her home. We couldn't come right away because there was too much else to deal with. The police said you were looking after Jock so we have left it until now to collect him"

"HE'S NOT GOING" Jennifer screamed with tears filling her eyes

"To be honest we are going to need to rehome him anyway. Unfortunately, my wife can't abide dogs, or any other domestic animals come to that. We felt it our duty to take the burden from you, thank you for your kindness. Now we have to make a suitable alternative arrangement for Jock but if you are keen to keep him, that would be a good solution for us all."

Jennifer looked at her mother with an intensity which Sheila had not seen before. Sheila was quite unnerved for a moment.

"Well to be honest Joshua, Mac, sorry Jock, has become part of our lives over the past couple of weeks and we would really miss him if he had to go. We would be happy to keep him if you are in agreement. I think you can see what he means to my daughter"

"I can and I know that she, and you, would take good care of him."

Jennifer ran to her mother and climbed onto her lap and squeezed her tightly still feeling full of emotion and embarrassed by the presence of strangers.

Ben who had sat in silence throughout this exchange sat forward. Perhaps when we have finished our tea, we can sort out something in writing, to transfer ownership legally to Sheila and Jennifer.

"Of course," said Joshua who took another sip of his tea

"I believe that Jennifer has changed Jock's name to Mac. Will you be okay with that as well."

"To be honest I think he looks more like a Mac than a Jock anyway." said Joshua "We have got some things back at Mums house which might be useful, collars, dishes, beds and other dog paraphernalia if you would like to drop by and collect them."

266

"I would be pleased to, thank you "Ben volunteered "There you are Jennifer; Mac is going to be yours legally from now on, so he can stay with you forever"

Jennifer turned her head slightly and through sore red eyes smiled, ever so slightly, at Ben.

Chapter 30

Outside a primary school near the canal in Croxley Green firemen fought with the flames issuing from the broken frame of the window of one of the classrooms. Close by on a narrow boat a young boy struck a match, lit the end of his cigarette and smiled, his mother dreamt an alcoholic dream oblivious to the actions of her son.

Ben had been to the old ladies' house and collected all of Macs belongings. He and Joshua had signed a letter of sale for the transfer of ownership. Ben took the letter of sale and Mac's belongings directly to Sheila on the boat. He was keen to be able to give them directly to Jennifer. Sheila reluctantly agreed, she didn't really want father and daughter to spend time together yet. Jennifer was absolutely delighted. She took Mac's belongings from Ben with great enthusiasm but was unwilling to enter any conversation with him. He explained that the letter meant that Mac now belonged to Jennifer and her mum and that nobody could take him away. "Thanks" she said and turned away; she didn't trust this man any more than any other adult. She disappeared into her bedroom with the dog's bed eager to reunite it with Mac.

Ben looked towards Sheila with some disappointment. "I thought she would be bouncing with joy!" Sheila shrugged her shoulders and said "It's her age, she is uncertain about people. I am sure she will grow through it"

"I hope so" Said Ben "we are likely to be working together, hopefully for a long time, I would like to get to know her."

"Yes well, let's see what the future brings. Don't feel bad about it though, the only adults she really gets along with are Mickey, Winnie and Rufus."

"It's none of my business I know, but what happened to her father?"

"It's a long story" said Sheila, jolted by the question but electing to pass the opportunity "and I need to get on. Thanks for all you have done for us today."

Ben recognised the dismissal and turned to leave. "We can be friends Sheila, can't we?"

"Yes, of course"

Ben called a goodbye to Jennifer but received no reply, so he left.

Spring arrived eventually along with April rain which sounded like a flock of seagulls tap dancing on the roof of the boat. Mac had become an established member of the family and had been a Godsend for Sheila. Jennifer was less problematic; her leisure time was consumed with Mac. On sunnier days Sheila let Jennifer and Mac play in the nearby woods, much less concerned that she might wander off at any time. The three of them went for walks along the towpath and often stopped to chat with Bert. For now, life was quite pleasant.

Grand Union Houseboats awaited the completion of its first saleable product. Those involved with the build and fit out got on with their responsibilities and meetings became fewer and further between. Spic and Span continued to grow slowly, whilst invisibly laundering Sweeneys money, little by little.

Jennifer was less troublesome at school; she had even had another one of the girls, Vanessa, from school come back to the boat with Annie. Their visit was driven by the desire to stroke Mac, rather than to offer a hand of friendship to Jennifer. It was taken by Sheila as an encouraging sign, perhaps another step towards Jennifer's integration.

Ben was busy getting to grips with his part of the business and found it a good distraction from the absence of any personal emotional fulfilment. Whilst the loss of a wife and two unknown children were still painful, they were beginning, slowly, to fade into the shadows of time. He was interested in Sheila. He found her attractive and enigmatic. She was a singular character who kept him at arm's length, perhaps wary of his intentions. He wasn't sure what he had done to give her such feelings. He had been very happy to meet her again. Once bitten, twice shy, perhaps? He had not intimated at forming any relationship beyond that of business partners. He even felt some resistance to that.

He had enjoyed meeting little Jennifer, particularly the night when Mac's owners had turned up. He saw an appealing feistiness in her. He had managed to get a brief smile and thank you from her but had seen little of her since that evening.

He had also started to develop some friendships amongst the electricians with whom he worked but most of them were in relationships, some married with young families and not particularly interested in socialising. His old friends from the RAF occasionally turned up to reminisce but the RAF, and all that went with it, were consigned to the back of his mind. It was all about the future now and building a successful business. He allocated an hour each evening to go running, knowing that he needed to regain the fitness which escaped him after Caroline's death. His new flat was in Kensal Town, he had moved from the bedsit in Childs Hill to get closer to work. The flat was not too far from the canal. He started to run along the canal which took him past Sheila, Mickey and Rufus's house boats. It was a good place to run, being flat and interesting. Much of the surroundings were static but there was movement on the canal and occasionally one of the houseboats would be gone from the berth that held it on an earlier run. Much of the canal path was unmade and puddled in the wet weather. He ran past Jennifer's den and had caught a glimpse of her several times, but carried on without stopping.

Running gave him clear headed thinking time. He could reference the boats around him from a business point of view. Taking mental notes of canal life. Piles of logs sat on top of the roofs, washing drying, either on, or around the boat, when the weather allowed. There were generators for most boats, often standing on the bankside, chugging away. Many of the boats stored those things that wouldn't fit inside, under canvas on the top, cans of petrol, bicycles, wheel barrows, the list was unending. Some tried to brighten their boats appearance with plant life, sometimes with the hope of cultivating vegetables.

Curtains usually stopped prying eyes from seeing the inner living areas from the nearside, boat dwellers preferring daylight from the waterside windows, only overlooked by infrequent passing boats. Occasionally a radio could be heard, often played unsociably loudly. The owners of the boats varied from arty beatniks, to down and outs struggling through life. The characteristics of the boats clearly represented the characters inside, few boats looked as if their owners were affluent. Ben resolved to try and change that. He hoped that Grand Union Houseboats would start a trend of presentable, tidy and well decorated boats which onlookers would consider an interesting, alternative home.

One evening as he ran past the copse containing Jennifer's den, he slowed to watch her playing with Mac. There was something familiar about her but he couldn't fathom exactly what it was. He listened to her talking to Mac, as though the dog was her best friend, which, at the present, he was. His exposure to Jennifer had been limited, he felt he was being kept away and couldn't understand why. Jennifer had enjoyed her eighth birthday in January. Ben had been aware of this through Sylvia, who continued to drink coffee with Sheila at the café every weekday morning. Sylvia continued to encourage Sheila to get involved with Ben. "You two are made for each other" she would say with a wink.

She reported to Ben about Sheila at any opportunity. Jennifer's birthday was one such opportunity. Ben felt that a birthday present from him would be unwelcomed by Sheila. He did check which birthday it was just out of curiosity. It was only that Sylvia had mentioned the birthday which made him ask. He had absorbed the information but it had no significance at the time, but now as he ran a penny dropped. He thought back through his life and counted the years. It was roughly nine years ago that he came to London. It wasn't long after that he went to that party and met Sheila.

"My God" he thought. He kept running. It couldn't be that he was Jennifer's father, could it? Surely Sheila would have told him. Her behaviour at the restaurant was extreme really but he had originally put it down to the surprise of his appearance. Maybe there was more to it. The more he ran the more he thought, the more he thought, the more things made sense. He stopped abruptly and put his hands on his knees. Everything seemed to make sense all of a sudden but Ben could hardly believe it.

"Surely Sheila would have told me "He thought.

He turned and headed back towards Sheila's boat which he had passed some five minutes earlier.

Sheila was in a good mood. Her day had gone well. All the cleaners had turned up at their clients and she had not had a single issue to deal with all day. She had delivered Jennifer to school without mishap and had even been acknowledged by two mothers at the school gates. She had collected Jennifer without intervention from any of the teaching staff, which made a pleasant change.

Jennifer had gleefully walked Mac back from school to the boat and gone to the galley for a quick drink. She and Mac ran off together, promising not to go beyond the copse. Sheila watched her all the way, comfortable to leave her playing with Mac for half an hour or so.

Later as Sheila was thinking about their evening meal, she called Jennifer back. Jennifer had been completely absorbed in play with Mac, half hour had quickly disappeared.

"Aw Mum, we've only just got here!"

"Mac will need his dinner. The poor dog hasn't eaten all day" Sheila used Jennifers love for the dog to entice her back on board. Jennifer accepted that Mac would need food soon, so she reluctantly responded to her mother's call.

Ben arrived at the boat as Jennifer arrived back with Mac. He was sweating from his run and perhaps from the prospect of confronting Sheila. As he was running back he had started to doubt his earlier conclusions but he needed answers. Seeing Jennifer reinforced his belief. Now when he looked at her, he could see similarities between them. He leapt aboard and clambered down into the heart of the boat.

Mac went straight to his bowl in the galley and set about noisily consuming his meal from one of the bowls Ben had brought home.

"Sorry to bust in like this, "said Ben." I was just running past and I thought I would stop by"

There was no pre planning or forethought into how this meeting might proceed but he was here now and he needed it to be confronted, not something he could do in front of Jennifer.

"I saw you in the copse with Mac earlier" he said directly to Jennifer, who rolled her eyes and otherwise ignored him"

"What made you come back. I noticed you run past a little while ago?" Sheila heard a certain bluntness in her own voice.

"Well, as I say I was just running along the towpath and I thought I would call in. I need to talk to you" he said earnestly

"Okay, here I am" said Sheila sensing some menace in his voice.

"Alone" he said

"Well, that's fine but you will have to wait till Jennifer is ready to go to her room"

"Don't worry I'm going" said Jennifer who called Mac from his now empty bowl. They both made their way into her bedroom and slammed the door shut.

"Is it about the boat design, because I've had a couple of new ideas come to me?" Sheila ventured

"No, it's not about boat design Sheila. It's not about anything to do with business. It's about you and me and Jennifer"

Sheila knew from his demeanour that he knew; she wasn't sure how to respond.

"What do you mean? she said.

"I think you know," said Ben

"Know what?" Sheila was running out of cover

"She's mine, isn't she?"

Sheila inwardly collapsed. Suddenly nearly nine years of stoicism was defeated. She felt relief. She felt anger. She felt lost. She didn't have words so she let emotion take over. Waves of emotions stored up for years flooded out, taking her breath away and reducing her to a shuddering, shaking wreck.

Ben sat down beside her and drew her into him, feeling her emotions through their physical contact. This was the point when he knew the truth. He was a father. Jennifer's father. He tried to gather his own feelings whilst comforting Sheila. She tried to speak but no discernible words escaped. Sheila was fighting for breath between sobs.

Jennifer heard her mother's distress from her room. She appeared at the door and for the first time Ben looked at his daughter.

"Whats wrong?" she asked almost coldly.

"Nothing really Jennifer. It's a grown-up thing. I will look after your mother why don't you go back to your room and I will come and explain in a minute" Ben tried to be reassuring

"Why is she crying?" Jennifer was reluctant to go.

"Something upset her a little bit, she will be all right in a minute"

Sheila gathered herself and said "I'm okay Jenny, go and look after Mac. I'll come and talk to you in a minute"

Jennifer, felt her concern for her mother was rejected, shrugged her shoulders and went back to her room "Okay"

As they watched her leave, Sheila realised that she was still in some form of embrace with Ben.

Ben let go and sat back.

"You okay" he asked

She nodded but didn't know what to say next. The tears hadn't finished coming and she wasn't sure what they were for. Not sadness nor physical pain. Perhaps relief or realisation of a necessary outcome. Whatever it was it hadn't quite left her yet and she suspected that some time would need to pass before she was completely over this moment.

"I'm taking your reaction as a positive answer to my question" Ben said

Sheila looked at the floor of the cabin and nodded.

"Why didn't you tell me before now?"

Sheila found some strength and looked up from the floor directly into his eyes.

"Have you any idea of what the past nine years have been like for me. Bringing up a child on my own. The whole world looking at me like some kind of prostitute. Moving from pillar to post, with no hope of anything changing for the good. Then Mickey came along and everything changed, except that I am not his type."

Ben gave her a sympathetic, knowing look.

"He's been a great friend and companion" she continued "and we have started to make a good business together. Then suddenly, out of the blue, you turn up. I don't know what you expected me to do? Introduce you to the daughter that you didn't even know that you had? I've not known what to do. It has all been quite difficult for me, believe it or not"

"I'm sorry" he said "I didn't mean to accuse you in any way. I am dumbfounded really. I went out for a run about an hour ago, I was a widower still dealing with the loss of my wife and unborn children with no idea that I would be standing here now talking about a daughter! I don't know how to feel. I'm guessing we are both going to need to do some serious thinking over the next few days"

"I have been doing that since you walked into the restaurant that night. Do you want a cup of tea?"

"Yes please."

He shivered "I don't suppose you've got an old blanket I could use; I am starting to get a bit cold." Ben was wearing running shorts, a singlet and his RAF plimsoles which was his normal running attire. He had worked up quite a sweat on his run but the past fifteen minutes had made him forget. The sweat had dried cold on his skin and he was suddenly cold.

"I'll get you one. Give me a minute I need to speak to Jennifer for a moment as well"

Sheila put a kettle on the hob and left to see Jennifer. Ben closed his eyes and threw his head back. His red hair was stuck to his forehead. He scraped it back and blew out his cheeks, he hadn't expected this today! He was in a state of absolute shock. Apart from anything why hadn't he put this together before now? How could he have missed it; it was all so obvious now. His head was in a spin. He thought about the past and the future but he also had to deal with the present. He stood up and went to the galley area where the kettle had started to whistle . He found a teapot and some tealeaves and proceeded to make tea. He could hear Sheila and Jennifer's voices but couldn't make out what they were saying.

Sheila reappeared with a blanket which she handed to Ben.

"She's alright" she said and smiled briefly. "Thanks for making the tea. Tea strainer and cups are in the cupboard to the right of your head. Spoons in the drawer below and milk down there in the fridge. We have all mod cons on here. Sugar and biscuits are in the cupboard below."

Ben wrapped the blanket around his shoulders, followed instructions and produced two acceptable cups of tea, each with two sugars and strong enough for a builder.

They sat back down.

"What do we do now" said Ben genuinely

"Drink our tea and think about what just happened" I suppose

They sat quietly side by side both looking ahead, both lost in their own thoughts.

After a considerable period of individual personal silence, Sheila broke the mood.

"We'll be having beans on toast later if you would like to join us" she said casually. "I think you and I need time to agree what we are going to tell Jennifer. But for now, why not stay and have some tea with us. Then you can walk home and we can pick this up again tomorrow, after we have both collected our thoughts. I think we should say nothing to Jennifer today."

"I've got nothing to wear" I can't sit around like this.

"I will pop next door and see if Mickey has anything which might fit you. You are both a similar build."

"Okay. If you don't mind that would be nice"

"I'll pop round now. Do you mind babysitting Jennifer"

"No of course not" said Ben quite mystified by the events of the past half hour.

Sheila checked her appearance in the mirror, wiped away any signs of tears and covered up with her powder compact.

"I'll probably be ten or fifteen minutes; Mickey will need some explanation and when he gets started, he can talk the hind legs off a donkey. I'll be as quick as I can."

As she passed Jennifer's room she called out "Just popping next door to Mickeys Jen, Ben is staying for tea, so you aren't alone. I won't be long."

Ben was left alone, wrapped in a blanket, still slightly cold and still shell shocked. He had become a father, again? He wasn't sure that his still born children actually qualified him as a proper father. He had never enjoyed a single parental moment with his still born daughter or son, other than the responsibility to name then bury them. He had named the girl Jennifer how peculiar was that. Just one of life's weird coincidences he supposed. He hadn't connected that thought to Sheila's little girl until now. Now he has fathered two little girls, both called Jennifer. With this thought in his mind Jennifer appeared at his side with Mac.

"Macs hungry can I give him a snack"

Ben looked at Jennifer and saw his mothers' eyes. He felt a lump in his throat and coughed to cover it.

"Yes, I suppose so. He's got a healthy appetite hasn't he. He only had a bowl of food a little while ago. Do you know where his snacks are kept."

"Of course, I do I live here don't I?"

"Yes of course. Where are they? Can you reach them?"

"I wouldn't have to ask you if I could reach them, would I?" Jennifer rolled her eyes "They are in that cupboard above the sink" she said pointing to a glass fronted cupboard, full of a variety of food stuffs." In a tin box with a picture of a dog on. You brought it from that lady's house!"

"Oh yes, so I did "Ben said, whilst discovering the dog biscuit stash

He held the open box out for Jennifer to choose what she felt would satisfy Mac's hunger, she took three biscuits and looked at Ben to see if she could get away with it. None the wiser Ben smiled and replaced the tin lid on the tin and the tin to the cupboard. Jennifer fed the first biscuit to a very contented Scottie.

"Why haven't you got any clothes on?"

Jennifer looked up at Ben and awaited his answer.

"Well, I have been out running, in my running clothes, before I stopped here for a cup of tea with your mother" It all sounded ridiculous

"Why were you running?"

This was not the first conversation he would have chosen for his newly discovered daughter but somehow this is where they were.

"I need to get fit again" Ben said

"Why"

"Well because I have put on a bit too much weight lately and that isn't very good for me."

"You mean you are fat?" Jennifer stated

"Well, yes I suppose I do"

"I think you are fat too. Come on Mac" and she left her father with his mouth open and the wrinkles of a smile round his tearful eyes.

Sheila called out to Mickey and climbed down into his boat. She was in a hurry to update him and get his opinion on what to do next. Rufus greeted her in his dressing gown.

"Hi Sheila, Mickey is taking a shower, do you want a cup of tea"

"No thank you I need to get back but I was wanting to borrow some of Mickey's clothes"

"That's an unusual request" Rufus said with a smile "I don't think anything of his will fit you and you both have very different styles!"

"No, it's for Ben" Sheila blurted out

"Well, what have you two been up to?" Rufus gave her a sideways look which said everything. Rufus could speak with his face; he had an expression for any occasion. He clearly had an occasion in mind now and was enjoying his discovery. "I didn't know that you two were a couple"

"No, it's not like that" she began and then realised that this could turn into a saga if she let it. Mickey appeared from the shower.

"Hi Sheila, sorry you caught us off guard" he looked at Rufus and then back to Sheila. "What brings you round"

"She needs clothes for Ben, her naked boyfriend" Rufus teased

"What?"

"It's a long story but Ben is on my boat in his running gear, he is going to stay for something to eat later but he wasn't expecting to and he hasn't got a change of clothes, so I thought he could borrow some of yours" Sheila spat out her explanation as quickly as she could.

"Ben? What Bright Sparks Ben?"

"Yes, Bright Sparks, Grand Union Houseboats Ben. How many Bens do we know?"

Sheila had hoped to find Mickey alone and give him a brief synopsis of what had happened, she was loathe to have the same conversation with Rufus around.

"Please can you lend him some clothes I will explain this all, in detail, some other time"

Rufus made a silent "if I'm not wanted" comment with his face but sat down to stay.

"Of course, he can" said Mickey sensing a moment. I'll get him some slacks, a shirt and a jumper. Just a mo."

Sheila had noticed that Mickey became more camp in the presence of Rufus. Unsurprising really but noticeable. Mickey came back with a bundle of clothes and promised to call round later. Sheila returned home.

Ben put on Mickeys clothes which fitted him rather well. Sheila prepared beans on toast while Ben sat on the, rather uncomfortably firm, couch. Nothing much was said, both were running through a range of thoughts. Should we tell Jennifer now? Should we tell her ever? If we do, what should we tell her? How does a newly appointed father behave? Are there financial implications?

Ben told Sheila about his earlier brief exchange with Jennifer.

"That was about as much as we have ever said to each other you know and the last thing she said was how fat I am"

Sheila smiled. "Jennifer has had a tough time you know. She doesn't find mixing very easy. All her life people have been hard on her for something over which she had no control. So, she avoids contact as much as possible. When she does talk to people it is usually very direct, often apparently quite rude and not usually for very long."

"I'm sorry," said Ben

"For what"

"For not being here for her"

"Did you know a daughter existed before today"

"No"

"Then you have nothing to apologise for"

"Didn't you try to find me, when you knew you were pregnant. I would have done the right thing you know."

"I already told you I looked for you after the party before I even knew I was pregnant but nobody knew you. I didn't realise I was pregnant till weeks later and then it was too late, if I couldn't find you before it was unlikely that I would find you then."

"I can't help feeling guilty" Ben said "I come from a strict Presbyterian upbringing, my family will be horrified to hear that I have made somebody pregnant and not stuck by her. I don't have their religious fervour but I do share many of their morals"

"You couldn't stick by me if you didn't know I was in trouble. We were both up for a good time that night. I just got unlucky"

"Or lucky, you have a beautiful daughter"

"Yes, I do and I feel that she is mine. I am not sure that I am ready to share her"

"Is our tea ready yet? "With that question Jennifer smashed the atmosphere.

The toast had long since popped up and the beans were bubbling unnoticed in their saucepan.

"Yes, it is" said Sheila "sit at the table and we can eat. Ben is joining us for tea tonight if you don't mind"

"I suppose not. Are beans fattening?"

Ben almost choked on his fork.

The next 30 minutes were magical for Ben. He looked at his daughter and her mother in equal shares. Through the mist of confusion, he believed that this was a good thing and that everything would work out for the best. They chatted about Jennifer's day at school, about Mac, about living on a boat and how lucky they were, eventually it was time for Jennifer to go to bed, Ben wished them both good night and left.

"Why did he stay for tea mum?" Jennifer asked

"Oh, he was just passing by" said Sheila which was enough for Jennifer who wrapped her arm around Mac and went off to sleep.

Sheila felt exhausted, the cat was out of the bag. She supposed she was relieved but knew that life would get more complicated now. She expected Ben would want some involvement in Jennifer's life now and hoped that he wouldn't start sticking his nose in where it wasn't wanted. On the other hand, she still found him attractive and was pleased at the way he had reacted so far. Clearly it had been a bombshell to him but considering the enormity of the news he had received he had behaved impeccably. What would the future hold.

Chapter 31

The Watford fire station was relatively close to Croxley. The school had discharged its pupils, some time before the fire had been discovered. One classroom had been ruined and would be out of action for some months but the rest of the school could manage to resume normal activities after a couple of days and the all clear from the local education authority and the fire brigade.

An investigation of the site after the flames and smoke had been dealt with concluded that a fire in a wastepaper basket under the teacher's desk had been the point of ignition but there was no explanation as to why a fire should start there unless it was a malicious act. The teacher, Bob Baker, was a smoker but had all of his smoking paraphernalia on his person. There was no evidence to go on, everyone was perplexed as to who might hold a grudge against the school. The pupils in the class in question were in their final year and subject to the eleven plus to see where they would move next, grammar or secondary school. Bob Baker had an inkling who might have been responsible.

John Elton was new to the class that year his mother had moved to the area on her narrow boat and taken a permanent berth nearby. John had moved from his school in Kilburn. He was streetwise and tough. In his previous school he was just another kid and found it difficult to mix. His best friend it turned out was a girl two- or three-years younger, who also lived on the canal and who had an equally difficult time at school.

His arrival at Croxley Junior was a changing point for him in many ways.

John was not unintelligent but he had managed to remain uneducated. He was returned to his mother many times having been found by truant officers. Sometimes he would hide around the canal which he knew well. Sometimes he would venture into London or Notting Hill. When he was returned, truant officers usually found a drunken mother who swore blind that she had delivered her son to school on each occasion and promised that she would give him a piece of her mind, and ensure that it never happens again.

The authorities were informed and started to take an active interest in Mrs. Elton's parenting skills. Mr Elton was not a role model parent either. He lived in Camden in a flat and worked as a milkman. He only saw his son when the fancy took him and that was often just to antagonise his estranged wife. He was no stranger to a bottle of rum and his family visits usually ended in a violent scuffle, after which he took his son back to his flat as "she" was obviously not fit to bring up his child. When he sobered up in the morning, he realised that he couldn't look after his child, so he gave him some money and sent him back home to his mother.

When the authorities started closing in Mrs Elton, Primrose to her friends, decided it was time to move on. The Narrow boat had seldom moved but she was fairly sure that she could navigate it to a new life away from "that bastard". He caused her to drink and he was the reason her son was so badly behaved. She would take him away from the area, the school and start a new life. With some help and advice from Bert she managed to get the narrowboat started and following a rather eventful journey, berthed alongside the towpath near Croxley.

She did manage to stay sober for some weeks, not alcohol free but sober. The authorities in Kilburn were relieved to be rid of one of their problem families and provided scant detail to those taking over in Watford. It was as close as Primrose would get to a clean break. She really intended to give her son a chance and she knew there was every chance that if she didn't, he would be taken away from her. So, she tried.

John was unperturbed by his relocation. He would miss Jennifer but that wasn't a big deal. His mother had decided they would escape one night shortly after the ten-shilling robbery. He still had the money and many of the other items that they had pilfered over the weeks. For a seven-year-old Jennifer had been good fun. It was John who introduced Bert to his mother and asked him if he could help them start up and manoeuvre their boat from its mooring.

He was quite happy with his new location. There was plenty of open space for him to investigate and he had been welcomed into the school by his new classmates. They were falling over themselves to be friends with the new boy. This was a new world for John and one which he relished. He established a small gang of friends and for a while behaved like any other child. He was frustrated by lessons. His education to date had been sporadic, which to a large extent was his own doing. He was not interested in learning and was far behind the levels of his new class mates. Grammar school was not on his horizon.

The gang marvelled at Johns freedom to come and go whenever he pleased. They would meet at the weekend at a nearby park and he would stay as long as he wanted. He was not subjected to the same rules and boundaries that their parents imposed. He taught them to smoke, to incinerate insects and generally opened doors that they would never have dared to open before. Their theft started with apples from a local orchard. It seemed innocent enough. They were apples, how did they belong to anyone? Johnny gradually introduced the excitement of shop lifting until his gang became regulars in sweetshops, newsagents and outside greengrocers.

Bob Baker was a fifty-year-old, long in the tooth teacher. He sported a bushy moustache which was waxed to a point at either end. He had a ruddy complexion born of his enjoyment for outdoor pursuits, rugby, fishing, shooting even some bird watching. He was happiest in the open air. He was rarely seen without his bulldog pipe gripped tightly between his teeth. In class he had a penchant for flamboyant neck ties each of which he announced to his class at the beginning of the day and accompanied it with a warning that it was likely to signal a certain type of behaviour that day.

"Today my tie is purple. You might find I get angry very quickly with a purple tie on – Beware!!"

Bob Baker was not a teacher to be messed with and he liberally applied the plimsole which he kept under the lid of his desk. He had identified Johnny as a troublemaker early and Johnny was in regular receipt of a thwack with a plimsole, or a rolled-up newspaper. Johnny rolled with these punches, he had much worse from his mother and father. Aggression from this schoolteacher in front of his peer group gradually became a badge of honour. He was building an enmity for Mr. Baker as he was picked upon time after time. The final straw came after school one afternoon.

Johnny and his gang were in a newsagent near to the school. The usual game of distraction and theft was in operation when in burst Bob Baker. He had arrived to collect his monthly copy of Anglers News and his Rugby Weekly, along with a pouch of pipe tobacco.

"Elton, what are you up to" Baker roared

"Just buying some sweets sir"

But Bob Baker was nobody's fool and had seen Johnny pocketing a chocolate bar as he entered the shop.

"Come here lad" he said grabbing Johnny by the collar and thrusting his fat hand into Johnnies pocket. He pulled out a Frys five boys chocolate bar.

"Has he paid for this?" he asked the shopkeeper, who rather meekly said "No I don't believe he has"

The shopkeeper was pleased the boy had been caught but was not enjoying the fuss. He was not cut out for confrontation even with a gang of schoolboys. The teacher in front of him was clearly in his element.

"Right, you lot line up over here and empty out your pockets". Johnny and his three accomplices stood in front of the counter and ruefully disgorged the contents of their short grey trousers and scruffy blazers. Each child produced stolen merchandise to the surprise of the shopkeeper and to the delight of the teacher. Bob Barker beamed. Right give back everything you have stolen and report to me at the headmaster's office tomorrow morning straight after assembly. He scribbled a note of the boy's names so as not to forget in the morning.

"I am surprised at you Jenkins" he said looking at one of his normally brightest and best-behaved pupils, you shouldn't be mixing with this ruffian. Now off home all of you. Your parents will be informed about this and I know the headmaster will have something to say. I am going straight back to report all of you now, look lively!"

The boys scarpered, which is what boys of their age do. They all went their separate ways wondering how to explain this to their parents. All except Johnny. He tried but failed to regather the gang, in order to all to agree their stories and not own up to other misdoings to which they had all been party. The boys ignored him for the first time and set off for home. Johnny was more concerned for his loss of power than any repercussions. He had been punished many times before, it was part of his life's pattern.

Johnny held back and watched from a distance as Bob Barker, magazines and tobacco in hand, headed excitedly back towards the school. He had news for the headmaster which would be the buzz of the staffroom tomorrow and he was relishing the moment. Johnny followed him from a distance back to the school and watched him enter the classroom, when he re-emerged, he was without his magazines. He had set them down on his desk before presenting himself to the head. He practically ran across the playground and into the building containing where he would find the head.

Johnny seized the moment and ran to his classroom where he found the prized magazines of his nemesis. He picked them up, started to tear them into pieces. He gleefully threw the confetti into Barkers litter basket. It was taking longer than he had imagined. He remembered the book of matches in his pocket and threw the remainder of the magazines into the waste bin. Out came the matches. Carefully he set fire to page one of the Anglers Times. Once aflame he put it into the waste bin with the rest of the despoiled magazines. He turned and ran for the door, making his escape, unseen, across the playground.

Back at the narrow boat Johnny was unsurprised to find his mother asleep in her dressing gown. He made himself some bread and jam, then sat at the front of the boat and lit up a cigarette.

The next day Johnny decided not to go to school. He would spend the day in London at a cartoon cinema in Piccadilly. He had been there before when playing truant. The underground at Croxley was easy enough to get to and he still had money from various thefts committed over the past months. He said good bye to his mother who blew him a smudged crimson lipstick kiss and set off for town where he spent the rest of the day. The other pupils at his school were sent home, either, in most cases, with their mothers and an explanation about the unfortunate fire, or with a letter explaining what had happened, with an expectation that they would return to normal classes on the Monday to come.

Bob Baker gave the local constabulary the benefit of his insight and suspicions. Each of the boys involved in the thefts the previous night suffered a visit from a uniformed policeman at home. They were each given an opportunity to explain themselves to their parents and confirm their whereabouts at the time of the fire to the police. Rita Elton, Johnny's mother, was enjoying a cigarette and a glass of sherry in her dressing gown when her turn for a visit came around.

"Thank God I put some make up on this morning" she thought as the policemen boarded her boat.

"Good morning, Mrs Elton, thank you for seeing me this morning"

"You're welcome" she said "Whats it all about?"

"Is Johnny here?" the policeman asked.

"No, he's at school of course"

"I don't think so Mrs. Elton". The policeman began to explain what had happened and that the school had been closed for the next couple of days.

"Well, that explains why he's not there then?" her slightly addled brain was pleased with her logic "Thank you for advising me about the school. He is probably at the park with his mates. No need to worry"

"I am afraid there is a little bit more to tell you." Details of Bob Baker's testimony were shared and the policeman asked about Johnny's whereabouts after school yesterday.

"He was here with his mother" Rita Elton had no idea where her son was at that time but she was not going to let him be accused of theft and potentially arson.

"This is a very serious matter Mrs. Elton and we will need to talk to you with Johnny when gets home. Somebody will call back this evening. Will five o'clock be convenient?"

"Do what you like constable I can assure you that you are wasting your time." The policeman considered that there was little point in extending this interview and decided to send someone back later. He didn't want the hassle of a drunken mother defending her child for which he would have to write up notes. He was off shift at three, so he left.

Rita finished her sherry and resolved to stay sober today, for the benefit of her son. She would give him a piece of her mind and probably a backhander when he came home. In the meantime, perhaps one more wouldn't do any harm.

When Johnny returned, he found his mother asleep again. He'd had a Wimpey and chips and his favourite desert, a Rumbaba, whilst in London. The cartoons had been fun and he had seen off the rest of his money in a penny arcade. He had no idea that he had almost burnt his school to the ground but he knew that Bob Baker would be angry about his magazines. He smiled contentedly lit up a cigarette.

"Is that you Johnny" his mother's voice cut through the peace of the canal bank like a chainsaw. Johnny threw his cigarette butt into the canal and went in to face his mother.

"Hi mum"

"Where have you been all day?"

"School of course"

"Don't lie to me Johnathan Elton." His mum resorted to calling him Jonathan when she was really angry. It made little difference, Johnny was unmoved.

"What makes you think I am lying"

"I had a visit from a policeman who tells me you have been stealing from shops and might be involved with the school burning down"

"You're having a laugh." said Johnny slightly unnerved

Rita's head was throbbing and her mouth was parched. "Do I look like I'm kidding? Wait a minute while I get a glass of water. We have got some serious talking to do before that policeman comes back" Rita poured herself a glass of water and gulped half of it down without a breath.

"Well, you haven't been at school because it's been shut today. One of the classes burnt down yesterday. Where have you been?"

"To the park"

Rita smiled; she knew it "That's what I told him. I expect you went there with your mates when you found out the school was closed"

"You know me too well mum. I didn't want to bother you with it, so I went straight to the park"

"And what this I hear about you stealing from the newsagents"

"It's rubbish I had a bar of chocolate that I was going to pay for but Barking Baker accused me of stealing it. I was going to use that sixpence that you gave me yesterday morning"

Rita knew there was an explanation, she had no recall of giving him a sixpence, but she had no recall of anything that happened most days.

"And what happened after Mr Baker accused us. He sent us all home and said he was going back to the school. Actually, I think he brought some matches for his pipe. I came back and saw you, you remember"

"Yes, I do "she lied to herself as much as to her son

When the police returned that evening, Johnny was nowhere to be found. It took several minutes to raise Rita Elton from her alcoholic coma. No sense could be made of her drunken ramblings so the police contacted the local authority about the situation.

Over the course of the next week Johnny eluded discovery by any authority. He lived on his wits and stole what he needed to survive but he needed to get back to the boat from time to time. One time proved to be his downfall. He was grabbed by a well-meaning social worker who was assisted by a policeman. There was no foster care available for him so Johnny was taken to a residential detention centre until his future could be decided. He was accused of theft and arson and detained at her majesty's pleasure in Rochester borstal where he remained until the age of fifteen.

Chapter 32

Ben spent some time dealing with the shock of the discovery of an eight-year-old daughter. He had to examine his feelings. Immense shock of course. Guilt definitely. Joy undoubtedly. Concern for the future, yes. His overall feeling was of great happiness. He understood the challenges that lay ahead. He viewed Sheila as a strong, well intentioned young woman who had battled through difficult times with fortitude. He reminded himself again that she was an attractive and personable lady who he was beginning to get to know better and he liked what he was discovering. They had both matured significantly since that party. Perhaps there might be room for romance at some point.

He was getting ahead of himself and refocussed his thoughts on Jennifer. He saw a lot of himself in his daughter when he thought about it. She had his colouring for a start, fiery red hair, white complexion and a generous helping of freckles. He hadn't seen her smile much; she didn't express any emotions particularly strongly. She was a child who kept herself to herself, sulky, which was as he remembered himself in early childhood. He would like to get to know her more and breakdown some of the defences she had erected.

He resolved to meet with Sheila and agree how they should proceed, but he was clear that he wanted to be a part of Jennifer's life both emotionally and financially. He had lost one daughter called Jennifer and was now gifted another; his religious upbringing tugged at him. Without a real understanding of why, he thanked God. Perhaps everything was for a reason.

Ben, Sheila, Jennifer and Mac spent the next Saturday in Regents Park. Ben arrived at Sheila's narrow boat on his motorbike. He left it parked along the towpath making a slight obstacle for passers-by. Mickey agreed to keep an eye on it. They took the bus together at Bens suggestion. Sheila prepared a picnic. Jennifer was not greatly enthusiastic about the outing but was persuaded that it would be great for Mac. She took responsibility for his food and water and started to warm to the idea. Ben was still a relative stranger to her, someone about whom she felt nervous and uncomfortable.

It was late April and the weather was kind. They walked around the lake and watched the boaters manoeuvring themselves around the water, some with aplomb others with difficulty. It seemed it was more fun if you had no idea what you were doing with a pair of oars in your hands, laughter was certainly more forthcoming from the less talented oarsmen. Jennifer was issued with a set of rules for guidance of where she and Mac may and may not go, then left to enjoy playing freely with her dog. Ben and Sheila watched them. Mac was not really a dog for chasing a ball but he did take great interest in every other dog that approached. Jennifer was content to run around at Macs behest.

Ben and Sheila took the opportunity to talk.

"So, what now?" Sheila said

"Well, I know this will take some time but I would like to be a part of Jennifer's, and therefore your, life. I am really happy to have found out about her and would like to be involved with her in the future both emotionally and financially"

"We don't need money," said Sheila

"Of course," said Ben feeling slightly reprimanded "but I would like to help if I can. I am her father and it only seems right that I help you to provide for her. Apart from that, I would like to develop our relationship. We were naturally attracted to each other when we first met and I still find you attractive and interesting. Until now it has all been a little bit tense and traumatic. Let's relax and see where it takes us"

"What about Jennifer, do you think we should tell her?" As Sheila spoke, she felt she was slightly handing over control and didn't feel completely at ease.

"Not yet, I suggest we let her get to know me better and wait for the time when she is more comfortable with me. We can agree when the right moment is together. What do you think"

"I think that sounds like a plan" Sheila said happy that Ben was choosing to defer to her.

The four of them spent a lovely family day in the park. When it was time to go Ben hailed a taxi, which delighted both Sheila and Jennifer, a taxi was an extravagance in their lives. Ben saw them all to the boat, gently stroked first Mac, then Jennifer's hair and finally stole a kiss from Sheila before hopping onto his bike and disappearing into the night.

Sheila was delighted. The day couldn't have gone better as far as she was concerned, she felt a deeper warmth for Ben than ever before and believed that the future held promise for them all. Jennifer had not exactly warmed to Ben but she had accepted his presence all day and not made a fuss.

Days and weeks passed. Ben became a regular visitor to the narrow boat and continued to try to win Jennifer over. She coldly accepted his bribes in whatever shape or form they took but gave little in return. Jennifer had a life of rejection and misfortune built into her and it would take more than material gifts and a few visits to mend the wounds. Sheila was more malleable and allowed herself to become more relaxed and accepting of the father of her child. They started to meet for lunch when Ben found himself at the office, a situation which he increasingly manoeuvred. They shared each other's highs and lows. Ben was always keen to talk about what was going on in Jennifer's life and of course they talked about Grand Union Houseboats.

The first venture had been a great success and the business had made a tidy profit. Bobby had decided that now was the time to return to Birmingham. Grand Union Houseboats had invested in the next phase of their business plan by taking on two boats, one of which was going back to Coventry with Bobby who would individually fit out the interior as far as he could and seek local assistance when necessary. The other would follow the same path as the first designed by Rufus to meet a specific target market. Ben had decided that he would be the next customer, so the profile and customisation were more straightforward for Rufus. He and Ben had several design meetings. It was at the end of one of those meetings that Rufus took Ben into his confidence.

"This will be the last design I can do for a while Ben"

"That's a pity Rufus you are so good at it. What's changed?"

"Ben, I am an artist and whilst I do enjoy this work when I am commissioned, it is not what I dreamt I would be doing. I am an artist and I need freedom to paint and express myself. I am going to Paris to give my work a chance there."

"I see, what does Mickey think?" Ben had never had personal discussion of this nature before, with either Rufus or Mickey.

"I haven't told him yet. I think it will break his heart but I think we have run our course and I want to give Paris a try whilst I am young and have the drive to do so. I know it will be hard on both of us but I think the time is right. Artists have to suffer for the sake of their art?" Rufus tried to force a smile.

"When are you going to tell him"

"Soon, just as soon as this design is finished, I have a few things to tie up with regard to the gallery and my rental of "Freedom" also needs to be terminated."

"Freedom?" Ben was slightly perplexed

"Yes, the boat where I live is called "Freedom" I rent it from one of the chaps who comes to the gallery" Rufus explained "I was hoping I might enlist your support with Mickey."

"How do you mean?"

"Well, I think he is going to take my leaving really badly and I know he has a great friendship with Sheila"

"Yes" Ben wondered what was coming

"Well, he is going to need her a lot more in the next few weeks and I know that you and Sheila are spending more time together, Mickey told me, he tells me everything. I hoped that you would allow him some space with Sheila so they can talk things through when he feels the need, which I know he will"

"Of course, I will, it's not as if I live there or anything, Sheila and I share a similar friendship to Sheila and Mickey"

Rufus raised his eyebrows and gave Ben the benefit of his expressive face.

"I don't think it's quite the same but that's none of my business is it"

"I won't be in the way" Ben assured him "Do you want me to tell Sheila what you have told me"

"It might be a good idea but wait for me to give you the okay, okay?"

One day at lunch out of the blue Sheila said "I think we should tell Jennifer!"

Ben was slightly shocked that the time had come in Sheila's mind. "She must trust me to behave appropriately" he thought but he was not entirely sure exactly what "appropriately" would mean in their situation.

"Okay if you think it's the right time, I will be very happy to tell her. I am nervous about her reaction but we will have to face it sooner or later. If it's good, that will be great. If she reacts badly then, we will know what we have to deal with and can start to heal the wounds sooner rather than later."

"We need to decide exactly what it is that we are going to say "said Sheila" You are her daddy, okay but there is an eight year "where were you" issue here!"

"I don't think that anything we tell her should be fabricated. I think the truth is best. I did not know that she was going to be born when she was born. If I had known I would have stayed to look after her. You lost touch with me and couldn't let me know that she had been born, so you looked after her on your own. We can explain about our recent meeting and how we found out that I was her dad, I think that is straight forward."

"That sounds very easy" Sheila didn't sound so confident "I hope it goes as well as it sounds, but yes, I agree with the bones of what you are saying. I thought we had such a lovely day at Regents Park that perhaps we should do that again and tell here there"

"Sounds Perfect. I can make it this Saturday if it suits you."

The date and time were set. Both went away to worry about what Jennifer would think of it all but in particular, how would their relationship with her would change.

Chapter 33

On the Friday evening before the planned reveal Mickey arrived at Sheila's door. He was clearly upset and wanted to talk. Mickeys eyes were a reddish-purple colour through continuous rubbing, they were slightly closed and tearful. His breathe hung heavy with the acrid smell of alcohol. He threw his arms around Sheila. Jennifer watched his arrival with concern.

"Rufus is leaving" he said with great drama "He's going to be an artist in Paris and I won't see him again"

Rufus had not asked Ben to say anything yet so Sheila had no inkling that this was likely to happen

"What do you mean? What has happened?"

"He told me he wanted to follow his dream and go and paint in Paris and that he felt we had run our course. I don't want him to go." Mickey started to weep on Sheila's shoulder

"Why is he crying" Jennifer asked bluntly

"Because he is upset Jen, do you mind if I talk to Mickey on his own. Perhaps you could take Mac for a little walk"

"Alright we can walk down and see Bert"

"Yes but no further and don't be gone for long" Sheila didn't really want to send Jennifer out; it was seven o'clock at night but she couldn't have the conversation she needed with Mickey if Jennifer was there. Jennifer knew her way to and from Burt's boat like the back of her hand and it wasn't far.

Jennifer put Mac's collar on and left without further encouragement.

Mickey gathered himself together, Sheila had never seen him like this he had always been strong and seemingly in control of his emotions.

"Do you want a cup of coffee?" Sheila asked

He nodded and sat on the sofa.

Sheila went to the galley and made some instant coffee.

"What exactly happened "Sheila asked

"I went to Rufus' boat and found him packing some of his things into boxes. I obviously took him by surprise, which is what I intended, I had a gift for him. I couldn't understand why he would be packing things up, so he told me. He was quite nice about it but he said that as much as he liked me and living here it wasn't what his life was meant to be. That he had to do something now before his life slipped past him. I thought it was some sort of joke at first but he was deadly serious. I started to get upset, then he did and it all got really uncomfortable. We talked about it for about an hour but then he said I should leave, that he would come and say goodbye but that anything that we had was over, finished.

I didn't want to leave but he was horribly insistent and quite upset himself, so I left and came here, I didn't know what else to do and I didn't want to be alone on my boat. What do you think I should do?"

"Drink your coffee and calm down" Sheila had never seen Mickey like this before, he had always been the shoulder for her to cry on or the sage word when she had needed him. She was unpractised and uncomfortable about handing out advice, especially to Mickey.

"Has he ever said anything like this before" Sheila sked

"He has always said that he wanted to go to Paris and be a real artist, he said that Montmatre is "Shangri-La" for a painter and that his dream is to get a flat in the area, paint day and night. I thought it was just a dream I never thought he would actually go. I can't blame him for going but I will miss him terribly and he is bound to meet somebody else, so for us that is probably that."

"Not necessarily Mickey. I think it would be if you tried to stand in his way. If you accept that he has been wanting to do this for some time and for him it is necessary to happen in the near future, let him go with your blessing. When he comes back, he may well come to you."

Mickey knew that this made sense logically but he wasn't feeling very logical at the moment and his emotions were overwhelming.

For the next twenty minutes the two friends talked it through. Mickey regained some composure and even managed to joke about taking a French lover as a reprisal. Sheila suddenly leapt to her feet.

"Jennifer's not back. she should be back by now"

"Oh God this is my fault "said Mickey instantly changing demeanour. "I'll run down to Bert's and get her; you wait here in case she went the other way."

Sheila remembered the tightening of her gut last time Jennifer had gone missing and now she was back on the receiving end of Mickeys advice. She actually preferred it this way round but would not relax until she saw Jennifer.

Fifteen minutes passed before Mickey, Jennifer and Mac arrived back at the boat.

"I wasn't long" she said, "we were trying chestnuts. Bert was cooking them on a fire. The smell was lovely and I have never had one before"

"They were sitting at Bert's talking" said Mickey seemingly a bit more like himself." She seems to find plenty to say when she is with Bert, I don't know what they talk about. Look I will leave you now, you've had enough of my woes and you have got bedtime stuff to do. I feel a bit better now! You are right I need to support him going and get on with my own life, but I still don't want to. Thanks for listening and for your advice, perhaps I'll see you tomorrow"

"Are you sure you are going to be okay Mickey"

"I'll be fine, I am a big boy now and you have helped me get things straight. Don't worry about me. Get that sweet thing to bed" He kissed Sheila and Jennifer both on the cheeks, rubbed Mac's head and made for the door.

"Mickey we may be out tomorrow, we are going to Regents Park for a picnic with Ben, not sure when we will be back but not late so if you want to talk, feel free,"

"Thanks Sheila."

Sheila started to make ready for Jennifer to go to bed.

"Why was he crying?" Jennifer hadn't forgotten and wasn't going to let it go.

"He was upset because Rufus is going to live in another country and he will miss him. It's a bit like if Mac had to go away, you'd be upset wouldn't you"

"Rufus isn't a dog"

"I know but it's the same sort of thing"

Jennifer shrugged her shoulders; she didn't understand grown-ups.

Next morning Sheila heard the growling of a motorbike as it pulled up alongside the boat, there was a final red-blooded roar of the engine as Ben turn the accelerator rapidly to full before switching the ignition off. Relative tranquillity returned to the canal. Sheila's petrol generator chugged meekly on, briefly upstaged by the 500cc menace.

"Good morning" Ben arrived with flowers for Sheila, chocolates for Jennifer and a bone for Mac. Jennifer was more pleased with the bone than the chocolates, although the sweets were also well received. A thank you from two ladies, a wag of the tail from the dog and a peck on the check from Sheila. The day had started well.

"Is everybody ready for a picnic"

"I am" said Sheila with a smile, Jennifer abstained with her silence whilst Mac sensed the excitement and wagged his tail excitedly.

Sheila produced a shopping bag apparently bursting with food fit for a Regents Park family picnic "I think we will eat very well"

"I've brought cider, Pepsi cola and water for Mac" said Ben "And a surprise for everyone"

Jennifer was intrigued but refused to show any enthusiasm.

"Come on let's get going"

Mickey extravagantly called a taxi again, this time it was for their journey to the park. There was a nervous tension and silence between Sheila and Ben as they drove past Lords. They looked at each other but found no words, each thinking through the monumental moments to come.

Unexpectedly it was Jennifer who broke the silence.

"Mickey was crying last night because Rufus is going away"

"Jennifer, that is not very good manners, we don't talk about other people like that"

"But it's true, he came round to the boat crying and you said that Rufus is going away"

"I know but we don't always tell everybody what happens to us all the time." she turned to Ben and said "Sorry, Jennifer shouldn't have said that"

"So, you know?" said Ben

"Know what?"

"About Rufus"

"What about Rufus?" Sheila felt confused and compromised she didn't want to share Mickeys private life nor that of Rufus.

"We met recently to go over the plans for the next narrow boat. He told me that he was planning to leave and go to Paris at some time in the near future but he asked me to stay quiet about it until he had a chance to tell Mickey. He was going to let me know when I could warn you, but he has never contacted me since so I have been waiting for his all clear"

"So, you knew before me?"

"Yes, I knew a few days ago!"

There was something that didn't sit well with Sheila about this. Mickey was her friend and anything to do with his world she felt entitled to know first. She also knew that this was a ridiculous envy she was feeling that Ben knew before her, non the less she felt it.

The taxi fell silent for a chilly moment.

"Let's think about our day" said Ben "I thought we could get out one of those rowing boats. Do you think you could row a boat, Jennifer?"

"Yes, but who would look after Mac, can he go in the boat?"

"I'm sure we can take him on board, after all he lives on a boat doesn't, he?"

The taxi arrived at the gates of the park and they all climbed out. Ben settled the bill and they made their way into the park to find a spot for their picnic. It was a clean bright day and the sun was shining. The grass had been recently mown and the smell was fresh and light. Sheila laid out her blanket and they all sat down. All around people settled down to their days adventure. Mac was off the lead and strayed away to another family group with a feisty Jack Russell. He was trying his best to make friends but the Jack Russell was snappy and wary of the sniffing of a strange dog. Mac's persistence finally won through and the two dogs allowed each other's noses free access.

Jennifer was running not far behind Mac.

"Don't do that Mac" she said as she arrived with the dogs' owners

"They're okay let them have a sniff" said the gentleman of the party

"Is that your dog" the question was asked by one of the girls sitting on the blanket guarded by the Jack Russell. The girl spoke with a lisp.

"Yes, his name is Mac, what is your dog called?"

"Timmy" came the answer. The owner of the lisp was Susie, a young girl of a similar age to Jennifer and the two seemed to connect. They chatted about each other's dogs, breed, age, favourite food etc. and after a short time decided to take them off for a walk together.

Jennifer remembered to ask Sheila if it was alright to go and Sheila readily agreed within a set of rules. The girls and dogs ran off but remained in sight as instructed.

"How are you feeling" Ben asked Sheila

"Alright I think it will go okay. I want to tell her soon though it has been on my mind for too long."

"Me too. Since I found out Jennifer is my daughter, I have only wanted to be her father and until she knows, it won't be possible, so I can't wait to tell her. I assume it is you that will actually tell her?" He asked already knowing the answer

"Of course," Sheila had never imagined any other scenario.

"What have you told her before about her father?"

"I told her you had gone away before she was born and that I didn't think you would ever be coming back"

"Did she ask where I had gone to?"

"Yes, she did lots of times over the years. I told her I didn't know and I decided to stick with the same story, which is basically true, isn't it. Eventually she just accepted that she would never have a father and has not asked about you for probably two or three years now"

"So, what will we tell her?"

"The truth, you didn't know that she was going to be born before you went away so you didn't think there was any need to come back. Let's tell her what actually happened, obviously we don't need to go into the bedroom details, our story is very romantic in many ways."

"Sounds like a good plan to me" Ben agreed

It was twenty minutes before the girls came running back with their over excited dogs

"Can I have a drink please" Jennifer was breathless, as was her new friend.

"Of course, would your friend like one?"

"No thanks I will go back to my Mum and Dad for a while and have a drink with them."

"You 're not going, are you?" Jennifer was obviously enjoying her company and not keen to say goodbye.

"No but I will just go back and say hello and have a drink. I'll come back afterwards"

"Okay" Jennifer turned back to Sheila to take the drink being proffered

"She seems nice" said Sheila "Come and sit down here with us for a moment there is something we want to talk about"

"Yes, she is nice, her dog is called Pip and they got him from a rescue home six months ago"

Jennifer sat and drank her orange juice

"Jen, you know that Ben and I have become friends recently and he has been visiting us quite a lot really"

Jennifer nodded but was more interested in tugging at Macs lead as he tried to play with her.

"Well, Ben and I have actually known each other for a long time. We met at a party long before you were born"

Jennifer continued playing with Mac, hardly interested in her mother's words.

"Jennifer, Ben is your father" The words seemed to escape accidentally and landed with a thump!"

Sheila had Jennifer's full attention now. She looked at her mother with incredulity as if she had misunderstood. Slowly her face turned towards Ben "No he's not, my father went away and is never coming back, you told me!"

"I know and that was what I thought, but he has come back and he is so happy to have found us!"

Sheila looked at Ben who was smiling his best smile for Jennifer and wondered if her words were accurate, was it "us" he was happy to have found or just Jennifer.

Jennifer got to her feet and looked at Ben with disgust "He's not my dad!" and she ran off towards her new friend with Mac trotting happily behind oblivious to the turmoil that his young human had just entered.

"Jennifer" Ben jumped to his feet and started after her.

"Wait" said Sheila "I think we will need to give her a little space to absorb what she has just heard. I don't think we should go after her and add pressure to what is going to be very difficult to take in."

"We can't just leave her" Ben was feeling inadequate and disappointed in himself he hadn't said a word during the encounter. He felt that he had let himself and his daughter down.

"She'll be fine, we do need to keep an eye on her but she is a tough little cookie and has been through some very difficult times. This is just another one, for her to deal with, a big one I know. Once she has taken it in she will come back. If she doesn't, I will go and get her and bring her back for lunch. This was never going to be straight forward and nobody knew how things would play out. We will have to be patient"

Ben watched as Jennifer arrived with the other family who were only some twenty yards away, there were a couple of other groups between them. She stopped and said something and then turned to look directly at him. Her eyes were hostile and unbelieving. She turned quickly away and sat down with the other family who seemed to warmly welcome her presence.

Jennifer sat there for an age and then got up with her new found friend and ran off playing with their dogs, apparently oblivious to the news she had just received. Ben and Sheila watched in silence not knowing what to say to each other except reassuring each other from time to time. It was an agonisingly long time before Jennifer's friend was summoned back to her family to eat their picnic. Jennifer looked across at her newly announced father and screwed up her face. She walked back to the space which Sheila and Ben had made theirs and sat down. She looked at Ben and said "You are not my father. I don't have a father."

"I am sorry Jennifer to upset you like this and I want to try and explain to you what has happened" Ben was trying to find the right words and the right tone to get his daughters attention but she turned her back on him, crossed her arms and looked back at the family she had just left.

Sheila gestured for Ben to leave it. Jennifer refused to eat and sat with Mac in her arms looking across at the new family that she had met.

"That's what a real family is like" she thought.

Through her life Jennifer had become accustomed to not having a family. Most of the other children had mums and dads and the few that didn't, knew what had become of their missing fathers or in one case mother. Accidents and illnesses had taken them away. Jennifer had always been different. She had never known a father and had always been treated differently. She was a bastard and had been called it many times. Being a bastard, didn't mean much to her except it made her different to all the others. Someone not to be respected or trusted, someone who was in some way dirty. Apparently, her mother was considered a tart or a scrubber, she didn't understand either of the words but when she heard them spoken it was not in a nice way.

She had spent the past years building barriers around herself to defend herself against abuse. The foundation of her barriers was built on her mothers' words. "You are unique and you are better than all of them. You may not have a father in your life but that will make you a stronger person." These words had proven to be powerful weapons of defence and using them as a mantra had made Jennifer the person that she was. Now here was some virtual stranger trying to undermine her foundations, undermine everything she had come to believe. She was not having it. She had met many challenges before and she would meet this one face on.

She turned and look at Ben "I haven't got a father" she repeated and burst into tears.

Bens attempts to wrap her in his arms were firmly refused. Jennifer moved away from him nearer to her mother whose arms she accepted readily. Sheila's eyes told Ben to back off. Jennifer had been through enough for one day and Sheila would need to reset her compass which would likely take a few days. Jennifer sobbed into her mother's chest.

"It's not true, it's not true" she screamed and tried her best to hit her mother. Sheila held her tightly and tried to soothe her with soft sounds and words. Eventually Jennifer gave in and slumped into her mother's embrace.

"I'm sorry Jenny I didn't want to hurt you but we had to tell you as soon as we could. It wouldn't be fair not to" Jennifer sucked in some air and shuddered more tears out. "Ben, your father had to go away to the royal air force and he didn't even know that I was going to have you. He would have stayed if he had known, wouldn't you Ben?"

"Of course," he said "I am so sorry that I didn't know about you. I would have loved to help bring you up. I would have definitely stayed if I knew that you were around, but I didn't! I want to make it up to you both as best as I can and I would like us to all be a happy family"

Sheila flinched, what did he mean by that.

Jennifer was listening but unconvinced.

"Why didn't you stay with mummy like all other dads"

"I lost her and didn't know where to find her, a bit like little Bo peep!"

Sheila squirmed Jennifer had never really taken to nursery rhymes.

"That's just a stupid Rhyme "Jennifer said

"You're right "said Ben enjoying the opportunity for dialogue. "I was just trying to explain, why I was not here for you. I am here for you now and want to do everything I can to make your life happy"

"Come on "said Sheila let's eat our lunch "We can talk about this all later"

Jennifer could not be persuaded to eat anything until Sheila produced a small Chocolate cake and cut three large pieces. Chocolate cake was too nice to resist and Jennifer didn't. She sat and looked at Ben as though he had just landed from another planet.

Gradually Ben and Sheila manufactured the best version of what had happened to them. They made it sound romantic and wholesome rather than tawdry and sad. As they unfolded their tale, they both started to buy into it themselves to some extent.

Actually, it could well have been something romantic if fate had dealt them better cards. Jennifer was exhausted by all the running around earlier and now this emotional upheaval. She finally fell asleep at Sheila's side. They decided to end their picnic and head back to the boat. Ben scooped up Jennifer and carried her to the park gates, Sheila followed with the picnic paraphernalia. At the gate they hailed a black cab and took themselves back to the canal.

Ben and Sheila decided to leave things as they were for the time being. Ben said his goodbyes and promised to come round tomorrow to see how things were going

Chapter 34

Jennifer was confused. She had spent all her young life fighting off the verbal and sometimes physical attacks to which she was subjected. She had learnt to put on a brave face and convince herself that she was special rather than peculiar because she had no father, Of course, she had been envious of the other children she knew. She had spent a lot of time with Annie. Her parents Winnie and Liam seemed very happy together. Jennifer called Liam by his name which didn't sit well with anybody. It was clear that he took no responsibility for her. He was polite and kind but far from loving. In many ways she was an incumbrance on their family, the outcome of Winnie being too soft hearted. Through his Catholic eyes Sheila was contemptable for having a bastard child and Jennifer couldn't help but hear some of his comments to Winnie whilst she was in their home. Until Mickey came along, Liam was the closest thing she had experienced in terms of a male relationship. A sort of cold kindness and authority without any love.

Mickey was relatively new in her life and was more like a jolly uncle. He was a welcome addition but no more of a father than anybody else. He didn't lay down any rules and was warm and friendly. Jennifer was suspicious at first but had warmed to him. He expressed only affection to her and her mother, made no demands and she never heard him utter a bad word about either of them, or anybody really except perhaps Sweeney.

Suddenly a relative stranger called Ben was telling her that he was her father. It was clear that her mother agreed with him and appeared to quite like him. She was going to have to put up with him but he was going to pay. If he was her father then she currently held him in contempt. His arrival re-energised the rebelliousness that the arrival of Mac seemed to have dampened. She lay on her bed that night and for a long time she cried. Then for an equally long time she started to plot how her father would be made to pay for his absence.

When Ben arrived the next day, it was a Sunday. He had surprised himself by feeling the need to go to church and quietly think things through. The situation he found himself in was surreal in itself and the apparent vitriol expressed by Jennifer had shocked him. He had expected a reaction but he was unprepared for what had happened. He had nobody really close with whom he could discuss how he felt, perhaps he might find some spiritual guidance; he didn't really know what took him there but he did find it calming. The pastor smiled upon Ben as he did all of his congregation and was very engaging as Ben left the church. He hoped that they might see more of him in the future. Ben made some appropriate noises about the sermon and made his way to Sheila's boat not sure what to anticipate but not really expecting as friendly a welcome as he had just enjoyed from the Pastor.

It was a bright blustery day with the threat of showers. The canvas flaps on a nearby barge were engaged in a battle with the wind. Sheila stood on the front of the boat with a coffee cup in her hand and a headscarf keeping her hair protected from the wind. She had spent some time making herself look nice, lipstick, foundation and mascara, she had made an extra effort for him this morning. Ben, noticed that she looked very attractive this morning and found himself smiling at the prospect of spending more time with her. As he clambered from his motorbike, he realised she was unaware of his arrival and was watching Jennifer play with Mac on the wasteland close by.

"Morning" he called

"Oh Hi" Sheila clearly hadn't heard him arrive, despite the roar of his motor bike. She was lost in thoughts of the future.

"How is my daughter this morning" Ben asked with a sense of pride but also of trepidation.

"She is okay. She slept for a couple of hours in the afternoon and didn't mention you when she woke up. She wanted to take Mac out so we went for a walk along the towpath. I did try to bring the subject up but she clearly didn't want to talk about it and I didn't want to push it. We had tea, listened to the radio for a while and then she went to bed. There was not a peep from her last night once she had settled down. This morning we had breakfast. I asked how she was. She said fine. I reminded her that you were coming today and she just shrugged. I suppose that is slightly better than where we started but it's going to take a long time!"

"I know. I didn't know before yesterday, just how long. I was really disappointed with her reaction. I suppose I was hoping that her eyes would light up at the news that I was going to be her father and we would all enjoy a lovely family picnic, laughing and playing together. She soon burst that bubble, didn't she?"

Sheila smiled back at him and noted the use of the family word again.

"Let's see how it goes today!"

Sheila and Ben enjoyed a coffee together before Sheila went to bring Jennifer back. She asked her to be on her best behaviour and be nice to Ben. Jennifer nodded but said nothing as they walked back, Mac trotting happily behind them.

"Hello Jennifer" Ben greeted her as she reached the boat.

"Hello" she replied without looking

"It looked like you and Mac were having fun over there"

"Were you watching me?" she asked

"Well, yes, your mother and I were enjoying seeing you and Mac playing"

Jennifer said nothing

"He's a great little dog, isn't he?"

Nothing

"Do you know what breed he is?"

"Yes of course I'm not stupid"

"No, I know that, but perhaps I'm a bit stupid because I'm not sure what breed he is?"

Jennifer rolled her eyes. "He's a Scottie, that's why we called him Mac"

"Of course," Ben conceded "That was probably why his last owner called him Jock"

It was a mistake to mention that Mac had enjoyed another life before arriving here. Jennifer ignored him again and went to her room.

Whilst Sheila prepared a late breakfast Ben sat in the lounge area and stared out of the window, he wondered what his mother and sister would make of all this. He knew they would not be happy about it all. No doubt he would have to tell them at some time in the future but it was not something for the near future. The sizzle of bacon in a frying pan was comforting and the smell took him back to special occasions at home. Bacon was a rare treat reserved for occasions.

Eggs, bacon, tomatoes and fried bread were the order of the day. Jennifer stayed out of the way until she was called. All three sat down at the meal table pleasantly, anticipating the meal. Jennifer had tasted bacon before and knew she liked it. Mac sat at Jennifer's feet, his tongue hanging from the side of his mouth, salivating.

The meal was uncomfortable, Sheila and Ben made polite conversation about anything they could bring to mind. They tried painfully to engage Jennifer whenever they could.

Sheila and Ben washed and dried the dishes together.

"Do you think she would come for a walk with me on my own?" Ben suggested

"You can try" said Sheila "But I doubt she will go"

Ben went to find Jennifer in her room.

"Jennifer, I am going for a walk down to Thomas's newsagent to buy a Sunday paper. I wondered if you would like to come with me and choose a comic and perhaps some sweets. You can bring Mac.!"

Jennifer looked at Ben suspiciously.

"I suppose" she said hesitantly "Is mum coming?"

"No just us. We might be able to find something for Mac as well if you like"

A treat for Mac pushed her over the edge. "Okay" she said but I'm not holding your hand"

"Only across the roads"

Ben was delighted, this felt like a major breakthrough.

The trio set off down the path with Sheila waving them a worried goodbye.

Their visit to the shop was a minor success. Little was said but they spent some time together. Jennifer and Mac were duly rewarded and they all returned to the boat without major drama.

A breakthrough indeed. Ben and Sheila decided that little and often was the strategy to adopt for the foreseeable future.

At lunchtime Mickey arrived. The three adults chatted for a few moments together avoiding any of the current personal challenges they were each facing. Obscurely Mickey had been reading about the Russians doing widespread nuclear testing which he had read about in the papers that morning. They all expressed their concerns about what it might mean to the world but concluded there was little they could do and what would be would be.

"I think there is enough in our lives to worry about and actually I should be going" Ben announced "I'll leave you two to sort out the world's problems." This was a tactical escape and they all understood. They would see each other at work at some point during the week anyway.

Mickey and Sheila sat and talked about their problems for two hours, whilst Jennifer amused herself, firstly in her bedroom, and then alongside the boat on the towpath, within earshot of the boat.

Sheila was happy to put her worries to one side for a moment and listen. She wanted to know the latest on Rufus and how Mickey was handling things. She did want his view on the events surrounding her over the past couple of days but was happy to wait.

Mickey seemed to be in control and less emotional than she might have expected.

"He is going to Paris next month. He has found a bedsit near Montmatre which is within his price range. He has got two friends over there, a couple from art college, so he has some reference points, I think he will be alright. We have agreed to write to each other and that I will try and visit him once he has settled. Maybe in a couple of months. We are free to meet other people, obviously, and I fear that Rufus is open to another relationship, if it comes along. He is very romantic that way."

Mickey was beginning to struggle a little.

"I am sure it will all work out" Sheila assured him

"I hope so Sheila, I know he has to go and fulfil his dream so let's hope it's for the best for both of us."

Mickey took a deep breath, shrugged his shoulders and moved on.

"So how are things going in Sheila's world"

Sheila told him about the events of the past twenty-four hours.

"Well, that's not so bad. At least the worst is over, you've told her." Mickey tried to sound convincing. "She will get used to the idea as time goes by. Do you want me to say anything to her?"

"Only to be supportive if she talks to you about it. Don't bring it up yourself please I think that Ben and I need to work through this together"

Mickey raised his eyebrows and gave her an enquiring look.

"How goes it with Ben?" he asked

"I don't know" she said "he keeps referring to us as a family unit when he talks to Jennifer but there has been nothing actually happening between the two of us"

"Do you want something to happen?" Mickey knew the answer but the question was hanging there to be asked.

"Yes, I do "Sheila surprised herself with the speed of her answer. "I think it would be for the best for Jennifer."

"But that's not all" Mickey invited her to open up a bit more

"No, you're right. I liked him from the first time I saw him at that party and that feeling came back to me. I'm getting to know him a lot more now and beyond the character that I met that night, is a kind caring and compassionate man. I would like know if he has any feelings for me but it is all a bit complicated with the situation with Jennifer"

"I know but part of the Jennifer problem might be resolved if she saw you as a normal mother and father, as a pair. She doesn't see that at the moment, does she?"

"I suppose not but I don't know how to approach it with Ben. We have relationships on lots of different levels now, friends, business associates, parents, how do I move it on from there. I don't want to make a fool of myself"

"Why not use your female guiles. Invite him for a meal to catch up on Jennifer stuff, I will have Jennifer and Mac overnight, I could do with the company anyway. Use the evening to talk about you and him, candlelight and all that."

"I don't think we are allowed candles on the boat, are we?" Ben had always advised Sheila against candles.

"You know what I mean. Set up a romantic dinner. Put on some perfume, wear your best frock remind him who he met at the party and talk about each other instead of Jennifer "

Sheila smiled "I think you're right, and besides what is there to lose" maybe he felt the same way as she did and they were both holding back.

The couple talked for a while longer before realising that their attention had been drawn away from Jennifer. After momentarily remembering previous disappearances and panicking, Sheila was relieved to hear Jennifer and Mac climb aboard the boat full of energy and apparently carefree.

"Would you like a drink"

Mickey talked to Jennifer and Mac for a while and suggested the idea of a sleepover and midnight feast. Jennifer was excited by the idea and asked if she could have popcorn.

"Of course, popcorn is a must. I'll tell you what let's go to the west end and watch one of those cartoons, there is a cinema in Piccadilly where the cinemas only show cartoons. Mac will be ok on the boat for a couple of hours. We can have a Wimpy out and bring some popcorn back. What do you think"

Jennifer's eyes lit up. "Sounds great" she said "Thank you uncle Mickey"

Sheila hadn't seen her smile like that for a long time.

Ben arrived on foot at Shelia's boat early the next Saturday evening. It was a twenty-minute brisk walk or a thirty-minute amble from his bedsit. He had been able to pop in briefly once during the week to say hello to Jennifer who had given him her cold shoulder routine. Sheila had suggested dinner to him one day at the office. She had asked Sylvia to let her know when he came in and Sylvia of course was delighted to be part of a scheme to promote romance, which she instantly recognised. Ben also sensed a different tone to this invitation and felt comfortably warmed by the prospect.

Carrying flowers on a motorbike wasn't really an option and he didn't want to risk oil or grease on his best suit so he had opted for the stroll along the canal path. He had passed the still empty berth which Johnny and his drunken mother had once claimed as their own. One or two enthusiastic runners and cyclists passed him by and several dog walkers enjoyed an evening stroll. The evening was still and warm, the canal smelt of petrol and rotten fruit. Ben was not sure what to expect this evening. He felt that there would be more to this dinner than there had been to any previous meetings and it seemed right to him. He found Sheila attractive and would like to start a romantic relationship but he wasn't sure if the feeling was mutual.

Sheila had taken Mickeys advice, best frock, bold red lipstick, scented candle light, mood music and a bottle of wine. It wouldn't take Einstein to recognise what was going on here. This was a do or die situation, kill or cure.

Ben presented Sheila with the bunch of flowers.

"Thank you they are beautiful. I don't remember anybody ever buying me flowers before." Sheila was twenty-seven now and had never been bought flowers. She was moved to tears and kissed Ben, leaving the shape of her scarlet lips clearly on his cheek.

Ben felt the strength of emotion of the moment and hugged Sheila closely to him. The flowers were slightly worse for the encounter but the nervous tension was broken and replaced by breathless anticipation of the evening ahead.

"Can I make a suggestion for this evening" Sheila asked almost shyly.

"Of course," Ben was on a high and ready for anything.

"I suggest that much as we might love her and much as we might be tempted, we don't talk about Jennifer all evening. There will be lots of time for that in the future."

"I agree to your terms" said Ben with a chuckle "but first where is she?"

"She and Mac are babysitting Mickey for the evening and having games, a sleepover, midnight feast, anything which will divert Mickeys attention from Rufus"

"Great, so I literally have you to myself this evening"

"You do" agreed Sheila "Would you like a glass of wine?"

Ben and Sheila relaxed into each other's company. They explored each other's pasts again and laughed about some of their now mutual colleagues. Sheila even opened up about Sweeny and the Sweeney money. She wasn't sure this was a good idea but the relaxed atmosphere and the wine to which she was unaccustomed loosened her tongue. Ben appeared to take it in his stride and referred to it as a windfall and nothing to be ashamed about. The evening flew by. Sheila coyly invited Ben to stay, she had not had sex with anybody since the night at the party but had often relived their encounter in her mind. The tension was unbearable as he led her to the cramped narrowboat bed.

"Are you sure about this" Ben waited, they laughed " you know what happened last time!"

"As long as it doesn't make you go out and punch somebody afterwards, I might not see you for another ten years"

They both laughed and fell into bed.

Chapter 35

Ben became a regular overnight guest on the boat. Jennifer reluctantly accepted his visits but gave little ground emotionally. She allowed him to walk with her and Mac. He could take her to the park which was a little further afield, but she treated him rather more as a manservant than a father figure. She accepted his gifts and abused his attempts at reconciliation by demanding more and more by the way of treats for herself and for Mac. Ben was happy to be included and went along in the hope that there would be a change of heart somewhere along the way.

Sheila was overflowing with happiness. She had long ago given up hope of ever reaching a normal place in society, a home and a partner. A successful partnership in a successful business. Her daughter was not yet where she would like her to be emotionally but all the pieces were now in place for them to become a family unit. As time passed her relationship with Ben got stronger and more fun came into her life. Ben even came to the school to talk to the headmaster when Jennifer had one of her outbursts which sadly hadn't gone away. He was introduced as Jennifer's father to the disbelieving teaching staff and word soon travelled round the school gates.

Ben made a point of collecting Jennifer from school each Friday and started to build friendships with some of the other mothers. Sheila was not entirely happy with this situation but he had become so loving towards her that it hardly seemed a threat.

Jennifer still harboured a revenge plan and patiently waited for the right moment.

Mickey got on with life without Rufus and started to develop other friendships in the homosexual circle that he had entered. He did get a couple of letters from Rufus keeping him up to date with his progress but then the letters stopped. Mickey was upset but realised that he must move on. He planned a weekend visit to Paris for the Autumn, wrote to Rufus and waited for his reply. In the meantime, he became more liberal with his favours and found himself becoming something more of a party animal. He spent most Sunday afternoons with Sheila. This time was a mixture of business catch-up, Sweeney money review, emotional outlet for them both and time for him to spend with Jennifer.

One afternoon Sheila and Mickey were wading through the forthcoming weeks rota and discussing the pros and cons of various of their cleaners. Jennifer decided that now was the right moment to stir things up for Ben.

"Mum" Jennifer interrupted.

"Yes Jenny"

"You know you say that Ben is my father"

"Yes, he is your father" Sheila repeated for the umpteenth time.

"So, is it all right for him to touch me?"

"What do you mean touch you?" Sheila's heart stopped for a moment

"You know, touch me"

"Well, you hold his hand sometimes, don't you?"

"Yes"

"And sometimes he wants to cuddle you to show you he loves you"

"Yes"

"Well, that sort of touching is lovely"

"Okay" said Jennifer and went back to Mac.

Mickey and Sheila looked at each other quizzically.

"What was that about?" Mickey mouthed silently

Sheila shrugged and wondered.

The thought stayed with Sheila all night and she woke up several times during the night with images of Ben creeping into Jennifer's bedroom under the cover of darkness. It had been three months since that night of romance had changed everything and life had begun again. Surely Jennifer's question was perfectly innocent. She was sure about Ben but she had heard lots of stories about child molesters coming from the most unexpected places, often in the family, uncles and brothers. Surely Ben couldn't molest a child, let alone his own child!

It was Friday and Ben would bring Jennifer home from school tonight, perhaps Sheila could bring the subject up. She wasn't sure how and she didn't want to but Jennifer's question was gnawing on her mind. Ben arrived at about four o'clock with Jennifer who rushed to her room to find Mac, who was asleep in his bed.

"You're a bit later than normal" Sheila suggested

"Yes. I had to go in and see Miss Williams. She said Jennifer has been causing trouble again and asked me to go in to talk to her and the headmaster. He seems a little over keen on the cane as a solution as far as I can see."

"What did she do?"

"She slammed the desk lid down onto the hands of one of the boys in class"

"Why"

"I don't know, they don't know. Jennifer said he deserved it and that was all she would say. The teacher said that there was no excuse for that sort of behaviour and sent Jennifer to the headmaster."

"What about the boy. Did they ask him what happened?"

"He just said she slammed his fingers in the desk because she didn't like him."

"What did Jennifer say about that?"

"She said she hated him in fact she said she hated them all."

"Apparently his fingers were very bruised and he was taken off to hospital to get them checked."

"Did she get the cane"

"One on each hand. The head was there to tell me when Miss Williams invited me into the classroom. He said he was sorry that it was necessary but that she is an unruly child who needs to learn the difference between right and wrong"

"What did you say?"

"I said I thought that he was a bit heavy handed and that Jennifer is going through a difficult time at the moment. Perhaps it will do her some good, but she didn't seem the least bit broken by it she just sat and looked straight ahead whilst we spoke about her. I said that I would talk to you about it when I got back here. Mr. Hudson said that this was the type of behaviour which should be dealt with by the father and that the absence of a father figure through her life until now was undoubtedly at the heart of her problems. They had hoped that my emergence would start to have some effect but they have yet to see it. I felt like I was on trial or something. What could I say. They are probably right."

"You don't think I've been a very good mother then?"

"I didn't say that. I think you have been incredible in a very difficult situation but Jennifer can be very single minded and naughty and that is to do with your circumstances not you're parenting. Anyway, the teachers don't really help the situation. Miss Williams is a frustrated old spinster who takes her frustrations out on the children and as for Hudson he seems like a sadistic old man with a grudge against society in general.

They turned to see Jennifer standing at the galley door.

"I can hear you, you know" she said "You think it was my fault as well don't you. Everybody is against me."

"No, we don't" said Sheila in a soft sympathetic tone "tell us what happened"

"I slammed the desk lid on Jack's fat hands, it was funny and it made him cry."

"Why did you do that?"

"He called me Nodad again like he always calls me. I told him he was wrong that I have got a dad. He said I can't have because I'm a bastard. Then he went to get something from his desk so I smashed the lid on his fingers, and that was that. Miss Williams came running over to poor little Jack. She didn't ask what happened, just sent me out and while Matron took Jack away to look after him, she took me to see Hudson. He hit me with a stick but it only stung a bit."

Ben hadn't ever heard Jennifer talk for so long.

"Jenny, you can't mete out your own punishment to the other children. You will just get more trouble coming your way" Sheila couldn't be angry with her daughter's behaviour she knew exactly what she was suffering. Admonishment from her mother didn't seem fair at this point. Ben wanted to add a father's firm hand to the situation but he was not accepted as "father" yet and was still trying to find affection. He too had some sympathy with his daughter's predicament.

"He got what he deserved" said Jennifer and went back to her room.

"I don't know what to do with her" said Sheila "she is capable of being very vicious and doesn't seem bothered by the consequences."

"I am afraid that's some of my blood." said Ben "Remember that night at the party? I just hit out against what I thought was unjust and found myself in hospital. I used boxing to take out any anger that I had. Shame she's not a boy, a boxing club would probably teach her some discipline and allow her to let off steam"

"She's not a boy though is she, so perhaps we need to find another outlet for her. Oh God I thought all this would go away when you turned up. I thought the other children would leave her alone."

Jennifer lay on her bed and looked across the canal to the copse where she used to play with Johnny. She hadn't seen him now for nearly a year. She knew he would have done the same thing to that fat bully Jack.

"I wonder where Johnny is now"

He would know what to do about this man Ben who has suddenly appeared from nowhere. He wouldn't trust him either. He didn't trust his own father, or his mother either, he had to look out for himself and she was like Johnny. Johnny had managed his own life with a mother and father who didn't live together or have a proper marriage. She still wasn't sure she believed that Ben was her father. He was nothing like her, except perhaps her hair and maybe the freckles, but he didn't look like her otherwise and he certainly wasn't going to tell her what to do. Johnny seemed to have made his father go away and live somewhere else, this man was spending more and more time with her mother, who was paying more attention to him than to her. Something needed to happen to get rid of him.

Ben and Sheila quietly discussed their options for Jennifer. The school was not helping the situation and Jennifer would never have an untarnished reputation as long as she stayed there. First step they decided was to take her out of that school and find another, where she could have a fresh start. An opportunity to make friends and be a normal child with a mother and father. This was a clearly a positive idea and gave them heart.

Maybe we could go away for a holiday all together. We could spend some of Sweeneys money. This idea was very appealing and became step two. Sheila had never had a holiday herself and thought it would be a wonderful opportunity for them all to get closer. Let's go to the Isle of Wight I've heard it is lovely there. The gloomy atmosphere was lifting and the future looking brighter again.

"Maybe we should think about getting married" Bens words landed like a World War Two bomb.

"What?"

"Maybe we should get married. I feel like we are right for each other and I am sure it would work out better for Jennifer in the long run."

"But we've only been together for two or three months"

"I know but we are really getting on, we have a daughter and I think that we love each other enough to make it work"

Ben had not set out this morning with an inkling that by the end of the day he would have proposed to Sheila, he almost heard the words escaping from his mouth and couldn't stop them leaving. As he spoke, he felt more comfortable that this was what he wanted. Part of him felt that it was an enormous rush and far too soon but he did want the stability of a family. He had always been attracted to Sheila and his life without a partner since Caroline's death had been pretty empty.

Sheila couldn't believe her ears. Fifteen minutes ago, they were talking about their daughters' behavioural problems, suddenly she was on the end of a marriage proposal. It wasn't the romantic scenario of which she had always dreamed but she was long passed expecting that now. He was asking her to marry him and she was overjoyed.

"If you really mean it, yes I think that's a great plan"

They hugged and kissed in the living room whilst Jennifer lay in bed scheming.

Chapter 36

They decided to speak to the local authority in the next couple of days and find out what the possibilities were for them to move Jennifer from her current school to a new one. In the meantime, she would have to carry on where she was. There was only a month left of term time and she had been through enough to carry her through four more weeks.

Sheila dropped her off at school and made her promise to be on her best behaviour. Jennifer made all the right noises, she knew how to play the school gates game, it didn't mean anything, whatever happened in class happened and she couldn't help it. Sheila promised to come and collect her and speak with Miss Williams after school.

"A lot of good that will do" Jennifer thought but agreed with her mother and trudged off to another dreary, long day in the classroom. Jack wasn't in school today which pleased her no end. She must have really hurt him, good.

At the end of the day Sheila arrived early, Ben had decided to join her and put on a joint front for the teachers. They stood together at the school gates until the bell sounded. Some of the mothers were clearly gossiping about them, shifty eyes and speedily redirected looks made it clear that they were the main topic of conversation. As the children left the class Ben and Sheila moved in. They collected Jennifer who was first out and took her back to her class to meet Miss. Williams.

Miss Williams eyed the couple as she might have eyed a skunk.

"Can I help?" she said coldly

"We wanted to talk about Jennifer, if you have some time"

"I am surprised that you would be interested in the views of a frustrated old spinster"

Ben and Sheila looked at Jennifer whose expression didn't change, bored disinterest.

"We wanted to talk about Jennifer's future." Ben ploughed on despite the setback

"Would you like me to invite the sadistic old man with a grudge against society?"

Ben couldn't believe he was hearing his own words repeated so accurately back to him."

"I am sorry Mr. Macdonald and Miss Johnson but I really don't have time for this today perhaps you could make an appointment with the secretary and we can arrange a formal disciplinary meeting for you to air your concerns. I think the local authority would like to hear your opinions of their staff."

With that she picked up her hand bag and brushed past them into the corridor.

They both looked at Jennifer.

"What did you say?"

"Only what you said last night. I remembered it quite well because I thought it was very funny."

"You shouldn't have repeated it here" Ben curbed his anger

"You said it, not me" Jennifer looked him right in the eye.

"Right let's go"

Phase one of the plan had been dealt a blow.

Later in the week the couple visited the offices of the council's education department. The reception they received informed them that the events earlier that week were already known, no doubt including the reported character attacks delivered behind closed doors on the boat. The meeting was very formal a stern looking lady and two equally stern young men listened to their plan and with some reluctance and strong warnings agreed to seek a place for Jennifer elsewhere. It seemed the school had suggested that she be moved already. Wheels were put in motion for the September term and it was agreed that Jennifer leave her present school with immediate effect. Details of what was left of the school curriculum would be provided and the parents should ensure that Jennifer was up to the required standard before she entered her new school.

As they left Ben was astonished to see Squadron Leader Cummings leaving the same building.

"Squadron Leader Cummings "he called quite formally. He didn't know how else to address him even though he was in civilian clothes.

"Macdonald, what the devil are you doing here?"

"It's a long story Squadron Leader, this is Sheila, a friend of mine. We have been in to see about her daughter"

Sheila didn't like Ben not taking ownership of his daughter.

"What about you?"

"I took retirement from the RAF shortly after you left. I was very sorry to hear about your wife. Tragic really."

"Thank you, sir, yes it was terrible, I still miss her"

The words cut into Sheila again.

"Of course, you do" said Cummings eyeing Sheila

"So, you are retired then?"

"Heavens no, I'm out of the RAF but I couldn't sit at home and vegetate. No, I am working with the government helping with young offenders. My role is to reintroduce them into society after their term at her majesties pleasure. They're not all bad you know.

It's often their background which does for them. Given a new opportunity and some guidance many of them go on to be good citizens"

"Sounds like interesting work"

"Yes, it is, listen, I have to dash, perhaps we could meet up for a drink sometime, talk about the boxing and all that?"

"That would be great, can I give you one of my business flyers it has phone numbers and address on it. Give me a call when you can and we'll arrange a drink"

"Will do. Lovely to meet you, Sheila. Ben I'll call you." And with that Squadron Leader Cummings was gone.

"Who was that?" Sheila asked. Ben told Sheila about Cummings, and all that they had been to each other in the air force, as they made their way back to the office. They would have to make arrangements for Jennifer not to be at school from the next Monday so with that and the demands of their work Cummings was soon forgotten.

Winnie's child care side of the business was doing very well. The business employed six part time helpers who covered the hours between eight and six every weekday and eight to one on a Saturday. Winnie agreed to take Jennifer for the next three weeks. She knew how to handle her and actually thought she would be helpful with some of the really young children. This was a cost-free solution for Sheila and she was always comfortable with Winnie looking after Jennifer, she was like her second mother.

The council came up with a new school for Jennifer, it was a convent. The mother superior insisted that Jennifer would need to take part in all of their religious activities. She was reluctant to take a child whose parents professed no faith but were persuaded that this child could actually be brought into the Catholic faith. The council provided some inducement involving extra funds for the convent which helped her to make her decision. The education officials knew that the nuns would not be messed about and the environment would provide the best opportunity for Jennifer to be tamed. Sheila had her reservations but was persuaded by Ben that they could manage the religious bias and that the strict regime might be good for her. So, it was decided that Jennifer would start at St. Mary Madeleine's catholic school the following September.

Part two of their three-part strategy was a week's holiday on the Isle of Wight. Ben found a bed and breakfast run by a family with four children of their own. They were happy to allow Mac to go along as well. Jennifer actually got very excited at the prospect of a holiday, especially since Mac could come. She enjoyed the train journey and crossing the windy Solent.

The idea of a holiday was all very new and very exciting. It was difficult not to soften her feelings to Ben just a little. The bed and breakfast had a long thin garden with a shed at the bottom which the owners had allowed to become a play shed for their children. Jennifer was accepted as just another little girl and joined in with the children's fun and games in the garden. She enjoyed herself so much that she was reluctant to go out to the beach with her parents. When they did get her away, they had a lovely family holiday together. Jennifer on one occasion let her defences slip and called Ben "dad". Ben and Sheila were overjoyed and he beamed with pride and hugged Sheila joyously.

There was just the third prong of their attack to complete and Ben showed no sign of backing away from his rather spontaneous proposal. On his return from holiday, he took Sheila to meet the minister at the presbyterian church which he had visited some weeks ago. The pastor was welcoming and happy to marry them although they made no mention of Jennifer, they hoped that she might be seen as somebody else's child on the day and not cause any complications to their suitability to be married in church. Ben explained how his previous marriage had come to a tragic end and the pastor was very understanding and welcoming to Sheila.

They decided upon a winter wedding just short of Christmas and a date was set. Ben realised that he would now have to bite the bullet and tell his mother and sister all of his news. He had stayed away from his place of birth for some time now and probably hadn't spoken to either his mother or his sister for over six months. This would all be a lot for them to take in and he wasn't sure how well the news would be received. He decided that a letter would be best. There was the added complication that mother and sister had such close relations with the church. He was being less than honest in his approach to the local pastor. He knew that his mother would undoubtedly make a beeline for the pastor at the first possible opportunity, and without any shadow of a doubt would want to discuss the morality of children born out of wedlock. He would just have to hope he could stave that eventuality off, at least until the ceremony was over, by which time there would be no turning back.

Ben and Sheila decided to co-habit before they got married. It was financially beneficial, they spent much of their time together anyway, so why not? When September came and Jennifer had to go back to school, she was reluctant, to say the least, but of course she had to go. Sheila put on a brave face when she left Jennifer with a stern-faced nun outside the walls of the school.

The school was an old Victorian brick building with few windows. Jennifer's thoughts would have to be confined to the room. Perhaps it would help her focus.

At the end of the day Sheila, Ben and Mac waited nervously for their daughter to emerge. To their great delight she came out talking to another girl of her age. She was animated and brought her friend across to meet Mac. It seemed that the change of environment had been a success. When they arrived back at the boat they sat down to talk about her day. Apparently, she found her new friend Lily early in the day. Lily also had a Scottie and the two girls soon found a lot to talk about. The rest of the all-girl class were friendly and welcoming. This was something completely new to Jennifer who was used to being practically alone all day, every day. The nuns were strict but that did not intimidate Jennifer. She had grown a thick skin over the years and didn't mind being told what to do. She had hated being excluded from the group. It seemed she had found somewhere where she could grow and was welcome.

Ben and Sheila decided to leave it for a couple of weeks before announcing that they would both be getting married and Ben would be moving onto the boat. After two weeks school life had stabilised, Jennifer had warmed to although not completely accepted Ben, she would at least talk to him. It was decided that the Wimpy Bar was the best place to share their plans with their daughter and Jennifer was surprisingly calm about the news, not excited but not angry either. The three-point plan was working. Jennifer remained a difficult child but there were many fewer problems at school and the nuns knew how to deal with them better than the previous school had managed.

Ben went home and visited his mother to see how the news had been received. Both mother and sister were pleased to see him but were not at all sure about the mess in which he found himself. They were less judgemental than he expected. Perhaps they had mellowed over the years. They were not happy with the fact that Ben was now co-habiting before getting married but they agreed that marriage and contrition were the best weapons to keep the devil at bay. His mother was actually very happy at the idea of having a grandchild and looked forward to meeting her.

During the next month Ben moved in with Sheila and Jennifer. The situation was okay for the present but they both agreed that they were in good shape now, to find a house and make a proper family home. They would start to look in the new year after the wedding. When they told Jennifer she went into a screaming rage.

"NO, we can't leave the canal we love it here, Mac loves it her, I always want to live on a boat."

Ben and Sheila decided back off for now and try and lead Jennifer gently to seeing that a house would be the best for them all in the long run. It would clearly take some persuasion but there was time.

Jennifer had dropped her plans to get Ben into trouble, her life was getting better and actually he seemed alright.

Chapter 37

Squadron Leader Cummings arrived unexpectedly at the offices of Bright Sparks one morning in October. He was fortunate to catch Ben behind a desk doing some of the paperwork which was taking up an increasing amount of his time.

"Good morning, Ben" he said in his booming Squadron Leader voice.

Ben looked up and smiled. He was delighted to see the Squadron Leader.

"I am so pleased that you called in. I was wondering if you would follow up on our chance meeting."

"Of course, Ben, always delighted to see one of my old boys, especially the boxers. Are you still keeping fit?"

"Well, I run a little but nothing like I used to, I am too busy with this "he indicated the pile of papers in his in tray. "I came back expecting to be an electrician again but I seem to spend most of my time chasing up electricians, chasing up payments, writing schedules of work and quotations"

"Quite a big business then?"

"Not really, we have 11 electricians with two apprentices, me and Sylvia here in the office. Oh, and we have Grand Union Houseboats which is a joint venture with the company next door, Spic and Span"

"Sounds pretty big to me. Listen I might have a proposition which could be to our mutual benefit. Can you spare me an hour some time?"

"Certainly, sir" Ben couldn't help feeling subordinate "But it will have to be this evening I am afraid I am snowed under at the moment."

"Absolutely, perhaps we can have a pint somewhere after work. Oh, and you will have to start calling me Lionel, I am no longer your squadron leader after all"

"Ok Lionel, I will try but I feel you will always be Squadron Leader Cummings to me. Tell you what, the Black Lion is just up the road we could meet there. It will give us a chance to chat about the old days. Six o'clock, okay?"

"Perfect, see you there"

Ben met Sheila for lunch and told her about the Squadron Leaders visit. Sheila still remembered Ben not taking ownership of Jennifer when she first met the Squadron Leader, it left a bitter taste but things had changed since then.

"I hope the meeting goes well, perhaps he might like to come to eat one evening"

"Maybe, let's see what happens this evening. I will probably be late. He likes his beer!"

Later in the evening Ben and Lionel spent the first two pints catching up on their old comrades. Lionel brought the conversation back to business.

"You will remember us meeting at the council offices recently," Lionel reminded Ben "I think I explained then that I am working for the government"

"You did but I don't think you were specific about what you are doing"

"No, well if I am honest that's what has driven me to your door today. I work with the young offender's team at the home office. They thought my man management skills aligned with my service background and aptitude for discipline makes me ideal for dealing with young offenders."

Ben was intrigued.

"A lot of these young tearaways are fundamentally good; many have just been dealt a duff hand and gotten off to a bad start. They end up in institutions at a very young age and mix with other troubled young people. The government is doing what it can to reintegrate these people back into society. I only deal with the boys, who account for by far the largest proportion. My role is to place them in worthwhile employment with the opportunity to learn and grow. There have been some great successes before me and I am hoping to make a good mark of my own"

"I am sure you will make an excellent job of it, Lionel."

"Thank you. My association with the boxing fraternity is already proving invaluable. Where I can, I find employment and introduce the youngsters to a boxing club close by."

"That sounds like a good combination" Ben wasn't sure where this was going.

"It occurred to me that you might be interested in getting involved"

"Oh, I see" the penny dropped "I haven't boxed for a long time Lionel and to be honest I wouldn't have the time demanded to do it properly"

"That's a pity but it is not the main reason for contacting you. You are a partner in a relatively big business who takes on apprentices and give young men a start in life."

A second penny dropped.

"I see," said Ben

"I was wondering if "Bright Sparks" might be interested in taking on an ex – young offender from time to time. They are fully supervised and selected carefully to meet the business requirements of our partner companies."

"I suppose I would not be opposed to it in principal but I do see some pitfalls. For example, increasingly many of our electricians work in people's private homes and are entrusted with access to individuals' personal property. I am not sure our clientele would take well to us sending proven young offenders into their homes"

"I can see that. I believe that a proportion of your work is of a commercial nature or working in empty properties"

"That's true but this isn't something I can decide upon myself. I would like to help but we would need to go through the pros and cons in some detail and we would need to engage all the partners"

"Of course, there is a process to complete and everybody must be happy that there is benefit for all concerned. To be honest I think that without conscription a lot of the chaps in the RAF could have found themselves on the wrong side of the tracks. Most of the young offenders I have met are decent boys who have lost their way."

"Actually, I could see a number of our electricians as young scally wags back in the day." Ben laughed as he thought through his roster, none of them were angels. "Let's set up a meeting and see where it goes."

"That would be marvellous" said Lionel "It's quite a long-drawn-out procedure even after a business has agreed in principle.

We probably wouldn't be in a position to start for at least six months. Can I leave it to you to set up the meeting"

"Yes Lionel, you can. By the way where is the local boxing club?"

Ben told Sheila about his meeting with Lionel and was unsurprised to hear her enthusiastic support for the idea. She felt it was backing the underdog and had much empathy with their plight. It actually didn't occur to her that there may be some evil amongst them, she just saw downtrodden hard done by kids and she had some experience of that.

It was several weeks before Lionel was able to meet all the partners. Bob made a special trip down from the Midlands and was very keen to take up the idea.

"It's pretty much what I've been doing from the start really. I wonder where you two would have ended up without this business!"

Ben and Jim looked across at each other and smiled, they knew what he meant. All parties were happy to trial an ex young offender. Living arrangements would be made by the young offender's office and regular feedback would be provided in both directions. Lionel set things in motion. Somebody else from his office would have to vet the business and ironically investigate the partners backgrounds to ensure they were suitable for the responsibility. It was agreed to readdress how they split the business moving from a geographical north, south boundary towards separate commercial and private divisions. In this way there was less risk of offenders being tempted to steal from the clients. There was no point introducing temptation if it was unnecessary.

Ben found his way to the local boxing club and started to take a hands-off interest, spending a night training in the club each week. All was going well.

December came and the wedding was all set. Sheila thought that she didn't have many people to invite. When she had finished listing the members on her cleaning staff, she found that she was more connected than she knew. Each was invited to attend. Winnie, Liam and Annie of course all came along in their best outfits

Mickey was to give her away. Rufus made an appearance which was both good and bad at the same time. Sheila was pleased to see him, Mickey wasn't sure. All day he was an emotional wreck; he had started to see somebody else who was also at the wedding and Mickey found it difficult to sort out his feelings. Sheila made herself ignore his plight and focussed on having the best day that she could. Jennifer's first term at the convent school had been considerably better than any other school experience to date. She had accepted Ben as her father but kept a healthy distance from affection. Jennifer was allowed to invite two friends from school which pleased her immensely and made her feel much more part of the wedding. She was brought a new outfit which, she personally, could take or leave but it made her feel special on her parents' special day.

Ben's mother and sister came and caused far less trouble than he anticipated. They made a huge fuss of Jennifer who lapped up the attention and began to quite like the idea of having a slightly extended family. This was as close to a normal life as she had ever experienced.

Ben invited friends from the RAF and the Squadron Leader, Lionel, was on parade and brought along his wife who Ben had never met. Ben invited Caroline's family who politely refused but sent their best wishes for a happy future. Jimmy and Bobby came with their wives plus some of the electricians with whom Ben had developed a close association.

The occasion was not lavish but it was a nice event. Sheila and Ben said a quiet thank you to Mr. Sweeney whose money had been so helpful for Sheila, she almost felt a fondness for his memory.

So, they had come full circle, from a chance meeting at a party to this. Both were very happy.

Chapter 38

The Macdonald family settled into a relatively healthy pattern. Ben and Sheila grew closer and closer as the years started to tick by. Jennifer established a working relationship with her father but was never able to bring herself to love him. She had suffered too much. In some ways, now, he had taken the mother she was used to away, to be replaced with a happier version. Sheila was more focussed on Ben than she was on Jennifer and Jennifer was acutely aware of it. At least she had a balance with the girls at school now. They treated her with equality and shared a lot of interests which they grew into together.

The Catholic School structure allowed them to continue together into senior school. Jennifer was never a model pupil but her behaviour was significantly better than before and she was no longer singled out as a troublemaker, there were plenty of others testing the patience of the nuns.

The girls were reaching puberty and their interests were taking a different form. Beatlemania was taking a grip and Jennifer and her thirteen-year-old friends enjoyed the apparent anarchy which it seemed to offer. The nuns were less than enamoured with the music trends and all that came with it but found it impossible to contain.

Grand Union House boats delivered its twentieth completed project with another eight in the pipeline, four in the north with Bobby and the rest in the south. Each of the businesses Spic and Span and Bright Sparks were very successful and everybody was enjoying relative wealth. The young offender's apprenticeship scheme had proven to be a great success. Underlining what could be achieved the first recruit, having qualified and been with the business for four successful years, was given a junior partnership. Spic and Span joined the scheme, although the skill sets were less challenging, none the less the office cleaning business provided opportunities for work for youngsters seeking to establish themselves out of residential confinement.

In the spring of 1963 Ben and Sheila sat Jennifer down and gently broke the news that she was to become a sister. The doctor had confirmed that Sheila was six weeks pregnant. Ben and Sheila were delighted. Jennifer wasn't. Life had reached a balance for Jennifer which a new baby would definitely upset. She had managed to forestall her parents plans to leave canal life by screaming every time it was suggested. She knew her parents just wanted a quiet life.

This news however was different she could see that there would be little option but to move from the canal to accommodate another little human. She also realised that her stranglehold on her mother and fathers' emotions would be loosened and thus her power over them. The announcement came at a time when Mac was struggling with his health. He was reluctant to leave the boat and was no longer the active play mate that Jennifer had first enjoyed. He just lay in his basket with his sad face resting on his front paws looking up with doleful eyes, waiting for the inevitable. Jennifer was sad and worried about her faithful little companion.

The announcement that they would be leaving the canal was shocking for Jennifer but unsurprising. She did her best to make enough fuss to interrupt plans but knew she was doomed to failure. The new baby when it arrived would be born with everything which she had be deprived of as a child. The more she thought about the future the angrier and more depressed she became. Her friends were now her saving grace she had two particularly close friends both made at the convent school. Both were rebellious, despite coming from relatively stable backgrounds. Rita Marino was the daughter of an Italian immigrant who had worked hard to build his life in England. He and his wife ran a restaurant having worked all hours waiting tables for others whilst saving every penny that they could. They were buying their own maisonette but spent most hours of the day at the restaurant, leaving Rita in charge of her little brother for most of the evening. Jennifer was a regular evening visitor to the Maisonette, as was Bridget Malloy.

Bridget was the daughter of an Irish labourer. Her father worked hard all day and drank hard all evening. His wife was a diligent and dutiful mother with five other children, mostly younger than Bridget, so whilst Bridget was required to help look after her younger siblings the discipline and control for her own behaviour was left largely to the nuns.

Ben and Sheila had met Rita's parents and were happy that they were solid and reliable. Bridget's mother had previously been in the employ of Spic and Span and was known to Sheila as an industrious reliable cleaner. It was on the arrival of her fourth child that she had left Spic and Span to concentrate on her family.

Jennifer was allowed to visit and sometimes stay with Rita. This was always pre agreed. Ben and Sheila were quite happy to have more time to themselves and it may well have been on one of Jennifer's sleepovers with Rita that her future sibling was conceived.

The three girls sat in Rita's bedroom smoking and listening to their latest records. Rita's eleven-year-old brother Gino was aware what was going on in the bedroom but was happy to be left to his own devices. There was a black and white television for him watch and he had plenty of his own interests to pursue, not least football in the park with his school friends.

The girls would talk about their favourite groups and who was the best looking. John, Paul and George were shared amongst them with each, happily, having a different favourite. Ringo didn't get a look in on the romantic side of things although he was, they all agreed, a great drummer. Jennifer was a little more of an Elvis girl, she liked the wilder nature of rock and roll and would take Elvis before any of the Beatles. Walls were covered with posters of their idols. Make up became a covert pleasure, none of their parents encouraged it, which made it all the more delicious

Once a week on a Friday the girls would be allowed to attend a youth club at the catholic church. It was the activities before and after the club which were of more interest. Cigarettes and flirtations in the park. Boys had become an exciting mystery since the girls spent their days in the company of Nuns and other girls. Both boys and girls were uncomfortable with each other, both encouraged their friends to engage with the opposite sex and both were open to experiment. Jennifer's first kiss was with a spotty boy for whom she had no attraction whatsoever. She found herself on the end of a dare and unable to pull out without losing face. It was brief, slightly exciting but ultimately very disappointing. Jennifer put it down to experience and avoided any similar situations in the future.

Ben knew some of the boys from the youth club now because his interest in boxing had been rekindled. A night at the gym had become a fixture of his week. Every Thursday he would be coaching the young boys and helping them develop both their skills and their personalities. Several of the boxers had come from the young offender's programme, Lionel had done a great recruitment job for the club and believed it to be a powerful means of rehabilitation.

Lionel popped in from time to time, and chatted to Ben about the boxing, the boys and the scheme. One evening he was chatting to Ben about the scheme and sounding out the possibility of a new opening for one of his boys. Ben was open to the suggestion; it had all worked very well so far and a couple of the boys who they had brought through had moved on to start their own businesses. There was room to take on one or two more.

Lionel described the background of the potential next recruit. He had some common ground with Ben as his formative years had been lived on a narrow boat. He had suffered the misfortune of a being the child of a broken marriage where both parents were alcoholic. The mother had made no improvements in fact she was hospitalised and unlikely to see the outside world again. The father was completely out of touch and uncontactable.

The boy had been involved in an arson attempt which had somehow gone wrong but had resulted in the burning down of a part of a school. The boy was apologetic and claimed to have been under stress at the time of the incident. He had been in care for four or five years now and had gradually become calm and more accepting of the self-discipline which was required to adapt to the out-side world. He would need to be strong to look after himself and disciplined to control his behaviour. Lionel and the authorities thought he was ready. He also thought that Ben and the apprenticeship would give him a perfect opportunity to take a second chance. It was a bonus that the boy knew the area, having been brought up in the vicinity. He had also shown some promise in the boxing ring whilst confined.

"Whats his name?" Ben enquired

"Johnny" said Lionel "Johnny Elton"

Lionel put the process in motion and after a couple of meetings with Ben and Jimmy, Johnny Elton became the newest recruit to Bright Sparks "Fresh Start" initiative. On his first day Johnny wore a second-hand leather jacket. His hair was loaded with hair cream and combed back into a quiff. He wore tired old winkle pickers and drainpipe jeans with a slightly grubby white tee shirt. All of which he had picked up from a kind hearted borstal clothing provider. He was far from the model of a middle of the road, home spun, boy next door, who might ordinarily have been selected by an employer.

Ben found Johnny a little difficult socially. His ability to interact was limited, which, given his sad background Ben was not surprised about. It was all part of the reintegration into society process. exposure to more and more new people should start to have a positive effect on his social skills.

Johnny had been with the programme for four weeks and was progressing quite well. He was keen to learn about electrics and didn't seem uncomfortable with the skills required. He had spent time with three different electricians and was looking forward to helping out on a houseboat refit. Lionel turned up at the Bright Spark offices to see Johnny, he asked that Ben be there for the meeting. He had some news of which Ben needed to be aware.

Johnny looked dispassionate and unmoved as Lionel broke the news that his mother had passed away, two days ago, in the hospital.

"Oh well" he said, he didn't know what else to say, he had put his mother out of his mind long ago. She hadn't bothered to visit him in the borstal more than once. At first, he took the news of her death in his stride until he looked at Ben and saw the sadness reflected in his face. Johnny suddenly collapsed into Bens arms in floods of tears, he sobbed manfully, completely out of control. Ben's shoulder was the first he had been able to cry on for many years and the backlog of tears flooded from his body. After some time, Johnny pulled himself together and apologised for his behaviour. He wiped his eyes and spoke

"Sorry, that shocked me more than I thought it would. I think I will be okay now"

Ben suggested that he take some time off to come to terms with his emotions and to take stock of what it meant to him.

"Thanks Ben but I lost my mother years ago and have been living without her since. I would prefer to carry on working if that's okay with you. I will be fine now."

"Whatever you want Johnny" said Ben "But please let me or one of the others know if things get on top of you. I know what it is like to lose somebody so close. You may need to take some time. Let me know"

"You don't need to worry about the funeral arrangements John" Said Lionel "the authorities will handle it all. I will let you know when it is all sorted out and I am sure that Ben will allow you some time to attend if you choose to do so!"

"Of course, "said Ben

"Thank you "Johnny said "Can I go back to work now please?"

Two weeks later Johnny attended the funeral. It was a hot day at the beginning of June. He wore a clean white shirt with his jeans, as he didn't have many clothes to his name. Ben chose to go with him to offer some support. The funeral was a very sad affair. A representative from the hospital, one from the local authority, Johnny and Ben were the entire congregation. Johnny watched as his mother's body was lowered into the ground and wondered what life could have been like. He shed another tear, threw a single rose onto the coffin and turned and walked away to get on with his own life.

Chapter 39

Johnny had expressed an interest in the Grand Union Houseboat business. He and his mother had lived much of their life on a rather dishevelled boat which was moored in Croxley Green near Watford. His mother had nothing much to leave to her son and was never in a state of mind to consider the need for a will, but the boat, and all the junk within it, was hers. The local authority was happy to allow Johnny to inherit what to them was a problem and made the necessary legal arrangements.

Johnny viewed the boat with a strange affection and determined to keep it. Perhaps with some of the skills he was learning with Bright Sparks he could turn it into a viable home. For now, it was locked up and somewhere to visit at the weekend, when he could start to clean out the junk and make it habitable. The journey to Croxley from his bedsit was relatively easy on the underground and Johnny started to go each weekend. He enjoyed being back on the canal and set about clearing the boat with enthusiasm.

Ben was happy to assign Johnny to the Houseboat team. He saw the glint in Johnny's eye and thought such enthusiasm could only be a good thing. Passion for the work he did would help Johnny to turn his life around, and the fact that he had a boat of his own to look after was a bonus.

Grand Union Canal Houseboats completed another conversion. Johnny was part of the proud team who as had become custom met at the site of the new conversion and smashed a quart bottle of cider across the bows. Somebody had suggested it as a cheaper alternative to champagne and the idea had become a tradition. The Houseboat team gathered to drink a toast to the completion and to wish success to those would be fortunate enough to live on board. There were sandwiches and cake and the event was an opportunity to socialise. Winnie, Liam and Annie were always invited and Jennifer enjoyed the rare opportunity to see Annie who went to a different school now. Jennifer had never really been a fan of these occasions but she went along knowing there was an opportunity to see Annie.

The celebration was only a twenty-minute walk down the towpath from Sheila and Mickeys boats. A new permanent berth had been secured which was essential for a straight forward sale or rental. As Sheila, Ben, Mickey and Jennifer arrived at the site Jennifer's eyes were drawn to a young Elvis lookalike. She knew instantly who it was. Her heart started pounding and she gasped for a breath. Jennifer had never forgotten Johnny and often wondered what had happened to him. He was standing alone with a glass of coke in his hand looking bored. Jennifer wasn't sure how to behave. Johnny's attention was taken by a duck and her four little ducklings swimming past the boat. He hadn't seen Jennifer's group arrive.

"Hey Johnny" Ben called to him; Jennifer looked away.

Johnny turned to see Ben and his party climbing aboard the boat. He instantly recognised Jennifer and a broad smile ambushed his face. He made his way towards Ben.

"Johnny, this is my wife Sheila, my daughter Jennifer and you know Mickey. This is Johnny everybody. He is one of our newest recruits and had a hand in finishing off this lovely boat."

"Hello Johnny, nice to meet you. Good work, the boat looks fabulous" Sheila shook Johnny by the hand.

"Hello Johnny" Jennifer smiled "Nice to meet you"

He looked her straight in the eye and they both knew, "Nice to meet you too, was it Jennifer?"

"Yes, Jennifer"

"Well, we'd better get on with launching this boat it looks like everybody has been waiting for us." Ben said and left the group to find Bobby.

"What parts of the boat conversion involved you Johnny?" Sheila asked politely.

"Well, lots of different bits really. I am just learning but I have been focussing on the electrics mainly." Johnny felt quite proud to be considered part of the team

"Well done" Sheila said "It all looks smashing to me"

"Thank you, "said Johnny

"We'd better catch up with Ben" said Sheila "Come on Jennifer"

Jennifer followed her mother but looked back and smiled at Johnny as she passed him. Johnny smiled back and followed her with his eyes.

The launch ceremony went without hitch and all about the boat were enjoying a glass of something and a bit to eat. Bobby had said a few words to launch and name the boat. Following a smattering of applause people broke into smaller groups and chatted excitedly about the boat. Jennifer found Johnny.

"What happened" the words spilled from her mouth. They had been waiting to escape since she first saw the empty berth his mother's boat had left several years before.

"Wow you've grown up" were Johnny's first words. Jennifer was maturing and growing into her body. She had started to fill out and was becoming quite shapely.

"So have you. I like your quiff"

"Thanks"

"So, what happened"

Johnny gave Jennifer a short history of the night his mother decided to start a new life somewhere else and told her much of what ensued. Jennifer shared a potted history of events in her life. Time seemed to slip by. Johnny and Jennifer were suddenly back to their comfort zone. They completely understood each other and the intermittent years were forgotten.

Later in the afternoon they heard

"Jennifer, we have to go now." It was Sheila.

"Aw Mum, can't I come back home later on my own"

"No, you can't. Come on now say goodbye and let's get going, nice to meet you Johnny"

Sheila turned and left.

"Can I meet you some time?" Johnny asked.

"Of course," said Jennifer and she gave Johnny details of the youth club, times, address and details of the park where they met beforehand.

"I'll see you Friday" he said.

The week dragged by for Jennifer. She couldn't wait till Monday to tell Bridget and Rita about her exciting meeting with Johnny at the canal. She gave the girls the full history of their relationship, even describing their thieving exploits, which the girls found thrilling. They couldn't wait to meet him and he became the focus of conversation for every spare moment of their week. Each day past agonisingly slowly. On Thursday Jennifer casually mentioned to her mother that Rita had invited her to stay on Friday after the youth club because Rita would be babysitting. With numerous assurances Sheila agreed leaving the evening free for Jennifer to spend with Johnny. She had no intention of going to the youth club that night.

Friday came and the three girls spent the early evening dressing up in their favourite clothes. Mascara and lipstick were applied aplenty. Rita's little brother was speechless when the girls emerged from Rita's bedroom. He had seen them playing with make up before but this was a full makeover. The girls looked to him like young women.

"Where are you lot going?"

"Just to the youth club, we will be back at nine as usual" Rita said as if everything was normal

"Blimey" he said lost for any other words.

The girls set off for the park. As they walked down the street, they were getting more than a few heads turning to look at them. This hadn't happened before and they took it as a complement. Many of the thought inside the turned heads were about young girls being allowed out made up like tarts. The girls took the looks to be complementary and put a little extra bounce into their step. At the park they decided to sit in the shelter beside the playground and have a cigarette. Some of the usual lads arrived and started wolf whistling and calling out. Rita and Bridget were happy to be admired in such a way, Jennifer was just looking for Johnny.

Finally, he arrived. He had come straight from work and had no time, or inclination, to change. He combed back his quiff as he walked across the park towards them.

"God, he's lovely" said Rita before he reached earshot. "What are you going to do?"

"Don't know yet, let's see what happens, but I don't want to go into that youth club with him." Jennifer was looking at a working man, not a boy like the others who went to youth clubs. Johnny was better than that.

"Hi girls" Johnny was much more confident in the presence of three young giggly girls, he felt that he had the upper hand. The girls giggled and said "Hi" back. This was all very rock and roll, hi, not hello!!

Jennifer introduced Johnny to the girls as an old friend of hers who had just moved back into the area. The girls knew everything about Johnny already so the introduction was just to break the ice. Johnny sat down with them and got a cigarette out of his breast pocket and impressively lit up with the use of a cigarette lighter with a flip top. The girls were more impressed. They sat and talked about music, jobs, schools, boats and anything that came to mind really. Jennifer was enjoying showing Johnny off but secretly wanting him to herself.

"Shall we go for a walk" she said in the midst of Bridget's monologue about the Everly Brothers' music.

"Sure "he said

Rita and Bridget looked at each other and giggled. "Have fun" they said in harmony.

Johnny stood up and to Jennifer's delight took her hand in his.

"See you later girls" he said

"Mum and Dad will be back about eleven thirty" said Rita giving Jennifer and Johnny about three hours together.

They decided to stroll down by the canal and go and see some of their old haunts. Jennifer was walking on air; she couldn't believe this was happening. As they reached the canal Johnny turned and kissed her gently on the cheek. Jennifer took all her experiences with the spotty boy and employed it. She kissed Johnny full on the lips. Neither of them had any experience beyond this in the matters of romance but they had both had a million conversations with their friends about what happens between a man and woman. They soon found their way to a fully-fledged no holds barred French kiss. It was magical for them both. They both laughed with joy as their lips parted.

Jennifer thought of the spotty boy who had first kissed her and realised what a waste of time that had been.

The couple walked, hand in hand, along the towpath, laughing and reminiscing about the past. They remembered each boat that they had stolen from and compiled a mental list of swag.

"What happened to that ten-shilling note, I was furious with you for going away, but even more furious for stealing my ten-bob note" Jennifer laughed

"I felt very guilty spending it and I thought of you but I was far, far away so what could I do" Johnny lied

"Let's go to the hide" Johnny said

"No, we can't it's too near to our boat. I don't want mum to see me, she thinks I am at Rita's"

"Perhaps another time when your mum isn't around. We can go and cremate some spiders" They both laughed but both wanted to go back to those days for a moment.

"You know I have a boat of my own, don't you?"

Jennifer didn't know.

"It was my mother's but she died and left it to me so I am doing it up at the weekends."

"Wow where is it" Jennifer said "I can help you"

"It might be difficult it's up at Croxley which is a bit of a journey, I go there every weekend and do some work on it. It would be nice if you could come one time but I am not sure your parents would agree to it"

"Maybe" said Jennifer "Let me think about it, I might be able to escape for a day"

Johnny walked Jennifer to Rita's house. They spent fifteen minutes enjoying their new found kissing skills. They didn't want to stop but knew that mum and dad Marino would be back soon and they didn't want to be discovered. They said good night and agreed to meet again next Friday

Jennifer knocked quietly on the door and an excited Rita opened it up desperate to hear Jennifer tell her everything that had happened. They got ready for bed, where they sat and talked for the next two hours. Jennifer didn't mention the Croxley boat. That was going to be their secret. Jennifer listened as Rita told her about their evening. Apparently, Johnny's appearance had spurred some of the boys at the youth club to get a little bolder and both Rita and Bridget had enjoyed a kiss and a cuddle in the shelter, after the youth club had turned out. Rita's suiter had managed to get his hands inside Rita's bra which added a bigger thrill to the evening. Rita had quite liked it.

Another long week passed. Jennifer could think of nothing but Johnny and somehow getting to help him on his boat. They met at the park again and spent a similar evening Rita and Bridget's new "boyfriends" were schoolboys and somehow much younger than Johnny, who had no interest in meeting them at all. Much kissing was enjoyed but at the end of the evening Jennifer was a little disappointed that Johnny seemed to have no interest in her jumper at all.

"I think I can get away next Saturday and come and help on the boat if you want me to!"

"That would be great but what will you tell Sheila and Ben."

"They 're a bit focussed on baby stuff and finding a new home at the moment. They asked me if I want to go with them and help choose a house next Saturday. I said no and if they don't mind, I will spend the day with Bridget. They didn't seem to mind. To be honest I think they would be happier that I don't go. So, I can come to Croxley and be with you all day!"

"That's great as long as Ben doesn't find out. He'd sack me and I'd probably end up back in borstal"
said Johnny sounding uncharacteristically worried.
"They'll never know" said Jennifer "how could they find out?"

So, it was decided and a week later, Jennifer and Johnny took the underground to Croxley Green. Jennifer stole a little money from her mother's still substantial stash, knowing it wouldn't be missed. Johnny took Jennifer to the newsagents from where he and his school friends used to steal. The shopkeeper, who was the same man didn't seem to recognise Johnny and was happy to sell them cigarettes, he thought Johnny might be old enough. Johnny couldn't help stealing a box of chocolates for old times' sake. They both remembered the thrill of stealing and getting away with it. Johnny presented the chocolates to Jennifer who was thrilled at the romance of the gesture.

He then took Jennifer to see the school that he had burnt down. He told Jennifer about his old teacher and she agreed that he had it coming to him. Jennifer was suitably impressed and wished she had possessed the courage to burn down Miss Williams class and incinerate Mr. Hudson at the same time.

Jennifer and Johnny were not good company for each other but neither of them saw it that way. They were two children in maturing bodies, who had yet to fully grow up mentally. They showed off to each other without parental control.

Johnny took Jennifer to the boat and after a passionate bout of kissing the pair decided to do some clearing up. This could be a bolt hole for the future for them both. They would have to be careful but if they planned things right, they could enjoy each other's company without anybody interfering. They took to their tasks with enthusiasm.

Johnny had already cleared a lot of the rubbish from the boat, in particular all his mother clothes had gone on his first visit. He couldn't bear to think of her. He had started to work in her bedroom which was now relatively clear. The next room to attack was his old bedroom which was small and wouldn't accommodate them both.

"I'll clear this and you can start on the galley" Johnny said

Jennifer happily got on with the cleaning. Her mother wouldn't recognise her. The couple worked hard at their tasks. They stopped for lunch and took a walk to nearby Cassiobury Park before returning to the boat. The afternoon passed quickly and soon they realised that Jennifer would have to leave if her secret wasn't to be uncovered.

Johnny walked her to the underground station. They kissed goodbye passionately.

"I wish I could stay all weekend" Jennifer said

"That would be nice one day"

Jennifer boarded the train and made her way home.

She got in at about five thirty.

"Did you have a good time" Sheila asked

"Yes, we went to the park with two of Bridget's sisters and played with them on the swings and stuff"

"Aw that's nice"

"Did you find a house?"

"Yes. I think we are going to make an offer on a house in Burnt Oak. It's a lovely three-bedroom semidetached house with a lovely garden. I think you will love it."

"I doubt it. I like the canal. Is it near to the canal?"

"No not really"

"Is it near to my school?"

"Well, no you will probably have to change schools but think how well that worked out last time you changed"

"So, I won't see Bridget and Rita any more, typical, you never think of me do you. It's all about you and Ben and now that baby, I can go to hell. Well thanks." Jennifer ran crying to her bedroom.

Sheila looked at Ben, who shrugged his shoulders.

"She'll come round when she sees her bedroom. Leave her for now you won't get anywhere, you know how stubborn she is"

Sheila and Ben tried to approach the subject again on Sunday but Jennifer was not to be moved.

"I am going to lose my two friends; you know how horrible that will be for me"

"They can come and stay for the weekends. You won't lose them"

"Can I stay with them for the whole weekend as well? You won't let me stay all weekend now, just overnight"

"You are a little older now, so, yes if their parents agree you can stay all weekend" Sheila was unhappy with her words but she was in a negotiation and had to make some concessions. Ben would be happy for Jennifer to be out of their hair for a whole weekend, so he had no problem agreeing to this.

"Can I stay with Rita next weekend then"

"Well, yes I suppose so if her parents don't mind"

"Rita's parents like it when I stay there because Rita isn't on her own then"

"Okay Jennifer, here is the deal. You come and see the house with us and we will allow you to stay with Rita next weekend. I am sure when you see the house you will love it"

"Okay, deal" Jennifer smiled to herself. She would go and see their stupid house and then spend the weekend on the boat where she would rather be.

The house was actually quite nice as it turned out. Ben and Sheila took Jennifer in the back of Bens new company van. She had to sit amongst Bens tools and various electrical stores but the journey wasn't too long. The area was quite pleasant and green. Her designated new bedroom was relatively massive compared with where she slept on the boat. The garden was very appealing to Jennifer, ideal for her and a dog to play to their hearts content. Jennifer was slightly weakening. The house also represented the opportunity to spend more time with Johnny. That alone was a plus. Jennifer relaxed her stance against moving and Sheila celebrated a victory.

Jennifer met Johnny at the park next Friday and gave him a big kiss.

"Guess what?" she said

"I don't know, what?"

"I am coming to spend the weekend with you" Jennifer squealed and showed Johnny her duffle bag.

Johnny was a little taken aback.

"How come?"

Jennifer told him about her masterful negotiation.

"Every cloud has a silver lining" she smiled mischievously

"Well let's go then." Johnny said and they set off for the underground. It was raining which was unsurprising for a British summer, but they ran and splashed in the puddles excited for the weekend ahead.

Chapter 40

Jennifer and Johnny thought they discovered their adult selves on that boat that weekend.

The first night was a honeymoon and they discovered sexual appetites that they hadn't understood prior to the Friday. They hid away on the boat for the entire weekend. They still made a surprising amount of progress in the cleaning and clearing of the boat but they wasted no opportunity to return to the bedroom and the carnal pleasures it had to offer. Jennifer was still only thirteen. John was fifteen. They had both had suffered lives which most other children of their age wouldn't understand and the sense of finding themselves and their independence was overwhelming.

They returned to their separate lives on the Sunday afternoon. Jennifer lied her way through the inquisition about her weekend. Fortunately, neither Ben nor Sheila felt it necessary to check up on her and Jennifer had ensured she was back early enough not to cause any worry.

During the week Mac took a turn for the worse. Ben took him and Jennifer to the nearest vet for advice and treatment. The advice was that Mac was not enjoying life, there was no cure for his ailments, he was just on old dog and he should be put down. Jennifer was devastated. She refused to believe there was nothing that could be done. Ben had to make Jennifer see that bringing him back home would only prolong his pain and discomfort. Jennifer was left to say goodbye to Mac in a room all alone. When the time came, she cradled him in her arms and sobbed like she had never sobbed before as the vet injected death into her little friend.

Ben took Jennifer home. She was broken. She cried herself to sleep that night and refused to get up for school the next day. She went and sat in the copse opposite the boat, where she and Johnny used to play. Johnny was all she had left now. Her mother and new father were focussed on their new home and their new child. She was soon to move away from her two best friends to a place where she knew no-one, and would have to start again. Johnny was the best thing in her life.

On Friday she met Johnny at the park and despite their concerns about being seen, took him back to their copse. They were careful to stay out of sight of the boat. When they got there Jennifer had taken a blanket for them to huddle underneath and make love on.

"I only want to be with you Johnny. There is nothing else in my life. I want to run away and be with you"

"Jennifer, I want to be with you as well but I can't run away I've got to keep working and the authorities don't leave me alone till I am sixteen. I have monthly visits to assess my development. Anyway where would we go?"

"The boat, we could go to the boat" Jennifers eyes lit up.

"No Jennifer that's not going to work. We can go there for weekends but we can't run away there."

"I can. You can stay and work and I can run away and stay on the boat. I can look after you "

Even Johnny realised that this was delusional.

"No Jen, we're too young we would never get away with it. We would need a lot of money and we haven't got any. It's better the way we are for now. Let's keep the boat as an escape for just us. We'll go as often as we can and when I can leave and get a job somewhere else then we'll look at running away. I promise"

Jennifer cried again. She knew he was right but just wanted to get out of this world where everything seemed to go wrong for her.

"Promise me, we will go as soon as we can and that you will never leave me"

"I promise"

Jennifer and Johnny stayed together wrapped in the blanket until it was a reasonable time for her to arrive back at the boat. He left her out of sight of the boat and made his way back home. Jennifer trudged sadly back to the boat to await another week before she would see him again. She had to conjure up another reason for being away for a whole weekend without causing suspicion. She shouted hello as she climbed onto the boat and went straight to her empty room. Mac's bed lay forlornly empty.

As she lay in bed, she thought about the evening she had just spent with Johnny and all that had been said. "He promised to run away with me as soon as we can. We'll go somewhere that nobody knows us and make a new start." It never occurred to her that this was what Johnny's mother had thought five years ago before fleeing to Croxley. The canal to Croxley was paved with good intentions.

Jennifer sat up abruptly in bed. A thought occurred to her. Sweeneys money, mums stash was hidden away on the boat. She knew that she mustn't speak about it, so she knew that her mother shouldn't have it really. She had stolen it!! It wouldn't be so bad then if she took it so she and Johnny could run away together. Lots of thoughts went through her head. They could change the name of Johnny's boat and take it to another part of the country where nobody knew them. The money would last them for years and when it ran out, they would be old enough to work anyway.

She knew where the money was stashed and she could check it tomorrow. It was a Saturday and Ben and Sheila were bound to be out buying something for the new house. She would stay on the boat and see what money was left, after they had gone.

The next morning Jennifer discovered there were still hundreds of pounds left in the stash. She needed to tell Johnny. This changed everything. They could go at the weekend and not be missed for two days by which time they could be miles away. Sheila couldn't tell the police about the money going missing because it wasn't hers anyway. Nobody would have any idea where to look until they tied up Johnny's disappearance with hers and came looking for the boat. After that the police would look for a while but soon get fed up. They could keep travelling farther and farther away until they could never be found again, then they could settle down just the two of them a lead a normal life for a change.

Friday couldn't come fast enough and when it did Johnny's eyes lit up when Jennifer told him how much money there was. It was too much to resist for a fifteen-year-old who had never had money. They hatched a plan. That weekend he would change the name of the boat. He would do as good a job as he could painting over the existing name. They would call it "Scottie Mac" Johnny could buy some transfer letters to make it look professional. He had checked out the engine and knew it still ran. He would need to ensure there was enough fuel on board to set them on their way. He could get that from the boat works in Croxley just across form where he was moored. During the week they could meet secretly and Jennifer could give him her clothes in small amounts so he could take them directly to the boat. Jennifer would set up a weekend away and try and get her Mum and dad to let her stay away until after school on Monday. She could tell them that Rita's parents had a special function at the restaurant so they would have to work Sunday evening. They had asked if Jennifer would like to stay till Monday. She and Rita would travel to school in the morning so Shelia and Ben would not be expecting to see her until Monday evening. That would give her and Johnny three full days of travel before they even noticed she wasn't there. They wouldn't tie her disappearance to Johnny's for a day or two, so the couple could travel for five or six days before they even thought to look for the boat.

They could moor it in some backwater for two or three weeks and never be found. The hiatus would die down and they could all get on with their lives. She could send Sheila and Ben a letter saying she was running away and that she would be okay. Tell them to get on with their lives with their new baby and forget about their troublesome daughter. It was perfect. A perfect plan.

All went according to plan. Ben and Sheila once again were wrapped up in the excitement of their new home and acceded to Jennifers wishes with little or no resistance. It all sounded quite plausible to them.

Johnny and Sheila cast off on "Scottie Mac" the next Friday with all of Sweeney's money and high hopes for the future. They chugged along the Grand Union Canal with great anticipation of a great new life spent happily together, just the two of them, care free!

What they didn't know was that Jennifer was pregnant.

Authors Note

This story was a positive outcome of COVID.

When the weather was fine my wife and I walked the length of the Grand Union Canal from Paddington to Tring a few miles a week. We grew to love the canal. Its character changes, mile by mile. In my mind Jennifer and Johnny are still travelling some of that canal as I write this.

My hours trapped inside when the rain fell, happily introduced me to the joy of writing a story. I wrote firstly for the pleasure of writing itself.

Each of the characters became alive to me and begged to know what would happen to them next. I have had great fun writing about them and intend to continue their story which has many twists and turns to come. Jennifer and Johnny have interesting and challenging futures, as do Sheila, Ben Mickey and Rufus. All of whom are sitting still in their lives waiting for me to come back to them.

The story to date ends rather abruptly and leaves you to draw your own conclusions as to what may happen to each of the protagonists.

I hope you have enjoyed their story thus far.

There is much to come from Jennifer and Johnny's future lives. I may have to keep their futures to myself.

Let's see!

About the Author

Clive Lamb spent his working life in sales and marketing. In retirement he found the time and opportunity to write. He has always had an interest in words and for many years has provided friends and family with humorous pieces of poetry. Poetry of a more serious nature he reserves for personal reflection and catharsis. During the period of covid lockdown Clive initially wrote bespoke stories specifically for his grandchildren. Such was the pleasure found in the writing that Grand Union Story was born. The story offers the opportunity for several story extensions in the future. Clive is husband to Jane, father to Spencer, Matthew, Jessica and Jordan and "Grappa" to Marley, Lilah, Nathan and Emily.

Acknowledgements

Thanks to Jane for her patience and for putting up with my virtual absence whilst I was away in the world created in my mind. Thanks also for everything else she does for me. I fear my absences of mind will continue. Thanks to Janet Davidson and Patricia Chandler for their belief and encouragement and for reading my work as it progressed. Thanks to Christine for her help in editing and words of encouragement. Thanks to Graham Smith for taking the time to create the excellent cover work.

Printed in Great Britain
by Amazon